AN
IMPERFECT
PLAN

AN IMPERFECT PLAN

A Novel

ADDISON McKNIGHT

LAKE UNION
PUBLISHING

Text copyright © 2022 by Nicole Moleti and Krista Wells
All rights reserved.

Published by Lake Union Publishing, Seattle

www.apub.com

Amazon, the Amazon logo, and Lake Union Publishing are trademarks of Amazon. com, Inc., or its affiliates.

ISBN-13: 9781542037808
ISBN-10: 1542037808

Cover design by Shasti O'Leary Soudant

Printed in the United States of America

AN IMPERFECT PLAN

PROLOGUE

GRETA

2020

He was unrecognizable. The only things familiar to Greta were the tufts of brown hair peeking out from the gauze bandage. She only believed it was him because the hospital ID on his wrist read *O'Brien, Patrick B.* Attempting to take deep breaths, she looked at the nightmarish scene: his face, mostly hidden by an oxygen mask; catheters, IVs, and tubes snaking out of his body; an imposing line running out from his throat. The few visible patches of skin looked . . . oddly darkened. Greta shuddered, thinking about what the hidden parts looked like. The nurse's words from just moments ago played like a loop in Greta's head: *Ninety-eight percent of his body is covered in third-degree burns, but we'll do what we can.*

When the ambulance arrived at the hospital, the medics had rushed him straight to the burn and trauma ICU. Greta had run down the burn unit's hall still barefoot, her whole body trembling, her thoughts spiraling. Now all she could do was pray that his pain wasn't as torturous as she knew it must be.

The doctors and nurses hovering over him worked rapidly, moving constantly around his battered body. She strained to decipher their muffled words through the partition dividing her from them, pressing her forehead up against the glass as she searched every inch of his bandaged body, desperate for a movement, for any tiny sign of life. The whiteboard on the wall of his room said *Patrick O'Brien*, and her stomach turned both from seeing it stated so starkly there and from the sickening smell of burned flesh making the air rancid. Her nose and mouth covered, her breathing was still irregular as she whispered, "Please, God."

The heart monitor blared, its beeping aggressive and high pitched. She jumped, staring in disbelief at the flat line extending across the entire screen.

Hitting the window, she shouted, pleading with them to save him, to keep trying everything, to not even think about giving up. *They can't give up.*

The drama and commotion in the room slowed until it stopped entirely and the doctors and nurses backed away from the scorched, still body. The attending doctor pulled down his face mask, glanced over at the clock, and seemed to pronounce the time of death.

Greta's legs gave out, a primal sob erupting from deep within.

A doctor appeared before her. She was on the floor now, hyperventilating, as he apologized, explaining that they had done all they could but he had succumbed to his internal injuries. Shakily getting to her feet, she pushed past him and into the trauma room. Accusations flooded her mind; she needed someone to blame for this.

Closer to the body, Greta gagged at the overpowering smell of burned flesh, bile inching its way up her throat. Dizzy, she watched a nurse removing the tubes. Greta stepped to the edge of the bed and stroked his hair. "I'm so sorry, baby," she whispered. "I love you so much. I always will." Her voice caught. "We will find out who did this."

Her fingertips grazed his hand, and its coolness shocked her. It seemed too fast . . . and just like that, acid rushed into her mouth. Greta flew down the hall to a bathroom, just barely collapsing in front of a toilet before her stomach emptied itself violently. When her retching turned to sobbing, she slumped on the cold tile floor, unable to move. She pressed her now-icy hands against the back of her neck. Her grief invited in a stream of dark thoughts, and she wondered if this was her punishment for all her lies. Saliva caught in her throat as she breathed deeply, and she choked, coughing. She grabbed a wad of toilet paper to blow her nose and wipe the tears pouring down her face.

She was alone again, and the thoughts returned. Why hadn't she told him she loved him more often? Why hadn't she been more giving and present?

A forceful pounding startled her, accompanied by a voice bellowing aggressively from the hallway. "Mrs. O'Brien?" They weren't going to let her be.

"Just a second," Greta called, slowly wiping her face.

Before she'd even made it to the door, the voice commanded, "Mrs. O'Brien, come out. Immediately."

Greta's eyes narrowed, her heart clutching. The floor felt like quicksand as she opened the door and stepped into the hallway. She reached for the wall to steady herself.

"I'm Detective Morales. I have a few questions."

PART ONE

Chapter One

COLETTE

1984

"We can't have anything he'll come back for." Her mother's angry voice carried up through the weathered floorboards. "They told me to do this."

Colette's tiny fingers clutched her doll so hard her knuckles turned white. She tossed the doll onto the floor of the tree house and went on all fours, closing one eye and pushing the other to the hole in the wood. Her mother's voice was a growl now as she mumbled to herself, and Colette watched as her mother opened one of her father's brown bottles with the picture of the turkey on it and poured it all over the wooden swing that hung from the same large oak that Colette's tree house was built on.

"Mommy! No! I love the swing!" she cried as her mother's shaky hands peeled the plastic from the top of another bottle and then poured the amber liquid all over one of the only things in the world Colette cared about. Panic gripped her. She was safe up in the tree house; her mother would never climb up the rickety wooden ladder with the cracked rungs. But she could never be sure what her mom would do next. She carefully nestled her doll into the bed she had made out of an old sleeping bag she had found in the shed. She threw her legs through the opening and rushed down the ladder, jumping the final few feet when she was three rungs up from the ground.

"He might come back, don't pour it out!" Colette whined as she pulled on the back of her mother's worn nightgown. Two empty bottles lay on the ground near her bare feet, and she was opening a third. The smell coming from them was sweet and sour at the same time, and Colette felt sick.

Her mother's rough hand, slick with the stinking liquid, swatted back toward her and hit her cheek with a wet slap. "He's not coming back!" she snarled as she threw the bottle to the ground. Colette sat on the grass for a moment, stunned, holding her hand to her cheek, which was damp from tears and the remnants of her mother's smack.

The beautiful swing set that her father had labored over was standing strong with the setting sun behind it. The little tree house clung to the big trunk, held in place by rotting pieces of wood, the blue paint peeling away in spots. The window's glass had broken in a storm, but there was one big piece that was crack-free so Colette could keep a lookout. Every minute she could, Colette would run outside and swing on the swings and play with her dolls in the house. Especially on days like this, when she didn't know what kind of mood her mom would be in. She loved swinging on the wooden plank that hung from two thick ropes on the branch, looking out at all the trees lining the fields on their farm when her feet hit the sky. Even when he'd still lived with them, her father hadn't been around much; he was always working at the lumberyard or going to the pub with his friends. He never played with her or read her books, but he had made that swing and the tree house for her. With his own hands.

Her heart was beating like crazy as she watched her mother go back into the house mumbling something. Maybe she wasn't going to do anything bad after all. She really hoped not. The wet stuff would dry . . . it would be fine. She stood up from where she had been knocked to the ground by her mother's angry hand and made her way back up the ladder to the safety of the house.

She breathed in the sweet smell of the wooden floorboards and climbed onto the sleeping bag to hug and kiss her doll. "It will be okay," she whispered in the doll's ear. She really hoped it would be. She and Dad had worked hard on this.

He had collected the wood for a long time from the scrap pile at his job at the lumberyard. Some pieces were long and some were short, all different colors and scents. When he thought he had enough, he'd told her it was time to get to work. She had helped him by holding the nails in the small circle inside her palm and handing them to him one by one when he asked. Every Sunday for weeks, Dad would measure and cut the pieces of wood using his tools, and she had loved the sound of the measuring tape as it swooshed back into its holder. She would laugh so hard when he would try to tell her something with a nail stuck between his lips, his words coming out like gibberish. Each night when they were done for the day, she had swept up the sawdust left behind on the garage floor with the little pink broom from the kitchen set Aunt Lisa had bought her for Christmas.

She heard the back patio door sliding open and she peeked out. Her mother came storming back outside, still mumbling under her breath, and Colette watched, frozen in fear. Her mother stood at the bourbon-soaked swing and calmly stuck her hand inside the top of her nightgown and pulled a cigarette pack out of her bra. She placed a cigarette between her lips and lit it with a big square silver lighter.

Colette watched as the lighter, still alight with flame, left her mother's fingers and flew through the air as if in slow motion, landing on the swing. Little blue flames burst along the wood.

"Please . . . Mommy . . . please!" she screeched and dropped her doll. But it was too late. Colette watched as the wood burned slowly, inching toward the thick ropes that held it.

"Ya better get down from there," her mother said with a wicked smile on her face as she watched the fire creep up the ropes of the swing fast like lightning.

Within seconds the fire was licking the tree branch that led to the little blue house. Colette ran across the floorboards and threw her feet onto the ladder and climbed down into the smoky air. She dashed across the yard to get a bucket from the garden and fill it with water from the hose. Her mother's back was to her as she watched the blaze, her laughter filling the backyard. Colette ran over when the bucket was filled to the top with water, going as fast as she could, careful not to spill any. She threw the water with all her might up toward the branch that was engulfed in flames, but the little splash didn't even reach it. The fire was going to reach the tree house.

"Mommy! The house!" she screeched as she looked over to where her mother had sat down in a lawn chair, smoking her cigarette with a big smile on her face. *She's going to let it all burn, she's not going to help me.*

Colette realized with horror that her doll was still up there, and she flew like a flash back toward the ladder. Embers floated in the sky, and her feet left black soot marks on each rung as she scrambled up. One whole wall of the little house was engulfed in flames, and the heat hit Colette's cheeks as soon as she put her head through the hole at the top of the ladder. Smoke filled her lungs and she choked. Her doll was propped against the wall in the corner; her face was melting and her beautiful, silky blonde hair had disappeared. Black lines slid down her dissolving cheeks from where her eyes had once been, and her ears were dripping nubs on the sides of her head. Colette burst into furious tears of helplessness as she realized that she couldn't save her only friend. She pushed herself down the ladder, coughing on the thick gray air. She ran away from the fire and plopped down on the ground and watched while the solitary sign of her father's love for her went up in flames.

When Chief Morris came to the house because one of the neighboring farmhands had seen the smoke and called the fire department, Colette's mother wasn't laughing anymore. Colette watched curiously as her mother wiped tears from her cheeks and pointed at Colette and whispered in the fireman's ear.

She heard him say, "Okay, Connie—we will take care of it."

She watched as the fireman came toward her and wondered what he was going to ask her. She wouldn't dare tell him what her mother had done; she knew, even though she was just a little girl, that nobody should ever know how mean her mother could be. But still her stomach flipped in the one moment it took for him to reach her and crouch down to talk to her quietly where she sat in the grass in the backyard.

"Colette, what happened today could have been much worse than it was. You are a lucky little girl that nobody got hurt because of what you did," he said, and Colette was confused but relieved when she noticed that his eyes looked kind and he reached out for her hand.

"Your mommy wanted me to talk to you about how dangerous it is to play with fire."

~

1994

Even though it had been over a decade ago, Colette could never be near a fire and not think about the tree house. She stared at the hand gripping the red can of gasoline, jerking it up and down and allowing gas to spray out onto the logs that had just started to die out. Her mind flashed, and it was her mother's hands igniting fire on the beautiful wood so perfectly crafted. She jumped at the male voice in her ear.

"People around here don't realize how dangerous it is to play with fire," he said, and she turned to look at him, swallowing the lump that had formed in her throat at the familiar words. She smiled and shrugged, not knowing what to say.

"Everyone knows when you try to make a bonfire too perfect, it explodes," he said, pointing as the girl threw the gas can into the flames.

Colette turned toward him and prayed that he didn't notice the laughter she choked out was the nervous kind. She watched the fire rise and lick the sky in the reflection of his eyes. She pushed away the ugly memories of her childhood and focused on what was in front of her.

She couldn't believe that he was talking to her. Rob, the coolest guy in this little town. He had shown up her freshman year, two grades above her in school. They had never met, but she'd heard through the grapevine that he had moved there from New Jersey because his father had gotten a big job at the sub base. He looked different from everyone else at the party; his tan arms were lit by the glow of the flames, and his brown hair, instead of being tucked underneath a dirty trucker hat, was slicked back with gel.

"I was hoping you would be here," he said with a wink.

Colette frowned. "You were?"

"Yeah, I haven't seen you around in a while," he said.

"I . . . I . . . don't think we've ever met," she said, wishing she hadn't stuttered.

"Oh, I'm Rob. I could swear we smoked a cigarette together at a party a while back," he said, his eyes squinting in confusion.

"No . . . no . . . I don't smoke," Colette answered.

"Hmmm," Rob said. "Well anyways, happy to have a beautiful girl like you to hang with tonight." He took a pack of Camel cigarettes out of his fleece jacket and lit one before reaching toward her with the pack. "Are you sure you don't want one?"

She considered. This hot guy who seemed so different from everyone else in town thought he knew her. But he didn't. And there was a quiet comfort in that fact. *He doesn't know anything about me or my mother. He's probably the only one here who doesn't.*

"You know what, doll? I'd love one," she answered with a coy smile.

The beer and nicotine hit her, and the world was spinning. Nearby, a bunch of boys were digging a hole in the ground to put the keg into. They would bury it, letting only the tap stick out, an old trick just in case the cops came. The earthy scent of the soil, soaked from the hard rain the day before, turned her stomach.

"Oh God, that smell," Colette said, pushing her hand over her mouth and nose.

"The smoke?" he asked.

"No, the mud. The smell of it makes me sick," she answered and took a drag from the cigarette.

"Really? Why?"

"Because it reminds me of my mother." The words poured out of her as her fingers brushed against her scar. And then she was about to tell him why, but she stopped herself.

You just met this guy. Why are you telling him your secrets?

Rob looked at her curiously, taking a drag of his cigarette. "Care to elaborate?" he asked with a chuckle.

"Not really," she said with a tight smile. "I just . . . I just had a shitty childhood." She stuttered a bit, wishing she had never brought up her mother.

Rob tossed his cigarette on the ground beside him and pulled her into a hug and kissed the top of her head. "I'm sorry. That sucks," he said.

Electricity crackled between them, and his soothing voice calmed her instantly. He seemed familiar. *Had* they met before? She was cold, and she suddenly wanted to smoke again. She closed her eyes, and the starry night got blurry. In what seemed like seconds, she was in the front seat of Rob's car reaching for the door handle. *How many beers did I drink?* She didn't remember leaving the bonfire.

Colette watched as the door of the pickup opened before she had a chance to pull on the handle, and she wondered at the fact that nobody had ever held a door open for her before.

She was clumsy and awkward and her feet slipped on the footrail before she hopped down from the shiny leather seat that had stuck to the backs of her thighs. She landed into him, dizzy, swaying from the two beers she'd had at the bonfire, as her feet touched down on the mossy floor that had once been her driveway.

She started to shrug herself out of the fleece jacket that he had lent to her when he'd noticed her shivering at the bonfire. He touched her arm. Electricity ran through her again, and she shoved her hand in the fleece's soft pocket so he wouldn't notice she was shaking.

"Keep it," Rob said as he leaned in to kiss her. He smelled like chewing tobacco and Natural Light mixed with an expensive cologne, and her heart was beating out of her chest as they embraced and kissed more passionately. "I'll pick you up tomorrow at nine for breakfast, babe. We'll go to the casino," he said with a wink after they untangled.

She had never been to the casino that had been built a couple of years ago in the next town over—most of the locals grumbled about it and viewed it as an evil enterprise—but she would eat breakfast wherever he wanted to eat breakfast.

"Okay, thanks," Colette said as she glanced at her watch and did a quick calculation to figure out that she would see him again in nine hours. Aside from the chewing tobacco, he seemed so different from any other boy she had met in town. She watched as his shiny new pickup pulled out of the drive, and she blew air out of her mouth in a deep exhale. The world was spinning, with a symphony of crickets and frogs in the crisp night air of September in Connecticut. How had she gotten so lucky that he had chosen her at the party?

If she didn't know better, she would think Rob was from the "good" side of town, but that wouldn't make sense. There was no "good" side of Jewett City. A town a mile long, with just two major roads running perpendicular to Main Street. Each road led to farmland that ran as far as the eye could see. Before tonight, she'd never met one boy from Jewett City who seemed like anything special. Rob was different; he was like a breath of New Jersey air blowing through their sad little town.

She made her way up the creaking steps of the porch into the ranch that sat in front of miles and miles of farmland. Growing up in a small town where everyone knew everyone else, Colette had made it through high school without ever having a serious boyfriend. The forty guys in her graduation class hadn't piqued her interest. Most of them had grown up on farms, and their backwoods style—flannel shirts and work boots crusted with mud—and favorite pastimes, including drinking beer in fields and shooting the empties, weren't exactly appealing. She had hopped into her fair share of pickup trucks driven by boys who had drunk one too many beers, but that had never thrilled her. Whenever she'd found herself pressed against the front passenger side of a truck, she had pushed off her suitors and asked to be taken home to her family's ranch on a Christmas tree farm that had no Christmas trees.

Colette had grown up surrounded by pine trees that grew across the fields with nobody to prune or care for them, her father working day in, day out at the lumberyard down the road. She felt most comfortable alone at home in her room, away from her parents, away from the world. Playing with her dolls or catching frogs down by the pond on the edge of the farm when she was a kid. Once her father had left, her mother's mania worsened. When living alone with a small child had proven too much, her mother had been put away when Colette was eight years old. She had never gotten over it.

She was five years old when her father left, and she had lived through the fire as well as many other ugly episodes until her mother had finally gone too far. When her father was forced to come back because child services had sought him out when her mother was institutionalized, Colette could never shake the feeling that he was only there with her because he had to be. By then he was depressed and quiet, just a shell of the man who had once built his daughter a swing set with his own hands.

The door creaked open, and she prayed her father was asleep so he wouldn't smell the bonfire smoke and the beer that was a cloud around her and ask her obligatory questions even though he didn't care about the answers. The house was dark inside, just the fluorescent light over the kitchen sink blinking with age showing any sign that someone was home. The small kitchen, with its dark wood paneling and green Formica counters, smelled like chicken noodle soup from the can, and she opened the warped wooden cabinet doors, searching for chips to quell the drunken hunger pangs mixed with butterflies that were swarming in her stomach. She settled on a bag of stale oyster crackers and took them to her bedroom, where she lay on her bed in Rob's fleece jacket and stared at the ceiling, playing the night over and over. She had a feeling something magical had happened between them . . . but she couldn't quite remember any specifics. This always happened when she was nervous; it was like her anxiety took over and her memory became fuzzy.

She peered at the shell necklace that her aunt Lisa had given her where it hung on her lampshade and smiled. If this thing with Rob really happened, Aunt Lisa would be so happy for her. Aunt Lisa, her mother's only sibling, knew more than anyone what life had been like with her mother, and she also knew that living with her father was no picnic. She would be thrilled if Colette found someone she could share her life with who actually cared about her.

Colette glanced over at the windowsill directly in her line of sight from where she lay, her head on her thin, worn pillow, and saw her favorite childhood doll, which sat on the wooden ledge. This doll had replaced her old favorite that had died in the fire. How she had clutched her tight every night in this bed, wishing her father would come home and wondering if her mother would ever get better. She would eventually fall into a fitful sleep with thoughts of why or how. But tonight, she drifted off with the sweet smell of chewing tobacco and the salty smoke of the bonfire in her hair, dreaming of Maybe.

~

Colette's hunch had been right about the magic between her and Rob. After their first night together, they didn't spend many apart. He'd whisper in her ear each night, telling her how beautiful she was as he stroked her long limbs and ran his fingers through her dark-brown hair. He would pick her up and they would park at the Averys' farm, way out in the fields that were so far away from their house, the Averys wouldn't notice. They would have sex on an old blanket and then curl up together drinking Mike's Hard Lemonade under the stars. She'd started to believe Rob when he told her how special she was. She started to believe that she was beautiful and began wearing clothing that showed off her figure, her skin peeking out from distressed concert T-shirts she had torn in half. She stockpiled the vanilla-scented lip gloss that she bought at the Crystal Mall that he loved so much and wore her long hair down in loose, wavy tendrils, the way he told her it looked best. Even as she found herself getting more attention from other guys, she only had eyes for Rob. She'd do anything for him. Without question. He was her everything, her savior, her ticket out.

She went to her part-time job at the nearby hospital and started nursing school after Aunt Lisa helped her fill out all the paperwork for loans and grants, still leaving her with a hefty bill, which Rob promised to help with. She went through the motions, saving as much money as she could and spending every minute away from Rob thinking about him.

Colette had been so eager to get away, it hadn't taken much convincing on Rob's part when he suggested that they leave town together. She wouldn't be leaving anything good behind—no roots, no loved ones who'd miss her, no adoring and devoted mother and father waving and wiping their eyes as she drove away, no parents to speak of at all. In her dust would be only pain and heartache, fear and disappointment. She imagined being a nurse in New York would be a lot more exciting than being one near Jewett City. She'd been altogether captivated by Rob's lofty dreams and larger-than-life personality. They worked hard to save so they could leave town; their destination was "the big city," as soon as possible. So after a year of working hard, studying, and applying to finish her nursing degree at a school in New York, she had packed up her scant belongings and moved to the city with him.

With Rob by her side, Colette had believed she could be one of those people she saw on television who led fascinating and glittering lives in Manhattan. She'd had zero reservations about getting out.

As they pulled away from her house, she picked at her cuticle, watching the familiar landscape pass her by, and she turned to Rob and he grabbed her hand.

Colette had shared with Rob the struggles of her childhood. She trusted him with all the ugly details, and he had been horrified and supportive. When she had told him about the last time she had seen her mother—the time in the doll hospital—his disbelief and disgust had been palpable. His reaction had made her realize, with hindsight, how extremely disturbing it all was . . .

The sun shone through the threadbare curtain that hung in front of her window in the quiet house. She padded softly toward the kitchen, her sun-kissed feet barely touching the dirty wood floor of the hallway. Glancing into the small room off the kitchen, she saw her mother, who snored softly in her dusty-rose nightgown on the plastic-covered sofa, an overflowing ashtray and empty glass beside her.

Colette started her morning ritual. She stood on her tiptoes to rinse out the beer mug, her small body barely reaching the kitchen faucet. Her mother had continued to set the table every night for her husband, Colette's long-gone father, and poured beer in his mug.

In her bedroom, Colette still had the deflated pink balloon he'd given her on her fifth birthday, when he'd left them for the last time.

She knew it was going to be a bad day when her mother didn't wake for breakfast. The kind of day where Colette sat in front of the television watching cartoons, all but invisible to her mother, who walked around mumbling to herself. Sometimes she argued heatedly, doing both parts.

On the good days, her mother took her pills; hopeful, Colette counted them to be sure. Those days when she didn't have to worry or watch her back were blissful. She loved going to work with her mother at the doll shop, when her mother forgot to send her to school. She'd brush the dolls' hair and change their outfits while waiting for the few customers to make a purchase or deliver a broken doll to the doll hospital. Colette's mother charged them a lot of money to restore their old dolls. The room in the back was filled with "sick dolls" who'd never again see the light of day after being dropped off. Colette always felt heartbroken for them, but they scared her as well, so broken and sad back there in the dark. Her mother told her that people were too cheap to pay for their dollies, which wasn't right because they were like real babies. Colette always avoided that chilling room, which was dark and strewn with seminaked dolls missing their limbs or eyes or hair.

On one of her worst bad days, her mother had sat at the front desk pressing buttons on the old cash register, whispering to herself, while Colette took her favorite doll, Jenny, and bent her tiny body into the front cabinet that held the dolls' clothes and wrappings. After spending the morning dressing Jenny in beautiful gowns and coats, she heard her mother calling. Fearful, she remained still and quiet, which made her mother scream with escalating fury. Colette sat frozen until the door to the cupboard was ripped open. Her mother's rough hands ripped Jenny from her shaking fingers and pulled Colette out by her spindly biceps. The swift movement caused Colette to scratch her leg on the edge of the cupboard floor; she cried out in pain, unable to hold it in.

"*You heard me calling you!*" *she hissed. Her mother dragged her by her hair across the store's front room, screaming obscenities and threatening punishments to come.*

She pulled Colette to the back of the store, pushed her into the doll hospital, and slammed the door shut behind her. "You need to stay in there until it's safe to come out," she yelled firmly, drowning out her daughter's sobs. Colette pulled on the doorknob, pleading for someone to open the door, until she'd worn herself out.

She whimpered quietly against the door, listening for her mother. She tried not to look at the broken dolls, frightened to make direct eye contact with the frozen stares of their spooky glass eyes. So she counted—she closed her eyes, holding herself, and counted, hoping the rhythm, the monotony, would distract her. At some point, it must have lulled her to sleep, because it was like time stopped, and the next thing she knew, a nice policeman was opening the door. She was too embarrassed to stand up—as she came around, she realized she'd peed her pants, her jeans and socks soaked. She smelled like pee and sweat, like she'd been running around all day. Where her leg had caught on the cabinet, streaks of blood had dried to her skin. And her fingers were bloody, though she didn't remember picking and pulling at the door that hard. The dolls were thrown around like a tornado had come through.

Her stomach rumbled and her dry mouth couldn't make a sound as the policeman reached down and took her in his arms, and immediately she forgot about trying to figure out what had happened. Her mother was watching—her eyes glassy with a faraway look, her body swaying from side to side—from the safety of the doll shop. "Thank God! Colette!" she cried, as though she hadn't been the one to lock her in the small room. But Colette was focused on the police officer. The nice man with the soothing voice, who held her in spite of her accident, didn't yell at her and call her disgusting for it. He rubbed her back. Told her she'd be fine.

And she watched, feeling calm, as another police officer put handcuffs on her mother and pushed her out the front door.

"Do you still want to stop and say goodbye?" Rob asked as they drove away from Jewett City.

"Yes," Colette said, squeezing his hand and closing her eyes, willing her nerves to still.

They pulled up to the large brick building and she got out of the car. She stood and heard Rob's car door shut. She turned to look at him, conscious of the fear written on her face.

"No . . . thank you. I'll just go do this myself," she said.

"Okay, I'll be here waiting, babe," he said.

One foot went in front of the other in the sandy parking lot. When she got to the front desk, she reported her name and asked to see her mother. It had been over ten years. She had given up asking to go after a while. Her father always said she was too sick for visitors. In hindsight, Colette knew that nobody was ever too sick for visitors. But she had an overwhelming urge to say goodbye. She might never step foot in this town again, and she didn't want to have any regrets.

Fear gripped her as she waited. The nurse directed her toward a double door with glass panels.

"When she comes down, she'll meet you in there, the family room."

Colette peered through the glass. Patients were sprinkled throughout talking to each other or staring into space mumbling to themselves. Some looked downright catatonic.

The nurse came over and looked through the glass as a door opened inside the family room and a burly woman pushed through.

"Okay, you can go in. There she is," she said.

Colette was frozen. She couldn't push the door open. She watched curiously as a woman she didn't recognize at all sat down in a rocking chair with a doll cradled in her arms. The image spooked her. She watched as her mother spoke to the doll, bowed her head down to the blonde-haired baby, and whispered in her ear. Colette was going to scream. The image of her mother holding a doll made her insides turn. The last time she'd seen her had been so traumatic, at her mother's

21

doll shop, the police, the crying . . . She tried to push it all out of her mind. She couldn't face this person who valued a doll more than her own daughter. Years of resentment boiled to the surface, and she stared through the window with her hand gripping the doorknob. She couldn't turn the knob, frozen, a scared little eight-year-old girl again.

"Aren't you going to go in?" the woman asked as Colette backed slowly away from the door.

"No . . . no . . . I can't," she said as she turned on her heel and ran back to Rob. She threw herself into the car, out of breath and frantic. "Let's get out of here."

Chapter Two

GRETA

1996

Greta felt a surge of satisfaction as she stirred her coffee with her own stainless-steel flatware instead of the silver spoon she had been born with. Sitting at her patio, she held her cordless phone a few inches away from her ear as her mother rambled on, Greta barely listening to what Evelyn was saying. She was exhausted from her long flight back from Stockholm and still in shock—she wished she could go back in time and erase that one-night stand. Unless she could think of a solution fast, it could ruin everything.

"Come over soon," Evelyn insisted. "I have a derby hat for you."

"Okay, Mom. I'm on my way." Greta reconsidered her choice to accept a job only six miles away from her parents' $26 million English-style countryside estate. After having been in grad school in Sweden for the last few years, she knew the opportunity had come because of her last name, but her fondest memories didn't include her parents. The brightest spots of her childhood had involved playing hide-and-seek with the nannies, cracking jokes with her driver on the way to and from boarding school, and getting down and dirty with Jack, her on-and-off boyfriend during prep school.

When she arrived at her parents' annual Kentucky Derby party a half hour later, she heard her mother bickering with one of her lawn staff on the front terrace. "I told you to pull the weeds, but you pulled down half my wall of gorgeous ivy that's taken years to grow! How could you?"

Greta could tell there was a language barrier and stepped in. "Mom, let me talk to him. Go inside."

"Fine, you deal with them. I am going to fire my house manager—he's useless." Her mother stalked off, still huffing and puffing.

Greta turned to the man, who was visibly distraught. *"Lamento que mi madre fuera grosera,"* she offered as she waved goodbye to him, secretly wishing her problems were as superficial as her mother's. She was more concerned with her own problem—her pregnancy, the result of a misguided, unfortunate night in Stockholm, the identity of the father a blur. She was both upset with herself and frustrated that she didn't feel close enough with her mother to share what had happened. She longed for a mother she could be herself around.

She had contemplated terminating the pregnancy but was still in shock. Having an abortion and making her career a priority felt so much easier. She wondered if women her age, in her tax bracket, even had abortions.

Greta turned and walked into the house, where she found Evelyn contemplating hats laid out on the dining room table.

"How are you feeling? You must be exhausted from the long flight." Her mother placed one of the hats on Greta's head and kept right on talking. "It's too bad Audrey isn't coming. This will be the first derby party she isn't making."

"I know, she told me she felt bad about it, but we are getting together tomorrow." Greta wasn't going to be able to tell her lifelong best friend, who desperately wanted children, that she'd gotten pregnant by accident and didn't even want to keep the baby.

"Here, darling, this one goes with your beautiful auburn hair. Maybe it will make you look less washed out." Evelyn leaned in and centered the hat as she picked up a small clump of Greta's hair to examine the ends. "Do you want me to book you an appointment at David's?"

"I am thirty-two, Mother. I can book my own hair appointment," Greta said, pulling her hair out of Evelyn's grasp. She was grateful that her hat was less ostentatious than her mother's, which featured peacock feathers and fuchsia flowers and was punctuated with an oversize sapphire brooch. It was sure to bring lots of attention—as was clearly the point. "Where's Dad?"

"Oh, he's out with his friend Paul from Bedford. One of their racehorses was supposed to be in the derby, but it was scratched."

"Oh, that's too bad," Greta said.

Evelyn moved a large bouquet of fragrant stargazer lilies around the mirrored entryway console, as if searching for the perfect position. "Which horse was it?"

"If you're interested, you should talk to him about it. I mean, you never call him, and it might be nice if his own daughter showed a little more interest, don't you think?" Evelyn moved the flowers again. "Better?"

"Yes, perfect." Greta took in the aroma of the flowers mixed with the woodsy, musk-scented candles burning nearby, but she was too consumed with her unplanned pregnancy to enjoy anything. The last thing she wanted was to be home rearranging flowers like her mother, and having a baby right now made her feel as if she'd end up like her mom, even if that wasn't the case.

Evelyn pointed at a painting hanging on the wall above them. "Would you like to have a Renoir for your new apartment? This one is from Sotheby's; you went with Dad to the auction when you were little."

Greta remembered adoring her father but aching for him to show up at dance recitals, horse shows, and tennis tournaments, and it always felt like he was away at work—unless it was for Emily. Even her mother seemed to prefer bragging to her Junior League friends about Emily's popularity, and Greta got the message that being prom queen trumped her academic accomplishments.

"Sure, Mom. And it's not an apartment; it's a condo."

"Of course, dear. I had mentally earmarked this version of the original 1876 *Dance at le Moulin de la Galette* for you. My decorator told me it's good feng shui to hang romantic paintings, opens up the heart chakra or something. I told her you were having troubles with men."

Emily was younger yet had already settled down with one of the wealthiest men in Greenwich, and Greta was still single and childless. This fact seemed to bother Evelyn greatly.

"That's just super," Greta said, failing to keep the sarcasm out of her voice entirely.

The butler stepped into the room and announced that Greta's sister and brother-in-law, Marshall, had arrived. Evelyn whispered to Greta, "I hope she convinced her weekend nanny to take the kids. I don't need Megan and Connor running around the house breaking things."

Greta also hoped that Emily had come kid-free today. She enjoyed her niece and nephew in small doses, but today she was too upset to muster the energy.

"Emily? Is that you, darling?" Evelyn called out.

"Hi, guys, I've missed you!" Greta hugged her brother-in-law and noticed her sister avoiding her gaze, staring down at her compact and fixing her lipstick. Maybe it was because Greta hadn't flown home from Sweden for Connor's christening? She just didn't have the patience to keep up with her younger sister's temper tantrums.

While everyone else was chatting, Greta slipped into the butler's pantry and snuck a few crackers to tame her nausea as she watched one of the cooks blowtorching the grapefruit brûlées, then walked outside to the flagstone patio bar to get some air.

"I'll have a mint julep. Two, actually," Greta said to the bartender, assuming her mother could also use a drink. The Kentucky bourbon whiskey sitting next to the Baccarat crystal pitchers adorned with lemons, limes, and fresh sprigs of mint looked too appetizing to pass up.

The bartender handed Greta the two cocktails in stemless glasses etched with the Walsh monogram, and Greta handed one to Evelyn, who had appeared beside her. Marshall and Emily joined them a few minutes later. Their Bloody Marys, loaded with garnishes—olives, bacon, and grilled shrimp that peeked out of their glasses—looked delicious as well.

"Cheers!" they all said in unison as they clinked each other's glasses.

Evelyn turned to Greta and pointed to her hairline. "Can you see my scar? I just had some more work, and the doctor promised my scar would be faded by now, but I thought I saw a little red mark this morning, right here."

"All I see is your giant hat."

Guests began to pour onto the patio. The excess of madras plaid and blue seersucker sport coats, peach-colored pants, and bow ties annoyed Greta. The women had paired their hats with pink and kelly-green dresses, and most of them offered the same dry pecks on the cheek, chirping, "It's so good to see you!" as Greta struggled to remember their names.

She continued to mingle with anyone besides Jack. She narrowly avoided him as she made her way back toward the bar. The last thing she needed was to see her ex with his new wife, petite and plain looking and not who she had pictured Jack marrying.

Avoiding him caused a knot in her stomach, similar to the feeling she'd gotten when her sister had called her in Sweden to inform her that he was getting married. Even though she had left him, a part of her wished she could switch places with his wife versus being in her current predicament. How was it that she'd excelled on the tennis court and in the classroom but not in relationships? *No one in this town will ever accept a Walsh having a baby alone.*

She made her way back to the bar, where she was happy to see her father, and weaved her way through the crowd to give him a long-over-due hello. They didn't always see eye to eye, but Gerald Walsh was the only father she had, and she'd missed him.

"Dad," Greta said as she reached up and gave him a hug.

"Hey, kiddo. Staying out of trouble?" he teased.

"Trying to," Greta said as the pit in her stomach expanded.

Gerald motioned to the bartender and pointed at a champagne bottle off to the left. "Hey, pour a glass of that Armand de Brignac for my oldest," he ordered, then handed it to Greta when it was done. "Congrats. So proud of your new job, kiddo."

Greta soaked in the moment; it wasn't often that she heard those words from her dad.

"Thanks, Dad. I'm excited. I start on the thirteenth. I'm going to be working fifty hours a week like you."

"That's great. Get a couple of years in and your old man will be retiring. Then you can take over Blackwood."

Greta's eyes widened for a moment, then shifted down to the drink that she probably should have passed up. After a few sips, when no one was looking, she tossed it in the bushes and continued socializing. She didn't want anyone guessing that she was pregnant. Not here, not now.

Just as the champagne hit her stomach, she noticed her childhood tennis coach. She ran over to say hello, offering her first authentic hug of the evening.

"Is that really you?" She smiled widely at Norman.

"Greta! How are you? I was delighted when I'd heard you moved back."

"Yup, I'm back all right."

"You were overseas, right?" Norman asked.

"Yes, just finished grad school," she said, noticing how much he had grayed.

"Hey, I want to reintroduce you to my son; it's been years since you've seen each other." Norman tapped the man standing next to him on the shoulder. "Patrick."

Patrick turned and held out his hand. "It's a pleasure to meet you again, Ms. Walsh."

Greta's eyes moved from his lips to his two-day-old facial hair to his muscular chest.

"Oh, please, call me Greta." She blushed as she noted Patrick's tan skin and piercing green eyes, trying to remember the last time she'd seen him. Maybe when she was at prep school and he'd been in middle school. Whenever it had been, the change was shocking. He was gorgeous. Breathtakingly so.

"You still playing tennis?" Patrick asked as he took a small step toward her, even though they were already quite close.

Greta's insides fluttered; the words stuck in her throat. "Um, I, uh . . . I want to play tennis again," she said awkwardly, noticing her heartbeat increasing and feeling like an idiot.

"Greta has an amazing serve," Norman bragged. He glanced briefly at them both, then announced it was time to go grab a drink refill. "Really good seeing you," he said as he headed toward the bar.

"I haven't touched my racket since UPenn," Greta said apologetically.

"That's right, UPenn. Impressive." Patrick's voice was so soft and sensual.

"What horse are you rooting for?" Greta asked. She tilted her head and puckered her lips into a flirtatious smile. There was something charming about his carefree demeanor and natural confidence.

"Unbridled's Song. You?"

"Just here to have fun, not much of a gambler," Greta said. She preferred the more stable bond market.

"Hey, Patrick!" the bartender called out.

"Oh, that's my friend Joe," Patrick said. "Can you excuse me just a second? I'll get refills. Whatcha drinking?"

"A mint julep would be wonderful, thanks," she said, feeling guilty that she was drinking while pregnant and unsure whether she was keeping the baby. She watched him walk away and then spotted Emily heading to the powder room. She decided she could quickly freshen up and trusted Emily would know about Greenwich tennis gossip as she followed her.

"What do you know about Patrick O'Brien?" Greta asked as she touched up her lipstick and dabbed some perfume on her wrists and neck.

"What's that?" Emily asked, probably buzzed enough to forget she had been mad. "Smells amazing."

"It's Jo Malone. Marshall will love it. Here." Greta offered her sister a spray and decided her hat looked dumb. She pulled it off and flipped her head over a few times to get rid of the hat line pressed into her hair. Greta envied Emily's blonde "Rachel" haircut and wished she had a similar bouncy, square-layered style, especially after her mother's comments. Hopefully Patrick would think she looked sexier without the obnoxious hat.

"What do you know about Patrick O'Brien?" Greta asked.

"He teaches tennis and is *way* too young," Emily said, rolling her eyes.

"How old is he?"

"Like twenty-five? You need to find a real guy. You know, to have kids with."

Greta wondered why it was so important to have a "real guy" in order to have a baby but at the same time agreed that children deserved a mother and a father—better ones than her own. "I meant for tennis lessons," she lied.

Emily curled her upper lip as she turned to Greta and warned, "Mom and Dad will kill you if you sleep with the help."

Her family's snobbery bothered her and was a big reason she'd gone to Europe and broken things off with Jack. Part of her would always adore him, but she'd tired of him always talking about himself. She ignored her sister and went back outside to enjoy the drink her soon-to-be love interest was holding for her. He seemed so much less stuffy than everyone around him, and it was a refreshing change.

They instantly picked up where they had left off, laughing and inching closer to each other until Patrick's left side was nudging her right. A thrill went through Greta. It was as if she could see a glimpse into her future and imagined being a top hedge fund manager by day and walking on the beach with her lover by night. She imagined having it all.

From the big-screen TV set up on the patio, a bugle sounded. In a smooth baritone, the announcer said, "And . . . they're off." They listened to the frenetic play by play. "Unbridled's Song is off to a strong start. Prince of Thieves is coming around the bend . . . now in third. Grindstone is on the outside, and that looks like Cavonnier, yup, Cavonnier is continuing in the lead. This race is too tight to call!"

The sparks between Greta and Patrick were only intensified by the tension among the heavy-handed gamblers desperately awaiting the photo finish. Once the results were posted and everyone was debriefing and passing around cash prizes, they slipped down to the dock to take advantage of the breathtaking views of the sunset, and he finally reached for her hand. As the fading light began to give them a little privacy, their lips touched for the first time.

That first kiss felt like something out of a fairy tale. Their connection was dramatic and intense; Greta couldn't stop, not even when she glanced up and noticed Emily staring at them from the patio in the distance, judgment etched on her face.

Not even her unplanned pregnancy could prevent Greta from pressing up against Patrick and trying to forget what she would soon need to face. His masculine hands vacillated between gentle and firm. They could barely unlock tongues long enough to enjoy the orange-and-pink sky as the sun slowly sank lower on the horizon. Patrick brushed her neck and grasped her hair behind her head. His lips started at her forehead, briefly stopped at the tip of her nose, and then landed on her mouth. Greta was captivated; this was just what she needed right now.

Their passion was interrupted by a police siren, which grew increasingly loud. It felt so unfair; she was finally connecting with this incredibly good-looking guy who was interested in *her*, and now something was going on in her neighborhood to distract them.

The music stopped and she realized the lights were not in the distance; the authorities were at the party. Amid red-and-blue flashing lights, they grabbed their shoes and ran up the grassy bank toward the flagstone patio, where police officers were speaking with *her* father. Her jaw dropped. Stunned and out of breath, she watched as he was handcuffed and manhandled. She had always thought his wheeling and dealing would eventually catch up with him, but seeing it happen now, tonight, in front of her, was still a shock.

Her father was arguing with the two officers on either side of him. Greta, still carrying her sandals, tiptoed closer to see if she could hear what the officers were saying. She was concerned for him, but also embarrassed.

Her parents' guests circled around her in obvious disbelief. Greta heard bits and pieces of whispers. *What did he do now? Money laundering? Securities fraud? Insider trading?* She pushed the gossip aside, and Patrick did his best to help her direct the crowd away, but her eyes welled up. She was humiliated.

On the edge of the murmuring crowd, Evelyn stood, shaking as she clutched a teary-eyed Emily. Gerald being whisked away in handcuffs in front of all their friends had been unnerving. "They have no idea who they are dealing with," Evelyn cried as the police car drove off. "This is a huge mistake!" She caught her daughter's eye and screamed, "Greta, get me a Xanax!"

Greta looked at Patrick. "I'm so embarrassed. I need to help my mom. Wait here, please. I'll be right back. Don't move."

She let go of Patrick's hand and ran to fetch her mother's pills, her sister following her inside. Upstairs in her parents' bedroom, she opened the medicine cabinet. She began reading the labels on the rows of transparent plastic bottles and grabbed the antianxiety meds before turning to comfort Emily, who was gasping through her tears.

"I can't believe this. Can I lose my trust fund?" Emily sobbed dramatically. "Can Dad go to prison?"

Greta tried to offer her hysterical sister a hug, but truly, she wanted only to get back to Patrick, as he seemed like an answer to her most pressing concern—becoming a single mother.

After the party, Greta called her friends Eva and Melana in Stockholm and told them that she'd met an amazing guy who wasn't even fazed by her family's drama, that he might be "the one." They were both shocked that Greta was even thinking of settling down with one man.

She even called her therapist, Bette, to cancel their next phone session.

"I'm not sure that is such a good idea. Sometimes it helps to talk when you're going through a big transition," Dr. Arizmendi suggested.

"No, no, I'd have nothing to talk about, everything's perfect," she insisted.

A month later, Greta woke up in bed and looked over at the entangled sheets where Patrick had been lying and smiled. As she rubbed her eyes and stretched, he came back in with two coffees to sip on in bed. Greta had thought about coming clean and telling him the pregnancy was from a one-night stand, but he leaned over and kissed her belly between sips and said, "I can't wait to get married and start a family . . ."

Greta knew Patrick was traditional. And she knew, in order to keep him, she would have to lie. She really hoped the dates were close enough to pull it off; she did *not* want to lose him.

"Patrick, I agree with you about just diving in, starting our lives together."

"Yes, babe, I can't wait . . ."

"Well, I've never met anyone like you, and I want to spend my life with you. And I know it happened fast, but . . ." Greta choked up as the words she'd contemplated a thousand times in her mind finally came out. "We're pregnant!"

Chapter Three

COLETTE

1996

When they'd finally arrived in New York City, ready to take it by storm, reality had quickly set in. Rob and Colette couldn't afford rent, even in the grungier parts of town. So they'd settled on a studio apartment in the Bronx, right near the subway. The elevated train rumbled by their windows all day and night, and their neighbors weren't friendly. Colette was afraid of walking the streets alone, and she always double-locked the front door when she entered their cramped and crumbling place. She had not signed up for *this* life, and yet they'd been happy, had clung to each other in the homey nest they'd put together. If anything, their unwelcoming surroundings brought them closer and left them mutually reliant.

Rob and Colette had gotten married at city hall in downtown Manhattan soon after they had moved to New York. Aunt Lisa, the only genuine nurturer she'd ever known, had been the lone family member Colette invited to their small celebratory wedding dinner.

Growing up an only child with nearly no extended family to speak of, she'd looked forward to the two summer weeks spent on the

Connecticut shore with her only aunt. Those two weeks were always the best ones of the year. At home she waited each night for her dad to come home and heat them up Hungry-Man dinners. She actually enjoyed the dinners with her father, even though they never talked much; they sat at the table together, though, and her father always gave her his apple crisp when they ate the country-fried steak dinner. But when she was with Aunt Lisa and her husband and later her boys, they spent meals as a family enjoying lobster rolls and New England clam chowder from the Old Lyme Café after long beach days. She had been so touched that her aunt had made the trip to celebrate her marriage to Rob.

Colette had known her dad would never make the trip; he regularly griped about how much he hated the city. Even though they didn't talk often, she could sense a sliver of pride coming through his complaints or disdainful comments about her "fancy life in the Big Apple." Her heart soared when he mentioned once how different she was from her mother. *She would've lasted one hour in New York when she was your age,* he'd said. Colette's goal since she could remember was to be nothing like her mother.

After Colette and Rob were married, they were overjoyed to realize that the housing setback was temporary, lasting only until Colette landed a job with a decent salary as a nurse's aide at the biggest hospital in the borough. Rob had spent most of his time focused on studying for his Series 7 and searching for a job on Wall Street. Finally, one day he returned home ecstatic, whisked her out for a fancy dinner, and shared the news that he had accepted a position as an entry-level analyst at J.P. Morgan. They could finally move into the city.

Today was finally move-in day. Rob had offered to help unpack, but she encouraged him to go study at the library. She could tell he was stressed about his pending Series 7 test, which he had failed the first time.

"Are you sure?" he asked with his backpack weighing heavily on his shoulders.

"Yes, babe," she said, pulling him in for a long kiss. "You have to study. I got this."

He pulled her closer, and the kisses became more passionate. They were both on a high, living in the city, feeling success just at the tips of their fingers. Their future looked bright, and it fueled a quickie to christen the new couch they had just had delivered that morning.

She finally pushed him out the door, anxious to unpack and start putting together a bureau they had gotten from IKEA. She smiled as she peered down from the large window overlooking the busy Manhattan street and watched him walk down the sidewalk, disappearing around the corner.

Colette got to work on the bureau, and hours later she was done. She sucked on her bleeding finger where her acrylic nail had snapped off and used one hand to fold up her small pile of tanks and jeans, scrubs, and undergarments and fit them all into one drawer. Rob had stopped home in the afternoon, changed, and gone back out to a party with a bunch of guys from work. Colette had barely looked up when he told her, as she was so focused on the five-page instructions and the endless bags of screws and nails that came with the bureau. Rob's Ralph Lauren mock turtlenecks and sweaters and his Calvin Klein underwear took up the rest of the flimsy drawers. He'd discovered a newfound interest in fashion since starting his new job, and Colette had been saving a little bit of her paycheck each week to buy him the Hugo Boss suit he'd been pining for.

After their clothes were put away, Colette moved into the bathroom to unpack her toiletries. She placed the shampoo and conditioner on the edge of the tub, then reached into the cardboard box and pulled out a box of tampons. Struck by the realization that she couldn't remember the last time she'd needed one, she dropped the box and ran out the door.

When she returned, she raced straight back into the bathroom and ripped open the package in her hand, immediately peeing onto the pregnancy test she had just purchased. After staring at the results for what felt like forever, she wrapped up the evidence in toilet paper, buried it deep in the original packaging, took it to the incinerator room on their floor, and pushed it down the chute. It had been her first instinct, to hide the evidence from Rob and maybe from herself. But as she walked down the hall back to her apartment, she thought about being a mother.

The idea of a family floated on the distant horizon, but Colette had never allowed herself to really consider it now—it was something she could worry about in the future. In her dreams, she would have babies with Rob, and they would be healthy and happy and she would be a good mom. She would be nothing like her mother, she would make sure of that.

She could do this—with Rob by her side. They could do this. She was scared, but at the same time, she was surprised by the excitement she felt. Unable to concentrate on anything else, she paced the new apartment, flooded with happy thoughts, waiting for him to get home. After she'd paged his beeper for the fifth time, he finally called.

"Hi, babe," Colette said in the most casual tone she could muster.

"Yeah, what's up?" he asked between what sounded like long swigs from a bottle. "So we took the train to Connecticut, and I'm at this party in Greenwich with the guys from work. It's kind of important, so I can't really talk. I'll be late. Don't wait up."

Colette struggled to get words out without sounding disappointed. "Oh, sure . . . well, I can wait. I'm not tired. When do you think you'll be home?" She instantly had second thoughts about telling him—at least tonight.

"I don't know. You wouldn't believe the size of this fucking palace I'm at right now," he said in a hushed voice. "I'm at a party for this hot new hedge fund, Teiking. Anyone who's a big deal is here, and this fucking house is unbelievable. Maybe we'll have all this one day."

Colette could hear the hope in his voice but brushed off his drunken dreams, even if she loved the way he'd said *we*. "When will you be home?" she asked again.

"You are never going to believe who I saw tonight!" He sidestepped her question again. "Some girl Jilly from Jewett City. She said she knows you—her parents had that dairy farm down the road from yours."

Colette confirmed that she remembered Jilly; she had been one of the few girls in their very small class in grade school.

"So she's married to some guy who works at Wells Fargo, and she's here tonight! She looks horrible—they have two kids and it shows. Can you believe it?" His loud, drunken comments and laugh struck Colette as mean spirited.

"Oh. Small world," Colette replied half-heartedly.

"I'm so glad we're normal. If we had a kid right now, I'd off myself," Rob said.

Colette's stomach tightened at that. "Oh. All right, I'll see you tomorrow," she said quickly, hanging up. She rubbed her tan, flat abdomen. Sinking onto their new futon, she started to cry. She wondered if she should tell Rob at all. She couldn't ignore the voice in her head telling her to end the pregnancy to keep Rob happy, to keep him from resenting her. He had done everything for her—if it weren't for him, she would still be at home with her father, doing God knows what. And now she was in New York City with a good job and new apartment, with Rob by her side, and she had to understand that he just wasn't ready to be a father.

Her first instinct had been to hide the test. Maybe that was for a reason. Maybe she knew it wasn't the time to have this baby.

~

Days melted together as they settled in, and Colette lived with her secret, opting not to share it with Rob just yet. The days were fuzzy and she had no recollection of making the appointment, but she kept hearing a voice inside her pushing her to do what Rob would want. She ultimately walked into the abortion clinic in Connecticut alone, betraying herself even as her heart broke.

Colette felt disoriented when she received her discharge papers, and a nurse asked if someone was coming to pick her up. She lied, too embarrassed to admit the truth. She was numb as she slumped down on the curb outside, waiting for the cab that would take her back to the train station. She stared blankly at the paperwork for "C. C. Richards" that outlined the possible side effects of surgical abortion. Her eyes focused on the words "can cause scarring of the uterine wall or damage to the cervix. These complications may make it more difficult to get pregnant again." What had she done?

How had she gotten here? She could barely remember. She wanted to go back to when she felt joy and excitement. She envisioned herself sharing her positive pregnancy test with Rob and him embracing her. Even though having a baby was something she hadn't really thought of until faced with the reality of her pregnancy, now, suddenly faced with the possibility of *never* experiencing motherhood, an overpowering fear came over her. Her stomach turned, and she leaned over to vomit. When the cab pulled up, her legs felt like lead as she dragged herself to it, her arms heavy as she reached for the door handle and pulled it open. She sank into the back seat, her heart fluttering. What she felt with certainty and clarity was a profound sense of loss, a tragic emptiness.

∼

Even though Colette buried her decision deeply, thoughts of what she had done slipped into her consciousness all the time. Each month, she kept track of her menstrual cycle to ensure that it was "normal." If her cycle wavered outside of twenty-eight days, she became consumed with worry that her reproductive system was compromised in some way. She dreaded the thought of Rob discovering the truth, while simultaneously blaming him for the worst decision she'd ever made. The very first time she'd had a chance to be a mother, she had destroyed it—just as her own mother had.

As time went by, Rob became more obsessed with his job, repeatedly shooting down her appeals to start a family. After accumulating a heavy load of student loan debt, he had finally secured an excellent job and thought that he had plenty of time to worry about kids. He had his eyes on the prize and wanted to work his way up, he argued, urging Colette to do the same. Her drive for fortune had never matched his, though, and they fought about it all the time. Through it all, she continued to carefully stow away little bits of her paychecks each week for the future, one she believed would include him.

But as life unfolded in the slow burn of Manhattan, it became increasingly clear that Colette and Rob's original plans were not going to happen as easily as they thought and that their perfect life would be derailed in more ways than one.

Chapter Four

GRETA

1996

Greta continued to pretend that she wasn't two months pregnant with another man's baby. Patrick had been so thrilled over the news that she started to believe the baby was his. Did biology even matter? He wanted this baby more than anything in the world, and that was way more important than how their child was conceived.

If her mom could live in the land of denial, why couldn't she? Months after his arrest, her father was behind bars at the Federal Correctional Institution in Danbury, charged with several counts of insider trading. This made Greta want to cry; her strong father was now behind bars. Her mom had personally dismissed the evidence that clearly proved he'd made some unethical business choices, and this was hard for Greta, who'd always known her dad pushed the envelope but wasn't aware of how far. She wondered how her mother still managed to maintain her arrogance and force a smile during her weekly bridge club gatherings, assuming she let out her rage on their American Express Platinum Card.

Greta was fighting off morning sickness as she pulled into the prison lot. She parked in the FCI's visitor section and thought about locking her four-carat French-set halo diamond engagement ring and matching wedding band in the glove compartment but didn't. She may have paid for the ring, but she loved this man and wanted to show the world she was married, including her father. She and Patrick had tied the knot the week after she'd told him she was expecting, pretending she was pregnant with *his* child. She walked down the long path toward the prison entrance, in black heels with her Louis Vuitton purse hidden under one shoulder, and pulled open the front door, annoyed that as soon as everything was finally falling into place, she had to leave work early to visit her father, behind bars.

Being an analyst at Teiking meant she'd need to work ten times harder now that she wasn't guaranteed to take over her dad's company, Blackwood. She had done every graduate school assignment with her father's succession plan in mind, and now on top of working her ass off, she'd be trying to prove herself while raising a new baby. What at first had felt like a crumbling career plan and pregnancy out of wedlock was now a new job and a new marriage. Falling in love with Patrick had erased so many worries.

After checking in with a surly guard, Greta waited for her name to be called. She was directed toward a special light that revealed her prison guest identification number in invisible ink and was told that she couldn't bring her purse inside. Another guard instructed her to place it in a designated locker so she could pass through a metal detector, after which she was patted down and then finally buzzed in.

Her father's hair was overgrown, and he appeared pale and weaker than she'd ever seen him look. He offered a gruff "Hey, kiddo," along with a small smile, and her initial uneasiness subsided.

"Hi, Dad." Avoiding conversation, they watched the news on the TV that was hanging in the corner. There was a report about the financial market and then breaking news: TWA Flight 800 had crashed off Long Island, killing all 230 passengers aboard.

"Oh no, those poor people," Greta initially gasped, especially unsettled because Patrick was flying to Atlanta to watch the Olympics with his father. Once she remembered he was definitely on another flight, she joined her father in worrying that the S&P would sink as a reaction to the crash.

Gerald was stuck on the same thought. "They corrected the market for no reason. People say it's rising yields, but I don't buy it. This is why I don't fly anymore—damn terrorists."

"Maybe it wasn't terrorists. Could be a freak accident or something."

"Regardless, it's going to fuck up the market."

"Dad, um, I got married," Greta blurted, twisting her ring self-consciously, wondering if he had noticed the wedding band and hoping Emily was wrong about her father thinking of Patrick as "the help."

Part of her wished she'd indulged in a big wedding like Emily's, but she was so in love with Patrick that she wanted to dive in headfirst, and tying the knot quickly would ensure her baby was born with a father by its side.

"What? Oh no, no, no. To the tennis kid? Are you knocked up?" Gerald asked as he shook his head.

"He's not a kid." Greta defended herself, ignoring the second question but secretly worrying that Patrick *had* popped the question sooner than he would have if she hadn't been pregnant. She thought about Patrick's smile gazing up at her, down on one knee on the tennis court when he had proposed, and how the entire tennis club's staff had cheered at the news. She had paid for the ring, but Patrick had made the moment special.

"Married?" he repeated. "You'd better get a damn postnup."

"Dad, you should be happy for me. You have no idea how you've been dragged through the mud in the papers. Having a new last name has been a godsend."

Greta grappled with her father, who'd just been knocked off the professional pedestal she'd always put him on, now giving her personal advice.

"Oh, please," he said dismissively, waving his hands. "That man's like his father—a mooch. You'll outgrow him, kiddo, trust me." He shifted in his chair. "How's this gigolo gonna take care of you?"

"I can take care of myself, thank you very much."

Her recent disdain toward her father, coupled with the faint smell of institutional food that reminded her of dirty dishwater, made Greta's stomach worsen. She thought again about lying to Patrick about the pregnancy—she'd considered coming clean so many times, but she loved him too much to risk losing him. She wanted to excel at her new job, and she also wanted a husband and kids. Lying to Patrick seemed like the only way to have it all.

"Greta, listen to me! I need a favor," Gerald said, changing the subject as he grasped the corners of the tiny table between them and lowered his voice so only she could hear. "You need to go to my home office and get something from my desk for me."

Greta drew back a little in surprise.

"On the right side in the bottom drawer is a file labeled 'Personal.' I need you to grab it. Put it in my safe-deposit box; the key is hidden in my walk-in humidor. Do it without letting Mom know."

"Where in the humidor?" Greta asked as her weight shifted from side to side. She had a sinking feeling that she had inherited this same lie-to-your-spouse gene.

"The key's in the drawer just below my Padrón Serie cigars. It's hidden. It looks like another piece of cedar paneling, but if you press it, it opens. Get that key and get that file, and just go put it in my safe-deposit box."

"Fine," she said, feeling bad that her father was always trying to get one step in front of his lies. Would this be her life too? No. She was not her father.

"I can't afford to have anyone snooping through my shit."

She was curious about what her father wanted her to hide this time—another affair, perhaps? If her mother didn't leave him for spending company money on prostitutes, she probably never would. Years ago, Greta had caught him with his secretary, Bianca, and never mentioned it to her mother, or anyone else for that matter. Perhaps that's why he trusted her now with his dirty business.

Greta had initially racked her brain to try to figure out who would want to destroy her father. She worried it might have been Bianca, but knew this wasn't her mess to clean up and she needed to focus on her future, not his jealous secretary. Blaming whoever was behind this felt as pointless as blaming the girl that spun the bottle instead of the boy waiting in the closet. She accepted that her father's corporate panache masked some deep-seated demons that had finally caught up with him. She was more determined than ever to start fresh.

Greta had also convinced her boss to hire her ex-boyfriend Jack, her father's protégé, to work with her at Teiking. He was smart, attractive, and hardworking—she still considered him a family friend. They were both in love with other people now, so there was no reason they couldn't work well together. She knew her father had taught him the ropes, and she would likely get credit for introducing Teiking to such a valuable asset.

She asked her father point-blank, "Who do you think turned you in, Dad? Bianca?"

"God no," he said. It was clear he believed it. "I trust her with the whole business. It wasn't her."

"It's getting late," Greta said, "and I've got a lot of work to do. I want to get home now."

"You two fit in your little apartment?" Gerald asked, snickering.

"Now you sound like Mom. It's a condo. But if you must know, we're looking at houses."

"Well, when you buy this Peter Pan a house, make sure you keep the title in your name. Don't get yourself screwed over."

"Dad, you're so rude. Did you harass Emily like this?"

"Emily knew Marshall more than a week, and she let me walk her down the aisle. And she didn't chase after some preteen tennis coach. He asked me for my permission to marry her, you know, like a gentleman."

Greta let out a long sigh. "Whatever."

"Oh, honey," he added. "I'm just teasing. But I'm dead serious about the house—leave his name off the paperwork."

"Bye, Dad."

She stood up to signify that she'd had enough, but her tough-girl exterior melted away as she watched her balding father get frisked before being walked back down the long, narrow hallway to his cell. He turned toward her and said, "Bye, honey, thanks for coming," and then his hunched-over, diminished body disappeared down the corridor.

Why had her father asked if she was knocked up? *Was* that the only reason Patrick had married her? Her muscles felt even tighter than when she'd arrived, and she was dizzy from not eating. She retrieved her purse from the locker and headed back to her car, her dad's comments stuck on replay the entire drive home. What if Patrick had only married her because she was expecting "his" baby? Could she live with the guilt of having it and pretending it was his? And what if she never gave him a child of his own in the future? Part of her knew it wasn't 100 percent ethical, but a bigger part of her hoped it would end up being for the best.

Though it was late, she made a quick stop at her parents' estate. Her dad rarely asked her for help, so she felt obliged to honor his request. Her mom was out somewhere, so she grabbed the file and the thin gold key branded with the words GUARD 372 on it and got out of there before she ran into anyone she'd have to explain herself to.

When she finally got home, Greta drank in every sheet of paper in the file. There were typical overseas bank accounts, strange doctor bills, letters to lawyers, statements about her trust fund and Emily's, and then . . . another trust fund? Behind Emily's file were two 529 college fund accounts, set up to help her niece and nephew, Megan and Connor, but who was the third nameless account for? It wasn't like her father knew she was pregnant. She hoped her father would help her baby as well, and learn to love Patrick as much as she did—well, at least like him. He'd come around, she told herself.

She dropped the file on her kitchen counter and decided she'd bring it to the bank in the morning. She was glad that Patrick was out of town so she wouldn't have to answer any questions about her father's paperwork. Her stomach hurt, and she needed to just go upstairs and lie down. As she held her stomach and walked up the stairs slowly, she knew she needed to stop worrying about her father and focus on her unborn baby.

She lay down on her bed, and her lower abdomen began cramping in sharp bursts. In the fetal position, she hugged her knees as the searing ache shot through her. Her uterus contracted and she clenched her hands around the sheets. The throbbing was more intense than a period cramp. Worry swamped her thoughts. *What is happening?* She'd drunk at her parents' Kentucky Derby party—had it affected the baby? She recalled Patrick's face when she'd told him they were expecting and how excited he'd seemed at the thought of becoming a father. Panic consumed her as she tensed her groin muscles, trying to stop the pain.

Should she call her doctor to ask if this was normal? She dialed Audrey, but there was no answer. Her best friend had suffered complications after her miscarriage, resulting in a hysterectomy. Greta didn't want the same thing to happen to her. She hung up and had no one else to call. Her mother and Emily were never supportive. Maybe she should call Patrick and tell him about this excruciating pain—but what if she worried him over nothing?

Greta opened her nightstand drawer, wondering if Advil would hurt the baby. Maybe the cramping was normal . . .

She ran a warm bath and submerged herself in the water, but it wasn't long before she noticed the water turning pink and then red—she was bleeding heavily. The ache got so bad that she dunked her whole head underwater in hopes of finding relief. Coming up for air, she even wiped her face with her hands as she realized she was now bathing in a pool of her own blood. At first, she was too horrified to move but eventually stepped out and grabbed for a towel, still bleeding, as she just stared at the bloody water slowly draining.

Clumps of blood were coming out with each throbbing cramp. This unborn child wasn't just Patrick's fake baby; it had been her *real* one, and now she worried it was gone. What if this was their only chance? Patrick had told her on their third date that he wasn't open to adoption. It was the first time she didn't see eye to eye with the new love of her life. She was upset with him for caring so much about having a biological child, but at the same time, if that was so important to him, then maybe once the pain subsided, she would be able to accept that everything happened for a reason.

She crawled back into bed. The cramping and bleeding lasted all night and into the next day, as did her tears. She drenched her pad and leaked blood onto the 600-thread-count sheets. Greta tried to comfort herself and calm her growing sense of regret, but she also desperately wanted to erase the lies that surrounded everything that was currently happening. She imagined a future with Patrick that involved their biological children, and this vision carried her through the present grief. She hoped that if given the chance to become a mother, she'd somehow rise to the occasion, but for now she could focus on work.

The next morning she went straight to the doctor's office, where an ultrasound confirmed that she had miscarried. The doctor gave her a sad smile and told her she could try again in another two months, but she was suddenly scared of Patrick's response. Would she alone be enough for him? Why was she so confident everywhere else in her life yet so vulnerable when it came to being a wife and mother? He was so young and handsome, and in some ways, though her paycheck was bigger than his, she still felt as if she didn't measure up. She worried that part of him wanted a younger, more carefree companion and her career aspirations might somehow drive him away. She hoped she was wrong, because she liked that he was so much less uptight than other men she'd dated in the past and didn't seem to mind they were so different.

Greta drove home feeling empty and poured a glass of wine as she looked through the pocket-size booklet her doctor had given her on the way out: *Empty Cradle, Broken Heart: Surviving a Miscarriage*. She read it from cover to cover, rehearsing the facts and figures in hopes of assuring Patrick that they could still have children. Her pulse quickened as she picked up the phone and dialed his number.

"Honey, I have terrible news," Greta announced as she genuinely sobbed. She didn't want a baby as much as Patrick had, but she wanted to make him happy and had trusted that seeing his happiness would outweigh her dishonesty. She looked at a framed engagement photo of them with Patrick's arms wrapped around her, and her heart ached to have him back home with her.

"Our baby . ... We've lost our baby."

Chapter Five

COLETTE

2005
Nine Years Later

Colette shivered inside her thin wool jacket. The early storm had caught
her by surprise. She'd been running late that morning and hadn't been
able to find her heavy winter coat. Her hair stuck out in wisps under
her warm hat as she made her way through the snowy streets. Her olive
skin, which glistened gold during the summer, had somehow reached a
startlingly pale shade after so much time spent indoors. She had never
worked so hard in her life; utter exhaustion had become her new normal. She was supposed to be off today, her first day in two weeks,
but due to the weather and treacherous conditions, several nurses were
unable to make it in. When the hospital called at 4:00 a.m. asking her
to cover, she had considered saying no but then thought of the disap-
proving comments sure to come from Rob if she turned down a day's
pay. He worshipped at the altar of the almighty dollar.

　　Was it New York that had changed him? She couldn't be sure. She
had certainly found herself biting her tongue more, trying harder to
please him since they'd moved out of Jewett City. But she'd had a stark

moment of realization the other morning when she had been looking for something in the junk drawer in the kitchen and her eyes had landed on his old name tag from the Foxwoods Casino.

"Hey, babe, why do you still have this?" she had asked, holding up the golden nameplate.

"So I always remember what it felt like to be on the other side," he had said with a wink. It dawned on her then that he hadn't changed at all. He had always been hungry for money, prestige, class.

The Mashantucket Pequot Tribal Nation in Ledyard, two towns over from Jewett City, had opened a casino a couple of years before she met Rob. Rob had shared with her that he had been one of the first in line to get a job and had scored when they hired him for valet service. They had offered him ten hours a week, as they planned to open initially with limited hours. They never closed that first night, so bombarded by gamblers that they never found a window of time to close. And they'd been open ever since.

Rob had worked every chance he got, in between business classes at UConn, saving up for a new truck, chipping in for Colette's nursing degree, and then putting away every penny he could for his escape to the big city. When Rob told her with stars in his eyes about the expensive cars he parked at the casino and the big tips the rich people threw at him, she had joined in his enthusiasm because it seemed like the natural thing to do. She hadn't wanted him to know that she wasn't lured in at all by the shining lavender light glowing from the Foxwoods roof that she could see from the highest point on the Avery farm down the road from her father's. She hadn't told him then that money didn't excite her, and she wasn't about to tell him now.

"I wouldn't give that there casino one fucking red cent," her father would yell when he had one too many drinks with his friends. Many locals saw the casino as an imposing entity bringing traffic, drunks, and "lowlifes," as her father referred to the people who came in droves every weekend to gamble.

But Rob had embraced all that it had to offer. Colette wasn't interested in the casino life quite as much as he was, but she sure did appreciate him paying for her nursing classes with all the tips and overtime money he made.

And now here they were in New York City, where enough money was never enough.

Rob had been working later and later, traveling more than ever for work, and often not showing up when he said he would. She worried that there might be another woman, but she had no proof and didn't want to accuse him without evidence. Even when he was home, the tension was thick, as was the mistrust between them, like the old Rob and Colette from Jewett City were gone, and in their place were two people who had lost the stars in their eyes. It was as if she'd lost something somehow, like she now paled in comparison to the sophisticated, highly educated class of women he was working with. Her dream of having a family was getting more and more unrealistic, as their intimacy was infrequent. Though she had once dreamed of sharing the news that she was pregnant with an ecstatic Rob, when she thought of it now, she could only envision him being mad at her.

Sometimes when he spoke to her, his tone felt dismissive, and Colette found herself entertaining fleeting thoughts of leaving him. The thoughts dissipated immediately, though, because she had never lived on her own, and no matter what, Rob was safe. He had gotten her this far, and how would she ever live on her own in this big city? She didn't want to find out.

She hugged her worn-out messenger bag closer to her body as a woman with a Gucci purse walked past her. Watching the woman move with her confident strut in her furry, high Sorel boots, Colette cursed at her own cheap, ugly nursing shoes slipping on the sidewalk. No matter how hard she worked, she never felt like she was good enough in this city that Rob had said would be their answer to everything.

The shine had clearly worn off those distant moments of new romance. And now in the throes of working sixty-hour weeks in a busy New York hospital, with barely time to sleep or enjoy life at all, she realized that Rob's dream, for her, was a nightmare. She didn't "Love New York" like a proper New Yorker. But she was just starting to admit that to herself, and yet the thought of returning to Jewett City seemed even worse.

The WALK sign had started blinking the hand symbol, warning that it was unsafe to cross, but Colette decided to take the chance and run; she was almost late and a New York pedestrian, after all. No one who lived there actually waited for permission from the traffic lights. She knew halfway across the icy street that she'd made a grave error as she lost her balance on a patch of black ice. She smashed the wet pavement with her knee and shin. The pain was nauseating.

She tried to get up, putting weight on her leg, and the pain was so sharp, so searing, that it was like an out-of-body experience. She crashed back to the icy ground, the injury giving her a moment of pure clarity: *I can't go to work in this much agony. I can't live this city life anymore. I can't do this.* She was suddenly watching herself trying to regain her composure on the wet pavement, inhaling a large gulp of frosty air, watching herself struggle to her feet.

Then, seemingly instantaneously, she was at the ER entrance.

Confusion clouded Colette's already-stressed brain before upset roared in to take its place. This oddness had happened before, these missing pieces. Whenever it happened, she internally scolded herself for being so tired, so distracted, so stressed that her mind just wandered off. *I have to take better care of myself. I can't get sick.*

She'd learned in nursing training that some people blocked traumatic memories—they'd come into the ER and not know what had happened or how they'd gotten there. Of course, some of those people were drunk or on drugs, and some wanted to hide what they had done, but it had happened occasionally to her, so she knew it legitimately happened to others. Not knowing was so frustrating, even creepy, but she wouldn't obsess. Not right now. She was hurt and needed to focus.

Colette fumbled in her purse for her flip phone, causing a burning pain in her wrist, and dialed the nurse's station where her friend Chelsea was working. Moments later, Chelsea shoved open the door and came outside, shivering in her thin scrubs, a wheelchair at the ready.

"Do you want me to call Rob?" Chelsea asked while she lifted Colette's legs onto the emergency room bed.

"No . . . I don't want to stress him out." Colette brushed her off. "It's probably just a sprain."

The doctor ordered X-rays, Colette gasping when he examined her knee. It was swollen and already badly discolored. The wait for her results took forever. The pain was unrelenting, and she worried about how long she'd be out of commission.

"It looks like you have fractured your patella," the doctor grimly reported hours after she'd arrived at the ER. "You'll need surgery to repair the break, and we'll likely use some pins or screws to put it all back together. You'll be in a cast afterward, and you'll have to rest for around six weeks. After physical therapy, you'll get back to normal, though. The wrist is just mildly sprained."

The news was devastating to Colette, her life turned upside down in a few snowy seconds. She contemplated not even calling Rob but had the fleeting worry that something terrible could happen during surgery. *He's going to be so annoyed with me.*

But she had to call and tell him she was in the hospital and staying overnight for surgery. She was so nervous her fingers shook as she dialed the number. When Rob's voice came on the line, her stomach lurched and she started to feel dizzy.

"Hey, doll, I have some bad news."

Colette found relief only when the anesthesiologist came into the OR to knock her out. Counting backward from ten, she got to eight before the ache switched off—along with her worries, temporarily.

~

Colette struggled to make out the fuzzy image in front of her as she struggled to remember where she was.

"Colette? Hey, how are you feeling?"

"Like shit," she managed to say before closing her lids again, hungry to return to that deep, languorous sleep. When she next opened them, sunlight was piercing through the half-opened blinds, and someone was pulling at her arm.

"Good morning, chica!" Chelsea's high-pitched voice was singing as she wrapped Colette's bicep with a blood-pressure cuff. Colette stayed still and squinted against the harsh daylight while Chelsea pumped the bulb attached to the cuff.

"Vitals are great!" Chelsea said a few moments later, removing the cuff and pulse clip from her finger and jotting down notes into a chart. When Colette attempted to shift herself up so she could properly face her friend, a searing pain shot through her entire right side, and she slumped against it.

"Oh no, don't try to move too much," Chelsea instructed as she grabbed Colette under her arm and helped to comfortably settle her into the bed.

"Fuck," Colette mumbled. She was in bad shape. It all started flooding back to her, and the first thing she stressed about, once again, was the income she'd miss. Rob.

"Do you know if my husband called?" she asked.

Chelsea's face flushed slightly, and she busied herself jotting notes down on Colette's chart. "Um, yeah, he actually stopped in this morning, but he said he didn't want to wake you . . . He had something important at work to get to."

Colette changed the subject. "Did Dr. Neil say how long my recovery would be?" she asked, barely able to get out the words.

"Only three to six weeks." Chelsea's wide smile and peppy tone made clear that she thought she was delivering good news. She adjusted Colette's pillows. "You'll be back up and running in no time!"

Colette tried to run numbers in her foggy brain but couldn't add or subtract due to the worst pain she had ever felt in her life.

"Oh my God, I can't think straight; my whole right side hurts," she moaned.

"Well, we have a morphine drip for you today; that will help while you're here," Chelsea said, peering at Colette's chart. "You'll get oral pain meds when you go home." Chelsea went over to the morphine pump, which she unlocked with a key. She handed Colette the button to press whenever she felt pain, reviewing the instructions and explaining that the machine would not allow her to get more than what was medically allowed and safe, all things Colette understood as a nurse but all things Chelsea was required to tell patients. Colette pressed the release button a few times, hoping for quick relief. Though she was aware that pressing repeatedly wouldn't dispense a higher dosage, like obsessively pushing the button to call an elevator when in a hurry, she couldn't help herself. "You should feel much better soon," Chelsea reassured as Colette's vision started to blur. For which she was thankful.

The day passed foggily in morphine-induced sleep. Waking every few hours, at first Colette couldn't remember where she was and why. The next morning, more clearheaded, she tried to sit up without jostling her casted leg. Even though Rob had said he would try to come to the hospital last night, he was coming in from a conference in DC and probably wouldn't make it until morning. *Should I call him again? No. He's probably tired; he will be here soon.*

She was focusing on a tray of breakfast on her bedside table when Nellie, a nursing intern who had shadowed her for the past six months, opened the door.

Colette smiled for the first time since falling. "Hi, Nellie."

"Great news! You're going home." Nellie grabbed Colette's file from the rack at the foot of the bed. "I'm here to go over your discharge instructions. I'm so sorry this happened to you," she said sympathetically as she rushed to Colette's side. "I literally don't know what I am going to do without you here."

"You'll be fine," Colette replied. "You've learned a lot since you started here; you don't need me to hold your hand anymore."

"Ugh, I feel like I really do. Hurry up and get better." Nellie smiled as she poured water into a cup and held it out to her. "You're my work mom."

Colette smiled back before taking a sip. She knew most patients would be thrilled to be getting out of the hospital, but she couldn't ignore her nagging anxiety. How would she get by without the use of her leg for six weeks? If only she had a normal parent to come help her, she thought, allowing herself a moment of self-pity. Rob would never take off work to stay with her. Not even a single day. He had too much at stake at work.

Nellie began reading through the doctor's orders and went over cast-care details, but Colette was distracted. "Okay," she interrupted, "what time will I be released? I should call my husband."

"Oh, probably not until the afternoon. I can wheel you out if he just wants to meet you in front."

Resentment, which she'd been feeling far too frequently lately, enveloped her.

With tears threatening to spill from her eyes now, she told herself she was being dramatic. *Get it together and don't dare cry in front of Nellie. She looks up to me.*

She was down all day, waiting for Rob to call her cell. Though she knew the other patients had loved ones checking on them or anxiously waiting for visiting hours, Colette had no one pacing and checking the clock every five minutes. When it became glaringly obvious that he wasn't going to call, she had to pick up the phone. He apologized for not being with her—he'd had an important meeting, blah, blah, blah. He promised to be there by 4:00 p.m. to get her. She put the phone down, then grabbed it again, her fingers ready to dial her father, but she lost her nerve. Nellie returned and helped her to gather her things and get dressed with the bulky cast before getting her into the wheelchair.

"So, you have oxycodone for five days," she informed Colette as she wheeled her into the elevator and handed her the scrip. "It's three 5-milligram pills per day, once every eight hours as needed. By then your pain should be much better, but if you feel like you need more, I can hook you up." She winked at Colette, who awkwardly shrugged, thinking that Nellie was crossing a line.

Rob was out front, as promised, and he helped her get up to their apartment and snuggled into bed before running out to fill her prescription. Under her own covers, she pressed the blinking light on the answering machine by her bed to hear a message from Aunt Lisa. Her mother's sister had moved to Connecticut shortly after her mother had been sent away for the last time. Aunt Lisa had always made a point of keeping in close contact with Colette, from early on in her childhood. Colette remembered yearning for that day each summer when her father would drop her off in Old Lyme, where she'd spend the next two weeks in a rental home enjoying the sun and surf. Aunt Lisa shared normal, if not always happy, stories about her mother, which contrasted sharply with the ones her father always told. Even if it was just to sometimes jog her memory of times before her mother was really bad.

"Remember when your mom would read you your favorite book over and over again?" she would ask.

Colette would rarely recall these memories, and she would have to dig deep to remember a time before her mother was too sick to care for her with love or affection.

"*Corduroy!*" Aunt Lisa would remind her when she could see on her face that she couldn't find the memory. "You used to love that story!

And your mother would read it to you over and over and over!" she would say with a smile.

An unfamiliar pleasant memory fluttered on the outskirts of her brain. She could see the picture of the little bear in the bed inside the department store. And she remembered loving the idea of the bear getting taken home by a loving family. And she also loved it because the girl in the book who loved Corduroy was named Lisa.

"Yes . . . I remember," she would say with a tight smile.

In her new message, Lisa said she was worried about Colette (she'd called the apartment and Rob had filled her in on the state of things) and asked her niece to please call her soon and let her know if she could help. Colette called her back to thank her for her offer but assured her aunt that she was fine. In truth, she desperately wanted Lisa, who'd always been so warm and caring, so normal, to come stay with her, but it would be selfish to ask her to leave her two boys.

Rob arrived back sooner than Colette expected with a cheap bouquet of flowers, likely from the stand on the corner, Chinese food, and the pain pills that by now she desperately needed. She swallowed one and watched as he filled a vase with water for her flowers, his hair perfectly gelled and combed back, his arm muscles tensing as he held the heavy vase. It may have been the oxy, but she suddenly felt an old rush of attraction for this man she had run away with as a teen. Sure, they had gone off track lately, but maybe she'd been at fault, feeling sorry for herself and slacking while he was such a workaholic, doing it all for them. She needed to make a greater effort, to see to it that he looked forward to coming home to her. She had to cut it out with all the self-pity and frustration, she thought as she sipped on the wonton soup he'd brought her. She needed to pick up her game. After a few spoonfuls, she got cozy and gazed at the flowers on her nightstand.

"He loves me . . . he loves me not," Colette whispered as she began to feel woozy. "He loves me." She smiled before closing her eyes, enjoying the warm calm that came over her body like a much-needed hug.

Chapter Six

GRETA

2005

The windshield wipers pushed away the snow as Greta breezed through three yellow lights on the way to her doctor's office. Parking as close to the front door as she could, she rushed through the slush in her work heels, glancing left and right, hoping she wouldn't be spotted seeing an infertility specialist. She managed to make it to the front desk with one minute to spare, and after checking in and finding a seat, she pretended to read an issue of *Vanity Fair* with Jennifer Aniston on the cover, avoiding eye contact with the other women in the waiting room by flipping pages.

Greta hoped that her pregnancy was viable, but with her recent history of infertility, she knew better than to trust an at-home test. Feeling jittery, she took deep breaths to try to settle her nerves. Her thoughts returned to Jack as she realized she'd forgotten that they had reservations at L'Escale with potential clients. While she loved that she'd convinced her boss to hire Jack, and saw eye to eye with him on everything that was work related, that was where the friendship ended. She wasn't about to share her private infertility journey with him, or anyone in the workplace. She considered calling Jack to say she'd gone home sick but hoped he wouldn't ask her what was wrong when she returned to the office. Privacy was important to her.

"Greta O'Brien," the receptionist called.

She was led down the hall and into an ultrasound room. She lay down, and her heart sank into the examination table. They'd struggled for years, and she blamed their seven-year itch on the fact that infertility had taken a huge toll on the marriage. But she had matured, and remaining childless was no longer part of her plan. She had decided that she could become a more hands-on parent than her parents. She needed it to work this time.

Greta felt terribly alone and hadn't even been able to tell Patrick where she was going today; she couldn't let him know the lengths to which she was going to make their dream of having a family a reality. He knew about the IVF shots and, of course, had to make his own contribution by going and giving a sperm sample, but he didn't know the details, and she planned to keep it that way. Each year she excelled in the workplace yet failed to become a mother. She deserved the same American dream that every other woman in Greenwich had. Not having at least one child felt completely unfair to Greta.

She grasped the sides of the examination table to steady herself as dizziness hit. The ultrasound technician dimmed the lights, which helped, and Greta looked around at the blurry walls adorned with posters highlighting various aspects of women's reproductive health—she was worried about every topic mentioned. She focused on them to avoid small talk as the technician administered a transvaginal ultrasound. Feeling the cold gel below her gown, she closed her eyes and prayed for a positive outcome.

"Everything looks good. The babies are in there and look to be measuring perfectly with your dates," the technician said.

Babies.

She let out a sigh of relief and felt her lips curving into a triumphant smile, but the technician looked concerned. She angled the monitor away from Greta, who had a flashback of other times during her infertility journey when bad news was delivered. She prepared herself for the worst. She was pissed because the doctor had convinced her to use a donor egg and said it would exponentially increase her odds of having a live birth. She wished there were a way that didn't include more lies.

"What's wrong?" Greta asked, the hint of desperation in her voice plain to her own ears as she tried to read the technician's body language.

"Hold on just a minute. I'm going to have the doctor come in."

She was alone again. Her pulse quickened and her fists clenched as panic set in. If she was already tightly wound, she felt like she could fly through the ceiling when her doctor walked into the room and peered at the monitor.

"Greta, everything's okay," the doctor said warmly. "You're pregnant with multiples, measuring seven weeks. Why don't you finish up in here and then stop by my office to talk."

~

The doctor was sitting behind his desk, but he pulled his chair closer and leaned in to make eye contact with Greta as she sat down. "So, as you know, we fertilized a dozen eggs and implanted the best four embryos, and because it's resulted in a multiple pregnancy, it's also caused a little pregnancy-induced hypertension. It's nothing to worry about. This is very common when using egg implantation."

She stared at the familiar mahogany desk as he continued. "You are pregnant with three embryos, which is great news. We can't determine the sexes until around week eleven. However, because of your advanced maternal age and your high blood pressure, this is a risk."

Greta remained silent, as she thought he was making this out to be her fault.

The doctor paused and then asked, "Are you religious?"

"I'm Catholic, but not super religious. Why?"

"Carrying three fetuses to term at forty-one isn't ideal." He took a deep breath and said, "I think you should consider selective reduction."

Greta bristled at his second mention of her age. "Selective what?"

"Selective reduction. We can make you an appointment right now, and because all three embryos look good, we will just insert a needle in embryo C, the one farthest from your cervix, and eliminate it."

"You want me to abort one of the babies that you just put in my body?"

"I realize there is a bit of a moral dilemma for some. I just don't want you to risk them all. Your odds of success will be greatly increased if you carry two babies instead of three."

"Well, if I'm going to be honest, *one* baby seems like enough." Her gut clenched a little at having to admit it so baldly out loud, but it was true—while one baby felt like enough, she was grateful to potentially have two.

"I don't think we need to eliminate two," her doctor said. "One should be okay, and as I said, I will just do the embryo farthest away, instead of having you choose."

Why was her doctor so comfortable "reducing" by one embryo but not two? She was confused and scared, and it seemed like she had very little time to process all this.

"I know it's hard and that you'll want to discuss it with your husband, but the procedure needs to be done as soon as possible. If you decide to try to keep all three embryos, we'll need to discuss the potential health risks in more detail." He looked down at his notes. "I think it makes sense to have the procedure. We can schedule it later today."

Greta wished Patrick would understand that using expensive donor eggs and selective reduction were necessary evils in getting what they wanted, but he wouldn't.

"Let's do it." She couldn't afford any added risk.

Her doctor hid his surprise well, but she still caught it before he said, "Well, do you want to talk with your husband?"

"I'll call him," she lied, then added, "but I want to do it now, today."

"Very good. Go take a break, talk to Patrick, and come back in an hour."

Greta wanted to go home, change clothes. "How long will the procedure take?"

"It's quick, maybe fifteen minutes, but you won't be able to drive home after. Is your husband available?"

Greta said she'd take care of it and, instead of calling Patrick and worrying him, called Audrey as she walked out of the office. They'd been close since childhood and now lived next door to each other. Audrey agreed to accompany her, and the two women arrived at the doctor's office forty-five minutes after Greta had left it.

The procedure went smoothly, and Greta was relieved there were still two viable heartbeats at the end, but she hadn't been expecting the grogginess—nor the flood of emotions that erupted as she was wheeled into the waiting room. After years of waiting to find out she was pregnant and actually wanting the child, she felt as if she had to turn her back on one, and it wasn't fair. Her sister, Emily, merely had to look at Marshall to get pregnant and have a child, but Greta and Patrick had endured one hiccup after another, none of which she felt comfortable talking about. She'd accepted losing the baby she'd conceived in Stockholm, but then she got pregnant again and at eight weeks she'd found out there was no heartbeat. Through it all, Patrick had been her rock. Then she got pregnant again and was more closely monitored; that baby died at fourteen weeks, and the D&C revealed it had trisomy 13.

While the doctors tried to convince her it was her body's way of ridding itself of a chromosomal abnormality, she felt as if she were cursed. Why did something that seemed so easy for teenagers not wanting babies feel so impossible for her and Patrick? Part of her wanted to crawl under her covers and just give up. There was something about her infertility that felt shameful, and she didn't want anyone to know she was failing at this part of her life.

"Thank you, Audrey," Greta said as they walked to her car after the procedure.

"Don't be silly! You feeling okay?" Audrey asked.

"Yeah, a little out of it, but okay." Greta slid into the front seat and Audrey closed the door for her, Greta grinning as she thought about the fact that she was *finally* pregnant—with *twins*.

"Tell me about this procedure and what's going on."

But Greta couldn't wrap her head around sharing it all, so she said she was too wiped out to get into it and promised to fill her in later. Her happiness was quickly turning to grief for poor "embryo C," her emotions a roller coaster—she needed the drive to process it all.

Greta appreciated Audrey supporting her infertility journey. Audrey herself had adopted two kids from Korea, and while Greta knew it had been hard for Audrey, her family was now complete, and Greta envied her friend being on the other side of her infertility battle. She just wanted to hold her two babies; she wanted to make it real.

When Audrey pulled into the snowy driveway, she asked if she could walk Greta in, as if she sensed that Greta finally wanted to tell her about the day's events.

Greta sighed in relief. "Yes, please." Her own vulnerability surprised her.

Inside, Audrey began rearranging the cushions on the sofa to make a comfortable spot for Greta and then covered her with a sheepskin throw blanket. "Do you want me to make you some soup?"

"Thank you, no." She couldn't even think of putting a bite of food into her mouth.

"Oh my God! I saw Lauren Bowers. She had extensions and looked like she had some work done. I hardly recognized her!"

For a few minutes they gossiped, and Greta started to feel normal again. Even if it was temporary, she almost forgot about the difficulty of her day's decisions, which she hadn't regretted but which weren't easy. The wrenching details flashed back, and she couldn't hold her tears in any longer. "I was pregnant with three babies, and the doctor suggested I abort one. That was the procedure today."

Audrey stopped playing with the throw pillows and gasped. "Oh. My. God. What? That's crazy! But you're pregnant, um, like the IVF finally worked? I didn't even know you guys had tried again. Congratulations. Twins!"

Greta looked at her obviously jittery friend, who clearly didn't know what to say. She pointed at the wine fridge. "Grab that bottle of opened Chateau Montelena and pour yourself a glass, and I'll tell you the whole story."

Audrey gratefully obliged and poured Greta water in a matching wineglass.

After taking a few sips, though, Greta struggled to find the words to explain her day. "I did IVF with . . ." She tried to settle her thoughts. "Today was so freaking hard, Audrey."

The front door opened, and Patrick walked in. Holding back her tears, Greta put her index finger to her lips and whispered, "I haven't told him yet."

Speaking softly, Audrey said, "I should go. You need to tell him. He'll be so excited you're pregnant."

"I just didn't want to get his hopes up after miscarrying and our failed IVFs until I was sure at least one of the eggs implanted this time," Greta responded. "Please stay." She squeezed Audrey's hand, desperate to share more confessions, needing to unload. Greta had wanted to share more details with Audrey regarding how she'd come up with the pros and cons of lying about something so important, but she didn't think Audrey would be able to see her infertility journey separate from her own.

"Hey, Audrey, long time no see," Patrick said from the kitchen, making both women jump. The ice machine in the refrigerator rumbled as he got himself a drink and winked at Greta lovingly across the room. Despite the inevitable stress of their infertility challenges, there was still a spark between them.

Audrey waved hello and turned back to Greta.

"Okay, I can take a hint. I'll leave you two alone," Patrick said. Balancing his glass of water in one hand and *Tennis* magazine in the other, he walked over, leaned in, and kissed Greta on the head, then looked up at Audrey and smiled as he left the room.

"Don't you want to tell him everything you went through today?" Audrey asked. "He'll want to know you just had this huge procedure, Gret! We can catch up later."

"I am *not* telling him," Greta said, hiding her face in her hands. She let out a deep sigh. "And there's more."

"More?"

Before she could talk herself out of it, she blurted it out. "I used *donor* eggs."

She might not have been able to share her secret with her husband, but not telling a soul felt insurmountable. It was too big a burden to keep all inside.

"Oh, well, that's okay. Did the doctor say it would help your chances?" Audrey asked, clearly trying to be supportive. "I'm so happy you and Patrick decided to move forward, and a donated egg doesn't make you any less a mom. At least that's how I see it with my girls."

"Shhhh. Patrick doesn't know."

"What do you mean *he doesn't know?*" Audrey's eyes were wide.

"He doesn't know about the donor, and I am *never* telling him," Greta said, instantly regretting that she'd shared such a big secret with her friend. Audrey's friendship had always felt so unconditional; her reaction surprised Greta, who chalked it up to Audrey's blurring their infertility struggles and let her temporary frustration toward her friend go. Audrey had been through a lot as well and didn't even have a job she loved to distract her like Greta did. A job she was so grateful for.

"Greta, that is crazy. You *have* to tell him!"

"No, I don't. I brought up egg donation once, and he said no way. No discussion. He wouldn't consider adoption either. He said it wouldn't be his child." Greta instantly realized she was being insensitive by sharing this with an adoptive mom.

"Well, that's too bad," Audrey said defensively. "The girls couldn't be more our own." She diplomatically turned the conversation back to Greta. "What kind of doctor just mixes your husband's sperm up with a donor egg and doesn't tell your husband? That's unethical."

It felt like Greta had been slapped. "Why are you upset? It's my body."

"It was part of his body too. It isn't right," Audrey persisted.

Greta looked down at the floor. "But this doctor said it was my best option, and he has high success rates."

Audrey looked incredulous. "It isn't about success rate. It's about the fact that Patrick has a right to know."

"Not if he would say no and stop the whole thing. We want a baby, okay?" Greta had expected that Audrey, of all people, would understand how hard infertility was. Greta thought about how she had endured years of calculated sex with a thermometer on her nightstand and injected a needle into herself. She deserved children after those years of headache, even if that meant having a secret.

"This is seriously nuts! You have to tell him you used a donor. You have to tell the kids they're from donors once they're older; you can't hide it. Your kids deserve to know. What's going on, Greta? I know it's hard, and I struggled with an open adoption, but kids need to know the truth. Who's the donor? Your sister?"

"God no! It's a stranger; that's how I wanted it," Greta said. "Actually, if you must know, it was a horrible experience, and I just tried to get it over with as fast as I could. It felt like online dating, and it's crazy how many young women are just giving away their eggs."

Audrey looked bemused. "Well, I'm sure they get paid well. They're not just handing them out."

"I was hoping they do it because they want to help people who are struggling. It's so hard. You scroll through this website of donors at the clinic. It just didn't feel right to choose my babies' donor mother like I was arranging a marriage." Greta added, "I chose a Caucasian donor with no picture, no profile actually, an anonymous woman. It felt safer not knowing too much."

Audrey put both hands on Greta's shoulders and made her final plea. "You *have* to tell Patrick. He needs to know how those miraculous heartbeats came into your body. You've been through a lot—so much—but not telling him is wrong, honey. What if he finds out later? It's too big a lie."

"He won't. I made a very generous donation to the National Egg Foundation charity that my doctor's wife chairs, so I'm confident that we have an understanding; he will never rat me out."

"You can't just write big checks to cover up lies," Audrey said.

Greta thought about how she'd lied to Patrick when they first met and how that might have been part of the reason they'd gotten married, but she loved him so much. Now they would have the perfect family, so everything must have happened for a reason.

"Please be quiet! Patrick could hear you." Greta was pleading now, trying to keep her voice down. "He's a Catholic of convenience and would never have approved of my decisions. This was the only way I could figure out to give him a baby. A family is all he has ever wanted, and I was terrified he'd leave me if we didn't get pregnant." She hoped this statement wasn't actually true as she hugged a sofa pillow to her stomach protectively and thought about how despite all the tension the infertility journey had caused, she and Patrick loved each other deeply. However, she couldn't help but worry that without children to solidify the marriage, she and Patrick may outgrow each other like her father had warned.

"Don't be silly," Audrey countered. "He loves you. He's not going anywhere. He wouldn't."

"Well, I wasn't going to take that chance." She said it firmly, and Audrey gave her a sympathetic smile and a firm nod, as though that would be the end of it.

"He's such a great guy, and do you see the way he looks at you? I wish Tom looked at me like that."

Greta glanced at the wall toward the framed wedding photo that looked like museum-quality art. Patrick was tan and his face was beaming. She might not have had the celebrity wedding Emily had, but she was finally about to start a family. She couldn't let Audrey ruin it by making her feel guilty about how.

The snow was letting up as Greta handed Audrey her jacket and opened the door. "I don't want *anyone* to know these babies aren't mine. Please don't go blabbing this to anyone, not even Tom, promise?"

"Greta, they *are* yours. No matter—"

"Audrey. I don't want platitudes right now. I want your word."

Her friend nodded again and gave her a hug, which Greta didn't return, nearly slamming the door shut, upset that her secret had been met with such judgment. She didn't need her own fears and feelings of guilt maximized and confirmed . . . she needed a friend.

Racing upstairs, she opened the master bedroom door. Not wanting to let on to Patrick that there was anything amiss, though, she forced herself to breathe slowly, hoping the lie would be worth seeing his excitement.

Her eyes widened. "Patrick, sweetheart. I have the *best* news!"

Chapter Seven

COLETTE

2006

Walking down the hallway of the hospital alone, without the aid of a cane or walker, Colette reveled in how amazing it was to do anything independently, even these basic acts she had previously always taken for granted. She felt like a convict newly sprung from jail; she had taken a shower without help that morning, then gotten dressed with ease. She had been forced to learn how to do everything on her own or do without, as Rob had been predictably too busy to be much help.

He had stayed home for the first two days, working frantically on his laptop in the bedroom but popping up when she called for a glass of water or help getting to the bathroom. The third day, he'd said he had to go to the office and told her to call him if she had an emergency. He had at least called her a couple of times a day to check in and had come home right after work, skipping work dinners and travel. But unsurprisingly, he had reverted to being unreliable and uninvolved only a week after her hospital discharge. She'd made huge progress, out of necessity, but she was no less proud of how she'd adapted. Just this morning, she'd applied makeup to hide the dark circles that had cropped up under her eyes and swept her blush brush over her cheeks in an attempt to make her pale skin appear alive.

Her five-day oxycodone prescription had lasted fewer than three, leaving her with a hunger she had never experienced. The pain was dreadful—all she could think about was getting her hands on those pills. She needed them, but she also strongly desired something else they'd provided. She'd thoroughly enjoyed those days spent in bed in that blissful cloud of confusion. After the first prescription had run out, Dr. Neil had generously given her a ten-day supply, but that one, too, was gone in half the prescribed time.

As a nurse, Colette was well versed on the dangers of opioid medications, yet she'd quickly succumbed to what she had only read about for years. Feeling desperate, she'd taken Nellie up on her offer for a little extra help getting the meds. At that point, she had four weeks before she had to go back to work, and she figured she could relax at home, resting her knee in a pain-free trance. Nellie had come through big-time with 10-milligram pills, which were double her original dose. She paid handsomely for the supply, confident they'd get her through the next twenty days.

But with nothing to do at home except watch television—and the clock—she'd felt every inch of her body becoming restless as each pill wore off. She couldn't move around much because her leg was almost permanently propped up on pillows as she lay on the couch, but she'd itched to get up. Each time she'd tried to put off taking more medication, the pain had seared, shooting from her knee up through her thigh. By the time it was coursing through her veins and her head started to pound, she'd give in and pop another tablet in her mouth, sighing in relief. She promised herself that once she was up and about, she'd lay off the opiates, but by then it had been too late. Intellectually, she knew she was in trouble as soon as she started to count them.

In four days, she'd finished the supply she'd planned to have for weeks, and she needed more. She had been embarrassed to call Nellie again, but her intern had said she understood when Colette explained how much pain she was in. She got her thirty capsules this time, for $300. When she went to the ATM to withdraw the money, Colette had crumpled the receipt and tossed it in the garbage to avoid seeing her account balance. Feeling her control slipping, she'd made another promise to herself: once she went back to work, she would quit, cold turkey. She continued to hit up Nellie to replenish her rapidly vanishing supply until, when her time off was over, she'd spent nearly $1,000. It hadn't helped that Rob was not present enough to notice.

It didn't take longer than her first hour of being back to real life for Colette to realize she was in trouble. She felt blood rush to her face when she spotted Nellie in the hallway at the vending machine. Colette inhaled sharply and exhaled loudly as she walked toward the person who'd somehow, in just a few short weeks, become her new best friend. She sidled up to Nellie while she peered at the selection of chips and candy.

"I'm so annoyed. I forgot my lunch and I'm starving," Nellie said as she pushed a dollar bill into the machine.

Colette rolled her eyes and laughed. "I wish I had your problems."

A bag of chips fell to the bottom, and she grabbed it and turned up to peer at Colette, a serious look on her face. "C.C., you seem stressed. Do you wanna go out for a cigarette?"

Colette shrugged, trying to seem unconcerned as she inserted coins into the machine. She hated when Nellie called her that—her mother had called her that whenever she was having a bad day or when she was mad at Colette. She could hear her gravelly voice in her ear, waking her up from a deep sleep. When she was manic, she sometimes wouldn't sleep for days and she would find a reason to wake Colette.

"Wake up, C.C.," she would say as she poked her arm or slapped her face. Colette's mother would keep her up by making her scrub the floor or fold all the clothes in her drawer, and she would often doze off the following day at her desk at school. Colette shuddered at the memory but didn't want Nellie to notice her bristling; she needed the younger woman's friendship, her loyalty. "No, thanks, I don't smoke. I guess it's weird having all that time off, and it's just made me realize maybe I'm not where I want to be."

"Like in life, or do you mean at work?" Nellie inquired.

Colette grabbed a granola bar from the bottom of the vending machine and put it in her pocket. She pulled her hair into a pony-tail while considering Nellie's question. How could she explain to this twenty-three-year-old the cause of her stress? The list of things that kept her up at night was immeasurable: the future of her relationship, her career, worrying about her mother, feeling guilty for not calling her father more, wondering if and when she would have kids. Now that she was thirty, she could barely remember what life was like in her early twenties. The reasons why she told herself she needed a glass of wine every night—or two, or five—were endless. And adding to her standard anxiety, her newfound obsession with oxycodone had become a real problem.

"I just worry a lot . . . I've been worrying since I was a little kid. My mom was sick," Colette confided as the two turned to walk back to the nurse's station. "She was sick and then she went away when I was eight."

"That sucks," Nellie said, crunching on her baked chips. "I'm so sorry."

Colette shrugged. "It could have been worse, I guess." She was already sorry she'd opened her mouth. At the nurse's station, she looked through a stack of case files to signal that she was done discussing her past.

A nurse at the station saw them approach and called over to Nellie. "You just missed your mom, she dropped off your lunch for you. I put it in the fridge."

Colette kept her eyes trained on the chart she was studying. She tried to swallow the lump in her throat that had formed at the mention of Nellie's mother. She flashed back to her younger self, staring at the telephone on the wall of her childhood home, willing it to ring. Colette's father had come back home to care for her after her mother had been institutionalized. Even though her father had been gone for years, and she was happy he was back, she'd yearned to hear from her mother, to hear her speak in a voice that was lucid and happy and give her the news that she was coming home. Days of staring had turned to weeks and then years, until reality had set in. Her father spent his days working at the lumberyard, his nights alone in front of the television drinking scotch until he dozed off in his recliner. Nellie's mother bringing in her lunch reminded her that she'd never really known what it was like to have a mother who took care of her. She stretched her mind to find a memory of her mother making her lunch but came up empty. She thought about any good memories she had, and she thought of the pool.

The pool had been the very same pool her father had grown up with at the house. The fact that it was patched and sealed and held together for decades didn't matter to Colette. She didn't care that the faded blue lining was old, because she enjoyed talking to her father while he tinkered with the filter and helped him put the cover on when winter was coming. On hot days, she would come home from school and find her mother floating on a raft in it. If her mom was happy, floating and suntanning, Colette knew she was in a good mood, and she would toss her backpack on the ground and jump in with her school clothes still on. She would cannonball in, splashing her mother, who would erupt in loud laughs. So many happy hours were spent in that pool until the day her mother destroyed it.

The fateful day in question, her mother was talking to herself about the pool with an angry voice. Colette had a funny feeling in her stomach as her mother pushed her feet into her slippers, snatched up a set of old keys, and told Colette to follow her outside. She remembered sitting in a patch of dirt watching her mother, wearing only a flannel nightgown and perched on the rusty tractor, trying to make it turn on.

She had a soft-focused image in her mind of sitting next to her mother on the tractor while she drove it across the vast land as she plowed her way toward the backyard of their house. Tree branches scratched at Colette's legs and arms and drew bloody lines all over her little body as they drove through the jungle that the land had come to be. She cried when pain pierced her neck as her skin sliced open. Her mother yelled "Shut up!" as blood dripped down the side of Colette's throat, staining her father's old T-shirt that she had worn to bed the night before. Colette whimpered softly on her perch on the front seat, watching her mother spend the remainder of the day scooping up dirt from the backyard with the shovel on the front of the tractor and dumping it into the glistening, cool water inside the pool. She remembered being too scared to cry, the fear of her mother's wrath outweighing the relief her tears would bring. Instead, she sat quietly and tried not to squirm too much on the tractor's dusty vinyl seat. Blazing sun bore down on them as Colette's mother worked to complete her task.

When she finally turned off the tractor, she laughed loudly and wouldn't stop. Colette couldn't remember how long they had sat like that, with her dusty hands covering her ears to dull the sound of her mother's laugh. Finally, her dad had come home and run in the backyard and picked her up off the tractor. She was soaked with sweat, dirt, and dried blood, and the tears she had been biting back finally released while her father cursed out her mom. And then . . . he left.

Even though the memory reminded her of the loss she had felt when her father had left her there with her unstable mother, she felt guilt about not keeping in touch—she hadn't spoken to him in months. In hindsight, she'd been grateful to him for his emotionless reactions to her requests for her mommy, which had probably inadvertently protected her from getting hurt. She understood now that he was limited in his capacity to deal with his circumstances and that the TV and liquor were his coping mechanisms.

As an adult—a nurse, no less—Colette could recognize that her mother had not left her intentionally, that her mental illness was to blame. Yet the pain of abandonment could not be eased, and her resentment directly conflicted with a nagging feeling that she should forgive her. Even though she knew she should . . . she couldn't. And anyway, her new adult worries trumped her childhood trauma. She had a failing marriage on her hands, and she worried that her window of opportunity to become a mother was slowly closing.

By swallowing pill after pill, she found all her worries slipping away for the first time in her life, but she knew, now that she was back at work, she would have to cut herself off. *Don't blow everything you worked so hard for.*

In her early nursing days, Colette had found that treating the common cold and sprained ankles bored her; that was for school nurses, rent-a-nurses. She had always been interested in working in the medical field, likely because of the mystery that surrounded her mother's condition. And when Rob had offered to help pay for school, it seemed like it made sense. But once she had started her career, she felt an indifference. It certainly wasn't her passion, but if she had to do it, she definitely preferred the excitement of saving lives. After earning her degree by taking classes at night and working days as a nurse's aide, she'd finally gotten a job as a nursing assistant. She'd worked hard and showed up for every shift she could get until landing her dream job in the ER as a triage nurse. The adrenaline rush of adapting to critical situations, working autonomously, and thinking on her feet made her great at her job. Even though bloody bodies came in day and night, their lives in immediate peril, work was the only part of her life that seemed to diminish her anxiety. She would get back to a normal schedule and to being fulfilled by her work instead of the empty numbness that the pills provided.

She was still staring at the same chart, her eyes glazing over, when Nellie reached out and grabbed Colette's arm. "Listen, I don't want to add to your stress, but Todd said I should give you his number so you could . . . um, call him . . . you know . . . if you need anything." She slipped a piece of paper into Colette's hand.

Colette froze, imagining how she looked through Nellie's eyes, a pathetic older nurse with stress issues and an addiction to pills. But then she considered Nellie, a nursing student still living at home with a mother who probably washed her scrubs as well as made her lunch. By the time she was Nellie's age, she'd already lived a lifetime of hurt and disappointment. She had already left her father and lived with Rob for four years.

She often looked back, asking herself how and why she'd gotten swept away by Rob and his grand dreams and promises. At those times, she'd remind herself that what she had been leaving behind was far bleaker than an egotistical, domineering man who wanted to make a lot of money. The first winter she'd spent in New York City, they'd had heat and hot water the entire season. Only one of many comforts she'd enjoyed living with a man who was gainfully employed.

Colette knew that the piece of paper in her hand was a dangerous gift. She would become a statistic. Many of her colleagues had succumbed to the soft haze that antianxiety meds and pain pills delivered. These pills allowed them to robotically check in broken bodies on gurneys; they allowed them, without panic or despair, to pull sheets over human beings whose lives had left them in untimely ways. She had never tried such methods to get through the day. But for some reason, on that day, when she could have crumpled up the paper and thrown it out, she made the mistake of slipping it into her pocket—for safekeeping.

Just in case, she promised herself.

~

Within a few short months, Colette was in regular contact with Todd, Nellie's friend, in the grips of a serious need, an insatiable desire she had no control over. Her plans of starting a family and creating a life she had yearned for since she was young were becoming less and less likely. Though she had seen it a million times as a nurse, she'd never understood addiction before. She had pitied her weak, drug-addled patients and took pride in knowing that what they were losing to was something that would never happen to her.

She was exhausted all the time now and decided to skip cooking the romantic anniversary dinner she had planned for Rob; instead, she grabbed food on her way home. As she walked up the five flights of stairs to their apartment, the smell of the food filled the air and reminded her of their very first night in New York. They had placed beach towels on the floor and spread out their Chinese takeout. They had fed each other with chopsticks, reveling in the anticipation of what was to come. Now, she entered the apartment and left the bag on the small dining table, just inside the door. She set the table and lit two candles in gold candlesticks in the center, sank into the couch, and channel surfed while waiting for Rob. After an hour, she called him; he didn't pick up. After two hours, it was clear that her vision of a night of celebration was not going to happen. She considered eating alone, but the thought of heating up the cold, now-congealed shrimp with broccoli turned her stomach. She had lost a lot of weight since her accident; food didn't interest her like it used to. Instead, she headed to the couch with the bottle of wine in one hand and her empty glass in the other. She pulled the crocheted afghan she had brought from home on top of her. After taking three pills today, she had told herself that she would save her last one for tomorrow.

She found herself craving the feeling of numbness each morning when she woke. The pain and worry that she'd felt her whole life were gone. And the pills helped her not feel a flutter of panic every time Rob stayed out later than he said he would. Even though they had been together for over ten years, he still had a hold over her. She never wanted to push the envelope too much and upset him. If anything ever happened . . . she couldn't picture herself living in the city alone.

She'd stopped counting the days of her menstrual cycle, as her period had become infrequent lately. Yet that anxiety she usually felt each month, each year, that went by without getting pregnant was gone. Rob had forbidden her to stop taking birth control pills, and she yearned for the day she could stop, the day she could "start trying" again; she was desperate to find out if she could even get pregnant. She almost cared more about the ability of her reproductive system than she did about having an actual baby—at least right now. She would never know if she could have a baby until she actually tried. She didn't even have the energy anymore to fight with him; she didn't feel her heart breaking in two every time Rob said they needed to save more money and work more before she could have a baby. She couldn't remember the last time he'd shown any interest or touched her.

~

She felt her body being shaken and poked, but her eyelids were too heavy to open.

"Wake up!" Rob said and shoved Colette's shoulder so hard she sat up with a start. Seeing his face before her, she turned her body to the stiff velour couch cushion to go back to sleep.

"Colette, it's five o'clock and your alarm has been going off for twenty minutes," Rob barked, pushing his hand hard into her back to wake her. Her eyes popped open and she turned to look up at him. He loomed over her, wearing only boxer shorts, his eyes puffy and his mouth sneering with disgust. "Are you late for work again?"

She tried to get her wits about her as she looked at the cable box under the television. It was 5:10 a.m. and her shift started at 5:45. She would definitely be late *again*.

"I guess I was tired from waiting up for you," she snapped as she stood and pushed her way past him, rubbing her shoulder that he'd hurt. She rushed into the bathroom and glanced at her tired face, bloated from months of opioid abuse and lined from the thick seam of the couch cushion. Her black T-shirt hung loosely on her thin frame, her sharp collarbones poking through the fabric. She grabbed her bra from the back of the bathroom door and noticed it hung loose around her breasts as she hooked it. She had no time to shower. She splashed water on her face, brushed her teeth, and scrambled to find her scrubs. She pulled open her underwear drawer and shook the last pill from the bottle into her hand. She would worry about that tonight; she would have to live on one pill today. She had already received several warnings about being late, and she knew her supervisor was keeping close tabs on her.

As she looked around for her keys, Rob followed close behind her. "You know what, Colette? Yeah, I forgot about dinner last night, but quite frankly, I didn't feel like sitting across the table from you while you dozed off and slurred your words. It's getting old."

"What are you talking about?" she demanded as she pulled her sneakers on frantically. "I just fucking woke up and you're already yelling at me? You're the one who never shows up. We haven't had dinner together in like two weeks, so don't tell me this is my fault."

"Right, because I like going out after work to blow off steam, and all you want to do is sit in this two-by-four popping pills and watching television. Sorry that I actually want to socialize and interact with other humans. Look around this place. What the fuck did you do last night?"

She tried to play it cool and not respond to his accusations. Part of her was shocked that he had noticed her behavior over the last few months. Colette had been proud of her ability to function without anyone noticing her problem—or so she'd thought. She'd hidden her pills from Rob and told him that her knee felt like it was completely healed. She'd once ducked out in gym clothes to go to the ATM to get money for her fix, telling Rob she was going for a run. She'd splashed water on her face before returning to the apartment, hoping she looked sweaty when she returned with a pill case hidden in her sports bra. He had never let on that he knew—but he was right about the apartment. Shaking, she looked down at shards of glass on the floor below where she had thrown her wineglass against the wall. She felt a small triumph that, in a pill-induced haze last night, she'd made a mess for him.

But now, her head was pulsing and she just wanted him to shut up. She grabbed her keys and her work lanyard and slammed the door behind her. She ran to the stairwell and rushed down all five flights as fast as she could. If Rob was mad at her now, he would really be pissed if she lost her job and wasn't bringing in any money—especially if he realized how much her little pill situation was costing them. Her income was the only thing about her that carried any worth in his eyes anymore; she knew it. He saw her differently these days. She missed the time when he had looked at her like the prettiest girl in Jewett City. Now, without her paycheck, Colette was of no use, worth less than nothing.

Which meant they'd be finished. Which meant she'd be alone.

Chapter Eight

GRETA

2006

Looking down at the puddle of water between her legs, Greta called Audrey. "How do I know if my water broke?"

"How would I know? I've never given birth," Audrey said, exhaling her frustration loudly.

"Well, I'm at work and I just took a couple more steps and more water's coming, so I'm scared. I'm not scheduled for a C-section for two and a half weeks. What should I do?"

"Call your doctor right now. Is Patrick on his way?"

"I haven't called him yet," Greta said, realizing that her best friend had a point. Shoot, she should have called her husband first. "Okay, I'll call him, but can you go pack a bag for me? Like some non-thong underwear and some baby clothes from the nursery? I haven't prepared anything, and Patrick won't know how, and I'm scared."

"Calm down and don't worry. I've got it; everything will be fine. I'll go over, but please call Patrick immediately!"

Greta sat down and tried to devise an exit plan, assuming that as long as she made it to the lobby, Patrick could pull his car up and take her to the hospital to deliver their twins ahead of schedule. He seemed to arrive within seconds after she'd called him, with the bag that Audrey must have packed. In a flash, she was being wheeled into the operating room. Things were happening fast—too fast. But then there was a pinch from behind a curtain, and she began to lose sensation in her lower half.

Excited and happy, but feeling out of control at the same time, she asked the nurse, "What are you doing now?" The nurse explained she was inserting a catheter that Greta was too numb to feel.

"You'll feel some tugging, but it won't hurt," a doctor said. Greta lay on the silver operating room table as Patrick squeezed her hand. He began to share bits and pieces of their struggles with infertility with the doctor, possibly just nervous talking, but Greta wanted to change the subject. She was riddled with anxiety about her secret, worried that her new babies might not resemble her. Patrick had expressed wanting a family, and she wasn't going to deprive him of that.

"Exciting that you're having twins today," the doctor said cheerily. He had been Greta's physician before their infertility journey had begun.

"I can't wait to be a dad," Patrick gushed as he grabbed Greta's hand and kissed her, and Greta's nervousness around becoming a mother subsided. This one sentence reaffirmed all her decisions, all her lies. Everything was going to be perfect. She had bought several books on parenting, but work had gotten so hectic that she hadn't had time to read them.

Greta was busy trying to secretly convince herself that she could do this, and Patrick's attentiveness made her feel as if she could. She felt warm, but her fingers were cold and numb, and she was trembling. "Is this normal?" she asked.

"Yes, it's just from the spinal block. It will wear off."

The doctor leaned back behind a sheet that was drawn over the operating table, dividing Greta's present fears from her unknown future. "I know it's a strange sensation, but everything is looking good."

"Patrick, I'm freezing." Greta's voice shook.

One of the nurses standing behind the doctor handed Patrick a warm blanket and then began preparing two compression devices to wrap around her legs. The nurse explained that they would help Greta's body temperature come up and prevent potential blood clots.

"Pick any names yet?" the doctor asked.

"We're thinking of Patrick Jr. for one of them," Greta responded. "Or Logan, maybe? Or Liam?"

"I like Liam; we just had a Liam delivered this morning. Is that short for William?"

Greta wanted a unique name, not the same as a baby born just hours earlier. So they decided it would be Logan, not Liam. And Patrick had suggested Brayden because his grandparents on his mother's side were O'Bradain, so they would name the firstborn Patrick Brayden and have him go by his middle name.

The doctor interrupted their name discussion, and Greta basked in the fact this was *really happening*.

"Patrick, I know this was a long journey, but thank you for being by my side the whole way," she said, wiping a tear.

"Greta, you worked so hard, found the best doctors. You deserve this."

"Thank you, baby," she said as more tears streamed down her face. Her stomach was numb, but her heart felt alive. She was proud that she'd persevered and felt fortunate that she'd been able to afford using a donor without causing any financial strain on her and Patrick.

"Here he comes. You can hold him," the nurse said. Not a moment later: "And here is your second son. Congratulations!"

"We did it, oh my God, we did it," she said through tears. Not even the guilt of using an egg donor could dull her present joy; she was officially a mother.

The doctor and nurse smiled as they carefully balanced the boys to show them to their new parents, but their manner was reined in, cautious—the babies were struggling to breathe on their own and needed ventilators, they explained. Panic shot through Greta as she watched her new sons, her miracles—her deepest secrets—rushed to the NICU.

"It's going to be okay, babe," Patrick said, stroking her hair and placing a few red strands behind her ears.

"Are you sure?" she asked, praying he was right.

Helpless and unable to move, Greta was overtaken by aggressive nausea as the doctor explained that he was just sewing her up and that the babies were in good hands.

Patrick had accompanied the newborns to the NICU, and Greta was glad he was gone so she could sneak glimpses at the battle wound stretched across her lower abdomen—a thick red line with silver staples across it—before they bandaged it. She felt like an empty vessel, hosting deep-rooted secrets and layers of deception. They had looked like two small, wet monkeys, but bittersweet tears streamed from her eyes.

"Promise they will be okay?" she asked, her worry morphing into panic.

The nurse said, "Greta, your babies are doing well, and once you're stable, you can go and see them."

She held out a plastic mauve-colored container shaped like a lima bean, into which Greta vomited. As the nurse helped her clean up, she told Greta that the doctor had ordered a blood transfusion because she'd lost a lot of blood and that this would help her feel better. Greta was too exhausted to argue. Though feeling like crap, she was elated. She imagined her two tiny bundles in Patrick's arms and realized she'd finally done it; she was a mother.

Thirty minutes later, Patrick returned beaming. "Honey, the boys are both stable, and both so precious."

"I'm so happy. I can't wait to see them," Greta sang.

"My parents are here. They wanted to come in to see you, but I thought you should rest."

"Did my parents come?" she asked, knowing that "parents" meant only her mother. She'd been distant with her father since his corruption conviction and two-month sentence years ago, but even more distant since he'd hardly congratulated her long-awaited pregnancy. She was focused on climbing the hedge fund ladder, and while she'd thought of reaching out to him for favors a few times, she resisted. And she'd accepted that it was sort of his style to skip out on important life events, to busy himself versus expressing admiration, but their lack of connection hurt.

"Your mom is on her way. Oh my God, our boys are incredible," Patrick bragged.

"You're so proud," Greta said, genuinely happy that Patrick was basking in fatherhood and they were officially parents to twins.

~

Greta was ecstatic, but equally wiped out and sore. She did her best to balance napping and visits with her newborns and was discharged two days later, though the babies needed a few more days for "lung development." Greta choked up as she left the hospital without them.

The NICU nurses encouraged her to use a breast pump, even though her milk hadn't come in yet, and at home she tried in the babies' perfectly decorated nursery. But once she finally figured out how to hook herself up to all the contraptions and get the bottles ready and start the pump, her nipples felt uncomfortable and her abdomen started cramping—so much that she thought she was having an appendicitis attack. Part of her wanted to nurse because her mother had told her not to bother with it. She felt like she wanted to do what every other mother seemed to do with ease. Plus she had read that you lose your pregnancy weight faster by nursing than just by vowing to drink more water and eat salads. Yet after trying to pump for a few days, it didn't seem worth all the aggravation. She had almost given up completely, and when her mother had said, "Greta, what are you trying to prove with this nursing?" she had thrown in the towel.

A few days later, when she was visiting her babies, she brought in some watered-down formula in a breast-pump bottle so the nurse would think she was pumping—but the NICU nurse caught on to her antics. She pulled Greta aside. "Why don't you meet with our lactation consultant again?"

Greta gritted her teeth. "I'm not nursing!" She hoped that Patrick was at least pleased that she had given it a solid effort. She was so happy when he said that nursing seemed harder with two babies than if they had only had one and offered to help out with bottle-feeding.

The next days were a blur of trips to the hospital and lots of takeout. Greta's stitched area began to heal, and she was able to get some rest, *finally*. Being at home, childless, was not part of her plan, but she tried to be patient and reconnect with Patrick after a stressful pregnancy. Part of her wished she could stay at the hospital with Patrick and their two children by her side.

In a few days, Logan's and Brayden's lungs were strong enough that they were able to be discharged from the hospital, and she and Patrick drove them home together, both smiling.

When Greta got home, she looked at her two sons, and they were miracles of science, but she couldn't ignore the discomfort from her swollen, stapled abdomen and the twinges of pain when she sat up. She ached when she went to the bathroom, and even her vagina felt swollen.

Her mother visited and pulled an envelope from her purse. "This is from your father and me. It's two 529 plans for the twins; college is important to your father. He wanted to come by the hospital, but hospitals scare him. I told him you'd understand."

Greta was sad that her father always seemed to have an excuse for why he couldn't be more present. She wondered if he'd gone to the hospital when Emily's kids were born but didn't dare ask. She thought back to the last Kentucky Derby party and how proud he'd been of her work accomplishments; she just wanted a father who was equally proud of her personal accomplishments. Hopefully he would come around, she thought.

"He could come by the house?" Greta suggested, trying to assess if he still disapproved of Patrick and hating that she cared and was always seeking external approval.

"I don't think he's much into babies; he hardly helped me with you and your sister. It wasn't trendy then. It's good Patrick doesn't have a real career; guess that's one perk of marrying a tennis coach," Evelyn sniffed. "This way he can tend to the babies if you need to get your nails done. I mean, the nanny might think two babies is too hard. Maybe you should have hired two nannies?"

"I think we're okay with one nanny, Mom."

"Emily wants to visit, but she thinks she might get in the way. I told her she should come," Evelyn said as she sat at the table sipping the chai tea that Patrick had made for her. "Have you even called her?"

"Mom, I've been sore; I've had surgery," Greta snapped.

"You're fine. It's good to move around, but you know, I can send over help," her mom offered.

"No, I'm good. Em will be mad I'm not nursing, she'll be mad I didn't book a photo shoot, and she'll be mad I'm going back to work. I'm not going to be able to deal with her."

"Well, she's just trying to be a good sister. I mean, her infant photos were spectacular. Think about trying to at least do that," Evelyn said as she took her teacup into the foyer and began rearranging Greta's photo display. "You should make their newborn photos a priority. And we need to schedule a baptism or your father will be upset."

"Oh, really?" Greta's stomach churned as she thought about her father. He had been charged with insider trading and then weaseled his way into a short sentence by using overpriced lawyers, but insisted her twins, who he didn't even visit in the hospital, be baptized. Why was her family judging her choices as if their own were 100 percent ethical? But she decided to ignore their hypocrisy.

"Yes, we'll set that up and send you both an invite," she said, secretly worrying that seeing a minister would trigger her existential dilemma about lying to Patrick and that someone would notice that her children didn't look like her "real" babies. Paranoia overcame her.

"I know you're tired, so I'll book you an appointment with Iris Photography. I have Jane's personal number. We just had her do professional photos of Dad's horse, and they came out amazing. The baptism can wait until it's warm outside so we can host the after-party."

"Great, Mom." Greta clenched her teeth into a smile, hoping if she dressed herself and the babies in coordinating outfits, no one would notice they looked nothing like her.

Evelyn finished rearranging the photos and then paused at the entryway console, noticing a new arrangement of lilies from a high-end florist. "Jack sent flowers?" She picked up the small white card that was attached and read. "It says, 'Congratulations, Gret!' He still calls you that? And why didn't he include Patrick's name? That's so rude."

"I don't know, Mom," she groaned. "I don't want to think about work." Part of her agreed with her mother, but she also missed work and trusted that Jack had her back while she was out on maternity leave.

The doorbell rang, interrupting the conversation, and when her mother reached for the door, in walked Greta's sister. "Emily, it's nice to see you," Greta said.

"Come in, Aunt Emily," Evelyn chimed excitedly.

Emily's arms were filled with Neiman Marcus gift boxes tied up with gold ribbon. "I'm not staying long, just dropping gifts and need to see the babies," Emily practically sang.

She stepped into the kitchen and placed the boxes in front of Greta, who forced herself to sit up straighter and try to appreciate her family, despite her exhaustion.

Emily glided into the living room and bent over the two white bassinets in the corner. The boys were asleep. She pressed her fingers to the sides of the babies' cheeks, one at a time. "So cute! They're dark, huh? But adorable!" she said, as if approving of her nephews.

Greta's fear of someone noticing her children not looking like her bubbled to the surface, and she worried when she looked at them, their dark hair and features. The stark differences were an evil reminder of her lie.

Emily joined Greta at the table. "I hope you booked Jane for photos. I had these in mind," she said, pulling out Burberry outfits from one of the bags she'd brought with her and dangling it on display.

"I'm so glad you guys came, but Patrick and I need a little 'us time' with the babies—to bond with them. Can you stop back later this week?" Greta said as Patrick picked up Brayden and walked around the kitchen bouncing him ever so slightly. He seemed like a natural.

Emily and Evelyn took the hint and let themselves out, blowing kisses back to the babies. Greta was happy she was now part of their circle of motherhood that she'd always felt excluded from in the past when her mother made little jabs about picking up stocking stuffers for her grandkids because "at least one daughter" had landed a man.

Greta waved goodbye and looked over and saw that Brayden was now asleep on Patrick's chest. She prepared a bottle for Logan and crept upstairs to give it to him alone in the nursery; she grabbed a book on the way. She sat down in the rocker and fed Logan as she perseverated on Emily's comments about the babies' complexions, suggesting that she didn't look like her sons.

The chenille slider was comfortable, but Logan began to fuss and she didn't know how to comfort him. She burped him and hoped he would fall asleep. As Greta rocked her baby, she thought back to the day she'd started dating Patrick. She'd had no idea she'd actually want a baby, or have to work so hard to have one. She remembered her father lifting a glass and saying cheers and letting her idolize him while he likely already knew he was in trouble with the law. His congratulating her on her new job at Teiking had felt like a major accomplishment, and she'd been so worried a baby would put a damper on his newly expressed pride. She attributed her miscarriage to the stress of her lies and worried that she hadn't learned her lesson.

She desperately wished she could just tell Patrick what she'd done; she got the eggs for *them*. Every time she looked closely at the babies' features, she saw glimpses of Patrick but nothing of herself. She'd read babies who come from donors can look like a combination of the donor and recipient, as cells mix, but her sons didn't look anything like her. Their features were more pronounced, their hair and skin dark. She couldn't help but be reminded of her lie every time she looked at them.

Even Emily was a constant subconscious reminder of what "good mothers" look like and her limiting belief that "good mothers" don't work. How could Greta ever succeed at motherhood? And why wasn't she allowed to love her job and her babies? She already missed feeling on top of her game like she did in the workplace.

Was she going to get any better at this? Or would she be haunted by her secret forever?

Chapter Nine

COLETTE

2006

Ringing penetrated Colette's heavy fuzziness. She lifted her head from her arm, which was stretched out on the small kitchen table next to her laptop. She looked around the apartment, searching for the location of the sound, then bolted from her chair when she realized that the phone was buried under the couch cushions. Already out of breath, she answered on the fifth ring.

"Hey. So, I have clients tomorrow. I'm going to stay in New Jersey on Saturday and Sunday, and I have a dinner tonight." Rob's emotionless voice still held so much power over her, she longed for the days when he'd called her "babe."

"So you won't be home at all this weekend?" Colette asked as she looked at her watch. "I mean, you're just finding this all out at three o'clock on Friday?" As was the case now whenever Rob had to spend weekends "traveling for work," Colette assumed he was cheating. As time had passed, she cared less and less about this—about anything he was doing. Or so she tried to convince herself. She was stung and humiliated by his disinterest, but she wouldn't show it. No way would she give him the satisfaction of knowing he still mattered, that he could still hurt her, as fucked up and lost as she was.

"Correct," Rob muttered robotically, his distaste palpable. "So, did you get a job yet?" he asked.

"No, but it hasn't been that long. I'm all set up and going to work on getting résumés out for the next couple of hours. I've already found a few things that seem perfect," Colette said, forcing confidence into her voice to hide her panic. When Colette had gotten fired for "time and attendance" issues, Rob had not been pleased, and the underlying current of stress that was already fizzling their bond had intensified since. Who would hire her? How would she replace all the cash she'd pulled from that ever-dwindling bank account before he found out? Each day she woke up with great expectations and resolve, yet once the pain started, she found that all she could focus on was getting her next pill. And once she had the pill, she was too chill to worry about her career. And now her whole life had spiraled out of control in such a short time.

"Okay, well, I gotta go." Rob clicked off before she could share some more sunny details about her barely existent job search. She felt like a loser but tried to focus on her computer screen, praying she'd find something—anything—to stanch the financial bleeding.

She and Rob had agreed to dump money into a joint savings account when they'd moved to New York ten years ago, the hope being that someday they'd have enough put away to buy their own place. They'd contributed whatever they could from each paycheck; the account had grown slowly but steadily, to $12,000. She had also been hopeful she would get pregnant again, but the longer they waited, the more she worried. She chose her battles wisely, often waiting until he had been drinking or seemed to be in a good mood to bring up having a family. After a while her nagging paid off, and he finally he gave in—in his own way.

"Colette, give it a rest. Nobody in the city is having a baby at twenty-eight years old. Only girls from home do that," Rob said one time.

She wasn't even sure if she wanted to have a baby so much at this point. She wanted to just know if it was possible.

"Why? I'm not a Wall Street girl. I can make my schedule at the hospital, and I can pick up an extra shift or two to pay for childcare."

Rob had looked at her through drunken eyes with pity, a look she had gotten used to that said, *You are beneath me.*

"A couple guys at work were talking about how their wives were freezing their eggs so they could use them later. Just do that and we can worry about it in a few years," he had said dismissively. "Everyone else's wife in New York wants to have a career, and I'm the only one who has a wife that wants to have a baby in her twenties."

Colette had to seize on this small win.

"Okay, I'll do that." She spoke with false defeat in an effort to hide her excitement so he would think he'd won. "But it costs money. I don't know if we can afford it." Colette hung her hopes on the fact that Rob would want to keep up with the Joneses. If his hedge fund buddies could afford it, surely he could too.

"I'll pay for it if you promise to shut the fuck up about babies for a few years," he had said with a laugh.

When the bill came in, Rob had balked but begrudgingly told her to use their savings for her $4,800 egg retrieval. He had no idea that the crux of her worry about children was deeply rooted in her guilt about her abortion. He also had no idea that she'd secretly taken an additional $500 for unlimited storage. And after years of worry, Colette had been able to sleep at night.

Colette had been draining the remainder of their savings recently, but it had been easy to pass off because Rob never checked their joint account. It was out of character for him, and whenever it was brought up and he had no idea how much was in the account, she wondered if he had his own secret savings that he was far more invested in. Over the past six months, between her lack of employment and the growing cost of her pill habit, Colette had nearly wiped it out. When she'd lost her job, Rob had demanded to know how she intended to pay her portion of their bills. By then, he was earning big bucks, but he was as stingy and money obsessed as ever.

She had lied, and her deception had continued to fester. "I have a rainy-day account for emergencies that I'll use to get me through a couple of months, if need be," she'd explained, every word untrue. He had mumbled something nasty and then thrown a pile of bills on the table in front of her and walked away. She had mastered his handwriting and was in charge of signing his name on all his bills, and she sometimes felt like nothing more than his assistant. The sum total of their relationship now consisted of scenes like this. What were they doing, she wondered, and why was he sticking around? Was it guilt? He'd brought her to New York with big promises and had moved on without her. She was nothing more than a noose around his neck, a drain, a mosquito he wanted to get rid of.

Colette had been certain she would find a new job soon, so the first time she dipped into the savings, she had considered it borrowing. She would replace the money the following month when she had a new high-paying nursing position. The same scenario had played out the following month and every one since. Making matters worse, Rob had given her his half of last month's rent in cash. She had tucked the $1,500 into her purse, fully intending to send a check to the landlord. Instead, it had all gone to Todd for pills. The $3,200 left in the account could go toward the rent, but that would mean they'd be down to $200 left and still be a month behind.

Two hours later, after sending out résumés, Colette, able to exhale for the moment, felt she'd earned a break. A sense of calm came over her the second the chalky film of the tablet hit her tongue. She had a couple left, but no way to pay for more.

Maybe that would work in her favor, she thought as she washed the pill down with a glass of wine and sat on the couch. With no drugs and no money, she'd have to go cold turkey. To force her own hand, she wrote a $3,000 check for one month of rent and, before she could change her mind, stuck it in an envelope and ran down to the lobby, where she stuffed it in the landlord's internal mailbox.

She felt relieved and even good about herself, but then there was the dread hammering at her about facing Rob when the shit hit the fan. He would find out; it was only a matter of time.

The night went by in quiet solitude, Colette glued to marathon episodes of *Law & Order*. She loved the police investigations but was riveted by the legal cases and presentations. She'd always been drawn to legal thrillers and police procedurals; she used to devour one after another back when she could focus long enough to read without going over the same sentence again and again. She fell asleep on the couch and woke to an empty apartment, as usual.

Still having some difficulty walking, she hobbled into the kitchen. She was especially stiff in the mornings, her knee requiring an hour or two to warm up. In front of the dirty coffeepot sat a handwritten note: *See you Monday.*

She tore it into pieces, made a fresh pot of coffee, grabbed the phone, and dialed Chelsea's number. Getting her friend's voice mail, Colette left a message asking if she had plans for the weekend and for a call back. A wave of loneliness hit her as she watched the slow drips of coffee fill the pot. Her focus turned to the two pills in her drawer. She could take both now, but that would mean a rough night ahead. Or she could try to go without and save them for an emergency. Impulsively, she ran to her room and shoved both into her mouth, telling herself that she'd have to deal with the withdrawal that would start in the afternoon.

Despite her lofty morning plans, Colette fell onto the couch, where she remained all day. Chelsea called to say she was on the hospital schedule both Saturday and Sunday. By 5:00 p.m., Colette was jonesing and determined to secure a fix. She picked and chewed her cuticles until they bled, leaving her fingers shredded and throbbing with pain. She paced the apartment, back and forth, trying to talk herself into reading a magazine or taking a hot bath. She *could* call Todd. She had that money in the account. She'd probably hear back from one of those jobs on Monday, which would mean a paycheck the following week. She could start paying back all the money, and Rob would never be the wiser. But what about the rent? No, forget it. She'd stay home and sweat it out. It wouldn't be easy, but she'd studied this in nursing school and knew she would just need to stay hydrated; it would only be a few days of feeling sick. She'd probably be right back to normal within a week.

Restless and perspiring, she tried to take a nap but couldn't sleep. She tried to watch television but couldn't pay attention. She walked through the rooms again and decided to call Rob. Sweat glistened on her upper lip; she swiped it off with the back of her hand, her fingers trembling as she dialed his number. No answer, so she called again. And hit redial again.

By ten that night, she was agitated and hugging the toilet bowl after vomiting repeatedly. Soaked in sweat, she splashed cold water on her face and started to sob. She threw herself into her empty bed, trying to ignore the aches and pains that radiated throughout her body. Cramps piercing her abdomen, she rocked herself, dozing off for frustratingly short catnaps in between running to the bathroom. By morning, she couldn't get herself up from the bathroom floor, so she laid her head on the cold tiles. By noon, she had no choice but to call Todd. She would ask for just enough to get her through a couple of days. Weaning herself off the pills would be better than this. It had to be. She'd be okay; she had to get through the day.

Todd said he'd park his car on the corner, and they agreed to meet at 4:00 p.m. She'd never been so weak; she couldn't imagine how she'd walk outside. She forced herself to drink water and eat a couple bites of a banana, which she threw up minutes later. It was like she had the worst flu ever. She needed to walk two blocks to go to the ATM to pay Todd, which seemed unfathomable. Somehow managing to pull on a pair of shorts and slipping her feet into flip-flops, she headed outside.

She was assaulted by a wave of heat as she opened the lobby door. Sunlight blinded her even through her sunglasses; she hadn't been outside in days. In her old life, she had slathered oil on her long limbs and sunbathed on the roof of her apartment or in Central Park with Rob. She wondered what Rob was doing at this moment. She pictured him laughing it up and relaxing while she was holed up, dope sick, greasy, and all alone. When she finally reached the bank, a sudden jolt of nausea rocked her, and she raced to a garbage can on the corner to vomit. The stench coming from the trash made her gag and retch all the more. Her stomach empty, she burst out crying, gained her composure, then went to the ATM and withdrew $160. After their rent check was cashed, that would leave a shameful $40. At the corner, she leaned against the side of a building and waited, taking deep breaths, aching to wash a magic pill down her throat. Still drenched in her own funk, she was horrified by her breath and body odor; she couldn't remember when she had last brushed her teeth.

A black Honda Civic with tinted windows pulled up, and the window rolled down. She forced herself to approach the car; she was detached from her frail body as her feet moved one in front of the other through the thick haze of smog on the busy city street. *How am I going to do this?*

"Hey," she said. In the past, she had just stuck her head into the passenger-side window and taken whatever he handed her, but today she would have to be a bit bolder since she was short on funds. She had a strange feeling as she opened the car door and sat down on the leather seat, thankful for the gust of air-conditioned breeze on her face.

"Paper or plastic?" he asked as he folded a hundred-dollar bill in half, not looking at her.

Colette had learned this lingo referred to the packaging of street drugs; paper meant heroin, plastic meant coke. She watched as he folded the bill again and started biting it. She could hear his teeth crunching into something.

"No, I actually need ten tens," Colette answered.

"Nobody wants tens, hon, they're like Tylenol. All I have are thirties," Todd said as he unfolded the bill, revealing a crushed powder. He snorted the powder and looked over at her for the first time, his eyes narrowing as the drug worked its magic. Colette squirmed against the chills she felt roll up her spine.

"Shit, you look like you need a bump," he said, wiping his nose with one hand and handing her the bill and a straw with the other.

Colette was taken off guard; she had never done this before, but she was desperate. She leaned over, snorted the powder through the straw, rubbed her nose, and handed the bill and straw back.

Almost instantly, Colette felt better than she ever had. Euphoria filled her body and soul, and she felt a sudden love for Todd. She was outside her body watching, waiting.

"Do you want the thirties?" Todd asked, taking back the powder.

"I don't think I have enough money. How much are they, doll?" she asked, her voice coming out stronger than usual.

"Thirty dollars per pill, but . . ." He glanced back at her, as if assessing the situation. "There are always ways to get a discount," he said in his thick Queens accent. He reached for his belt buckle, gesturing to his crotch. Colette wanted to react with righteous indignation, but she was feeling so good, she never wanted it to end, and she would do whatever she had to. She was strong; she could handle this. She thought of Rob for a nanosecond, then pushed his image out of her mind. She needed to hang on to the last of her cash—a fact she focused on as she leaned forward across the seat. Todd pulled himself out through his zipper, and she opened her mouth and took him inside. She kept her eyes closed, and when she released him for a few seconds to gasp for air, Todd's rough hand grabbed her head and pushed it back into his lap. Seconds later, she gagged, her throat catching as his stream of grossly salty hot liquid burned her throat. She tried to compose herself while

Todd readjusted his clothing and buckled his belt. Wiping tears from her cheeks, she turned to face him expectantly. Something inside her had shifted.

"Do you have a cigarette, doll?" she asked.

He lifted himself from the seat, straightening his leg enough so that he could reach into the front pocket of his jeans, shook out a Newport Light, and tossed it at her. He stuck one in his mouth too, and she leaned toward him as he flicked his lighter and held it out. She inhaled the menthol smoke slowly, savoring it. She opened the window on her side and exhaled, watching the smoke slip through the crack. The drag hit her and she felt light headed.

"God, I don't remember the last time I had a menthol cigarette," she said, taking another drag. "Okay, doll, hand it over." She aimed her mouth away from him as she spoke so the smoke would drift out the window.

Todd reached over to the glove compartment, clearly oblivious to the shift in her demeanor, grabbed a small bottle, and tossed it at her. "Here are five thirties, on the house," he said magnanimously, as though donating millions of dollars to a children's charity. She grabbed the vial and hungrily opened it while stepping out of the car. Leaning back, she shut the door with her hip, just as her bad knee gave out and caused her to stumble. She fell onto the sidewalk as Todd's car peeled away from the curb, her precious hard-earned pills spilling out onto the street. She watched in horror as one rolled into a sewer grate and let out a scream loud enough for pedestrians to turn and look her way. She grabbed the four remaining pills and popped one into her dry mouth, still on her knees on the dirty pavement. A wet clump of her hair stuck to her cheek; she picked it off and wiped her hands on her shirt as she stood up, gaining her balance.

She was humiliated when she noticed a mother clinging to her small child's hand, pulling the toddler away from her as they stood on the corner waiting for the light to change. The little girl gazed back, clutching a doll that hung limply. Colette drew a sharp breath as she noticed the doll had one crystal-blue eye that seemed to stare through her and only half her once-golden hair sitting aside bald patches on her head. Looking at the doll, terror engulfed her, but she took a deep breath and remembered that nothing could hurt her anymore. She peered at the mother as she dragged her child across the street. Colette watched, keeping the doll in her view until she was out of sight, her heart palpitating. She closed her eyes and leaned down into the pavement. The girl reminded her so much of herself at that age, and the doll clutched in her little hand reminded her of the last day she was in the care of her mother, before she got sent away.

~

Colette lifted her head from the pavement, confused and disoriented, with no idea how long she'd been lying on the street or why. She saw the bottle of pills in her hand but had no memory of how they had gotten there. She pushed down on the cap to open it and saw three beautiful pills. Despite her fogginess, she relished the elation that arose in her from having enough pills to get through one more day. Ignoring the stares from people on the street, she hobbled home.

Emotionally drained and struggling to see straight, Colette noted, curiously, that her throat burned and her mouth tasted like a dirty ashtray. She gulped vodka from the bottle in her freezer to calm her nerves and rid her mouth of the rotten taste. She struggled to gain clarity as she simultaneously enjoyed what was left of the high from the pill. She enjoyed the rest of the evening, happily watching a legal drama, hoping to get caught up or lulled to sleep. Though nursing could be rewarding, she sometimes wished she'd had more guidance in her teens. She had only Aunt Lisa to bounce ideas off regarding her career path, and her aunt had been enthusiastic about her idea of becoming a nurse. But what if she'd had someone who really believed in her? Who had been willing to help her apply to college? Maybe she could have been a lawyer. In her fantasies, she was a courtroom attorney, building cases on forensic evidence and righteously fighting for the downtrodden and victimized. Being empowered and making a difference.

She was startled from her slumber, woken by the violent banging of her drawers being opened and thrown on the floor. Rob, in a frenzy, stepped over the piles of clothing and stormed toward the kitchenette. He opened the silverware drawer and rummaged through it before ripping it out and dumping it on the floor, causing a booming crash. Colette watched, wincing.

"Where's all the money?" he demanded, storming toward her. She cowered against the couch cushions, terrified of his rage. His strong hands reached for her arms and pulled her up so she was standing facing him. She gazed into his eyes, which only showed his utter hatred and disgust for her. She'd known this day would come but was still shocked at his fury. She had never seen Rob like this before.

"I got a phone call from the landlord while I was away on business trying to fucking work, Colette. He wanted to know when we would be paying the last two months' rent. I gave you cash, you stupid bitch. Where the fuck is it?"

"I forgot to pay it, but I put a check in the mail yesterday," Colette said, her hands shaking.

Rob let go of her arms, took a step back, and looked her up and down. "For both months?"

Panicked, she tried to reason with him. "Well, I got a little behind, so just the one."

"Exactly why are you behind? It's this shit, isn't it?" he said, grabbing the pill bottle from the coffee table and rushing to the window. He opened it and shook the pills into the wind.

Colette was frozen in shock; she wanted to scream at him, to cry, but she just stared at him, openmouthed.

"Have you looked at yourself lately? You are utterly disgusting. Inside and out."

She tucked her unruly hair behind her ears and wiped under both eyes with shaky fingers, her nails topped with black moons. The faint smell of stale nicotine wafted from her right hand.

"I just woke up, you fucking asshole," she yelled back, anger and resentment boiling up inside her.

"When was the last time you showered?" Ashamed, she was silent, and he continued. "You not only look homeless, but you smell like shit. Why do you think I never want to come home? You make me sick."

She had no response to his accusations—all of them were true, though she also knew full well that he'd lost interest in her long before she'd become a drug addict. She watched as he rummaged in his work bag, grabbed his laptop, slammed it down on the coffee table, and began typing.

"What are you doing?" Colette asked nervously. "Tell me," she demanded. He pressed the keys, ignoring her.

"Where is all the fucking money?" Rob was in her face, turning the laptop and shoving it toward her so she could see the dreaded bank account page that showed all her withdrawals and the paltry remaining balance.

"Well, I haven't had a paycheck in weeks and I had to pay the bills!"

"I gave you cash, you fucking liar. I knew it. I knew I couldn't trust you." He slammed the laptop shut and started pacing like a caged lion in front of her, holding his head in his hands. "And there was $6,700 in savings the last time I checked. And now there's forty fucking dollars in the account. Ever since your fall, you have become a completely useless piece of garbage." He kicked her pocketbook, which was lying on the floor, the contents flying all over the room, lip glosses, lighters, and prescription bottles rolling on the wood floor.

"So now we have no fucking money, you have no job, and it's apparently up to me to clean up after you. Ya know, if it weren't for me, you'd be in Connecticut with your mentally deranged mother and your alcoholic lumberjack dad, living in a two-room ranch where you belong. I should have never brought you here. You are a fucking loser, Colette, a pathetic . . . junkie . . . loser." He sharply emphasized each word, pointing his finger in her face.

As she sat back on the couch, Colette felt strangely liberated—he hated her, resented her for impeding his dreams of wealth and success. The truth was out . . . and she was still breathing. She didn't care if he left her. She just wanted to be alone, to no longer have to worry about disappointing him. She took a deep breath and waited for what was going to happen next, looking back at Rob with a careless shrug. Her indifference only infuriated him further, and he grabbed a garbage bag and started filling it with her stuff, huffing and puffing and shaking his head, his rage coming to a head.

"You think you are going to sit here in my apartment popping pills and stealing from me? I am so done." He was screaming now. "You disgust me. I am not living with a slimy addict for one more day, let alone paying for the privilege of your sleaziness while you suck my blood. You need to fucking leave." He threw the trash bag at her; it hit her in the face and landed in her lap, spilling T-shirts onto the floor. He sat on the other side of the couch and leaned his head back with resignation and rubbed his eyes. He opened them and looked at her where she still sat, not knowing what to do next. He leaned toward her with hate in his eyes.

"I'm not kidding, Colette. Leave! Now! Get out!"

Instead of feeling despair, Colette was thrilled that she had an excuse to leave the apartment and go look for her pills on the dirty New York street. She bent down to pick up the contents of her purse, grabbed her phone and keys, and walked across the apartment that had once meant everything to them. Opening the door, she looked back at the man who had promised to love her till death did them part.

"Oh, and Colette: don't think I'm gonna forget you owe me nine thousand dollars."

Chapter Ten

GRETA

2007

Greta walked into the boardroom and took a seat beside Jack. The twins were finally sleeping through the night, and she was getting back to feeling like herself again, though it had taken longer than she'd expected. She glanced at Jack, worried about how much she had missed him, and hoped it was just the work itself she missed. She tried not to compare Jack to a relationship that she knew had been strained by years of infertility treatment and the stress of newborns.

The high-energy presenter introduced himself and launched directly into his pitch. "This fund is going to explode. Wait until you hear what industry we're going to invest in. It's so insane how much money we're talking. Our researchers predict that in 2027, this industry could rake in forty billion in sales; it's raking in twenty billion now."

Greta was stunned by the unprofessionalism of his presentation, and he hadn't even gotten to the proposed industry yet.

"Infertility!" The word was suddenly splashed on the wall projector screen, and the analyst pointed his red laser pen at it for extra emphasis. "There are eighteen start-ups that are all capitalizing on infertility. One company launched a product to address egg freezing, another an ovulation tracking system, and then there is big money with IVF financing, at-home hormone testing. The common denominator is that they are all financially successful. And now is the time to capitalize on these infertility start-ups."

He wanted to profit from what was a private matter for so many? Was this some sort of sick joke? Greta was used to being an outcast in a predominantly male industry, but this felt personal.

"Everyone's buying into it," he continued, "and I have some inside connections that are going to make Teiking's stocks skyrocket. These fertility companies are coming up with huge campaigns targeted at women under twenty, and the projected sales are insane." As if he were simply suggesting a blue-chip company, he concluded, "It's a surefire win. I want to be the first on board with its launch."

"Sounds promising," Jack said toward the end of the presentation. When the presenter finished, he said, "We'll review the market research and take a private vote." Apparently, Jack didn't care about preying on infertile women as much as she did.

Greta's pulse was fast at this point, her palms sweaty, but she tried to remain professional. "I'm not sure this company is in line with our firm's overall investment strategy," she said, "but thanks for enlightening us with the presentation."

She pulled a few mints out of her purse and began sucking on them in an attempt to ease her tension. Her left hand pressed against her chest, feeling her heart pumping through her black blazer. She had never experienced palpitations like this during a work presentation and had decided that when it was her turn to vote, it would be a confidential "no."

She kept checking her pulse on her wrist and her neck, just to see if relaxing her breathing would help lower it. This was all hitting too close to home. It felt as if the world was now playing evil tricks on her.

"We're not going to make money preying on women suffering from infertility. It's not right," she said, but then she second-guessed opposing, paranoid that everyone in the room would guess that she was one of those women.

~

Work was usually an escape from the stress at home, but not today; now Greta had the urge to reconnect with Patrick. She and Jack were always on the same page when it came to what companies to invest in; the fact that he would even entertain taking advantage of infertile women was making her wonder about his moral compass. She took a deep breath and dialed Patrick.

"Want to go to the spa tomorrow? We can just get away alone, maybe play some tennis?" Greta asked, remembering a fight they'd had when they were in the throes of infertility where he'd said he had thought she'd play more tennis with him. She had to get out of work and thought this might be a good opportunity to connect as a couple and bring back some of the love and affection they'd had in the early months of their marriage. A lie, a marriage, more infertility, a high-risk birth of twins. They had been through so much stress and undue hardship, and she was now trying to sustain her biggest lie yet. Perhaps a vacation would help, she hoped.

Patrick said, "I'm touched you thought about us, babe. Going away will be great!"

Next, she called Lucia, their nanny, to make sure she could come in the morning and stay overnight. Greta went home, packed up the car, and basked in the idea of getting away and getting *one* good night of sleep. She was a little nervous about leaving the boys for an overnight, but she trusted Lucia and convinced herself that staying connected to Patrick was important too.

When she got home, she felt a flutter of excitement about getting away.

"Did you see my dad dropped off his old Suburban? It's for Lucia. I was telling my mom that we were going away, and I mentioned I was worried about Lucia driving the twins around in her old car, and he just dropped it off this morning. Isn't that thoughtful? My parents were probably relieved that we didn't ask them to babysit," she said with a chuckle.

"Well, if you feel weird about Lucia, my parents would babysit anytime," Patrick said.

"No, no, the boys are used to Lucia."

"It doesn't even look old," he remarked, pointing at the "new car" in the driveway and adding, "Do you think she thinks we're insulting her car?"

"No, and who cares? It's our babies' safety that matters."

"Okay, but most nannies don't drive brand-new Suburbans."

"Patrick, it's fine, it's a used car. I think I'll buy an extra set of car seats, but for now, can you put the ones in your Jeep in Dad's car?"

"Sure, and then let's go. I can't wait to get you alone," he teased, and Greta smiled.

She rushed around trying to finish getting ready. As an adult, she noticed her father's flaws surfaced with more clarity, but so did the realization that he wasn't perfect, so she was able to slowly let go of the anger and resentment she'd been holding on to and appreciate that her father got her a useful gift and perhaps that was his way of showing her sons love. Despite their similarities, she always felt like the black sheep in the family, but sometimes he surprised her and did nice things. He'd said, "Want you to know the kids are safe while you're at work, kiddo." She could afford to buy her nanny a car, so she found the gesture particularly endearing and in many ways a symbol that his judgment toward Patrick had softened, and this made her happy.

"Why don't we just take my car to the spa and leave the Land Rover for Lucia?" Patrick asked.

"No, I want to take my car." Greta stopped herself from explaining that it would be embarrassing to show up at a luxury spa in a used Jeep. As much as she believed Patrick looked sexy driving a Jeep in the summer with no shirt on, her upbringing had conditioned her to be more comfortable in luxury vehicles. Although she had moved into a home that was below her means and less ostentatious than the mansion she was raised in, her affinity for the finer things still crept in from time to time no matter how hard she tried to push it away.

Greta jumped in her dad's old car and pulled it up closer to the house. She began scrolling through his GPS. Noticing an address under recent destinations, her eyes widened. She'd memorized the house number on Adee Street in Port Chester, New York, from the files she'd taken from his house and hidden when he was in prison. She wondered why she'd remembered this street more than a decade later.

She had to let it go, to focus on her own growing family rather than getting wrapped up in her father's past. She couldn't help but wonder what would have happened if she'd worked for him and then gotten in trouble herself. It was one thing for Patrick to dismiss her father's troubles, but if she'd ever gotten wrapped up in white-collar crime, he probably would have walked away. It was a blessing that she was working her way up at Teiking without needing her father's connections, and she was grateful she was married to Patrick and had excelled at work as Greta O'Brien versus having to be associated with her maiden name.

~

When Lucia arrived the next morning, Greta motioned her to park her car in front of the house and then pointed at the Suburban in the driveway and explained the car seats were in it just in case she needed to go somewhere. She also wrote down a list of the boys' schedules, even though Lucia already knew their routine. She felt a little more apprehensive about leaving them to travel and was nervous to be gone overnight versus just leaving them to go up the street for the workday.

"There is a double jogging stroller in the back if you want to take them on a walk in the park," Greta explained and handed Lucia the keys to the used Suburban, again feeling grateful her father had thought of this.

Lucia nodded, then made a shooing motion. "Go. Enjoy yourselves. You deserve a romantic getaway."

Patrick had already thrown his bags and their rackets into her car, hopped into the driver's seat, and rolled down the windows.

"Come on, sweetie, they will be *fine*. I want to get to our hotel room," he said, winking as she hopped in the passenger side and waved goodbye to Lucia. Greta knew what he meant when he brought up being alone in a hotel room; he kept suggesting that they get away alone, and Greta knew it was because she was always giving him excuses as to why she wasn't in the mood, exhausted by work and the two toddlers. She had packed Patrick's favorite pre-infertility red lace nightgown and was looking forward to not being woken up at 6:00 a.m. by her babies' cries.

As they drove away, she got a call from Jack at work; he let her know the firm had agreed that infertility investments were too risky at this point. He must have sensed her unease and felt it was worth interrupting her day off, and she very much appreciated the update. It immediately felt as if a weight was lifted, and the rest of the ride was fun and filled with laughter. Things were looking up at work and at home, so she smiled and took it all in. Greta and Patrick felt so right, and they were transported back to when they'd first met, reminiscing all the way to the Berkshires.

"I just read that the spa is dry," Patrick said.

"Don't worry. I packed some beer for you and La Marca Prosecco for me," she said, referring to her favorite drink.

When they finally arrived, Patrick's hands were all over Greta as they checked in.

She convinced him to let her have a drink first because she felt so out of practice when it came to their lovemaking, which happened only occasionally, when she forced herself to squeeze it in after a long workweek. She was always tired from caring for the twins and had been self-conscious about her postpartum figure over the last year, even though she was still a size four and Patrick didn't even seem to notice as they kissed and made love. She felt more relaxed with him than she had been feeling when they were home, but she still wasn't very aroused and wished she'd feel more of the spark she'd felt when they first met. She chalked it up to being in the throes of motherhood and tried not to worry.

"I love you so much," Greta said and meant it. She loved that they were a family. She was happy to curl up next to him and take a nap in the luxurious room. When she awoke, she nudged Patrick to get ready for their spa treatments.

"I've never gotten a massage. What do I wear?"

Greta laughed and explained. "There's a locker room, and they have big white robes, and we wear those into the waiting area." Moments like these made her realize they were so different.

When they got to the waiting area, Patrick sipped cucumber water and mockingly lifted his pinkie as Greta inhaled the scent of lavender-eucalyptus steam.

"Stop, you're embarrassing," Greta said.

"This water's cleansing my palate," he chuckled. "Let's skip the massage and go back to the room."

Greta remembered a time when she had laughed at every one of his jokes. Why did she now find him so immature for constantly joking about how little sex they had? And anytime she caught herself belittling his tennis coaching in her mind, she stopped herself and remembered how much she'd first admired that he chose to do something that made him happy versus being a workaholic.

She laughed and then said, "After our massage, we can play tennis. I'm so rusty."

Maybe if she took some time off work and played tennis with him more regularly, they'd feel more connected. She was willing to give it a try.

"We should play more at home," Patrick said, as if he'd heard her thought.

After the massages, Greta and Patrick walked back to their room to get changed and go play, but she noticed a missed call from Lucia.

"She's probably just checking in, but I'm going to give her a call to make sure everything is okay with the babies," Greta said as she dialed Lucia. She put the phone on speaker so Patrick could hear.

"Oh, thank goodness you called!" Lucia said. Greta could tell something was wrong from the tone of her voice.

Patrick dropped the two rackets in his hand and came and sat down next to Greta. He put one hand on her knee as Lucia went on: "Logan has a fever, and his whole body started shaking. I'm scared."

"Shaking how? What was the temperature? You used the thermometer that goes in his ear?"

"Yes," Lucia said.

Greta spoke clearly into the phone. "Call the pediatrician, and if they say it's okay, then in my medicine cabinet is baby Tylenol. Read the side of the box and give him a little in the dropper. Call me right back as soon as you get off the phone with Dr. Tyler. And call Audrey to come over and help you with Brayden."

After they hung up, Greta waved her own hand in front of her face to try to cool herself down. "Call the valet," she said to Patrick. "I think we should leave."

"Okay." Patrick patted her leg. "It's probably nothing; I'm sure kids get fevers."

Greta's heart was starting to speed up a little. She felt better packing up her things and heading home.

"I'm not sure where I put the ticket with the number," Patrick said.

"Oh my God, can't you keep track of anything?" she said, her frustration exaggerated because of her concern over Logan.

"Oh, here, got it. Greta, try to relax."

"Okay, you're right. I'm sorry. And I do want to play tennis with you at home."

"It's fine. We'll call Lucia on the way home, and I'm sure his fever will be down."

Greta quickly stuffed her toiletries into her designer duffel bag, and they headed to the main lobby.

~

An hour later, Greta called Lucia for an update. She was grateful the nanny was responsible enough to have noticed Logan was warm, take his temperature, and call her, but now she wanted to take over. Logan was a baby who needed his mother.

"We're almost home, Lucia," she said when the nanny answered. "How is Logan doing?"

"Oh, Mrs. O'Brien, he started shaking again, and his eyes rolled back in his head. I didn't know what to do so I called the pediatrician back, and this time he said to call 911. I'm waiting for the ambulance now and was just about to call you back."

Greta gasped, and she instantly regretted leaving them home so young.

"Ambulance?" Patrick said.

"Okay, Lucia, we're almost there. I will call Audrey to go with you or take Brayden or help. We'll drive there and meet you. Stay calm."

"They're here. Okay, maybe she can meet me at the hospital," Lucia said.

Greta hung up and took short, deep breaths as she dialed Audrey with shaky fingers. She breathed a sigh of relief when her friend said she was free and willing to go to the hospital and help calm Lucia down until she and Patrick arrived. Greta hung up, and Patrick put his right arm on her knee and squeezed. She was unable to take a deep breath.

When they finally arrived at the children's hospital, they rushed down the hall in the ER until they spotted Audrey talking with a nurse. As Greta neared, she saw her little Logan lying on a stretcher in a cur-tained-off room. His olive-tone skin contrasted with the stark white table. He lay completely still, an IV poking into his small hand. The sight of it made her sick to her stomach.

The nurse looked up. "Is this your son? What a little trooper. We're giving him some Ativan because he didn't come out of the seizure as quickly as we would have liked."

All Greta heard was the word "seizure."

"Oh my God, is he going to be okay?" Greta's knees were about to buckle. Patrick had leaned in to hug her, supporting her as she sank into a chair next to her son's stretcher, aching for him. "What's happening?"

"He had three back-to-back episodes. One at home, it sounds like, one in the ambulance, and one when he got here," the nurse explained. "We're keeping him overnight for observation, and we'll have a neurol-ogist evaluate him and rule out epilepsy. Let's stay optimistic."

Greta's knee-jerk reaction was to find answers. She said, "What caused the seizure? Why do you think it's epilepsy?"

The nurse gave her a solid squeeze on her forearm and said, "Seizures aren't uncommon in children under four. This could well be febrile in nature, but it's important to rule anything else out. Right now, he's in a typical post-seizure state of confusion. Don't panic."

Patrick sat in the chair beside her, their heads angling toward each other. "Thanks for driving so fast and keeping me sane," she said. She felt so guilty that she'd left her babies for a frivolous couple's spa trip.

Now she was scared there was something seriously wrong. She looked over, and Patrick was starting to doze off in his chair.

Greta couldn't imagine ever sleeping again, she felt so scared, guilty, and weighed down by her lie. Audrey hugged her and said, "He's going to be okay," but Greta worried nonetheless.

"Oh my God, honey, it was horrible. He was just shaking, and his eyes rolled up, and all I could see were the whites of his eyes, and his neck was limp," Audrey explained. "Lucia said the one at the house was the same. She rode with him in the ambulance, and she's still in shock. But I'm glad you called me. I told her to take Brayden home and explained you guys were on your way. She didn't have a bottle with her, so it's good she got him home."

"Thank you," Greta said, squeezing Audrey's hand and tapping Patrick so he could say thank you too.

A few minutes later, the doctor walked in, speaking as though they were in the middle of conversation already. "Normally I don't worry too much when kids have a seizure with a high fever. But his fever wasn't that high and he had three in a row, so we'll need him to stay overnight. Do either of you have a family history of epilepsy?"

And just like that, her anxiety skyrocketed.

She watched as Patrick slid a thumb back and forth over his mouth and took a moment to think. "No. I'll ask my parents, but I don't think so."

The doctor perched on a stool, his eyes fixed on the computer screen next to the bed. His expression grew intense, more focused. Greta felt heat flooding her face as she thought about "family" history. She clutched the armrests of the chair to hide her shaking hands as the doctor turned to face her.

"Is there any history of epilepsy that you're aware of, Mrs. O'Brien?"

Her mouth was dry as she croaked out, "No, sorry, not that I'm aware of." She hoped Patrick and the doctor chalked her weak voice up to her worry about Logan.

"Then it's probably febrile, but we're going to keep him overnight and have our neurology team explore what might have caused three back-to-back seizures, rule out epilepsy and other seizure disorders," the doctor said, turning back to the screen and shaking his head.

Acknowledging she'd lied hit hard. This might not be the first time her kids' genetics would come up, and she feared it was too big a lie to outrun. But how could she confess without it blowing up her whole life? *I really don't know his family history.*

Greta deeply regretted all the lies that had led to this one.

Chapter Eleven

COLETTE

2007

Colette couldn't pinpoint one thing she longed for—she longed for a lot, but she had given up on wishing long ago. When she opened her eyes, she simply blew out the candles. As everyone cheered, she looked around at the faces in this group—it was all people she barely knew. And yet, she was grateful that her friend had put together a little something to celebrate her birthday.

"Thanks, Chelse. I love you." Colette pulled Chelsea into an embrace. She'd taken to kissing her ass lately, hoping to offset the fact that she had been sleeping on her friend's couch. What had started out as a temporary favor, an emergency bailout, had quickly ballooned into six months with no end in sight. When she wasn't telling Chelsea how much she appreciated her or complimenting her clothes, hair, makeup, and weight loss, Colette was throwing money at her—to keep her only lifeline distracted and happy, and to prevent her from lecturing. Or worse, from asking her to leave.

After Rob had kicked her out of their apartment, Colette had no choice but to sell her wedding ring at a pawnshop in the Diamond

District. She'd walked away with no regrets and $9,000 in her pocket. She had suffered a momentary jolt after hearing the offer; Rob had painstakingly saved nearly $15,000 over the course of three years to buy it for her—but in the end, it had meant nothing. She had been relieved to have money to offer Chelsea at that moment, but she also knew it wouldn't last long.

"What did you wish for?" the eternally positive Chelsea asked.

"A job," Colette lied, hearing herself slurring, her arms still wrapped around her friend.

"Oh, I know you'll get something soon," Chelsea said, reaching out to cut the cake with Colette hanging on her. She slid a piece toward the birthday girl.

"Thanks, Chelse." Colette shoveled an obligatory bite into her mouth.

The night wound down early, and Colette was snuggled up watching mindless television by nine thirty. After reaching underneath Chelsea's couch for her stash of pills, she was dumbfounded to discover only one left in the bottle. She swallowed it hastily, then calculated how many she could afford to buy the next day.

The morning came too quickly, the apartment quiet and still. Chelsea and her boyfriend were often still there when she woke up, but sometimes, to Colette's delight, they worked the early shift at the hospital. She looked at her flip phone, checking for messages. Chelsea had called at nine that morning and left a voice mail. She was working a double and wouldn't be back until the following morning.

It wasn't until she went to retrieve a pill later that Colette remembered they were gone. She grabbed her pocketbook to lay hands on her precious envelope of cash; she needed a quick count. She fingered through the thin stack of tens and twenties and realized, with an anxious punch to her gut, that she had only $220.

"That can't be right," she said aloud, panic taking root. She recounted again and again, in need of a miracle. She needed to calm down; she also needed a fix as soon as possible, but she owed Chelsea more than $200, leaving her at nearly zero. Her latest round of job applications had yielded nothing, and impending doom overtook her.

"I can't do this anymore," she sighed, slumping onto the floor. Her head was pounding, and the constant worry about money and pills was wearing on her. She couldn't think straight, and every time she woke up and told herself she would quit cold turkey, it never stuck. She was spinning her wheels with no idea how to stop her addiction from fueling every choice she made. If she just had more money, she wouldn't have to be as stressed about it. She closed her eyes and tried to come up with a solution, and thought of Chelsea's "rainy-day fund"—a coffee can on top of the microwave. She'd seen her friend dropping bills into it regularly but had never dared to ask about or mention it. A little peek wouldn't hurt, she rationalized.

Counting it carefully, Colette was thrilled and relieved; there was $606 in the can. No way would Chelsea notice if $200 went missing. That would get Colette one last batch of pills, which would hold her until she had a job. She would *have* to have something by then. And then, she was done with the drugs and this lifestyle. She meant it this time.

She slipped ten $20 bills into her bra and called her new hookup, Desmond. Her habit could cost up to $100 a day, but with some scrimping and discipline, she could stretch her money for a few more days. She'd have to ration; that was all there was to it.

~

Three nights later, she swallowed her last pill before heading out with Chelsea, Nick, and some other friends from the hospital, this time to celebrate Chelsea's birthday. Tonight, the plan was to drink heavily to compensate for having no more painkillers, so she started with tequila shots. With her last fifty dollars, she bought a round for everyone and felt relaxed as the liquor started pumping through her system. Before long, the party moved onto the small open floor in the back of the bar so they could dance. Tired and foggy, Colette opted to stay at the bar. She laid her head down in the crook of her arm, just wanting to rest her eyes for a minute or two. *How am I going to get through the night without any pills? I'm going to be so sick tomorrow . . . I'm tired of living like a junkie.*

Colette woke when she felt tapping on her shoulder. She peered up at the figure above her with her eyes half-open, the tequila swimming in her gut.

"Desmond?" she asked, confused, her voice thick. She wondered how long she had been passed out. She looked around to see if anyone noticed and saw that her group was still on the dance floor.

"You called me and told me to meet you," he said. His voice was clipped with impatience as he shoved his hands in his pockets.

"Oh, right, doll. Let's go outside and smoke," she answered. She was glad the darkness of the bar would hide the flush of her cheeks as she followed her drug dealer outside onto the city sidewalk. The sounds of traffic surrounded them as he handed her a Marlboro Light and lit it for her. She inhaled sharply.

"God, I love smoking." She took another long drag on the cigarette and closed her eyes. She inhaled slowly and let it linger in her throat before exhaling. It felt so good after such a long stint of not smoking. "I haven't had a Marlboro in ages."

He gave her a strange look as he lit his cigarette. "You asked me for one the last time I saw you."

Colette pondered why she'd called him; maybe she was more wasted than she thought. The nicotine hit her and kicked up her buzz from earlier. She needed a pill. Even though just a short while before she had vowed to detox, acknowledging that tomorrow would be hard without it, she suddenly could think of nothing else but how she was going to get her next fix. Her stomach flipped as she remembered the last time she had been in this position, jonesing for a blue with no cash.

"I need some shit, doll," she said.

"I have whatever you need."

"Well, I might need you to take an IOU," she tried, knowing full well what his answer would be.

They hopped in a cab, and he was groping her before the car door was even shut. She felt numb as his fingers ran up and down her body, unhooking her bra. They disentangled when the cab arrived at their destination. Her body went cold as they walked toward his apartment building, his hand pulling hers to follow him. She knew where this was headed, and it made her sick. But she kept walking, because her need for drugs overpowered her self-loathing. He punched in a code at the front door, and when it buzzed open, they walked through a massive lobby adorned with mirrors and chandeliers and watched over by two doormen. If she hadn't been so consumed with what she was about to have to do, she would have been floored that this was where he lived. How many drugs did he sell, exactly?

"Good evening, sir," one of the doormen said, tipping his hat at them as they rushed toward the elevator. Desmond grabbed her hand and pulled her inside behind him, using his free hand to punch the button that said "PH." He pressed her close to his wiry body and shoved his hand under her skirt, ripping her panties aside and pushing his fingers inside her roughly. The pain caused her to catch her breath. She dug her fingernails into his back, and her stomach clenched as she considered what could happen once she stepped inside his apartment with the door locked behind them. She closed her eyes.

~

When Colette opened her eyes, bright sunlight forced them closed. Squinting, she spotted a clock she didn't recognize: 11:42. She slowly looked around a very large bedroom as her eyes adjusted to the light. The room had high vaulted ceilings, and long velvet drapes partially covered windows, open just enough to see the floor-to-ceiling panes of glass behind them with the New York City skyline in full view. She had no idea where she was.

She sat up and pulled the covers against her naked body. The soft silk felt unfamiliar. The room smelled like a mixture of sex and rancid cigarette smoke. She reluctantly turned her head, afraid of who she would find next to her in this strange bed. A shirtless man had his back to her. His shaggy brown hair reminded her of her drug dealer . . . but how could that be? Had he been there last night? She couldn't remember. She focused now, trying to lure back some details. When none came, she reached over to carefully pull the covers away from his face. She peered at Desmond dozing as a pit formed in her stomach.

She had to get out of there. She didn't want to face him, horrified at what she might well have done in exchange for pills. Fear ripped through her. This was the second time she had used her body for drugs.

But there were likely pills she could help herself to while her dealer slept. She might as well take what she could get and worry about getting a new dealer later.

Colette slid out from under the sheets, searching for her clothes. Partially dressed, she scanned the space, looking for her bra—and there, right on top of a marble bedside table, was her cosmetic bag. Resting on top was a beautiful bottle filled with alluring blue pills, 30 milligrams each. The relief at seeing them was overwhelming and helped to push her self-loathing aside. She bent to look under the bed for her bra, finding it next to a metal box.

Desmond's chest was still rising and falling steadily, so she quietly opened the box, which was filled with little wax paper stamp bags she figured must be filled with heroin. Colette quickly put her bra on and shoved the five stamp bags inside it. It probably wouldn't get her much on the street, but a hundred bucks was a hundred bucks. Even though she couldn't remember the details, she was fairly certain she had earned it. She stood and tiptoed over to a pair of jeans at the foot of the bed and slipped a wallet out of the back pocket. She carefully slid a credit card out, then put the wallet back. She threw a last look at the sleeping man before quietly opening the door to escape.

She had to walk around and find street signs to figure out where she was. As she edged along the sidewalk, the movement making her queasy, it became clear that she was still drunk, the contents of her stomach threatening to spill out onto the street.

Lafayette? She wrinkled her brow with confusion as she peered at the street sign. She walked a few more blocks and found a subway entrance, grabbing the first uptown train to arrive.

Colette felt herself sobering up as the train gently lulled her with its movement, her stomach finally settling and exhaustion starting to take over. By the time she arrived at Chelsea's, all she wanted was some water and some more sleep—and thankfully, the apartment was empty. As she sank down into the couch, she noticed a note on the IKEA cube that served as a coffee table. *Call me ASAP*—Chelsea's handwriting.

What had she done last night besides sleeping with her drug dealer? She stared blankly at the table, considering putting off the phone call, and eventually deciding she had to suck it up and get it over with. It was possible it'd be better dealt with over the phone than in person anyway. Rummaging in her bag for her phone, she saw Chelsea's coffee can on the floor next to the couch. The cover was off; inside, it was empty.

"Fuuucck," Colette breathed as she opened her phone to see she had three missed calls from her friend.

"What the fuck?" Chelsea answered after the first ring.

"Where are you?" Colette asked, trying to play it cool.

"I told you Nick was taking me to Atlantic City for my birthday," Chelsea yelled, "and that we've been saving gambling money for this for months."

Colette's heart sank. An apology sat on the tip of her tongue, but she stopped herself, knowing she would be homeless if she admitted what she had done. "Okay. So what's wrong?" she asked, playing dumb.

"First of all, where did you go last night? You disappeared."

"Umm . . . I guess I left with Desmond," she answered, trying to sound casual.

"Desmond?" Chelsea screeched. "I didn't even know he was there!"

Colette had put her foot in her mouth—she had been hoping he had at least been at the bar, but like a true drug addict, she'd hit him up for a fix and ended up sleeping with him. She remained silent.

"Whatever. Anyway, I can't have you staying with me anymore." Chelsea took a deep breath, clearly gearing herself up. "Get your shit and get out of my apartment today. I don't want you there when I come back." She sounded like she had practiced saying it. "I know that you stole my money."

"Oh my God! I didn't take your money! Are you serious?"

"Really? Nobody else has been in the apartment. I was hoping you would at least admit what you did." Her disappointment was visceral.

"I did not take your money. I didn't even know you had cash here!" She wasn't even sure why she was doubling down, being so ada-mant. Maybe it was just second nature—as an addict, she hid things and lied. But as she told herself that, a pit of guilt in her stomach expanded. She didn't want to hurt her friend. Especially the only one she had left in the world . . . but she couldn't seem to stop herself. *I used to be a good person . . . I used to have a husband . . . and friends. What is happening to me?*

"Colette, you fucking took the money. And I went through your stuff and found an envelope with thousands of dollars, which is fucked up. Nick and I agreed that you have to leave, so—"

"What? I don't have thousands of dollars!" Finally, something true she could be legitimately offended by. "I've been living off the money from my ring, and it's almost gone!" She was truly pleading now—she had nowhere to go.

"Stop lying, Colette. It's pathetic," Chelsea said with disgust.

Anger rushed through her, replacing the worry and fear. She *was* pathetic, but she didn't want to hear someone else tell her, least of all her only friend. "You're the one that's fucking pathetic, letting Nick tell you what to do. How dare you accuse me of stealing? I've given you money every week that I've been here. I thought we were friends."

"Fuck you, Colette. Get your shit and get the fuck out of my house." Chelsea's voice was quavering before she hung up.

And now Colette officially had nowhere to go. Though she had *borrowed* Chelsea's money, she was confused about the mystery cash Chelsea had mentioned. Digging in the garbage bag she had left her apartment with six months before, underneath gym clothes she hadn't worn once, she found the manila envelope of paperwork she'd taken with her when Rob had thrown her out: some random legal papers, her nursing license, her papers from her egg harvesting and freezing procedure, the papers from her abortion. She looked at that one a moment, her finger tracing over the "C. C. Richards" written in strong, unwavering black lines. Gazing at handwriting she didn't even remember executing, she wondered now how different her life would have been had she had the baby. With or without Rob, would she be in this mess if she'd become a mother? Blinking back sudden tears, she dug through the papers still in the envelope and found exactly what Chelsea had said was there: a stack of hundred-dollar bills.

Dumbfounded, Colette fell back against the couch. Where had this money come from? How had she forgotten she had it? And much, much scarier: What had she done to earn it? And how messed up had she been when she'd done it? If she'd slept with Desmond last night—God, she hoped that was all she'd done—for some pills, what on earth had she done to earn this much cash?

The nausea came roaring back and she ran to the bathroom, barely getting there before she emptied her stomach. She was rinsing her mouth out when her phone rang.

"Chelse?"

"No, Colette. It's Aunt Lisa."

"Aunt Lisa, hi!" Colette said with relief. Her shoulders softened and she exhaled, happy to have a reprieve from the stress of the night before and its aftermath, as well as the dizzying thoughts surrounding the discovery of the cash in her bag.

"How are you?" she asked, eager to engage in light conversation with someone who loved her.

"Not great, actually, Colette. I'm so sorry but it's your father." Her voice came over the line, and Colette was light headed. "A friend from Jewett City heard and called to let me know. He didn't really tell anyone, but your father was diagnosed with terminal cancer six months ago and he declined treatment. It's not good. He's at the cancer center in Rhode Island." Aunt Lisa's words came out rushed. "I will try to get there at some point if you need me, but I really think you should go see him."

Colette grabbed her small pile of belongings and the manila envelope before she could even finish talking. The word "dying" rang in her ears as she headed out the door for the bus station as fast as she could.

～

Colette chewed on her cuticle as she waited for her ticket to print; she had only a few minutes before her bus left. She sucked her thumb where she had torn the skin. The taste of blood turned her stomach. The credit card she'd purchased the ticket with was the one she'd just stolen from Desmond, and she panicked briefly that it wouldn't go through. *A new low, using a stolen credit card.* She exhaled when the agent slipped her ticket under the window. Colette snatched it and raced toward Gate B.

She was sweating as she hopped on the bus and struggled to catch her breath. She found an empty seat between two people, both of them reeking of stale cigarette smoke, which oddly made her crave a cigarette. Considering her current state, she'd have expected the smell to turn her stomach, but she fidgeted, trying to get comfortable, her body and mind both restless.

Her father had been sick for the past six months. They didn't have the type of relationship where they spoke regularly; she had called him on Christmas and they had exchanged brief pleasantries, but he'd not mentioned being ill. She knew he typically didn't give her any unpleasant news, but the fact that he hadn't told her he was dying was profoundly hurtful. She was partially to blame for the space between them. He'd been distant and emotionless in his parenting, but in this moment she tried to focus on his good qualities.

Colette laid her head back on the seat and watched the landscape pass by and wondered why she hadn't tried harder to have a relationship with her father. She treasured the small moments they had shared where he had been loving, but by the time Rob came into her life, she had given up. Her father was too hardened from their life together, and at that point it was a lot easier to focus on loving Rob than perpetuating a relationship with her father, who was forever detached.

Escaping from Jewett City had been unexpectedly bittersweet. When she had thrown her last bag into Rob's car the day she left, she'd turned back to take one last look at the small, dilapidated ranch in the poorest part of town, her heart skipping a beat when she saw her father watching from the bay window. On a whim, she'd run back into the house and grabbed him in a tight hug from behind. Though she'd known he would not return the gesture, she'd kissed him on the cheek and told him she loved him. When he had patted her hands and muttered, "I love you too," she'd nearly choked on emotion. He was uncomfortable with the intimacy, though, so it had lasted only a moment before he'd pushed her hands away and, his voice catching, said, "Now go make something of yourself."

That was the only time Colette remembered her father voicing any sort of affection for her, and she'd clung to it. He had, on numerous occasions, spoken of the time her mother had locked her in a closet. He'd gone to work in the lumberyard when Colette was three months old, and when he'd arrived home, her mother was at the kitchen table, talking on the phone. The phone cord was twisted around her fingers on one hand; in the other was a vodka tonic. Her father could hear the muffled sound of a baby crying and had tracked it to the small closet under the stairway, where he'd flung open the wooden door to find Colette strapped into a car seat, her face red and her mouth wide open as she screamed. Her mother had said that voices had told her she had to hide the baby because someone was coming to kill her.

Growing up, Colette had loved the story because her father had rescued her. Her mother's leaving had left a scar, but waiting for her father to love her was an endlessly gaping wound. The story, disturbing as it was, had assured her that he cared, that he would be there when she needed him. Now, she realized just how disturbing it was that this was a good memory for her, and it made her start to question everything she'd built since then: an unhappy marriage, a dependence on drugs, a life with no clear ties anymore. Her own issues were being thrown into stark relief by this return home.

She dreaded seeing him in her current state but was oddly comforted by it. At least he, of all people, couldn't—wouldn't—judge her struggle with addiction, having struggled with it himself.

Colette managed to doze, and when she woke up, they were out of New York. The familiar route was reassuring in a way she couldn't pinpoint as the bus sped past the Trumbull exits, where her aunt's house was. It was as if she were going back in time. As the bus got off at an exit, they passed through lower-income areas that brought up memories of her hometown.

Though she'd grown up lonely and in pain, in hindsight, she was sure her father had done the best he could. She had less than a handful of vivid memories, one of him pretending to be lost driving and her telling him where to go: "Turn right. Turn left." She would direct him until he finally pulled into their driveway—it wasn't until years later that she'd recalled the beer tucked between his legs, and she'd wondered if he'd not been playing a game but had legitimately needed to know how to get home. Still, she missed those days of being her father's navigator, of belonging, of doing something right for him. She missed their bond, flimsy though it may have been. She wanted to see him one last time.

When one of the people she was sandwiched between got off at the first Rhode Island stop, she spread out and placed her backpack on the adjacent seat. She was coming down off her breakfast of oxy and Diet Coke and felt sick to her stomach. She was exhausted and buzzing with thoughts about Chelsea, the only friend she'd had left, and how she'd fucked everything up. Now, as she sat there, heading toward family, toward "home" for all intents and purposes, she tried to convince herself that the tears dripping down her face were from sadness about her father's diagnosis—pancreatic cancer—but the truth was that she wished it were her instead. Not to altruistically save him—no, she wasn't that good a person. But to put herself out of this misery, to perhaps gain a little sympathy from others, as opposed to just pity and disdain.

As the bus entered the station at the final stop, she threw on a hat and gloves, steeling herself for what came next.

~

As Colette stepped into her father's hospital room and saw him lying in bed, her throat tightened and hot tears flooded her eyes. He was hooked up to various wires and IV tubes, his body stiff; she breathed a small sigh of anxious relief—for the first time in her life, she didn't feel vulnerable around him.

She had taken one of those glorious blue pills right before walking in. Now, she sat in the chair next to her father, waiting for the familiar calm to spread through her body as she gazed at him. Once he was gone, she would be an orphan. Her mother was technically still alive, but she had long considered herself motherless, and soon she would be fatherless as well. It made her feel invisible, unmoored.

Her father opened his eyes and moaned a loud, guttural sigh, his body shaking with spasms.

She adjusted his oxygen and grabbed his hands, in tightly clenched fists by his side. "Dad, what's wrong? I'm here."

"Colette," he whispered hoarsely, squeezing her hand. "Help me . . . I am so glad you're here. I can't . . . I . . ." His eyes drifted closed again, and he groaned as his body wrenched in a fit of visible pain.

"Dad, what do you want me to do? Should I call someone?" she asked, skimming the whiteboard above his bed that listed the names of the doctors and nurses on duty.

"No, no," he whispered between gasps of breath. "It's time for me to go. I want to die." He swallowed, the pain etching lines in his face.

Colette squeezed his hand and stroked his cheek. "It's okay, Daddy. I'm here," she said as tears dripped down her face.

He struggled to raise his head from the pillow and meet her eyes. "Colette, make sure these people know I have a DNR," he said gruffly before laying his head back down with defeat.

The entire day, she sat with him. Aunt Lisa came in the afternoon, making the hour-long trip from where she lived. Colette appreciated that she had made the effort more for Colette than for her father, whom she had never been close with. Nurses moved in and out, offering morphine and ice chips, palliative care, Colette knew. They offered comforting pats on her shoulder. After a few hours Aunt Lisa announced she was heading out and pulled Colette in for a hug, making her promise to come stay with her for a while before she made her way back to New York.

"Colette, you don't look good," her aunt said, pulling away from their embrace and peering at her eyes. "Are you doing okay?" Her brows furrowed with concern.

Colette smiled as widely as she could. "Yes, yes! I'm fine. I just had a party last night. I'm hung over." She looked back at her father's body in the hospital bed. "And sad," she said with a shrug as tears pooled in her eyes.

"Okay, just make sure to get some rest," Aunt Lisa said, giving her a kiss on the cheek.

Colette promised she would and reiterated that she would come stay with her for a while, but her first thought was how she would stay with her aunt and successfully hide her addiction.

In the afternoon, her father seemed lucid and pain-free suddenly. He looked at her, his eyes glassy, his face sweat coated.

"What are you going to do with yourself, Colette?" he asked pointedly.

She was taken aback. "Um . . . I'm not really sure, Dad. I guess I'm trying to figure that out." She had told him that she and Rob had split up but had kept the specifics to herself. Now she told him she was going to be staying with Aunt Lisa.

"Colette." He paused, his voice losing strength with each syllable. "You beat the odds . . . you got out of Jewett City." The last few words were a whisper, and Colette leaned forward to hear him. "You aren't your mother. You can have a great life. You're nothing like her."

But I might be like you, she thought. When she thought of her naked body next to Desmond's that morning, her stomach lurched. How far down this rabbit hole of addiction would she have to go before she found a way to stop?

He dragged in a breath as he kept talking. "You got dealt a shitty hand. God gave you a mother with schizophrenia, a mother who wouldn't get treated, wouldn't stay on her meds. But you're okay, Colette . . . you're a good girl." His chocolate-brown eyes gazed at her.

His words had shocked her into silence; he had uttered "schizophrenia" only a handful of times. The word itself had scared Colette when she was little. She realized now, judging by the knot in her stomach, it still did. She had spent her whole life worrying that she would end up like her mother and had been hugely relieved when she'd discovered only 1 percent of the population was diagnosed with it. There was a genetic component, but that in no way guaranteed she'd get it. And she desperately needed to not get it. It was a disorder that did not engender sympathy or compassion—there was too much stigma attached for that. It made people act bizarrely and sometimes aggressively, even violently.

Armed with the statistics and research, she had been careful to show her father that she was not her mother, that she bore no similarities to the woman whom he resented so much. She'd collected information in bits and pieces about her mother's likes, dislikes, and habits, storing them away and making a point to behave exactly the opposite. Her mother hated the beach, so she professed a love for the ocean; her mother laughed too hard and too loud, so Colette practiced a soft, coquettish one.

Her father declaring that she was nothing like her mother allowed her a peace she'd been waiting for her entire life. The burden she'd carried for so long was released so suddenly that sobs racked her as she held her father's fingers in her own while he slept. It wasn't until darkness overtook the room that Colette realized the entire day had passed. She wandered out of the room and headed to the nurse's station.

"Excuse me, I have some questions about my father, Cliff Richards."

The nurse came around the desk. "Of course, hon."

"He seems to really be suffering. I was just wondering, if, um, well, is this the end? Will this last a long time, the pain?" Colette foundered, trying to find the right words. Her nursing career hadn't prepared her for this. She cared about all her patients, had been good at comforting them, caring for them, but faced with her father's pain, his imminent death, she felt lost.

"There's no way to tell, honey," the woman said, grasping Colette's hands in hers.

Colette closed her eyes, enjoying the woman's comforting hold on her.

"There's no way to tell . . . but you know what to do."

But there's no way I can do what he wants me to do.

~

Colette woke what seemed like a few hours later from the light in the room, her head resting on her father's bed, his heart monitor emitting a loud, uninterrupted beep. She'd been there, sat with him, held his hand so he wouldn't be alone as he went into the great unknown. Heart breaking, she kissed his sallow cheek, stood, and walked out the door just as a nurse came racing in. "Please don't forget, he has a DNR on file," she said as she continued down the hallway, tears silently pouring down her face.

A disorienting sense of being unmoored washed over her. She had nothing left—no parents, no job, no home, no husband, no friends. She stepped out of the elevator and out through the revolving door, finding herself outside on the icy sidewalk. She vaguely wondered how many days she had left until the bottle of pills she had would be gone, considering the fact that she would have to find a new dealer. She shoved her hands in her pockets, the fingertips of her right hand brushing something. She pulled out a matchbook from the bar she had been in two nights before with Chelsea—with Desmond. She furrowed her brow and tossed it into a nearby trash can.

Drained emotionally and mentally, she collapsed in a heap on a bench as she cried, her breath coming in fits and starts. When she had no more tears or voice, she slowly rose, wobbling. And there in front of her was a neon sign flashing: OCEAN STATE REHAB CENTER.

Chapter Twelve

GRETA

2009

Every time Logan got a fever, Greta watched him like a hawk, praying that he wouldn't have another seizure. The doctors had tested for epilepsy and were fairly certain he'd had febrile seizures two years ago, telling her to keep an eye on him and that he'd most likely outgrow the condition.

Lucia was singing as she prepared snacks and looked after the boys while they played with clay, making mountains, dinosaurs, and airplanes. The boys adored the nanny, and Greta felt good knowing that Lucia was now knowledgeable about seizure protocol.

Greta placed her oversize Ferragamo bag on a clay-free section of countertop and sifted through the mail while she watched her boys. She could never stay home with them, reading picture books aloud, doing puzzles, coloring, playing with action figures, watching the same movies over and over again. She loved them deeply, in a way she hadn't been prepared for, but that hadn't changed her fundamentally—she didn't have the patience for playing with them all day. Even now she wished the messiness of the kitchen and the smell of the homemade clay didn't irritate her. Her maternal instincts were what most in society would have deemed paternal instincts—she loved them, wanted to take care of them by going out and making a living. On Lucia's days off, Greta often put the television on and confined the boys to the family room. She worked hard to not be like her critical mother and her cold father but wondered if it was impossible to escape her Walsh DNA. She never knew what to do with the twins and felt like she was failing.

"How was the picnic?" she asked brightly.

"Great!" Lucia replied. "They played and ate and had a wonderful time. We made ice pops with organic juice when we got home; they should be ready soon."

"I wike wed," Brayden said excitedly.

Lucia translated: "Yes, you like the cranberry juice better than orange."

Logan chimed in: "Lulu lookie."

Lucia turned to Greta. "I'm taking a child-development class on Tuesday nights. They say that at this age, they should know twenty words. Are you worried that their speech might be delayed?"

Greta felt her face flush. "Well, they were preemies, so I think it's fine." What the hell could Lucia know about speech patterns in toddlers from one class? Greta was careful not to verbally attack Lucia, who was probably only trying to help. But she felt defensive and worried that Lucia knew her children better than she did.

"Sure, that makes sense," Lucia responded, but Greta heard it as patronizing. She let it go because she wanted her kids to have a nanny who cared about them.

She said, "Oh, can you get some more cream of tartar? They love this homemade clay you make."

"Sure," Lucia said.

"Here." Greta pulled a credit card from her wallet. "Actually, you and the boys can go to the market tomorrow. I'm on deadline with a huge project for work." She blew past the woman's slightly surprised look and kept talking. "Actually, could you start doing some simple errands for us, especially now that the boys have started their toddler program?"

Lucia nodded. "Of course. I'd be happy to."

"Great. I'll leave a list. Just remember to look at labels, because I don't like giving them anything with chemicals."

"Absolutely."

"And just throw the receipts in here," Greta said, pointing at a top kitchen drawer.

Greta was proud she'd hired such good help for her boys but strangely envied her nanny's stress-free life. This girl had no deadlines, no grays to pluck, no wrinkles to obsess on, and didn't even seem to have to work hard to elicit smiles from *her* boys. How did she make raising her sons look so effortless when Greta found the job so daunting?

They discussed the boys' schedule for the week and agreed that Lucia would run errands after she put a load of laundry in the wash; she could put it in the dryer and fold after picking them up from preschool. Greta had only signed the twins up for the preschool program because Emily had insisted that Megan and Connor were geniuses because of it, and *she* had put the boys' names on the Greenwich Montessori's waiting list. Greta didn't like to admit that she was so removed from the school she didn't even know their teacher's name, but she'd put Lucia in charge of their school schedule and attending those events and told herself she'd really start getting involved when the boys were in grade school and it mattered more.

Brayden and Logan had stopped making things with clay and were now staring out the window as if mesmerized. They seemed joyful and bonded as they babbled to each other in their own secret language.

"Oh, your mother phoned and said to call her after you put the boys to sleep. She said it was very important," Lucia said.

"Okay, thanks. Maybe I should just call her now?" Greta suggested, wondering why the boys needed to be in bed for her to call her mom.

Lucia looked uncomfortable for a moment before saying, "Well, she sounded like she was crying. I can stay longer and put the boys to bed if you need me to."

"That would be wonderful," Greta said, grateful that she could focus on her mother, who rarely called crying. She dialed and waited for her mother to pick up. "Hey, Mom. What's going on?"

"Well, you're hard to track down," Evelyn said, and it was evident in her tone that she was upset.

"Sorry, you could have tried my cell. Lucia just told me you called the house."

She cleared her throat a little and ignored the comment. "Listen, honey. Please sit down."

"What's wrong?" Greta asked—with her mother, a serious issue could encompass any number of nonemergencies.

"Your father and I are getting divorced," Evelyn said, beginning to cry. Before Greta could process this, her mother kept talking. "Not a *real* divorce, but we're staging one so we can separate our assets. We started this process when your father got in a bit of trouble."

"You mean when he went to jail," Greta said, tiring of her mother's denial.

After a few seconds of silence, she went on. "Yes, well anyway, I'm putting the Nantucket house in your name—don't worry, we have renters in it all summer to offset the expenses."

"Wait a minute. Mom, slow down," Greta said, finally sitting down. "Why?"

"When your father was arrested, we lost a lot of clients, and thus our assets got hit kind of hard, and . . ."

"So do you think it's smart to hide more assets? Seems kind of risky," Greta said.

"I know you don't always get along with your father, but he's still your father, and he was in a lot of trouble and he worked hard to fix it.

It was his idea to get divorced and give you the house so that if the Feds come after him—us—you and Emily are okay," she said.

Greta just wanted a normal family and vowed never to get involved with any shady dealing at Teiking. She wanted to comfort her mother, but she blamed her father for putting them both in this position.

"I know he lost clients, but he can start over. I can give him some leads."

"Blackwood is completely folding," her mother admitted.

"I thought they said if he did time, the insider-trading changes would be taken off his record? Or was that only the conspiracy and securities-fraud charges that were dropped? Are you sure it's that bad?"

"Yes, it's bad. I called our lawyer, and he said if we liquidate our seventy-five million, we'll owe millions in capital gains taxes."

"Mom, it will be okay." She had no way of knowing this and actually thought it unlikely, but she needed time—and to placate her mother. Greta resented having to comfort a mother who had rarely comforted her when she was going through hard times, but she tried not to keep score and looked for her good side.

"I bet it was that Jack that ratted him out to the FBI; you need to stay away from that man," Evelyn said, nearly hyperventilating.

Jack? How did he get involved? "I don't think Jack would do that," Greta said. "Besides, he's not worked with Dad in years."

"Jack must have been jealous that Dad wanted you to run Blackwood," Evelyn said. "He thought you were going to get married, and he was pissed it ruined his career planning."

Greta took a long breath and sighed. Her dad had wanted her to marry someone rich like Emily's Marshall, and Jack was likely an ideal candidate. Oh well. She had no idea if Jack had his eyes on running Blackwood. All she knew was that she didn't want her boys to be brought up with all this drama. The older she got, the more flawed she realized her parents' marriage was. She only looked up to small parts of their character: her father's brain, her mother's refinement. But she wanted her sons to admire her overall character, not just bits and pieces. She didn't want them to feel belittled the way her mother and father often made her feel.

"You're smart to live in that tiny house," Evelyn said.

Greta bit back a retort—a four bedroom wasn't "tiny," but it wasn't a hill to die on in that moment. "I'll sign the papers to transfer the house, but are you sure it will even matter if he's already been arrested? The police could figure out pretty easily that the Nantucket house is yours," Greta said.

"No, no, we have it all under control. And don't tell anyone about the divorce."

"I don't know how you deal with all this."

"Greta, now you listen to me. There's nothing about your father that you know that I don't." There was a loaded silence before her mom continued. "*Nothing.* I know all the details of his mistakes, so please don't be fresh. I have stayed with him because family is more important than a mistake here or there."

This was the closest her mom had ever come to saying anything about her father's affair, and it surprised her a little. She'd always thought of her mom as purposefully naive; apparently she was just forgiving—or pathetic. "Right, Mom. Got it. I hear Patrick coming in, but I'll stop over soon." Patrick wasn't home, but she needed to find out more about what was going on from someone other than her mother. Maybe she could call Jack.

~

An hour later, when Patrick actually did walk in, his shirt was stained with sweat from his tennis coaching. Greta hid that her eyes rolled as she accidentally compared him to the men in suits she interacted with all day.

141

"Hey, sweetie," he said as he gave Greta a rushed peck on the cheek and ran to greet the boys with open arms. Greta followed him and explained that Lucia was staying later because her mother was a wreck after her father's latest shenanigans. She helped him reheat his dinner, left in the fridge by Lucia, while she looked for her keys and was secretly grateful to skip the bedtime routine to help her mother. She hated doing dishes and sometimes wondered why she didn't just treat herself to full-time kitchen help like her parents did. And after baths it was exhausting to play three rounds of Memory with Brayden after a long workday, so she welcomed the night off.

She needed to eat dinner with Patrick more. Even if she still wasn't feeling connected to him in the bedroom, she should try harder to have them eat as a family versus having Lucia feed the kids and letting Patrick fend for himself while she ate a bowl of Kashi cereal by her laptop. She had wanted to create the all-American family, to have a fulfilling marriage and dote over her boys, but being a wife and mother didn't always feel natural, and she wanted to blame her own upbringing for it. She knew that was lazy, the old "blame the parents for your emotional issues" trope, but considering what was currently going on, it couldn't be denied that her parents' relationship was odd at best and unhealthy at worst—not the best of role models when it came to creating that healthy family dynamic she had yearned for. She'd try harder, she promised herself—just as soon as she figured out what was going on with her father's business. She wished she could talk all this over with Patrick, but she needed to see Jack, someone who knew her father professionally and may be able to provide insight, if not answers.

"I guess I'll go check on my mom," Greta said. She was too tired to deal with Patrick's usual passive-aggressive comments regarding Jack as her "old high school flame" or "new hedge fund honey," and she was only meeting up with him to find answers. No sense inflaming that old nerve.

She blew him a kiss goodbye, feeling guilty that she hadn't told Patrick the truth.

~

When she arrived at MacDuff's, Jack had a glass of house wine waiting for her. She hugged him before sitting down.

"I heard. How bad is it?" Jack asked.

"Pretty bad," Greta said, gulping half her glass at once.

"I'm sorry," Jack said.

"I hate people knowing I'm a Walsh. When you Google my dad, the first thing that pops up is his mug shot. It's embarrassing."

"Okay, but people know you're different. And you should be proud of all the clients you've brought to Teiking without your old connections."

"I'm just glad I'm not a Walsh anymore."

"I kind of wish you still were," Jack said as he leaned toward Greta, smirking.

"Stop." But she said it teasingly. Jack was handsome, and she couldn't deny she was reminded of their high school fling and enjoyed the attention. Looking at him, she tilted her head a little and said, kindly, "Why does my family think you called the FBI?" Part of her wondered too—was Jack still upset she'd broken up with him or that he'd never own Blackwood? This put their past in a new light and made her even more grateful that, despite the recent tension in her marriage, she'd married for love and not money.

Jack didn't miss a beat. "Your dad probably worries that, if Blackwood folds, I'll go after his clients, but I swear, I think of him like a father." He lowered his voice suggestively. "Sometimes I wish he were my father-in-law."

Greta shook her head and leaned away from him. She gave him a mock stern look and then caught the bartender's eye to signal for a refill. It was comfortable being with Jack; she had known him for years. They had history and a common language, since they worked together as well. But she didn't like when he crossed the line.

"I do," Jack said, putting his hand on top of hers, and Greta was surprised to feel a flicker of something she hadn't felt since they were both young. She stopped herself from letting the feeling sink in—they had an amazing work relationship that she'd never want to risk changing.

"Thanks," Greta said to the bartender as he dropped off her new glass. It hadn't escaped her notice that he hadn't *really* answered the question. It seemed to her, though, that he thought it was as ludicrous as she had, the idea of him turning in her father, and probably didn't feel the need to defend himself.

"Are you happy?" Jack asked, moving slightly closer.

"Yes, I am," she said as she convinced herself that was a goal of hers. Her smile was a little rueful, but she was telling him what she wanted to make a truth. She was successful, had her two beautiful boys with her handsome and athletic husband, and in spite of this embarrassment with her father, her life was good.

He leaned back but kept his eyes fixed on hers, his hands still close enough that they probably looked like a couple, which made her feel uncomfortable. She was merely reaching out to an old friend, not hitting on her coworker.

Her family had enough secrets; she didn't need one more. But she had felt so asexual recently, so not attracted physically to Patrick. She couldn't keep blaming infertility and motherhood. Maybe it was a real problem that she'd eventually need to face? Her entire marriage was built on lies, lies that would likely catch up with her.

Greta wanted her toddlers to grow up with *two* parents. Motherhood and being a wife didn't always come naturally, but she'd succeed—there was no other option as far as she was concerned. Patrick was a good husband, a perfect father; she wouldn't ruin that. Jack was her closest friend at work—or maybe just the closest thing she had to a friend at work—and understood how complicated her family was.

"High risk, high return," Jack said confidently, brushing his hands through his hair, which was just starting to gray at his temples.

She secretly worried that her father was right—she was outgrowing Patrick, and Jack was more her type—but she suppressed that thought and stayed strong as she responded, "All I can see are the risks."

"Okay, fair enough. If you're happy at home, I'll back off."

"Yes, things are good," she said, putting both hands around her wineglass. She focused back on what had brought her to wanting to meet up: her father. She knew exactly what conspiracy and securities fraud meant but still admired her father nonetheless. She had a hard time facing that the skills she'd admired her whole life were now peppered with deception.

Jack leaned back. "Gret, your dad's firm is a feeder fund to this guy Barney Maxwell, who is in even more trouble than your father, and the FBI is so tied up on his case that your dad got off easy. Trust me."

Greta turned that over for a moment, wondering if she should research this Maxwell. Jack also sounded like he did know more about her father's case than he was letting on. "I just hate seeing him this old and behind bars again. He made a lot of mistakes, but he also worked hard, and now, right before retirement, he's losing everything." Shaking her head, she took a deep breath, trying to keep her emotions in check. "I make my own money and Emily will be fine, but my poor mom and all the shit she's put up with—I think she even knows he's had this long affair with his secretary."

"Your mom's good people," Jack said.

"Will his assets be seized?" Greta fumbled for mints in her purse, putting a couple in her mouth and nervously tapping her foot on the bottom of the barstool. At the last moment, she grabbed her car keys, too, to signify that she was ready to go.

"I wouldn't worry too much," Jack said. "He has a great lawyer." He placed his hand on top of hers again, and Greta felt the same electricity she'd felt the last time he'd done that. She pulled her hand away and placed it on her lap instead.

"Who leaked this?" Greta said.

"I don't know, maybe a plea bargain? It might not have been pure revenge," Jack said, but Greta knew it was Bianca, and her father had likely told her he was never leaving her mother and she was so jealous she ratted him out.

"Do you think it was Bianca?"

"No, she was like the backbone of that company and close to your dad," Jack said, and Greta was annoyed he was giving a secretary that much credit.

Greta wasn't surprised that Jack knew about her father's affair; they weren't exactly the most discreet, and Bianca and Jack had both worked at Blackwood at the same time. She wondered if he knew any details, but she wouldn't go there.

"My parents are getting a divorce just to hide his assets. They're putting the beach house in my name. My mom's out of her mind to put up with him and deal with all of his lies." Saying it aloud reinforced her will to avoid turning out like him. Her father had consistently lied to his family, specifically his wife, for years, disrespecting her. She would not become her father.

"If you need to take a few days off work, I can cover for you," Jack offered.

"No, I'll be fine," she insisted. "Does Bianca have kids?" she asked, the papers from her dad's secret file suddenly clicking into place.

"I think so. A girl . . . in her twenties, maybe? I haven't talked to her since I worked there, though, so I could be wrong about her age."

Greta grappled with the idea of potentially having an illegitimate half sister, and the idea that *if* this were true, it wasn't just a meaningless office tryst. If her father put the effort into setting up a college fund for this girl, then he likely had some genuine feelings for this woman, this child. That *had* to be who the other trust fund was for, but she wasn't going to air any more of her family's dirty laundry. Jack already knew too much. Besides, it felt a little "the apple doesn't fall far from the tree"—not the cheating, obviously, but she did have two children with Patrick that had not exactly been conceived in the way he'd been led to believe.

"She must have been worried about something to call the FBI and risk her own job, right?" Jack said. "Maybe they offered Bianca a plea?"

She wondered briefly whether Bianca had turned her father in—she couldn't think of anyone else who would be mad at her father. Was she in love with him and jealous he wouldn't leave his family for her? But even if they were having an affair, it didn't add up. She worked for him, so what would bankrupting him do for her? "I'd better go," Greta said, getting up from her barstool. She was suddenly anxious to be home, away from Jack and with her husband and children.

"You sure?" he asked.

"Yes, we have an early morning," she said, which was true. But she was also feeling a bit off-kilter now that she'd thought about how similar she and her dad were in some ways. She needed to be around her family and show herself that her secret was safe, her family was solid, and that she was not her father.

Jack closed their tab and held the door open for Greta, and they walked toward their parked cars. He stopped next to her car and lightly placed his hands on her shoulders and let them run down her arms to her hands. He didn't grasp them, but she thought he might, thought she might grab his. "You sure you're okay to drive?"

Greta chuckled. "Are you kidding me? I'm Irish."

Their eyes locked, and Greta felt guilty that she liked Jack. She'd just need to ignore the feeling. She loved her family. More than anything, this had proven to her that whatever was wrong in her marriage was her failing, not Patrick's. Any problems they had were likely due to her own lies, and the lies she told to cover them up. Patrick deserved her loyalty.

She needed to get home to the family she had worked so hard to create.

Chapter Thirteen

COLETTE

2009

"Wake up, Colette!" a squeaky voice whispered in her ear.

She rolled away from it, keeping her eyes shut until a little hand pushed her shoulder softly.

"We need to go see if Santa came," the small boy said excitedly. She opened one eye to peer at her cousin's face as he poked her. She'd thought for a split second that her own child had woken her, that she was this lovely boy's mother—which had felt amazing, wonderful—but now wakefulness was sinking in. With both eyes now open, she searched the room and everything clicked. She was in Aunt Lisa's guest bedroom.

She tightly hugged her ten-year-old cousin, Anthony. "Merry Christmas, buddy. I think I actually heard noise on the roof last night!" she teased. She was putting on a brave face, but what she was actually wondering was how she was going to get through Christmas without drinking or taking any pills. *Will I ever wake up and not immediately think about taking something to get through the day?* "Let me just brush my teeth and I'll be down in a minute."

She headed into the bathroom, leaving the too-bright lights off and rubbing her temples. Since leaving rehab, she'd struggled to get a good night's sleep. She had grown so accustomed over the years to just passing out after days and nights filled with booze and pills. Falling asleep sober was decidedly different, her worries keeping her from dozing off. Cupping water in her hand, she thirstily drank from the faucet and downed three Advil. She hoped the ibuprofen and a black coffee might just do the trick of killing her pounding headache (a lingering symptom of prolonged withdrawal)—not to mention get her through this holiday morning with family.

She had been to inpatient rehab twice now; the first time hadn't stuck, but this time she was really trying. Her addiction had spiraled out of control almost immediately after her first rehab stay, and she had come to crash at her aunt Lisa's enough times that it was clear to all that she was homeless. When her aunt had generously invited her to move in, Colette jumped at the offer. She'd bounced around the city for close to a year and a half after securing a part-time nursing gig in Yonkers. It was a huge get—she loved the work and had secured ongoing access to pills. She got another part-time job bartending at the Branch, a bar near the courthouse in Bridgeport, to supplement her meager nursing income.

Even though she had thought of her nursing job as the risk given that she was an addict, it turned out that working in a bar had been just as risky a choice for a substance abuser. Colette's drug problem allowed her to fit easily in with the bar's staff and many of the regulars; she had become fast friends with the bar manager, Melissa, and Bunny, a cocktail waitress. She had a great time with her new social circle, always staying out drinking and drugging with them, until they were all completely blasted. Every morning she promised herself she'd get clean, she'd do better. She really meant it too—until nighttime.

As she pulled a bra on, she thought about how much she missed her old life at the bar. Her nursing job had been a means to an end, helping her to pay her bills and gain access to pills. But it was at the Branch where she felt most herself and had the most fun. Sweat dripping from her brow, slinging drink after drink to the happy crowd of thirsty lawyers, lobbyists, and paralegals in the sticky air of the bar that had a perpetually broken air-conditioning unit. No matter how hard the work was, before she knew it each night, the hectic rush was over and she was counting out $500 cash, tipping her busboys and pouring herself and Bunny a shot of tequila. The lawyers bought them drinks and shots all night, so by closing time, 2:00 a.m., usually they were pretty wasted, but it was nice to be able to sit down on a barstool and enjoy a drink with friends. And by friends, she meant Bunny, Melissa, and their diehard regulars, Jerry and Frank. The guys were young hotshot lawyers who worked for the state's attorney's office, essentially running the notoriously corrupt court system in Bridgeport. Though both were married, they seemed to spend every spare moment with Colette, Bunny, and Melissa. Bunny and Frank had been involved on and off for years. Melissa and Colette were always urging her to break it off for good, but night after night they all found themselves in a pill- and booze-induced state, repeating the sins of the previous evening—all of them.

She had worked there for eight months, and for Colette it felt like home, her new friends like family. Everyone who worked there was an addict in some way, either an alcoholic, drug addict, or both, which made Colette feel less anxious and ashamed of her demons. She had progressed from popping pills to crushing them on the dirty bathroom sink in the bar and snorting them, after her new friends had assured her it was the best high. When she woke up without memories, she no longer worried about what she'd done. She trusted her friends to keep her in line or, at the very least, not judge her for it. The days of worrying about hiding her true self from Rob or Chelsea were long past. Of course, she still hid it from her family, but eventually hiding five pills a day became difficult. When her aunt confronted her, Colette hadn't even tried to deny it, collapsing in a heap of tears and begging for one more chance. That night, she'd cried herself to sleep and woken up shaking with chills; she'd vomited for hours. She was dope sick and ready—at long last—to admit she needed serious help. Her aunt had driven her to a thirty-day program and she had completed it, vowing upon graduation to do better this time around. *And here I am again.*

Colette took a look at herself in the bathroom mirror, where one glimpse of her face set her off. "You look like shit," she said to her tired thirty-three-year-old reflection. She had dozed off the night before without washing her face, and the concealer she had applied the day before was long gone, revealing violet half moons under her bloodshot eyes. Her olive skin had a grayish pallor to it that no amount of bronzer could hide, and her smoky eye makeup was smudged under her lash line, her lip gloss dissolved, leaving behind dry flakiness. She ripped her hair out of its elastic, ran her fingers through it, and put it in a bun.

Colette made her way downstairs, missing her friends, wondering if she should reach out to say merry Christmas, and the thought sent cravings through her body; just the thought of a Bloody Mary had her mouth watering. She thought about Bunny and Frank and considered how lonely Bunny must feel on holidays when Frank spent time with his wife instead of her.

She knew she shouldn't reach out to her friends from the Branch— if she did, it would likely result in rehab visit number three eventually. She had come home only a couple of weeks ago from her latest stint, and she was determined to avoid temptations—no matter how much she craved them. She had cut them all off. Maybe someday down the road they could reconnect, but now she had to stay focused on her own sobriety. When she got downstairs, she found her aunt and her uncle Arturo waiting for her, their boys, Anthony and Freddy, beaming and surrounded by presents.

"Can we start opening now?" Anthony squealed.

"Absolutely," Lisa said.

After a few minutes of watching, Colette made her way to the kitchen. She grabbed the handle of a cabinet, images of her childhood Christmas mornings swimming in her mind. She remembered wishing each morning that her mom would be there just like she had asked for. The disappointment each Christmas morning she felt upon seeing her father sitting by the tree alone, a drink in his hand, two or three gifts by his feet, was a punch in the gut over and over. The joyful noises of Aunt Lisa's family echoed through the house, and Colette opened the liquor cabinet slowly and grabbed a bottle of Smirnoff vodka. She held it, closed her eyes, and took a deep breath. When she heard her aunt walking in, Colette put it away and shut the cabinet quickly, turning toward the coffeepot to lift it and pour herself a mug.

"Don't you want to watch the kids open their gifts?" Aunt Lisa asked, eyeing her niece.

"Of course I do. I just really needed some coffee. Late night—I couldn't sleep." Colette forced herself to smile as she sipped.

"It must be hard for you to be here on a holiday," Lisa said, concern in her voice.

Colette instinctively swiped at her nose, which still burned occasionally from months of abuse. "I'm okay."

"Really?" Lisa didn't exactly sound convinced. "Maybe later we can call your mom and wish her a merry Christmas." She looked at her niece meaningfully and headed back to the living room.

Colette didn't want to think about her parents and her lifetime of sad Christmas mornings. "Yeah, maybe," she said to her aunt's back as she followed her into the other room. She had never once considered going to see her mother since she had made an attempt the day she left Jewett City. The image of her with the doll behind the glass had stuck with her as a lasting memory, and she had not wanted to go back there ever again.

"This one is from you!" Anthony said to Colette as he ripped the wrapping paper to reveal a box of Legos Colette had carefully saved seventy-five dollars for. "It's the *Star Wars* one I wanted!" He sounded sincerely grateful and excited, even as he quickly tossed the box aside to reach for the next one. It made unexpected tears spring to her eyes—not because he was ignoring the present for the next one but because he had so many. This wonderful family—her aunt who was nice enough to take her in, who, along with her husband, was a caring parent who saved enough money to treat their children on this day. It made her heart feel like it could burst.

"Merry Christmas," she said, full of emotion. "Thank you so much for having me here."

"Oh my goodness," her aunt said softly, pulling her in for a hug. "We wouldn't have it any other way. Merry Christmas, sweetheart. We are so happy you're here. We love you." She leaned back and gave Colette a big smile, then grabbed a stack of gifts and handed them to her.

The much-needed clothes and gift cards were like a tiny miracle, but she couldn't help but feel a little embarrassed and small, worried she could never repay her aunt for all that she'd given her. The struggle to hide the grim and ugly facts of her life was crushing, an ever-present, nagging fear of destroying her one last truly human connection, one that now meant everything.

"I know things have been tough, with Rob filing for divorce and all of these lawyer bills hanging over your head. And I just want you to know that I am so proud of you for getting sober, and you have helped us a ton with the boys since you moved in. This is going to be your year. I know it!"

"Oh, I hope so," Colette answered quietly, her eyes roving over the small bounty she'd just been given. She felt her face warm a bit as the slight embarrassment sank in.

"Are you still up for making the trip to see your mom next week?" Aunt Lisa asked as she helped Freddy undo the wiry ties holding a new toy inside its box. "Now that I finally got her moved to the hospital closer to us, it's only about an hour away."

"Uh, sure." Colette shrugged, feeling her aunt's eyes on her. She wished she'd never agreed to the visit when her aunt had asked her weeks ago.

"She'll be so happy to see us . . . and it's the holidays," Lisa said, sounding as though she were trying to convince herself as much as Colette. "Plus it's been too long. When was the last time you saw her?"

Too long was an understatement. "I don't know . . . I think I was maybe nine or ten? I don't really remember."

"Colette, I can't help but think that a lot of the trouble you have had lately is deeply rooted in what you went through as a child. I was thinking it might help you to see your mom. Maybe confront your fears or whatever might be bothering you?" Lisa's words came out as a question asked carefully, and Colette just shrugged in return.

"Okay . . . yeah . . . maybe," she said. Uncomfortable, Colette stood abruptly and headed toward the kitchen, saying she wanted to give Uncle Artie a hand with breakfast. He was placing a huge plate of pancakes next to a platter of bacon and sausage on the kitchen island as she walked in.

She plucked a piece of bacon and took a bite as she asked, "Need help?"

"Nope, just eat!" he said cheerfully.

"Artie!" Lisa yelled from the other room. "Can you take my sauce out of the freezer?"

"Yup, got it!"

Colette had learned so much about her Italian heritage from living with her aunt. Her grandmother, whom she had never met, had emigrated from Naples and taught her daughters how to cook authentic Italian cuisine when they were growing up. Whatever Colette's mother had learned she'd likely not retained, so Colette had never tasted real Italian food when she was a kid. She was looking forward to a Christmas dinner of homemade manicotti with her aunt's sauce and baked stuffed shrimp, followed by Italian cookies and cannoli—all a far cry from the microwave dinners she'd lived off her entire life.

"I forgot one of your gifts," Aunt Lisa said brightly, coming in from the other room with a little box.

"Another?" Colette felt ashamed about the one gift she had gotten for her aunt.

"Open it," the boys chanted as they stormed into the kitchen behind their mother and hopped into chairs next to Colette.

Inside the small box was a beautiful gold necklace with a heart-shaped locket, the letter *C* engraved on it. "Oh my God. I love it!"

"It was your mother's. She left it at my house the last time she visited, when you were just a baby, and I've had it all these years. I was waiting for the right moment to hand it down," Aunt Lisa said as she leaned over to help Colette put the necklace on.

For the rest of the day, Colette tried to relax, savoring the first Christmas she could ever remember with a "normal" family. The necklace, however, made her feel increasingly claustrophobic. As soon as the last dinner plates were cleared and she had helped Uncle Artie load the dishwasher, she excused herself and shot up the stairs. Shutting the door to the bedroom, she pulled off the necklace frantically, her nails digging into the clasp, and threw it onto her bureau. She lay down on the twin bed, taking deep breaths. She had mixed emotions about her mother's old necklace. She was happy to have it, a piece of something from her mother's past. Her past. But she didn't want to wear it. The guilt for not wanting her aunt's thoughtful gift was almost overwhelming, but the shared initial with her mother . . . it was choking her, reminding her of their similarities, the failure Colette had managed to become. She rolled over on her side and welcomed the darkness of sleep that began consuming her.

~

On New Year's Day, Aunt Lisa woke her at seven so they could be on the road by eight. Coffee churned in her stomach as she sat in the passenger seat looking out at I-95, willing herself to be calm and open to embracing the woman who had given her life. Her aunt chatted incessantly for the entire ride. The conversation was one sided; Colette was too anxious to engage in idle small talk.

As they arrived at the facility and headed to the visiting room, Colette chewed on her cuticles. Various games were set up on tables, and a television in the corner blared *The Price is Right*. Patients sat in scattered rocking chairs and couches. There were dolls on many of the chairs, which made Colette even more uneasy, remembering every unpleasant memory she had associated with dolls from her childhood.

"We just finished up with Connie's doctor, and we're going over her meds," an administrator with kind eyes noted as she closed a file folder and placed it on the reception desk. "I'll go get her. Please, make yourselves comfortable." The woman left the room, and Lisa took a seat, Colette flipping open the folder with her mother's name stamped across the front once Lisa wasn't paying attention. She scanned through pages of words that meant nothing until finding one that stood out. "Schizophrenia" was written in bold print across the page.

"What are you doing?" Aunt Lisa demanded in a scolding tone.

"I just wanted to see," Colette protested, but she flipped the file closed and sat next to her aunt. Seeing the diagnosis of schizophrenia for the first time in writing gave her mixed feelings. Part of her had secretly hoped that her father was being dramatic when he called her mom a "schizo" all those years. But now a wave of sadness hit her, though she took comfort in knowing that her mother, in fact, did have a disease, an identifiable disease that Colette could put her finger on, and she breathed a sigh of relief as she sank deeper into the old couch.

"It's going to be okay," Aunt Lisa said, grabbing Colette's hand.

The wave of comfort she derived from her aunt's touch threw her back to the summers they had spent together. "I know." Colette pulled on the locket, which felt tight around her neck; she'd put it back on the day after Christmas, not wanting to hurt Aunt Lisa's feelings.

"There's my baby girl!" The loud, boisterous voice startled Colette as Connie barreled through the door. Before Colette could even register what was happening, a woman with brown, wiry hair sprinkled with grays, wearing loose, wrinkled pajamas, had wrapped her arms around her, clutching her too tightly in a bear hug. Colette's arms were stuck to her body, and she was overwhelmed by the overpowering stench of cheap perfume.

"Hi . . . Mom," she managed to spit out as her mother held on to her. The shock of seeing her after nearly a lifetime clutched at her throat, and unexpected tears welled as she noted the sagging skin on her face and the dull pallor of her complexion that Colette remembered being bright and always flushed with manic excitement. She trained her gaze away from her skin and met her eyes when Connie finally let her go and sank down into an armchair next to the couch.

Colette peered at her curiously. Her eyes looked kind, like she remembered them being when she was having a "good day" from her childhood. She looked nothing like she did in the few pictures Colette had found at her father's house. In those, she'd been decades younger—less puffy, not tired looking. Fresh off the revelation of her diagnosis, Colette thought her mother had probably been manic when the photos were taken.

"Ohhh, I knew you were coming!" Connie exclaimed loudly. "I told Margaret. I said, I had this feeling . . . I always get feelings, ya know?" She leaned over with a serious look. "I woke up last week and I just knew that you were coming. I told everyone." Connie finished her announcement with a cackle of inappropriate laughter.

Colette fidgeted uncomfortably and picked at her cuticles, her hands shaking. Aunt Lisa must have noticed she was triggered and broke the ice.

"You're wearing the lipstick I got you," Lisa said. The color had bled outside of her mother's natural lip line, leaving a pink stain all around her mouth, making her look clown-like.

"Oh yeah, and the perfume! But some of the other stuff you sent I gave to my friends, because I don't need all of that fancy stuff in here," Connie said, rolling her eyes and laughing uncontrollably.

"Well, you know I'm a makeup artist, so I get lots of free samples, and I'm happy to keep sending them if you'd like," Lisa said. Though she was speaking to her older sister, her tone was the same as if she'd been speaking to a child.

Connie didn't answer, her laughter stopping as she turned to face Colette. "You know what else? On that day that I knew you were coming? I found out something about this place that your aunt had me locked in." She curled her lip, sneering as she looked back at Lisa.

"Oh no. Are you not happy here, Connie?" Lisa asked.

"Come here," Connie ordered, gesturing to her sister and daughter.

Both obliged by stiffly leaning in a little. Colette made eye contact with Lisa, and her widened eyes stared back at her. Colette pushed away the growing sense of disappointment as her mother rambled on, making less and less sense. *What did you expect? She was crazy when you were eight, and she never got out of here . . . Did you expect her to be the "normal" mother you had always dreamed of?*

"Do you know who owns this place?" Connie asked with wide eyes. "Saddam Hussein!" She was so loud that other people in the room looked over at them with seeming alarm. She sat back, arms crossed over her huge bosom, as if pleased with herself and waiting for their reactions.

"I don't think so," Aunt Lisa said gently, smiling sideways at Colette. "He died a few years ago."

"Yes, he fucking does, Lisa. He's alive and he's in hiding. Don't tell me about where I live," Connie insisted, clearly agitated. "Someone told me they saw him in the kitchen last week, yelling at one of the girls that works here." She leaned in again and whispered, "She's Muslim. If anyone finds out, they might have to shut this whole fucking place down. I could get killed!" Her eyes were wild, darting back and forth. "I might have to move in with you," she warned.

"Connie, he's dead. You don't have to worry about that anymore." Lisa reached over and took her sister's dry, scaly hand.

Colette noticed that her mother's nails had been painted but were now covered with small chips of polish. She looked away from the unsightly image, wondering if someone at the facility had painted them or if she had done it herself. She ached for a mother who was put together, who cared about her appearance.

"Lisa, do you believe everything you watch on the news? He's not dead. Mark my words." Connie sounded desperate for her secret to be accepted as truth.

"Why not catch up with Colette?" Aunt Lisa suggested, looking sympathetically in her niece's direction.

Colette turned stiffly toward her mother and looked at her expectantly, willing the interaction to be normal. She smiled softly. Her mother stared at her with disdain.

"So, what happened to that husband you never bothered to introduce me to?" Connie snarled in Colette's direction. Before Colette could even open her mouth, her mother spit, "I guess he left you like your father left me." She laughed maniacally again.

Colette was stunned. Even if she'd wanted to answer, she couldn't have. Her aunt had obviously shared details of Colette's life with this unknown woman, which surprised her. She wasn't sure how she felt about that, but she did know she felt protective of her father. She couldn't state the obvious—that her mother's mental health had deteriorated and caused the destruction of their marriage and her ability to be a mother—so she just stared back at this creepy stranger who thought she knew something about her.

"Well, too bad for you, but you're probably better off," Connie said, waving her hands around as she spoke.

I do that, Colette thought as she watched her mother talking, her hands flailing about. She studied the woman closely for evidence that they were related. She peered into brown eyes that, although a bit flat, likely due to meds, she saw her own brown eyes in. Connie's brown hair hung over her shoulders in disarray, and Colette realized that if she never dried or styled her own hair, it would look like that. The resemblance between her and this woman made her feel sick. *I don't want to be anything like her.*

She stared off into the distance for a moment, jarred by the image. One of the dolls caught her eye and she startled, staring at it, absorbed in the disturbing memory of her mother's doll hospital. When her mother unexpectedly shook her leg, laughing at something only she thought was funny, Colette came out of her thoughts and saw the light in the room had changed. How long had they been there?

"So, Lisa, I have a bunch of letters that need to get to the White House," Connie said, switching gears again. She reached into the pocket of her robe and pulled out a stack of greasy, crumpled envelopes and pushed them toward Lisa. "Mail these right away; they'll be furious when they find out what's going on around here. Hussein hiding out here and all. I think someone will probably have me come talk to the FBI, once they know the truth."

Lisa gently placed the envelopes in her purse. "I'll take care of that for you."

Colette took this all in, dumbfounded as her aunt spoke tranquilly to this woman who used to be her sister. As a nurse, she'd dealt with her share of people with mental disorders, but seeing her own mother like this, Colette was . . . embarrassed. The strong distaste it stirred up in her for her own mother made her anxious and jittery. She wanted to leave—needed to. After enough inane conversation had ensued that she felt her duty had been fulfilled, she grabbed her purse and stood. "Don't we have to bring the boys to that birthday party?" she said directly to Lisa with a pleading look.

Aunt Lisa smiled back at her with obvious understanding. "Okay. Connie, sorry to cut the visit short, but Colette has to get back."

"All right, then, see you two in another ten years," Connie said sarcastically, rolling her eyes again.

In that moment, for the first time since they'd arrived, Colette felt an unexpected empathy for this woman she barely knew. She, too, used biting remarks as a defense mechanism, and for the first time, she really saw herself in her mother and not in a horrifying or frightening way. Her shoulders softened, and she exhaled deeply as they walked to the car in silence.

"Did you feel like that went okay?" Lisa asked, pulling Colette up short.

"No . . . well, yes, I guess it could've been worse," Colette replied.

They climbed into the car, and Aunt Lisa looked over at her now as she put the key in the ignition, her gaze fixed on her for an uncomfortably long time. Colette could tell Lisa wanted something more from her, some sort of bigger response after such a long time of not seeing her own mother, but she was so drained, she couldn't muster up the energy to say much. Lisa turned her eyes to the road and started driving.

Finally, her aunt said, "It seemed like you connected with her there for a bit. I know it must have been hard to joke about Rob like that, but you made it seem like common ground for her. That was kind of you."

Colette wasn't sure what to say to that. Awkwardly laughing while her mom said she was better off without Rob hadn't seemed like joking, but she nodded. She turned the radio to a pop station and settled in for the car ride, closing her eyes, desperately wanting a pill to numb her from the horrors of this day and wishing her body would melt, piece by piece, until she was no longer there.

Chapter Fourteen

GRETA

2009

"Good morning," Patrick said, slipping a water bottle into his tennis bag.

"I'm so bummed I have an important meeting today. I completely forgot the kids' preschool conference." Greta sighed. "It is what it is; I work." She sipped what was left of her coffee in one gulp. "You'll report back for me, right?" She thought about her bonus check and felt like she'd better not share with Patrick how big it was. On the one hand, she worked hard to be able to build a legacy for her family, but on the other hand, she worried he'd feel threatened. He'd never said anything, but she sensed that underneath some of his sarcasm, he resented she was the breadwinner. She could pay for both of her sons' college expenses with this one check and didn't want all that hard work swallowed up in shame.

"Stay and finish your coffee," Patrick said, pouring himself a cup and giving her a *slow-down* gesture.

"Don't forget we have a family photo shoot tonight."

"You've reminded me like five times," Patrick said, smiling.

"Okay, I laid their outfits out, in case I'm running late."

"Got it," Patrick said.

"Lisa's doing my makeup. Can you get the boys dressed so they're all ready when I'm home?"

"Yes." Patrick sighed.

The twins came running into the kitchen, both tugging on the same stuffed animal. Greta poured them each a glass of juice and popped waffles in the toaster oven.

"I told Miss Renee we would both be at their conference. Do you think she'll think I'm a bad mom?" she asked, hoping Patrick understood she'd be there if she could.

"It's fine, babe, they're three," Patrick said.

"She probably thinks Lucia is their mother."

"I can call you from the conference and put the teacher on speakerphone."

"Yes, I have a million meetings, but I'll try." She secretly wished Patrick hadn't suggested this and just offered to fill her in later. *He is the one who reminded me they're only three.*

As much as Greta loved her job, it was moments like this where she felt as if she were failing them, and she wanted the kids' teachers to know she cared even though she couldn't be there.

"Don't be dramatic. Lots of the other families have nannies. And if you're really worried, why don't you just stop in and introduce yourself to the teacher another day?"

"I will," Greta said, liking Patrick's solution and feeling happy that at least he wasn't judging her. For now, she still wanted to do something, even if no one noticed. "I'm going to make a huge anonymous donation to the Montessori gala."

"Good idea," Patrick said, his eyes now on the newspaper.

"Just explain to her that I have work? Okay?"

"Okay. Enough. I'll call you. Stop worrying about it. I don't exactly think their 'student-teacher' conference matters at their age." Patrick came up behind her, soothing her and leaning over to kiss her on the cheek. They had made love last night even though she wasn't in the mood, because she really needed him to be up for family photos.

When her phone rang, she picked it up, covering the mouthpiece and stepping away from the kitchen just as the toaster oven dinged. She pointed at the waffles and gestured for Patrick to take care of them. "So, a value equity fund . . . macro fund . . ." She grabbed her car keys and walked backward toward the door. *Bye*, she mouthed, blowing a kiss to Patrick.

∼

A few hours later, when Patrick called her at work, Greta ducked into her empty office for some privacy so she could listen in on the conference.

"Hey, honey, I'm here with Miss Renee," Patrick announced.

"Good morning, Renee. It's lovely to chat with you. So sorry I couldn't be there."

"Hi, Mrs. O'Brien," the boys' teacher said. "So, I'll start by reviewing their progress reports. The boys are learning about famous impressionists, playing with the wooden geography puzzles, and using the abacus." As the teacher rambled on, Greta was glued to her laptop, working hard.

"They both love painting," Greta heard her say. She perked up and smiled, thinking about her smart toddlers.

"So before we go into their academic growth, I have a question: What do they do in their free time?"

Greta fumbled for a moment. "Well, they like tennis, right, Patrick?"

"Yes, I know they're young, but I do play with them," Patrick said proudly.

Greta thought about how bonded Patrick was to the boys and felt deeply envious. She just didn't know what to do with three-year-olds— or boys. They were so loud and rambunctious. She was a girl with a sister, so nothing had prepared her for the noise or the smells or the energy levels.

Miss Renee cleared her throat. "Let's start with Brayden. He loves singing and poetry and art."

Greta was worried about not being prepared for her work presentation, but she really wanted to listen to how her sons were doing.

"Logan is a joy to have in the class too, and he loves art. We've given him some left-handed kinder scissors, and he really likes cutting paper."

"Shouldn't you encourage him to use his right hand?" Greta asked, worried how her left-handed kid would fit into a right-handed world.

"Oh, no. There's nothing wrong with being left handed, and we follow the child's lead. But I do see him struggling in class. I'd almost recommend a zero-to-three evaluation with a developmental pediatrician, just to rule out some concerns."

Greta tried not to bristle. She knew the woman was only trying to help, but it was hard not to be defensive. "What concerns? He's three."

"Well, he doesn't interact with other kids at school. He just kind of strolls around and talks to himself."

"I'll inform our doctor," Greta said, hopeful this was something he would just outgrow. She'd never noticed this, but perhaps she didn't know what to look for because she wasn't around kids much.

The teacher continued: "He spends a considerable amount of time sitting in what we call the observation chair so he can watch what the other kids are doing, and then he seems to emulate them. He's also tired a lot of the time. Is he sleeping okay?"

"Well, we can put him to bed earlier, right, honey?" Patrick offered.

"Of course," Greta said. She cared about this, about her children. She really did. But these observations seemed inconsequential, bordering on absurd. Logan was a child, and no, he didn't always go down for naps well, but he didn't wake them in the middle of the night or anything.

"Is there a family history of it taking a bit longer to develop socially on either side? How was his birth?" the teacher asked.

"No. And C-section, a minute after Brayden," Greta answered quickly, her pulse racing. She wondered if she would be like this for the rest of her life anytime someone mentioned the boys' "parents" in this context. Why hadn't she thought about this when she had picked the donor? Why did it not occur to her that she would want to know about their genetic health risks? But she knew why—she had been more worried about the woman trying to find her, had been concerned about the secret, and hadn't thought through all the other possibilities. She was so desperate to start a family with Patrick that she wasn't thinking about the long-term consequences; now she was living with the aftermath of regret.

"Were they premature? Any hospitalizations? Sometimes there can be a connection."

"He was a little premature, as I was assured many twins are, and he did have febrile seizures when he was a year old, but there have been no issues since." She looked at her watch and decided she was done. "We'll handle it from here. Thank you."

She hung up. She didn't care if she was being rude. It felt like the woman was not only challenging whether Logan was healthy but also whether she and Patrick were good parents. She'd talk to Patrick, and Lucia, about it all later, though she felt like the teacher was overstating the issues, possibly feeling like she was required to, to justify her outsize salary for essentially being a babysitter.

Greta rushed through the rest of her work so she'd be able to leave early and get her hair blown dry and her makeup done before the family photo shoot.

She arrived home seconds before the photographer was due to arrive, relieved Lucia from her nanny duties, and noticed boxes of Thai takeout on the counter. She grabbed a plate as the boys ran to her and grabbed her legs.

"Hi, Mommy!" "Hi, Mama!" they screamed in unison.

"Go wash your hands, boys." They ran to the bathroom, and Greta heard them goofing around and pushing each other off the small stool in front of the sink.

The photographer arrived, toting professional lighting and props up the driveway. Greta rushed to hide the evidence of their takeout dinner. She reapplied her new lipstick, lit the half bath's Nantucket briar candle, and replaced the hand towel with a fresh one. Jane, the photographer, had been to her sister's as well, and Greta wanted the woman to be impressed with their home.

When everyone was ready, the photographer snapped away for a while.

First she took family shots, then just Patrick and Greta. Greta smiled at Patrick, and the photographer commented on how in love they looked, and Greta felt connected to Patrick as they stared into each other's eyes as if it were a wedding photo. Hot sex was overrated, she told herself.

"I have enough of the happy couple. So it's your turn, Logan, and then I want to get some shots of just you, Brayden." She instructed Logan to lean back on an antique stool that she had placed in front of her canvas backdrop.

"Do you think they'll be as good as Emily's?" Greta whispered to Patrick. She didn't understand why she always felt inadequate around her sister. She knew she was smarter and more driven, but she envied how put together Emily was as a mother. It wasn't necessarily something she'd aspired to, but she found herself disliking coming in second at anything. She found Emily shallow at times, yet she walked on eggshells every time she might disappoint her and was jealous that Emily and her mother were so similar. Her mother and her sister talked about each other to her, but she knew deep down they were closer than she was to either of them, and as much as she tried to be like them, she was more similar to her father. However, she was coming to terms with his flaws and his own lies and secrets that she desperately hated and subconsciously emulated.

"It's not a competition," Patrick said in a normal voice.

"I know. It's just that they've been through a lot lately, and I want to give them a bunch of framed photos. My mom will love that."

"Instead of displaying photos everywhere, they could come to a school event or come see them play?"

"Shhhh," Greta said, not wanting the photographer to hear that the boys had deadbeat grandparents. She glanced at Brayden's feet. "*Why* is he wearing sneakers?" she barked.

"The dress shoes were tight, so we just decided it didn't matter," Patrick said.

"My sister will notice." She hated herself a little for even thinking that, let alone saying it. She raised her voice and directed her comment to the photographer. "Can you just do a headshot?" Patrick's schedule was so light compared to hers, and she suddenly resented the fact that he hadn't run out to buy the boys new shoes, hadn't helped with this shoot at all.

"I know my parents could do more, but they really gush over photos, and my mom just reminded me that the boys can come play on their courts anytime."

"Last time we went there she asked me to resurface all of the courts, and I explained that the club hires contractors to do that."

"Well, she doesn't know. Your dad used to resurface our courts, didn't he?" Greta said, shrugging.

"No. He hired people to do it. I told her she needs to caulk and seal the expansion joints."

"Maybe you could send the contractors you use at the club over there. They'd appreciate you helping."

"It's like ten thousand. I thought they were having money issues?"

"Well, it's not that bad. They still need to take care of the courts," Greta said, and then her voice turned into a whisper. "Once these photos are done and framed, we can stop over and impress them with how gorgeous we all look. And you can pass the contractor's name along to their new house manager. They'll appreciate the tip."

Really, it wasn't just about impressing her parents and sister; she wanted the photos to be perfect for herself too. She had waited so long to have these children, she deserved to bask in each moment of their growing up, she thought.

The photographer nodded. "I could shoot these sweet boys all day." She leaned over to show Greta some of the shots on her camera's viewing screen. "The boys look just like Patrick; they have his *exact* smile. I bet everyone tells you that. But their skin—they have such gorgeous suntans! Who'd they get that from?"

Greta tensed, but the woman seemed not to be waiting for a real answer. She hoped the charming photos would make up for her discomfort over Jane inappropriately commenting on her sons' skin, which was rude. She saw the photographer out and then her mind wandered to Audrey. *Are people always stupidly commenting on the fact her children are Asian?* she wondered. Part of her envied that while Audrey's children didn't look like her, at least they all knew the truth. She didn't know if it was the photo shoot itself or her secret, but she felt exhausted.

"That was great, but I really need to check in with work, read my SEC filings, and research a report, plus I blew off all my end of the day paperwork . . ."

Patrick said, "I can do bedtime."

Greta really appreciated his offer and opened her laptop and remembered she also needed to review price quotes before the market reopened tomorrow. She watched Patrick chase the boys up the stairs.

Brayden said, "Mom, after my bath, will you read to me?"

"Of course. As soon as I get a little work done, I'll be right up."

She went upstairs and got changed and did some work in bed with her laptop.

She loved to watch Patrick carry the boys wrapped in matching towels from their bathtub to their bedrooms, each with their hoods up and often a stray bath toy in tow. Logan had an imaginary friend that he asked to come take baths with him. When Patrick shared this, it cracked Greta up. They had really seemed to have fallen into a routine of him doing bedtime. Parenting came naturally to him, she thought, as Patrick made silly noises while he got the boys dressed in pajamas. She was reminded of how different he was from her father—a man of few words, a workaholic, who selfishly had affairs. He was more loving than her mother too, a woman who withdrew into herself, becoming more judgmental and negative with each passing day. Greta knew she didn't have much in common with anyone in her family, but despite her best efforts she feared following the same destructive footsteps. When a damp Brayden climbed into their king-size bed with her, she shut the laptop and read him a chapter from the book he was holding.

"Logan, you sure you don't want to listen?" she asked, but Patrick explained that Logan was obsessed with wanting to replace all the batteries in the home's smoke detectors, and Patrick bragged about how smart he was to even be aware there could be a house fire. Greta found it annoying that she'd give up work to read them a story and her son preferred to tell his imaginary friend to "stop, drop, and roll." But she wasn't about to let her irritation turn into unnecessary paranoia that her son was too quirky.

PART TWO

Chapter Fifteen

GRETA

2016
Seven Years Later

"Patrick, are you just going to sit there and watch tennis while I pack *everything?*" Greta said while looking over at her husband lying on their living room sofa with the television remote in his hand while she ran around the kitchen packing. Then she stuffed the "his and hers" Moncler ski coats she'd just bought into the top of her designer suitcase.

"This is your thing, babe. I don't know where you want stuff."

"Well, at least ask me if I need help. Can you put the skis in the cartop carrier I bought, or do something besides sit around? We need to get on the road soon, and I have to make a quick work call."

"Of course you do," Patrick replied, slowly getting up from the sofa to join her in the garage. Glancing at all the bags, he asked, "Aren't we just going away for a weekend?" He laughed at the piles of stuff spread across the garage floor. "You bought a rooftop carrier for one ski trip?" he added, amusement tingeing his voice.

"Yes, the boys need room in the car," Greta snapped. "I just called Smugglers' to confirm. I'm bummed that it's not really ski in, ski out like when I used to go to Stowe. We have to walk a few hundred yards from our condo to the base of the mountain, but the lady said we would want to be 'in' the village versus up on the mountain itself . . ."

Patrick grabbed a tennis racket off the garage wall, bouncing a tennis ball up and down, up and down.

"Are you even listening?" she yelled as she stuffed more bags into the back of her SUV.

"Did you sign them up for ski lessons?" Patrick asked, finally looking up.

"No, should I have? I figured their elementary school does ski Wednesdays; Lucia picks them up every week. So they're probably good enough, right?"

"Well, Vermont's a bit steeper than Southington's 'ski Wednesdays,' but I'm sure their tennis skills I've taught 'em will help. They're athletic nine-year-olds, should be good."

Greta stopped listening and then ran into the kitchen to grab the healthy snacks Lucia had packed and brought them out to the garage.

"Aren't you so glad we're doing this family trip?" Greta said, making a silent clapping motion as she checked out her new fur headband in the car's side-view mirror.

"Yes, I'm happy, babe, but it's still hard. I work weekends. I feel like you forget that's when my 3.0 women's team has their matches. The moms don't like when I'm not there."

"Well, tell them it's family time." She smiled, hiding that she was not equating his work responsibilities to hers. "And PS, Patrick, I'm sacrificing not-looking-at-work stuff too . . ."

"But you aren't on the clock like I am," Patrick snapped.

"No, no. Sorry, thanks for agreeing to this family getaway. It will be fun to ski together."

Patrick stood next to her, still staring at all the piles of stuff and shaking his head as he said, "You bought Chanel skis?" He lifted them into the Thule carrier, chuckling a little.

Greta shrugged and wished she'd gone to a sports shop and grabbed a pair that Patrick wouldn't judge.

"Grab those," he said, pointing to the dusty K2 skis she'd brought up from the basement that sat next to hers.

She handed the boys' skis and boot bags to Patrick, who fit them into the storage container on top of her car.

"I haven't skied in ten years. I hope it's like riding a bike," Patrick remarked.

"Logan, come here," Greta yelled from the garage into the house as she hoped their age gap didn't stop her from doing as well as Patrick on the slopes.

"Is this your helmet and this one's your brother's?" Greta asked Logan.

"I hate that helmet—I told you it's too small! And I don't want to ski. Can I snowboard?" Logan said.

"I just had the skis sharpened; we can snowboard next time," Greta announced. "I bought you the next-size helmet. See if it's less tight."

"This one is too big. I'm not going," he yelled, throwing it across the garage.

"Buddy, I know it's annoying that Mom's making you try on fifty things."

"Patrick, don't tell him his mother's annoying. Try to defend me versus instigate!" she said.

"Sorry, just wanna get on the road," Patrick said.

"He acts like this when you buy him that Gatorade, and now he's eating Swedish Fish. All this red dye is making him act this way. Plus he's tired. We need to stop letting him play video games all night so he's not sleep deprived and throwing things."

"Well, you buy them gaming chairs and then bitch when the boys act like normal nine-year-olds. Maybe you're moody?"

"Moody?" she said. "It's more than that. It's disrespecting things, like when he broke that tennis racket after playing poorly. He's spoiled! Oh God, forget it. I need to finish packing so we can leave already."

Greta knew there were things at home that needed to be addressed, but she couldn't do it all alone. She wished she and Patrick were more of a team. So often he just felt like another kid instead of an equal partner, someone who really understood her desire to work hard to support her family.

~

The first hour of driving went smoothly as they sipped on Starbucks drinks they'd stopped for while still in Greenwich.

"Tim wants you to help him invest. I told him you'd come by and give him some tips," Patrick said.

"Tim?"

"The *owner* of the tennis club."

"Oh, oh that Tim. Tell me more . . ."

"I told him you're a money whiz, babe. If he grows the club, maybe we could even partner someday; I'd love to be part owner down the road. Anyway, can you help him?"

Greta hesitated. "Well, my funds are typically higher risk and . . ."

"And what? He's not rich enough for you to give him advice?"

"No, no, I'll look at his portfolio as a friend, but I'm not a financial adviser, Patrick. I'm in charge of making investment decisions for a large pool of capital given to us by very high-end investors that meet certain net-worth requirements."

"Like how much?"

"Well, usually over ten million."

"Jesus, no wonder you're always glued to your phone," Patrick said.

Greta was surprised they'd been married so long and he didn't know this basic information about her job. She had likely just learned to shut it off as soon as she got home. That wasn't his fault. She tried to be a mom for those few hours in the evening, not talk about work.

"Yeah, the portfolios I manage are more actively traded than what brokers do, and I can't let days go by because of the volatility and what's at stake, you know?"

"Yeah. Maybe you can just chat with him and make a referral. He really wants to get more into investing."

"Sure, I'll help. I should come by the tennis center and we can chat. I can come on a Saturday when I'm off." Greta thought about how she'd be proud to tell her family if Patrick was part owner of the club. It seemed like something they'd respect more than merely coaching, but she pushed the thought away.

"Do you like working a gazillion hours?"

"Yes, I love my job, Patrick, and I feel bad I love it so much, but I do. I mean, it's hard when I miss events and stuff with the boys, but I get such an adrenaline rush when the markets open, and I love seeing if rumors of mergers and acquisitions pan out. Every day is new. I can be in my office interviewing candidates for a new analyst position, and then Jack will signal me about some arbitrage opportunity."

"Yeah, Mom missed our Author's Tea!" Brayden said sternly from the back seat, signifying he'd been eavesdropping. Both parents swiveled their heads. Greta was surprised he wasn't just glued to his iPad.

"Sorry I missed that," she said, wishing her son understood her desire to work, twisting to respond, and then looking forward again as she returned her gaze to Patrick. "But I'm good at schmoozing with CEOs and potential investors; I think I get that from my dad." She hoped she'd inherited only his intelligence and not his selfishness, because Patrick seemed way less helpless than her mother, who tolerated being ignored for work as long as she had an expense account. Patrick didn't care about money, and Greta knew from Audrey that all the "Greenwich tennis moms" adored him, so she vowed to start appreciating him more as they headed toward the mountains.

When they arrived at their Mountainview 30 condo at Smugglers' Notch, the boys immediately started running around and exploring. They went out onto the deck and started throwing snowballs at each other. Noticing colorful lights on the ski slope, Logan said, "Mom, Dad, there are, like, fireworks on the mountain."

"Yes, they told me it's called the Torchlight Parade. People ski while holding torches," Greta replied.

"I want to ski with a torch," Brayden said.

"Me too," Logan chimed in. "I want the room with the king bed and a door to run away in the night," he added, laughing and opening and closing the sliding glass door.

"There are four bedrooms, figure it out," Patrick said.

"Did you sneak this old CB jacket into the car?" Greta laughed, pulling it from one of the bags. "You don't like our matching ski coats?"

"They're just so puffy! Sorry, I didn't want to hurt your feelings, Gret."

Greta wondered why she cared. *It's just a jacket,* she told herself, wondering why she'd spent thousands on ski gear for them and the kids.

"Did you bring wine? I'll make a fire."

"Yes, there's wine and I packed your beers," Greta said, feeling smug.

Greta carried her bags up to the master bedroom and then unloaded the groceries she'd packed—something Lucia usually did.

"I brought cookies and brownies, and I picked up a lasagna from Joey's for dinner tomorrow," she commented, wanting Patrick to notice all her prep work for once. Still, she felt inadequate as she pictured stay-at-home mothers baking brownies from scratch instead of picking them up at the bakery.

"Wow, look!" Logan said, and then proceeded to jump off the second-story balcony into a pile of snow before hopping inside through the downstairs sliding glass door entry. "Brayden, are you chicken to jump?" Logan laughed.

"Stop! That's dangerous," Greta warned, worried about Logan's recklessness. "Look, they have Scrabble, Patrick," she said, pouring wine.

The boys ran downstairs and Logan yelled back up, "The condo has Wii guitars!"

"I thought we would get them off games while we were out here. Oh well, cheers!" Greta said, reminding herself that even though it wasn't great for them, the kids were easier when they were gaming. She clinked her glass with Patrick's beer bottle just as sounds of the boys arguing traveled up the stairs. Greta smiled at Patrick as she gulped her wine, in hopes it would block out their fighting *again*.

"Stop fighting! Wanna come play Scrabble?" Greta yelled down. "Or Brayden, I bought you that Diagon Alley Lego set you wanted. It's in my suitcase." Brayden was really good at Legos, which was counterintuitive, because he was so much more outgoing than Logan, who preferred to sit and draw over building anything. Greta thought it was cute that Logan would tell Brayden to build his when her parents bought them huge Lego sets and Brayden would do it for him for hours. She didn't care that Logan didn't like Legos; she'd never liked Barbies and Emily had loved them. She remembered trying to convince Emily to put the Barbies away and play with walkie-talkies and she'd pretend to be one of Charlie's Angels or the Bionic Woman.

"No, I'm not in the mood to do Legos and Logan breaks them and I only like playing Mastermind with you, Mom, because he cheats."

"But how about Scrabble?" she asked again.

"No, Logan only writes swear words when he plays Scrabble," Brayden yelled back.

"It's fine. Let them go play games and we can play Scrabble. Or we can watch tennis together," Patrick said, sinking into the sofa and perusing the trail map as she joined him. They sat gazing into the fire, the flames lighting up the outside just enough for them to see that more snow was falling. She sensed that Patrick was happy, but something inside her still felt as if her own happiness was forced.

"Skiing tomorrow should be great. Let's go right to Madonna," Patrick said, smiling and pointing to the tallest mountain on the map.

~

The next morning, Greta was proud of her renewed decision to make her family a priority. She rubbed some sunscreen on her face, then carried the tube downstairs to make sure the boys put some on so they didn't end up with windburn. They were already wolfing down waffles with Patrick and looked partially ready in their long underwear.

"Mommy, isn't there a monster that, like, eats kids in Lake Champlain, right near here?" Brayden asked.

"No, it only eats girls," Patrick said in jest.

Greta interjected, "No, that's just a made-up legend."

"Coffee, babe?" Patrick said, handing her a cup.

Greta walked over and stepped out onto the balcony in her long underwear and Ugg slippers.

"Isn't it so big?" Logan said as he pointed at the same mountain they'd seen the night before in the dark.

She replied, "I know, that's Mount Mansfield. Brayden, come look too." She twisted, beckoning him over. "That's Spruce Peak, and that's Sterling Mountain, one of the mountains we're going to ski on today!"

Brayden said, "No, Mommy, can we just go skiing already?" He began to pull on his orange-and-gray camo snow pants.

"Okay, come on. He's going to get hot, let's get out of here," Patrick said, also pulling on his ski pants and helping the boys finish getting dressed. Greta convinced the twins to pose for a couple of photos, then she and Patrick leaned in close so she could take a selfie. They looked like a picture-perfect Smugglers' Notch advertisement.

~

After a few hours of skiing, Greta's feet already ached. But they were all having so much fun, so she ignored the pain. She and Patrick kissed as they rode the chairlift up to the top of Madonna.

"I'm going to get this picture," Patrick said, lifting one leg and steadying his ski gloves as he pulled out his iPhone and snapped a photo of the backs of the twins' heads.

"Be careful!" said Greta, worrying he'd drop a glove or his phone. She felt queasy as she gazed down at a sheet of thick ice and sharp rocks jutting out of the mountain ridge below.

Patrick's carefree nature—one of the things that had first attracted her to him—now slightly irritated her. Was it really that important to take a picture of the backs of her sons' heads? She tried not to dwell on it. Then she felt the chair shake. Was the lift stopping again, this high up?

"What the hell is happening?" Greta said, grabbing Patrick's knee with one hand and trying to steady the swaying lift with her other, being careful not to drop her poles.

They both looked up, realizing at the same time that their own sons were the cause of the shaking. Logan sat in the middle of their lift and forcefully kicked both skis up and then back while Brayden was shifted all the way to the left side, causing the chair to lean.

"Stop!" Greta screamed at the top of her lungs. She'd seen her sons playing around, but this was different.

"Lower your voice," Patrick chided. "The chairs aren't going to fall off; my buddies and I used to roughhouse on the lift. They'll stop when a ski patrol scolds them. Calm down."

"Calm down? One of them is going to fall out." She looked down at the treacherous rocks below and, ignoring Patrick, screamed again, this time even louder. "Logan! Stop it *right now!*"

Logan twisted around toward them, laughing. He pressed one pole up against his brother and began banging the other pole against the metal of the chairlift, making an ear-piercing noise that echoed off the mountain face.

"Knock it off," Patrick finally said at the same time Logan retracted his poles and scooted to the right.

Now he was lifting the chair's safety bar. It was way too early; they weren't close enough to the top.

"What the fuck!" Greta screamed again. "Put the bar down!"

Skiers seated two chairs ahead twisted around, observing the boys' dangerous game.

Brayden was holding on to the chair with both hands overlapping tightly and his poles gripped between his legs, with his jaw dropped and his eyes wide open in fear.

"Put the bar down, buddy, it's not time yet," Patrick yelled, but Greta feared his words were getting carried away in the wind.

"Put it down!" Greta screamed just as two consecutive signs appeared that read KEEP SKI TIPS UP and UNLOAD HERE with an image of a skier lifting the safety bar.

"See, they're fine," Patrick said, patting Greta's knee as she exhaled shakily and fumbled to lift their own bar up. She grasped her two poles with trembling hands and skied down the exit ramp and to the left, where Logan was laughing at Brayden, who was in tears next to him. Greta wasn't sure if the cold wind or her son's behavior was what was really chilling her.

Angrily, Brayden grabbed Logan's neck with an iron grip.

"Let go, Bray, two wrongs don't make a right," Greta said, wanting to cry herself. What had she done wrong as a mother to raise kids like this? She thought about the conversation she'd had with Patrick on the car ride up. Numbers came to her naturally, but disciplining her sons *did not*.

"What was that? You scared the hell out of me, and look at your brother. What's the matter with you? You could have pushed your brother off or fallen off yourself!" she said sternly as she looked right at Logan.

Greta didn't know if she was madder at Logan for acting like a crazy person or at Patrick for not backing her up. Her blood boiled as she yelled at her son, "That's it! We're going back to the condo. You don't deserve to ski the rest of the day!"

"That's a bit dramatic, Gret," Patrick said. "Let's just have a do-over."

"Yeah, Mom, it's fine," Brayden said, wiping away tears. "I'll just ride up with you next time."

"Well, you are not riding on this lift with your brother ever again!"

"I'm sorry, Mom," Logan said, seeming remorseful.

"Come on, Gret, let's ski down Drifter and grab some lunch in the lodge. Maybe he's just antsy because he's hungry."

Greta was tired of Patrick always making excuses for them.

Logan pulled Brayden up with his pole and Brayden smiled, already recovered from his earlier fright. Patrick took off down the mountain and the boys followed as she grabbed her poles and hesitantly pushed off, still trying to catch her breath. The scene of her family in front of her looked like a winter postcard, but something didn't sit well with her. She wasn't convinced that Logan's internal thoughts and expressed emotions 100 percent aligned.

Maybe this was her fault. Maybe she needed a parenting class, or maybe this was because she wasn't home enough, or maybe they were just too spoiled. She had no idea what to do next. She tried deep breathing to calm herself. She pushed her breath from her throat down to her stomach purposefully. Her beautiful house of cards felt susceptible to the wind.

Chapter Sixteen

COLETTE

2016

Colette's hands were shaking as she unbuttoned her work blazer before sitting down in the metal folding chair that was set up in a semicircle in the musty church basement. She reached to massage the back of her neck, trying to release the stresses of her workday and shift gears.

Vic's large frame sank into the chair next to her with a thud, and he leaned toward Colette to give her a peck on the cheek, the scruff of his chin tickling her. Sweat glistened on his brow, and he pulled off his baseball cap and ran his fingers through his dark hair and placed the hat back on.

"Sorry I'm late, got stuck on a job. How was court today?" he asked as he took her hand.

She looked down and noticed that dried cement laced the inside of his palm, and specks of white plaster were stuck to his wedding band.

"Court went well," Colette said, relieved that the day was behind her and that Vic, her husband of six years, was now here, sitting beside her. As soon as he'd arrived, a sense of calm had washed over her.

Although her new career as a medical paralegal was fulfilling, her days were long and often extremely stressful. Even still, she wouldn't trade it for her long, hard days in the hospital or at the bar, where she knew she would never be able to stay sober.

It was a miracle that her luck had finally turned. She owed everything to Aunt Lisa for not giving up on her. After getting out of rehab for the second time, with no money, no friends, and very little hope, Colette had found a job opening at the state's attorney's office, where Frank Marciano, Bunny's boyfriend from the Branch, was a prosecutor. It had almost seemed too good to be true. She'd wanted the job so badly, and though she hadn't been sure she was qualified, she decided to try anyway. She had nothing to lose at that point in her life.

Whenever she thought back to that day, her stomach always did an uncomfortable little flip. It was one of the many events in her life that was fuzzy; she couldn't quite put the pieces together. It had happened all the time when she was still using, but it occurred even when she was sober with alarming frequency.

Colette remembered being in her aunt's house perusing job listings in her pajamas, chewing violently on her cuticles until they bled, chugging cup after cup of coffee, and sucking the blood from her fingers as she weighed her options. Two hours later, arriving in the lobby of Frank's office, her palms had been sweating and her heart racing. Yet she couldn't remember the ride there. She had already been feeling frantic, as she was nervous about this prospect of a brand-new career and potentially working for Frank, who knew her from her unsavory past. The fact that she had zoned out on the entire ride there unsettled her further. Looking back, she was proud of her tenacity that day, under such duress; she was able to take a deep breath and secure a job that meant so much to her.

The receptionist in the first-floor lobby had told her that Frank was busy all day and wouldn't be able to see her. She panicked, considered going straight home, thought that she couldn't do it, couldn't get the job. But something made her stay and fight.

Muscles had twitched and she ground her teeth before mimicking the receptionist's smile. Keeping her tone as even as she could, she'd told the woman she would wait in the lobby until his meetings were done for the day.

Another call was placed while she'd stood her ground, and she'd wondered if he assumed she was still an addict, just there to blackmail him for drug money. Though she wouldn't be blackmailing him, she had planned to gently remind him that she had never told a soul, namely his wife, about his affair with Bunny. She would do what she had to—she could not go back to the bar, and the thought of getting a new nursing job didn't appeal to her. She had lost what little passion she had for a medical career, and she didn't want to be tempted working in a building filled with meds. But she could use her degree to do something that she was very interested in. She'd practiced her speech in her head: *I'm a fast learner, a trained nurse, and willing to take any additional training to succeed as a medical paralegal. I need this job.*

Her next memory of that day was her facing Frank where he sat at a huge mahogany desk that probably cost more than Colette had made in the last three years but looked right in the luxurious office with floor-to-ceiling windows. He'd pulled a toothpick out from where it rested between his teeth, tossed it in a nearby garbage can, grabbed a gold cigarette case out of a drawer, and gestured toward the door.

"Let's take a walk outside," he said.

"I need your help getting a job, doll." Her voice was firm.

"What kind of job, Colette? We don't have a bar here." He chuckled while offering her a cigarette.

She couldn't remember the exact details of the rest of the conversation, but it had obviously turned out in her favor. She had been so nervous, her whole life riding on that one interaction. She remembered Frank standing nervously, stubbing out a cigarette under his black loafer and shaking her hand. She had what was left of a lit cigarette in her other hand, and she had stared at it curiously and stubbed it out as well. His palm had been damp and the air was smoky.

"Don't make me sorry I'm giving you a chance," he'd said before she'd turned to leave.

Those words had rung in her ears almost every day since.

She had zoned out, and Vic was nudging her. "It's time for you to speak."

Colette swallowed hard to soften the lump in her throat. She wasn't sure what she was nervous about; she had done this before, but it never seemed to get any easier. She closed her eyes and took a deep breath before walking up to the podium. She gripped a piece of paper in one hand and her seven-year chip in the other as she turned to face the small crowd of Narcotics Anonymous members. She introduced herself to the crowd as she unfolded the paper.

"Even though many of you know me and might think that I seem to have it all together, I am here to share my story today, because getting this far has been a struggle. I have a great job, and I am happily married to the love of my life, but every single day, I think about my sobriety. A lot of hard work, two stints in rehab, and the support of all of you and this program have led to this day that I am receiving my chip to signify seven years of sobriety."

Colette shared some of the details of her childhood, her marriage to Rob, and her spiral into addiction after a routine surgery.

"I put what little family I had through hell, and I lost pretty much everything. I realized when I spent my thirty-first birthday in an inpatient rehab facility that I wanted so badly to feel like my old self or, at the very least, to feel normal. I wanted a good job, a relationship, a family of my own. I realized that these things that I wanted more than anything were slipping away because I spent so much time in my addiction."

Everyone nodded in understanding.

Colette continued: "I've always wanted a family, because I never really had one. I know a lot of you had it worse, were in foster homes with abusive people, in terrible situations, and I . . . didn't have it that bad." It was true. She hadn't as far as she could remember, and she wanted to acknowledge that she knew that others had it worse and also take responsibility. That was one of the main tenets of NA: taking personal responsibility.

"But my mom had schizophrenia, and my dad drank. And I always saw the families my friends had and thought that when I grew up, I'd finally be able to make a family like that, one of my own where the kid was actually wanted and loved and cared for so much." Saying this aloud was like scooping out her intestines and laying them bare for people to sift through.

"I was lucky enough to meet my husband at a meeting," Colette continued, making eye contact with Vic and flashing back to the day he had walked into a meeting and that feeling of butterflies in her stomach had registered. She still marveled at how fate had worked out in her favor after all. She'd forced herself to face her demons by frequently attending NA meetings, had kept to herself and made a few acquaintances but no real friends, immersing herself in her work and wearing her loneliness like armor.

About a year out of rehab, Colette realized it might not happen for her—the family she'd wanted in the way she'd envisioned. It didn't make her as sad as she'd thought, but it had made her more determined to stay clean and be successful. So of course, it was a night not long after that when Vic, with his strong, brawny frame and his skin tanned from years of working outside, had walked into one of her meetings and sat next to her. She had been instantly attracted to him and caught herself staring at his dark eyes while he spoke to the group. He'd worn a T-shirt, torn jeans, and work boots, a sharp contrast to the men she was surrounded by at the state's attorney's office. Vic's quick spiral from a couple of pills a day into full-blown drug abuse was similar to hers—he'd been injured during a masonry job, his original scrip valid and necessary, just like hers.

When the meeting let out on the first day they met, she'd seen him heading to the table with coffee and stale pastries and intercepted him. They had gone out to a coffee shop that night and talked until the wee hours of the morning. They'd barely been apart since.

When Colette had learned she was pregnant just months later, she'd felt true joy for the first time in her life. They had moved in together and read baby books at night, reveling in this exciting turn of events that had surprised them both. They'd even started to work on the baby's room, setting up a crib that a coworker had given Colette and painting the room a creamy yellow. When she had started bleeding in her fifteenth week, her doctor had suggested she wait a couple of months before trying again.

Colette's entire body flushed hot, and she clenched her hands into fists thinking about the miscarriage. "We have had our share of hurdles in our effort to start a family, but we have each other and we have all of you. Thank you."

~

"I know that was hard, babe, but you did great." Vic squeezed her hand as they were heading home later that night.

"Honestly . . . I . . ." Colette stumbled over her words. She pressed the button to roll down the window, letting the air cool the warmth in her face before she continued. "I did fine until the end, when I was thinking about the miscarriage," she said, her voice wobbling as she burst into tears. They had been trying to get pregnant again for six months, and it wasn't working. When she had shared with her doctor that she had frozen eggs in storage, he had suggested that in vitro fertilization may be a great option for her. Though she didn't want to go through the grueling process, she was starting to doubt this was going to happen naturally for her and Vic. Maybe she shouldn't be a mother—perhaps, like her own mother, who'd had difficulty caring for her properly, infertility was a problem Colette was given to stop her from continuing the cycle.

Vic grabbed a napkin from the glove compartment and handed it to her. "We're going to be fine."

"I hope so . . . but . . ." She sobbed but then took a deep breath to calm herself, wiping her tears. "I think it's time for me to use my frozen eggs. I'm sick of just hoping for happiness. I'm calling the doctor first thing in the morning." If that didn't work, maybe she really wasn't meant to be a mother.

Chapter Seventeen

GRETA

2016

Greta pulled into the driveway of her Greenwich home and lowered the window to wave at the twins, who were shooting baskets while Patrick mowed the lawn with a beer in his hand. Greta raised her voice just loud enough for him to hear over the sound of the mower. "Honey, you know you don't need to mow the lawn. I can hire my parents' gardener."

Patrick turned off the mower. "I like mowing." He smiled.

She shook her head. "Well, hurry and get cleaned up. Audrey and Tom are coming over for drinks before the fundraiser." Greta went inside and pulled a bottle of Sassicaia from their wine storage to put on ice. Patrick came in a few minutes later and sat on the sofa in his sweaty clothing and put the Tennis Channel on.

"Come on, Patrick," Greta said as she tried to manage getting out of the house. "Boys, the pizza delivery is on its way." She put money for the pizza on the counter and said, "There are fruit pops in the freezer, but only one each, and be nice to your grandparents."

Patrick, overhearing her, said, "What is this fundraiser again?"

"It's called Under the Stars. It raises money for the hospital's neonatal intensive care unit that helped the twins. Honey, can you wear that shirt I bought you and not a tennis polo?" Greta said as she got out her charcuterie board filled with hard and soft cheese knives.

The doorbell rang and she quickly brushed the crumbs off and opened the door and motioned Patrick to hurry.

"Whatever you say, babe," Patrick said, taking the stairs two steps at a time. His tone was slightly patronizing, but he'd still do what she asked—he always did. But lately it seemed more out of obligation rather than actually being on the same page.

"Come in!" Greta said and walked Audrey and Tom to the kitchen and poured them a pre-event cocktail. "How is the redecorating going?" she asked.

"Oh my God, so great, you have to come and see. Kellie's a true artist. She wallpapered the girls' bedrooms with these gorgeous complementary Asian prints," Audrey gushed.

"Expensive!" Tom chimed in.

"Patrick's almost ready. Look at the photo wall Kellie did for us," Greta said, pointing at the hallway's gold-framed collage that showed off photos of the boys at two years old standing under an oversize wooden tennis racket hanging on a wall at the US Open, and outside their school at three years old, and at Magic Kingdom when they were five.

"I love that one that Jane took. They've gotten *so* big. Where has the time gone?"

Greta looked at the photo Audrey was complimenting of the whole family laughing in front of a vintage red truck. She wished she felt as happy as she had looked in the photo. She kept thinking happiness was around the corner; it was hard to be happy when your whole life was built up from a lie.

She sipped her wine and shook off the melancholy. "Kellie is doing the boys' bedrooms in tennis themes for middle school, and it will look great through high school. I haven't updated their rooms since they were babies."

"Yes, it was way overdue. I'm so glad I introduced her to you. She's fabulous . . . Oh, hi, Patrick!" Audrey said as he walked in, giving him a big hug.

"We'd better get going or there will be no parking. Here, Patrick," Greta said, handing him a cracker with cheese on it along with her keys.

"What kind of cheese is this? It's disgusting," Patrick said.

"Shhh, it's *caciocavallo podolico*. It's known as horse cheese, but can you be quiet and just spit it out," she said, annoyed that he had such an immature palate.

Patrick swallowed hard just as the doorbell rang. It was his parents, who'd offered to watch the kids and spend the night.

"Hi, Cynthia. Hi, Norman," Greta said, extending a hug to each of them as they came in, and she reintroduced her in-laws to her friends and yelled for the boys to come and greet their grandparents.

She whispered to Patrick, "Can you make them come up from the basement? They are being so rude."

"You obviously never played video games as a kid. My parents don't care; let's just go. You said we're running late."

"Okay, well, I give up," she said, rolling her eyes. "At least help your mother with her bags."

~

"Okay, where is this place?" Patrick asked as he typed the address that Greta had saved on her phone into his GPS.

"I know fundraisers aren't your thing, babe, but thanks for being a good sport," Greta whispered.

"Can we leave early, maybe go grab a drink at a real bar, a hotel?" Patrick teased.

Greta said "No!" in a playful tone, but she knew he wasn't kidding.

As they were walking in, Greta noticed he had on a golf polo under his sport coat instead of the dress shirt she had suggested. They'd been together twenty years now, and it seemed like not only had her passion for him died, but some of his acquiescing to please her had as well.

They were greeted with outdoor cocktails and a scenic view of Long Island Sound at the Riverside Yacht Club before entering the cozy farmhouse-themed tent.

"Jenni, hi!" Greta said as they walked in, recognizing the event's chairwoman. They clinked champagne glasses, and then Greta and Audrey snuck off to a corner to catch up as they listened to the live country-pop band.

"I love this event," Audrey said.

"Yes, and it's an excuse to drink." Greta chuckled.

"We really shouldn't let so much time go without seeing each other. I mean, we're neighbors! I know you work, but you really need to make time to see all the new decor."

"I will," Greta promised. The truth was, she didn't really care about Kellie's color palette boards like her mom, Emily, and Audrey clearly did. She almost wished she cared more about homemaking tasks. Her lack of interest sometimes felt like another way in which she didn't live up to what a "good mom" or a "good wife" did.

"Pretty color," Audrey said, pointing at Greta's toes peeking out of her dress shoes.

"It's called Just Busta Mauve. But God, what a nightmare I had at the salon today," Greta whispered, looking around to make sure Patrick was preoccupied with Tom. "These college girls getting pedicures were talking about egg donors. One said how much cash they could get if they donated their eggs, and the other one was like, 'No way, you can get cancer or even die.' The hair on my neck was standing straight up, and I wanted to get the hell out of there."

Audrey put her drink-free hand on Greta's shoulder. "People are judgy about that stuff. It's the same with adoption. Just the other day, some woman asked me if my girls were siblings. And people always tell me it's so 'honorable' that I adopted. You just have to ignore it."

"The one woman was reading an ad in the *Yale Daily* out loud and laughing about how 'old moms' pay a fortune for college girls' eggs. It was horrifying."

Audrey gave her a sympathetic look. "Oh, I'm sorry, honey, but think about how naive we were back in college, when we thought having biological children was so easy, we worried about it happening accidentally."

Greta felt a pang for the baby she'd lied about and miscarried, the wild night in Europe that had eventually brought her and Patrick together. Falling for Patrick seemed so long ago that it was hard to imagine the carefree feeling. "You're right," she said, giving her dearest friend a small smile. "We did think it was easy back then, didn't we? Let's drink."

"How's everything else? Patrick good?"

Greta tensed. She wanted to confess how she and Patrick had begun seeing a couples therapist but knew that even though they were going through the motions, nothing would likely change unless she confessed that their marriage was built on a web of lies. Greta had sought out a therapist to work on ways they could be more of a united front when disciplining the boys, but she wasn't sure why she'd bothered—she knew that deep down she was putting on the same facade for the therapist that she was putting on for the world. It almost felt like if she could pretend they were uncovering all their issues, it would help make them disappear, but she knew that telling her therapist, and her friend Audrey, half truths wasn't ever going to make up for the deeper lie buried within her.

"We're really good," she exaggerated out of habit. "How's Tom?"

"He travels too much, and the girls are growing at the speed of light. I feel like he's missing it all. And the girls are struggling a little with being adopted now. They keep asking me about their birth moms, and it's kind of hurtful."

"I get that," Greta said, and in a certain way she did. She wouldn't want her boys to know their donor. Greta secretly wished that Patrick traveled for work; maybe regular time apart would spice things up, she thought.

"You do?" Audrey said. "Did you ever tell Patrick about using a donor?"

"God no! It would be worse now that all this time has passed," she whispered, looking around again to make sure they were still alone.

"No, he won't even care. He's the most chill guy I know!"

"No. Trust me!" Greta realized she had kept this lie from him for ten years now.

Audrey shifted awkwardly. "I think the boys know. I mean, not the donor, but the IVF part."

"*What?*"

"Maybe Patrick told them?"

Greta was dumbfounded. "No . . . I . . . I doubt it. Why do you think that they know?"

Audrey suddenly looked a bit abashed. "Well, Patrick jokes around about how you guys had some 'help.' It came up because the moms in the clinic were talking about how their friend that wasn't at tennis was trying IVF. It's not as uncommon as you think."

"Oh my God, he told them!"

"Yeah, the boys know they were IVF," Audrey said.

Greta was pissed. And felt like running over to ask Patrick why he would even mention IVF without consulting her. And she wondered how on earth Audrey knew this when she didn't. Perhaps she and Patrick were far more disconnected than she'd realized.

Greta reached for another drink from a passing server and forced a smile as they walked around looking at the art on display. She wasn't able to open up to her best friend about her nonexistent sex life, but she needed to vent about a new topic.

"We did get in an argument last week because I want to put the boys on HGH to make them taller so they'll be more competitive in tennis. My attempts at expanding their diet have failed—they are the pickiest eaters ever. But Patrick accused me of being obsessed with body image," Greta admitted. She wasn't about to share this, but she also blamed herself for their small size. If she'd had children younger, married someone taller, and not used a donor, she likely would have had kids who were as athletic as she was. *Their inadequacies are all my fault.*

"What's wrong with being on the shorter side?" Audrey asked, disbelief tingeing her voice. "Putting them on human growth hormone seems a bit extreme. Tennis should be about having fun, especially at almost ten. My God, they aren't even in middle school. I have to side with Patrick on this."

Of course you do, Greta thought, wishing her best friend would side with her for once.

"Well, if I'm going to miss work and go to tennis matches, I think it would be more fun if they won. And HGH is very safe." Her father suddenly flashed in her head. His drive often overtook his ethics, and she wondered if that's what she was doing with this. She had been working so hard for years now to avoid becoming either of her parents, but she could have sworn she had just channeled him. And she was standing in the room of another fundraiser, just like her mother.

"It isn't safe." Audrey's somewhat shrill tone brought her out of her reverie. "It's a steroid."

"It actually speeds recovery. I mean, we can easily afford it, and the doctor wouldn't tell me it was okay if it was bad for them," Greta said, throwing back the rest of her champagne.

"It can make you aggressive, and the boys don't need that on top of their regular hormones. I mean, they just got in that fight last week."

"What?" Greta couldn't believe all these surprises were surfacing about her own children. How did Audrey know everything?

Audrey looked surprised. "Well, they had a fight with Zeke—"

"They did? Zeke seems so nice," Greta said, but she'd always had her secret suspicions that the boys' friend was a little too rough around the edges.

Audrey's brows pulled together. "I know, he's a great kid, but Logan really had it out with him."

Greta bit her tongue—she wasn't ready to get this feedback. She buried her own thoughts and listened.

"Where does Zeke live again?" she asked, knowing he wasn't from Greenwich but not sure how far away he lived. She'd vaguely remembered the boys saying he took a long bus ride to school.

"I think he's from Norwalk."

"But he goes to their school, right?" Greta was always embarrassed that she didn't know many of the details regarding her boys' friends and at times wished she were in the loop like Audrey always was.

"Yeah, he's bused in. Anyway, the girls told me they had a fight during lunch a few weeks ago, but when I asked Patrick about it the other day, he said everything's fine now."

"A fight? And Patrick knew?" So yes, it was Patrick's fault she didn't know.

"Yeah, Zeke had a split lip, and Logan had a black eye. Didn't you see it?"

"He said he caught a tennis racket to the face when they were goofing around after a game." Greta's ears were suddenly impossibly hot as embarrassment engulfed her.

Audrey looked nervous now. "Maybe he didn't want you to hate Zeke. They made up the next day."

"And the fight was about?"

"I don't know. I guess Zeke said Logan was skinny, something like that. The girls weren't specific about it."

Greta was angry at Zeke, but agreed that her boys were too short and too skinny and felt like trying this HGH was her only option. She was doing it so they'd have a competitive edge in tennis, but perhaps it would cut down on them being the target of bullying to boot.

Audrey set her champagne glass down, gesturing nervously while she spoke. "Maybe if you just came clean, then the boys would understand why they look so much more like Patrick than you."

Greta wasn't having it—Audrey wasn't going to twist this into being her fault. She wasn't happy that Zeke was bothering her sons, and she was equally embarrassed that she'd known nothing about it. She didn't know how to even respond but felt an urge to keep them apart. She would tell Lucia they needed to spend less time with this Zeke and more time on their schoolwork.

"I don't know about them hanging with a kid that gets into fistfights."

Audrey pulled back a little, her expression bemused "No, he's a nice kid. He's into tennis too. I always see him hitting off the backboard at their school, and Patrick told me he offered Zeke free tennis lessons all summer. Patrick said he's a natural."

"Patrick didn't even mention him . . . or the free lessons." Greta clenched her jaw. Why was she so out of the loop? Especially after couples therapy and her thinking they were making strides, finally, in their communication, here he was, making decisions without her.

Greta thought back to their last couples session, when they'd pulled into their appointment in separate cars but held hands on the way in and sat close to one another on the therapist's sofa as they each shared what was bothering them in compassionate ways. Patrick had agreed to go after Greta brought it up, and he admitted he'd like to because one of his male tennis clients explained it had helped him and his wife reconnect. But Greta continued to worry that going through the motions of sitting on a therapy sofa was pointless when she'd never reveal the seed that had planted them there. Regardless, she tried to get the therapist to side with her when it came to wanting more support. She also told Patrick she'd go but asked him to please stop talking about their pregnancy, their marriage, and their kids' conception with anyone at work. She didn't look like her children and didn't need any "tennis moms" connecting the dots. Greta felt that each session was like a small bandage on a wound she was still unwilling to face.

Greta leaned in. "What else do you and Patrick talk about?" She was trying not to show the frustration she felt.

"Oh, you know, just the kids mainly," Audrey answered quietly. "Between us, he did say he hates Jack, so I'd be careful with how much you talk about him."

"I'm aware." Why the hell was her husband sharing his insecurities with her friend? She'd thought they were parenting together, but now it felt like he was parenting and hiding things from her. She worried she did the same thing with Jack—he was so much easier to talk to than Patrick—but she didn't like when she felt as if the roles were reversed.

She said, "I wasn't aware you two were close enough that he'd mention it to you, though."

Greta hated the jealousy that was obvious in her tone by now, but she'd learned one pretty clear thing tonight: she had to pay more attention at home—to her sons *and* her husband.

~

The next day, Greta woke up with a plan: she would take her three guys and Zeke to her parents' house to go boating, maybe play tennis, and lie out on the private beach. Her father had dealt with everything through disinterest and then, when she did something disappointing, punishment. She would not be the same.

After cajoling Patrick into calling out of his Saturday tennis clinics and extending the invitation to Zeke's mother for her son to join them—thank God for classroom parent lists sent over email—Greta called her own mother to let her know they were all coming.

"For the whole day?" Evelyn asked. "This will be great. Your father can sit with the boys and we can go get massages."

Part of Greta wanted to think her mother's response was ridiculous, but honestly, on any other day she would have wanted the reprieve from their nonstop energy. So instead of scolding her mother, she did her best to use a kind tone as she said, "Not this trip. I want to spend time with them."

"Ohhh-kay," her mother said, stretching the word out, "but *all* day? I mean, they'll go out on the kayaks and we can pop out for an hour, honey, can't we?"

"Mom, they're in fifth grade. We have to watch them on the kayaks and make sure they don't go out too far."

"Okay, okay." She seemed to have good-naturedly acquiesced. "I'll have lunch ordered in, then, for a treat. Do your boys still prefer chicken tenders and hot dogs, or can I order grilled chicken and kale and brussels sprout salads?"

"They are still picky eaters. I blame Patrick for allowing this junk when they're on the road. And order one extra of whatever you get them. I'm bringing their friend Zeke. And Lucia's with us, of course."

Greta had thought about giving Lucia the day off and then decided it wouldn't hurt to have an extra set of eyes when they were around water.

In the car on the way to her parents' house, Greta told the boys about lunch. "And make sure you say please and thank you to Granny, or she'll think you have bad manners."

"They're polite kids," Patrick said. "You don't need to always remind them."

Most days she would have agreed—they *were* well mannered, but she had been in the dark when it came to her sons' fighting, so she knew she needed to do more. She quietly but angrily said, "Well, maybe they're polite because *I* teach them proper manners."

Patrick looked a little shocked but didn't say anything more. When they arrived, the sun was out, and Greta sprayed them all with sunscreen before they ran to a small patch of sand leading next to the water. The area had been set up with towels, snacks, and three kayaks, half in the water. Greta was happy to see her mother being pleasant. Greta had helped her father with a new media strategy that allowed him to come clean about the corruption charges but allowed clients to focus back on his long-term success. This helped him get back on track financially, and while she'd initially resisted engaging in this role reversal, she figured it was the least she could do after all they'd done for her and the kids. They'd even warmed up to Patrick.

Patrick leaned over and kissed Greta, probably partially out of genuine emotion but also partially out of a desire to smooth over whatever had gone on in the car. "It was a great idea to have us all take the day off," he said softly. "We should spend more time together."

She smiled. "I agree." She squeezed Patrick's hand and said, "And if we get a minute alone, I want to talk to you about something."

"No one is paying attention to us. What is it?" Patrick said.

Greta continued: "I want to put the boys in private school. Lots of boys repeat sixth grade, and then they will be so much better at tennis in high school and have more opportunities to play in college. My time spent playing tennis at UPenn were some of the best days of my life." Greta also thought about how, deep down, Patrick would be happy they were good tennis players too.

Patrick nodded as if he were taking it all in.

"Audrey said they got in a fight," Greta said, unsure of why she was even bringing this up, because her reasons for wanting to change schools were bigger than just this one fight. She believed that the private school she had in mind yielded opportunities to meet other families who valued education. The school prided itself on offering the most current, relevant learning experiences, and she felt her boys, especially

Logan, would thrive in a smaller classroom where they wouldn't slip through the cracks.

Patrick looked thrown by the topic change—or maybe he was just shocked by what she'd said. "Why? Sometimes boys fight. And they're doing great at school overall."

"A better education—and public schools are more dangerous."

Patrick chuckled. "They aren't going to join a gang in Greenwich Middle School."

This was one decision she was going to make alone; she went to private school and was now successful. She explained, "I know, but Logan's already having trouble turning in his assignments. He'd get more attention at a private school."

"I don't think that's necessary," Patrick said. He cracked open a beer and leaned back in a chaise longue.

Greta called out to Lucia, "Can you please ask Logan to stop kicking sand? It's going in my mother's Gucci beach tote!"

Patrick gave her an odd look. "Why don't you just tell him?"

"I don't know; they seem to listen to Lucia more," Greta hissed.

It caught her off guard, though, because she realized it was second nature to tell the help to do something with her own child. She hoped it wasn't too late for her to stop the inevitable slide into becoming her parents, but this didn't bode well.

Patrick handed her the book she had been reading and then got his own out. "The boys listen to you. You just don't say much directly to them." She gave him a hard look and he shrugged. "And I don't like the idea of private school. The boys already have so much privilege and things handed to them, they don't need that too. Besides, you hired that tutor to help Logan, and he's been doing better, right?"

The school had called about Logan not turning in homework, so yes, they had decided that she would hire a tutor to come and help him after school. What Patrick didn't know was that she had told the tutor to do the homework for him if she had to—grades were important if Logan wanted to get into the best colleges, and if he was too busy concentrating on his tennis on the weekend, this seemed like a perfect short-term solution. She had gotten straight As *and* won tennis matches, so part of her wondered why this was hard for her boys. She also believed that Patrick would be really proud when they became competitive athletes, so if nudging things in that direction was what she had to do, then she would.

"Well, I'm going to look into it," Greta said. She didn't want to fight—that would defeat the purpose of her having them all go out there today—but she had already made up her mind.

Beyond that, she needed Patrick to feel more connected to her so he would stop resorting to talking to her friend—the one who knew Greta's biggest secret—about their life and their sons, and leaving her out in the cold.

Chapter Eighteen

COLETTE

2016

After years of self-sabotage, Colette had truly been hopeful about this first day of her new life. Since she and Vic had made the decision to pursue in vitro with her frozen eggs, a weight of dread had lifted. Of course, it made perfect sense that a broken water main would threaten to derail what could potentially be an amazing day. She had waited three long months to get in to see Dr. Erikson, the best fertility doctor in Connecticut, and she'd probably have to wait at least that long again if she missed this appointment.

Sitting at the roadblock waiting for the traffic cop to wave her through, she gripped the steering wheel so hard her knuckles went white. She took a deep breath, unclenching her jaw, and tried to fantasize about the very real possibility of finally having a baby. *Babies*—their intoxicating, sweet smells, their soft skin, their innocence and promise. She yearned for motherhood. To fill that deep, unrelenting void in her.

A honk jolted her out of her reverie, and she opened her eyes and drove past the roadwork, her anxiety back in full force. She breezed through a yellow light just as it was turning red; she had only four minutes until she had to sign in at the doctor's office, which meant she ended up peeling into the parking lot and practically running inside before slowing to a fast walk to the receptionist's window, where she announced herself.

A young girl stared at Colette, glanced down at the schedule in front of her, and grabbed a file folder. She seemed annoyed as she slid the glass divider open to speak—maybe she thought it uncivilized that Colette was panting at her from the other side of the glass.

"You can have a seat; someone will be with you in a moment," she said flatly.

Colette exhaled loudly as she sank into the nearest chair in the waiting room. Across from her was a cheerful-looking blonde pregnant woman engaged in deep conversation with an older woman with whom she shared features. A familiar pang of envy shot through Colette while she watched the mother and daughter. She turned away from the women before they noticed her staring, closed her eyes, and tried to recapture the loveliness of her earlier daydream. Grasping for it, she came up empty and thought, *Anything, any thought that doesn't include Mom.* Yet another step in her endless efforts to calm her nerves and achieve peace.

She was thrilled to be interrupted by her name being called. It was the unwelcoming receptionist, whose face still looked bothered as Colette stepped back in front of her desk. "Mrs. De Luca, we left you a message about canceling your appointment," she said.

She flinched a tiny bit at that. "Um, well, no. I didn't cancel my appointment. I definitely wouldn't have; I've been waiting so long," Colette replied, her nerves tightening.

The receptionist shut the divider and rolled her chair back toward an older man in scrubs, to whom she showed the folder with the sticky note. The two spoke quietly, gesturing to each other, briefly glancing at Colette. Panic set in as Colette began picking at the skin around her thumbnail, biting at the cuticle pieces she could get purchase on, and tapping her right foot, never taking her eyes off them.

The receptionist made her way back toward Colette and forcefully slid open the glass window. "Mrs. De Luca, we tried to reach you." The woman gestured to the man in scrubs, who was retreating down the hallway. "Dr. Erikson suggested you might want to cancel the appointment."

"What? Why?" Colette responded. "I don't understand."

"It says here that your appointment was regarding starting fertility treatments today, but Dr. Erikson ran into a problem retrieving the eggs."

"Okay, but I never canceled the appointment, and I would like to see the doctor," Colette said, trying to keep her voice from rising. Her eyes burned as she fought the urge to cry. "Today. Now, for the appointment I've waited patiently for."

The woman stared back at her, then flipped through some papers, "It says here that you were using eggs from the Edison Fertility Bank in New York City."

"Yes, that's right," Colette answered, watching as the woman scribbled notes onto the paper.

"And the eggs were stored in 2004? Twelve years ago?"

Colette was taken aback. It felt like it was yesterday that she had painstakingly injected herself with hormones every single day and gone through the grueling process of saving her eggs. *How could that much time have gone by?* she wondered.

"Yes, I guess it was about twelve years ago," she answered.

"Okay, we'll figure this out. I'll have you speak with Dr. Erikson. Just come through the door on your left."

Colette exhaled, her glimmer of hope renewed. She nearly sang "Thank you" at the woman who, moments earlier, she'd wanted to scream at. She heard a slight buzz and realized the door was being unlocked for her, and she threw the straps of her black bag over her shoulder and rushed to follow the directions, as if any lapse or error on her part would undo the progress she'd just made.

"You can go into the first door on your right," the woman said as she followed behind Colette. She shoved the file in her hand into the holder on the outside of the door and said that the doctor would be in shortly. Colette was in not a typical exam room but instead an office with a big desk. She had thought she'd be getting an initial physical and then scheduling her hormone shots before egg implantation, but that was obviously not happening today. Sitting in one of the two leather chairs opposite the imposing desk, she switched back to taking deep breaths, trying to channel the young girl she'd been, so determined to save for her future. She'd been naive then, so full of hope and the possibility of happy endings. She'd yet to face the hell that would unfold and completely unhinge her trajectory.

But she was here today thanks to more than one miracle, and she would not leave without an appointment to have her eggs fertilized and then safely implanted inside her. Now, Colette's skin felt sticky under her work blazer and she took it off, not caring that she'd only worn a skimpy tank top that revealed her ample cleavage. She pulled her long brown hair into a loose bun, put two pieces of gum in her mouth, and took a deep breath. Fiddling with her gold-chain necklaces, she made a wish as she moved the clasps around to the back of her neck.

"Good morning," Dr. Erikson said as he rushed into the room and sat in the chair behind his desk. He opened the file folder and did a quick skim through the papers. "Ah, yes, okay. So, I did try to reach you, Miss . . ." He flipped to the front of the folder where her name was clearly placed. "De Luca."

Colette leaned forward on the edge of her chair, clutching her bag. "I didn't get a message. What were you calling about?"

"Well, I know that you wanted to start the process of implantation, and we sent over the request to the NYU Edison Fertility Bank to have the eggs transferred over. But there was an issue because . . ." He ruffled through the paperwork and pulled out a letter, pushing it toward her. "You sold these eggs eleven years ago."

Dumbfounded, Colette stared at the letterhead from the NYU egg bank. After years of paralegal work, she was trained to pick out the important words. It was clear that her eggs had been donated. But how? By whom? Sickness pooled in her gut.

"But . . . I never did this," she said, staring at the letter, praying for there to be some mistake.

Dr. Erikson started shuffling through the file folder again. "They sent over the donation papers as well." He slid the paperwork in front of her.

Queasy, she read through to see that, in fact, she had absolutely given away her unborn babies. She skimmed to the bottom, where she had supposedly signed her name, and her breath caught as she took in the familiar signature.

It suddenly came to her, as clear as day, as she stared at the paper. It wasn't her hand that had signed away the only thing she'd ever really had in the world.

It was Rob's.

Chapter Nineteen

GRETA

2016

Greta stopped at Greenwich Hospital on her way home from work. Her father had been admitted for shoulder-replacement surgery. He'd mentioned that although he hadn't wanted to retire yet, he was forced to, so he had no choice but to get in shape for men's tennis leagues. Most of his clients left after he'd served time in prison, so the last decade of his career was dismal at best, and Greta felt bad that her career was soaring at the same rate his was sinking, so she wanted to be supportive of his surgery. He even said things lately such as, "Gret, we need to get you out on the court with your old man." And she liked that he was being so pleasant.

She signed in to see Gerald Walsh and headed to his floor, passing Bianca in the hallway. Any confrontation wouldn't have been worth it right then, so she avoided even acknowledging the woman and continued to her father's room. Asleep in the bed by the door, her father looked frail. She walked to his bedside and gently touched his hand.

"B?" he asked groggily.

Greta assumed he was thinking Bianca was still there. "No, Dad, it's Greta, your *daughter*."

"My daught—sorry, Greta," he said, rubbing the sleep from his eyes. "How are you? Can you get my nurse? I need my pain meds." He grimaced.

Greta didn't want to confront Bianca, but confronting her dad was a horse of a different color. "Dad, what is Bianca doing visiting? Does Mom know you're still seeing her?"

"Sit down," Gerald said, sighing heavily. "And calm down. I ended things with her a while ago. Before things were dismantled, she grew that company with me . . . and people make mistakes."

She stared at him for a long time before saying "Fine" as she crossed her arms in a sulk. Truthfully, when she thought about her father and Bianca these days, she found herself less angry at him. It probably had something to do with the fact that she now realized just how much she was like him at times. The first time she'd seen him cheat on her mother, she'd viewed it as if he were a failure of a father. Now she knew marriage was complicated, and while outsiders would paint her the bad guy when it came to her and Patrick, they didn't know what it was like to be married to someone and feel unsupported and alone. Maybe her father was tired of her mother's constant desire for more money, houses, cars, and jewelry, and his wandering eye was just his way of searching for some appreciation. Greta wasn't sure, but at some point, her anger had involuntarily transitioned to apathy. She wasn't about to make excuses for him, but she accepted that there was probably a complexity that she'd been sheltered from. And seeing him so physically fragile made her more empathetic than normal.

She wasn't going to let him know that, though. "Mom's an idiot to put up with your bullshit, Dad."

"As I said, Greta, people . . . *I* make mistakes. Your mother is forgiving. It'd be nice if everyone were."

She flinched a little and looked at him, surprised. "Are you saying me? I should be forgiving of *you*? What am I forgiving you for? If Mom forgave you, that's between you and her." She raised her hands, palms out. "Your cheating has nothing to do with me."

He tried to sit up a little, then rested back, his face taut. "You need to forgive me because I did make a mistake that could affect you." He winced a little, and she couldn't tell if the pain was from his shoulder or what he was about to say. "Bianca . . . has a daughter."

"Good for—" she started, but then it hit her. The 529. *Oh God.* "Your daughter, you mean. She had *your* daughter." Heart in her throat, Greta grabbed her stuff. She had a half sister. Granted, it was a half sister she didn't plan on ever meeting, but this was too much. After reading the tax documents years ago, she'd suspected it, but much like the affair itself, it had never been confirmed, and she couldn't deal with how now . . . it was all out in the open. Her family functioned well with secrets, and that's how Greta had learned to function: in the dark and without mentioning anything that might pinpoint a flaw. She tried to push everything under the rug like she'd been trained to do, but the fact that her father's dishonesty had led to her having a half sister seemed unfathomable. She wanted to confront him, hash it out with Emily, do it all without hurting her mother. The complexities of the lie felt all too familiar. Like how she wanted to tell her own sons they were conceived because of another woman's generosity, a doctor willing to bend the rules, her willingness to put her need for family above truthfulness. Was that so bad? But her father's lies became a reminder that there was a chance for people to get hurt in the end.

"This was a . . . I don't have time for this right now. If you need anything, call me. I have to go back to work." Greta rushed out of the room and drove back to her office.

After working for several hours over dinner Jack had ordered, she reluctantly headed home. She realized on the drive that work was her sanctuary, a place where she could be herself. She worried that she and

Jack were getting too close but was proud she'd told him she had family in town and needed to go. She promised she'd make up the work he did for both of them. When she pulled into the driveway, she was eager to get out of her clothes that smelled like Thai takeout, shower quickly, and focus on her family.

Greta thought about how weird it was to have a half sister. The information was a reminder that affairs are selfish. As she washed up, she told herself she was doing the right thing by leaving the presentation in Jack's hands and not missing witnessing Cynthia, her mother-in-law, transform their dining room into Hogwarts. She headed back downstairs and watched in awe as Patrick's mother arranged the Quidditch pitch, candles, and Golden Snitch–shaped candies. Checking out the photo booth with costumes and wands was much more exciting than working late like her father always had. She tried to convince herself: *This is what good mothers do.*

"It looks absolutely fantastic! I don't know how you do it. Thank you so much, Cynthia," Greta said. "I ordered a Harry Potter cake from my mom's caterer and also balloons that say 'ten.'" She wanted some sort of credit, even if it was just for buying the right things. Maybe it didn't make her a "good mother," but it was how her parents had shown affection: by buying things. It was why she often turned to work when she was feeling inadequate. If she couldn't bond with them, then at least she could buy them things they needed and wanted, could take care of them financially.

"Is everyone we invited coming?" Brayden asked.

Greta had no idea; she'd lost the RSVP list, but she didn't want an argument. "Yes, all the boys in your class are coming," she answered, hoping she wasn't too far off.

~

The next morning, everyone woke up to the aroma of her father-in-law Norman's pancakes and Cynthia putting the final touches on the decorations. Then Audrey walked over from next door with her husband and kids. Then Greta's family arrived: her mother, Emily, and Megan; Connor was at lacrosse practice with Marshall. Greta wondered if her sons should be doing more than just tennis, but she focused on how proud she was to be having a party at home versus the lavish events her parents had for them growing up. She was proud of being more involved and living more frugally.

Greta didn't know many of the mothers who dropped their boys off, which made her feel like a deadbeat mom—she thought of her father again and how she had a sibling who she didn't even know but pushed the thought away. He wouldn't have recognized any of her teachers or her friends' parents when she was growing up unless they had invested with him. A few of the women were downright rude, pulling up and letting their kids out with hardly a hello. But she was thrilled that the children were all having fun, bouncing between the basketball hoop, badminton, bocce, and horseshoes. Some of the adults who stayed played croquet, but most were chatting and sipping cocktails.

Greta made a point of connecting with some of the mothers who had stayed, even those she'd overheard talking about the boys' field trip coming up that they were chaperoning. She secretly hated these perfect mothers yet longed to be more like them. Greta was happy that Audrey and Emily mingled with everyone effortlessly. They could be a buffer and hopefully make enough small talk with the other mothers, because they could help her decipher this stay-at-home-mom language.

Greta stood near Patrick and hoped he was giving her credit for doing all this.

Emily sidled up to her, joining her and her mother, and Patrick, the consummate gentleman, excused himself to get her a drink.

"How's Brayden's head?" Emily asked as soon as Patrick left. "Has he had any headaches?"

The question threw her. "His head's fine. Why?"

"I told you: when we took them out on the yacht last weekend, he hit his head pretty hard. I just wanted to make sure it didn't give him a concussion."

Greta was startled now. "I thought you said it wasn't that bad. Was it?" She hadn't been worried at the time.

"When Brayden fell, I assumed he'd slipped on the deck, and I didn't see it myself."

"Okay . . . so what did happen?"

"Marshall told me later that Logan tripped Brayden."

Greta nervously said, "Well, did you tell Patrick? Maybe he should speak to Brayden about it." She sensed a familiar pattern but thought if Patrick heard concerns from an outsider instead of her, maybe he'd be less dismissive.

"He did." Her sister nodded knowingly. "But Marshall was concerned that he just said 'Boys will be boys' and blew it off. Is he having any behavior issues at school?"

"Logan?" Greta faltered for a moment as she felt both defeatism and defensiveness; she always went back to blaming herself. She wasn't surprised by any of it but had no idea how to get support without Patrick's help.

"Well, he's good in school, and I hardly think brothers roughhousing is cause for grave concern," she said, hoping Patrick was right and that Emily would just drop it.

"Well, I do have a boy and a girl, so maybe they aren't as rough. I just worry because there was blood and he never even said sorry."

"I'll speak to him," Greta said, now irked and wanting Emily to stop talking about the incident. Today was about her sons' celebration, and she didn't feel like focusing on her children's imperfections.

Greta was relieved when she heard the purr of Jack's Porsche pull up in front of the house and excused herself from Emily's judgmental conversation as she met Jack halfway up the path to the backyard gate. Finally, someone that saw only her strengths. But Jack was too busy for birthday parties—he didn't even bring his kids. He just dropped off a gift for the twins that looked professionally wrapped and explained to Greta he needed to be very brief—he still had a ton of work to do on their behalf and was dropping off some files for her to look over tomorrow. When she took the files from him, she wanted to sneak into her office to read them right away but placed them inside on the kitchen island and came back outside knowing she would be up late tackling the work.

"Thanks," she said, wishing he would stay and chat about work, but he took off quickly, and Greta's mother caught a glimpse of him leaving.

"He doesn't even come and say hello; he was like a son. But who cares after what he did to Gerald," Evelyn said, her tone shifting toward anger. "He stole like half of Blackwood's clients after your father's troubles. So rude."

Greta wondered if she knew her husband had a child out of wedlock but didn't engage and accepted that her mom chose to live in denial as long as she could continue to shop. Who was she to judge anyone, she thought. "Come on, Mom, let's celebrate!"

"Have a seat, Evelyn. I brought you a Canadian Club old-fashioned," Patrick said, pulling up a folding chair and handing over her favorite drink along with a napkin.

Greta loved how thoughtful Patrick was; she needed to notice these qualities more often. She even noticed the other mothers sneaking looks at him when their less attractive husbands were grabbing refills. She worried these younger mothers secretly judged her and Patrick's age difference but tried not to let her insecurities show. She took a big sip of her drink and reminded herself that she was doing a good job. She was living way below her means, hosting a modest party in her small backyard versus at her parents' expansive estate. It was hard to feign interest in Junior League, but she was trying. She loved her job, so she wasn't even sure why she felt the least bit envious of their mom clique, but she did. Maybe mommy guilt was real. She couldn't compete with these stay-at-home moms who devoted their days to volunteering, watching their kids' sports, and creating Pinterest-worthy decor. But why did she care? She'd never wanted their lives in the first place, had she? These women reminded Greta of Emily and her superficial friends, of her own mother. She felt like an outcast.

She found Emily and confessed, "Mingling with these Greenwich moms doesn't come naturally, Em."

"I know, but they aren't that bad, Gret," Emily said. "And you did a great job with the party. Mom always went over the top; this is nice."

Greta wondered if she should tell Emily about their half sister—not here, but eventually she should probably know. Greta worried that she'd take it harder than she had and not be able to relate to her father's lies the way she secretly could.

"I wish I could be happy at home with the kids, fulfilled like you are."

Emily explained, "You can work and be a mom, but your career doesn't need to be as hard driving as Dad's. You don't want to get too obsessed with money and end up in trouble like he did."

Greta was defensive. "I would *never*." And then she felt the need to safeguard herself. "I am super ethical. I just heard from a very inside source that Apple is coming up with a car in the future and the stock's going to soar. I didn't even add Apple to my stock portfolio because I didn't want to end up like Dad. I'm careful."

"Well, can you add some Apple stock to my portfolio?" Emily giggled.

"Very funny," Greta said, and it felt good to laugh with her sister. "Hey, thanks for warning me about Logan's behavior on the boat. I do see some things too, but Patrick's so stubborn. Anyway, I have to go walk Audrey out. Be right back."

Greta was torn because this wasn't the first time she'd been tipped off over her son's behavior, but she convinced herself that maybe siding with her laid-back husband wasn't the worst thing in the world.

"We're heading out too," Emily said. "Love you. Let's get together soon." Greta gave Emily a quick hug, then ran and fetched two party favors that her mother-in-law had made and handed them to Audrey as she thanked her for coming. She motioned for Patrick to come over and help her see them out.

Audrey grabbed Patrick's hand. "Bye, sweetie. See you on Tuesday."

Too stunned to ask her friend what the hell that was, Greta found her voice only after she'd watched them disappear next door. "What's Tuesday?" she asked Patrick.

"Oh, she signed up for my Cardio Tennis clinic when she was dropping her girls at their lessons. I thought she'd mentioned it to you." Patrick seemed surprised.

"Oh . . . ," Greta said. "She might have. I've just been so busy with everything." But she knew Audrey hadn't said anything, and as she thought about it, her body went numb, her face flushing. What was Audrey doing? What was Patrick doing? Was something going on, or was she just seeing possible infidelity because of her father—and her own lies?

~

Greta was in a meeting three days later when she noticed her phone, on vibrate, had rung several times. "It's my mom," she whispered to Jack, and went into the hallway to take the call.

"Mom, what's wrong?"

"Dad's dead . . . Your father's dead!" she said between sobs.

In a split second, Greta seemed to feel everything—anger, shock, sadness, fear. It hit her physically and before she knew it, she was sitting on the floor. "How?" she finally managed.

"In his sleep, this morning. I've been trying to reach you for two hours!"

"In his sleep?"

"He fell in the bathroom yesterday, before he was released from the hospital. But he was taking OxyContin for pain management. They let him leave anyway. Isn't that absurd? It's malpractice. I'm going to get an autopsy and then we are suing the hospital!"

Greta could hear her hyperventilating. "Mom, I'm so sorry. I'm leaving the office to come over now." She held it together until she hung up; then she erupted, bawling her eyes out on the floor of her office hallway. She hated herself for never once leaving work early or canceling a meeting to make time to play tennis with her father. Now he was gone and she'd never have the chance again.

So much had been left unsaid between them, she and the man she'd been so angry at for so many years—the man who she was so much like. During their last visit he'd shifted, admitted his imperfections, and was seeking to make amends. Having a half sister she knew nothing about weighed on her; it reminded her of her own web of lies, and for the first time she was curious about what both her half sister and her sons' donor mother looked like. She didn't necessarily want to meet either of them but basked in the curiosity. She wondered why finding out that she had a sibling had triggered something inside of her that now had her second-guessing if she should really take all her secrets to her grave, but it did. Tears overcame her, and her feelings faded into ambiguity as her whole body ached at the loss.

Chapter Twenty

COLETTE

2016

Colette pulled over three times on her way home. The first two were because she couldn't see from the crying and to call Vic. The third time it was to vomit, the trauma of her appointment with Dr. Erikson too much to bear.

For the past seven years, whether she was struggling to stay sober, depressed after miscarrying, or mired in self-pity, she had drawn comfort from the knowledge that she had frozen her eggs—she still had that insurance policy. Now, at age forty, after a series of miscarriages, she had hung her hopes on using them. Never, even on her worst day, had she thought about the eggs not being there. She had been blindsided by the news and still couldn't comprehend Rob hating her that much.

Now her head was swimming, and when she got home she barely remembered the drive. Vic was waiting for her at the front door. He walked to the car and she got out, collapsing into him. He held her up as they walked inside, where she fell onto the couch, trying to wrap her head around what had happened. How and when had Rob done this? She tried to remember how he had gone from her savior to her enemy, but it was all so fuzzy. He had changed so much since the beginning, but how could she have known then that her fondest memories of their life together would always harken back to that crappy apartment with roaches and mice, that things between them would rapidly go downhill, that their dreams would shatter into a million shards of broken glass, cutting and scarring her? She'd been so foolish, so *grateful* to him for forgiving the $9,000 she had owed him when they were going through their divorce proceedings. No wonder—he had likely recouped more than that by selling her eggs.

Vic handed her a glass of water and sat beside her, rubbing her back. "It's going to be okay, hon."

"He's such a fucking asshole!" Colette shouted, holding the glass in her shaking hands.

"Did you ever consider that we weren't meant to use those eggs? I didn't want to say anything to you before your appointment, because I wanted to be supportive, but those eggs . . . those were your eggs for you and Rob. Maybe those eggs were never meant for us," Vic said gently.

Colette considered this idea and took a deep breath, trying to stop the panic and pushing aside thoughts of how good it would feel to take a painkiller right now. "But what if I can't get pregnant? Or what if I keep having miscarriages?" she asked Vic, searching his face for answers. She grieved all over again remembering the pain and disappointment when she'd miscarried her last two pregnancies. Both times she had blamed herself, the abortion she'd gotten two decades earlier, even the egg harvesting itself, which was as likely to have caused problems as the complication-free termination. Her doctors had said that there was no clear problem, that she should keep trying for a healthy, viable pregnancy.

At her first ultrasound for her second pregnancy, they'd found that the fertilized egg had implanted but a baby had not grown. A "missed miscarriage," what they called the miscarriage of a blighted ovum, had followed a week later. Now, after months of trying again, her vanity drawer was filled with pregnancy tests she took constantly. It had felt like her frozen eggs were her last real shot at motherhood.

"We'll have a baby, Colette, when it's the right time," Vic said soothingly. "We'll pray for our baby, and it will come. I'm not worried."

"But I'm forty years old," she responded, still crying as he held her tight, kissing the top of her head.

"I'm sure everything will be fine. You're such a good person and have overcome so much. We'll have a baby and you'll be a great mother, the very best," Vic whispered. "Now all we can do is have a lot of sex," he joked.

She sputtered out a wet laugh. "It figures that that's your silver lining." Taking a deep breath, she sat up and wiped her face. "Should I try to press charges against Rob?"

"It's up to you," Vic said, "but what will that accomplish? The eggs are gone."

Colette shrugged. "I can't just allow him to get away with this and think I'm not going to go after him. It's fucking insane. I feel like I at least deserve an explanation."

"Whatever you want to do," Vic said. "Now, are you hungry? Can I make you something to eat?"

Colette had envisioned herself coming home from the appointment and celebrating the start of their in vitro journey with Vic. Instead, devastated and pushing away the thought of popping a pill to take the edge off her emotions, she stood up and went to shower and go to bed. That image of her baby was getting fuzzier and fuzzier, but she needed to stay focused, not find a way to actually get fuzzier herself.

The next morning, she woke up to a bouquet of roses on the kitchen island with a note from Vic: *Our baby will come. I love you.* Her eyes welled up. Remembering that time in her life, that time with and directly after Rob, was hard—not just because she had done so much that horrified her now but also because there were huge gaps in her memory, times when she'd been so messed up on oxy that she couldn't remember where she'd been, what she'd done. Even with all that, she was full of rage at Rob for doing this to her. What could she possibly have done to deserve it?

~

Colette found herself dialing Rob's number and sending him emails long after she promised Vic she would stop. He had refused to respond to her messages, and when she'd tracked him down at a Wall Street hedge fund, his secretary had taken countless messages that were never returned. But she couldn't help herself. After everything he had put her through, the least he could do was answer her. She forced herself to stop for a few weeks and struggled to push it out of her mind. Finally, at Vic's suggestion, she called Rob one last time, telling him she needed the closure of being able to make amends with him. Rob had finally agreed—maybe he'd changed enough, or maybe he'd heard in her voice that she had.

It was step nine. She had made amends with most of the people in her life, but never Rob. That hadn't bothered her until recently, until she was faced with the reality that she had hurt him badly enough for him to apparently sell her eggs. Now, what he had done hung over her head every day, affecting her ability to think clearly, to be strong, to stay sober. Many things in her life had created challenges to her sobriety—some intense and some not—but this made her feel like she was on the cliff's edge, playing with her sobriety, and she could fall at any moment, so it was time to do something about it. If they both had the opportunity to finally clear the air, she would be better able to move on.

When the day finally came, Colette found herself checking her phone every few seconds as she searched the people in the Greenwich Starbucks, looking for a familiar face from her past. The smell of fresh-roasted coffee beans hung in the air, and there was a low buzz of conversation all around her in the crowded shop. She wondered if she would recognize Rob after all these years. And would he recognize her? She was a completely different person from the drug-addicted, malnourished young woman he had last seen in New York City. She glanced up each time someone passed through the doors, fighting the sinking feeling that Rob might not show.

She had left the house that morning unconcerned about the normal things one worries about when meeting with their ex—weight, hair, clothing—and instead had been preoccupied with keeping her temper in check, afraid that if he responded defensively—or worse, aggressively— she'd lose it. But she'd shown up with hope, looking around for a man she'd first met when they were just kids.

"Colette." His voice was quiet, but it immediately set her heart galloping. She gazed at him as he approached her table. He was no longer the young boy she had fallen in love with. The person who stood before her was a man with hair that was a little thinner, though a lot grayer. His middle was just a little softer, but it was obvious it was Rob, the man who had gotten her out of her small town and away from the childhood that had haunted her. He'd been a good guy once—maybe had become one again, she thought as she rose and he gave her an awkward almost hug with one arm.

She sat again quickly, nervous sweat breaking out under her arms and breasts. Calmly, methodically, just like she had with Aunt Lisa and her husband, with Frank, with Chelsea, Colette covered what she wanted to, itemizing her sins. It had been terrible the first few times she'd done it, but Rob would be her last, and though she was nervous, she wasn't ashamed like she'd once been. She was maintaining her sobriety, she was healthier than she'd been in years, and she had a lot to be proud of. Her past was just that, and it was time to let it go—all of it.

When she was done, she took a deep, shuddering breath and inclined her head toward Rob. "Do you have anything you'd like to say to me?"

He'd been calm the whole time, looking her in the eye—honestly, it was a courtesy not everyone had been able to offer her when she talked about her past behavior—but now he had a distinctly uncomfortable air. His eyes seemed unable to land anywhere for long as he spoke. "I guess, just, thank you . . . for saying all that . . . for admitting it. I know I wasn't easy to live with and was focusing on work more than our marriage. It's . . . not been until recently that I've found a good relationship, but . . . honestly? I don't really blame you. We were young, and we'd just gotten out of our small town and didn't really understand the world yet."

Colette wanted to be grateful, to be graceful even, but his ignoring it was too much. "Okay . . . but what about my eggs, Rob? Don't you have anything to say about that?" Her voice was tight. All the pain she'd gone through in her journey to become a mother seemed to overcome her. Rob had played a part in that journey, in that pain. Recovery was about taking responsibility, not being a victim, but dammit, she deserved to have him at least acknowledge that he played that part.

Instead, his brow furrowed. "Your eggs? I guess I'm sorry I wasn't ready for kids and suggested you freeze your eggs, but I don't think we would have made—"

"No, Rob," she practically yelled. "Why did you *sell* my eggs? I know I put you through a lot. I spent your money; I *owed* you money. But how could you have done that?" People in the café turned to look at them then, but she didn't care. She'd made her amends, and now he needed to make his.

He looked like she'd smacked him. "Colette . . . I didn't sell your eggs."

Something about the way he said it—his tone or his manner, or maybe both—made her think he was telling the truth. But that only confused her more. "You didn't?"

"No. You paid the bills, the storage, everything. I wouldn't have a clue how to give away your eggs, even if I wanted to. I don't even know where you went to do that."

He was right. But it didn't make sense. She fumbled in her bag and pulled out the paper the doctor had given her. "You forged my signature," she insisted, smoothing the paper out and putting it on the table between them.

His confusion was obvious and she faltered, just for a moment, her eyes flicking down to where her finger rested, right on top of the signature in strong black lines: *C. C. Richards.*

"How do you even know it's your paperwork? Wouldn't you have signed your full name?" Rob said, sliding the page back toward her.

Colette thought hard as she stared at the paper and considered whether she had ever filled out anything in her life with just her initials. She flashed back to other times she had seen this signature. It was familiar, but she felt removed from it. She thought about when she had moved and found her abortion paperwork and her father's death certificate in a box under her bed. Both had "C. C." signage instead of "Colette." She thought of that day in Chelsea's apartment when she'd found out her father had terminal cancer minutes after Chelsea had kicked her out—she'd found that stack of money and had never figured out where it had come from. The news about her father had made her forget about it for the most part, so where had it . . .

The fog started to clear.

"Oh my God." She'd looked up at Rob and felt a new reality settle uncomfortably over her. She whispered, "You didn't do this?"

But she didn't need to see him shake his head and confirm it. By the time Colette left the coffee shop, she was seriously confused. She didn't want to believe it, but she knew there was a very strong possibility that he hadn't done this. *But if he didn't do it, then who did?*

Colette went back and forth on believing Rob on the drive home. She found herself that night chewing violently on her cuticles where she sat across from Vic at the small kitchen island. His dark eyes squinted at her. The more she told him about her meeting with Rob, the more he looked as though he had been punched in the gut. She spoke quickly and rushed to defend herself before Vic could get a word in. She had shared how she hadn't been sure when she left the coffee shop, but now she was back to believing it was him. She couldn't figure out any other option. It was easiest to blame Rob. She didn't want Vic to have any doubt that she knew he'd done this.

"But I don't believe him when he says he had nothing to do with it. When I was with Rob, I never trusted him. When I used to accuse him of things, he would make me think I was crazy. Make me doubt what I knew was true . . ."

Vic sighed loudly and pushed his fingers through his hair. "But, Colette, the thing is, you say you can't be sure . . . that you don't remember." He chose his words carefully, searching her face for a sign of comprehension.

Colette's heart was racing. *I'm not crazy.* She shoved the paper in front of Vic again.

"Look at it! I don't know what happened, but I know that I didn't do this. I know that much. It's not my writing." She pointed to the signature at the bottom of the page.

Vic didn't look at the paper as he lightly pushed it away. "Colette." His hand reached for hers where it lay on top of the papers. His hand around hers stopped it from shaking, but the rest of her body was buzzing and she felt nauseated. He stared at her without speaking for long enough that she began to feel uncomfortable and looked away. He reached under her chin and pulled her face gently back to face him. "Colette," he repeated.

"What?" she asked in a whisper.

"We talked about this. It seems like you really don't know for sure what happened. You promised that if something like this happened again, you would get help." His face softened as he looked at her with a pleading behind his eyes.

Colette collapsed into tears, the strong facade she had been trying to keep up melting away. "But I'm not crazy! It's just . . . he probably did this." She wasn't trying to convince Vic at this point—she was trying to convince herself, and she was crying so hard she could barely catch her breath.

Vic jumped off the barstool where he had been sitting and wrapped his arms around her. "I know, but maybe if you talked to someone, you might be able to make sense of it. This isn't the first time that something major happened in your life that you can't remember. And you've been obsessing over this egg thing and you're not thinking clearly."

Colette pushed him away softly. "I am thinking clearly, and I know that I would remember if I had sold my eggs." She sniffed. If she let her guard down, if she even hinted at being unsure, what would Vic do? Would he force her to get help?

"Okay," he acquiesced, "but I think it's time for you to talk to someone. Will you? You promised." He wasn't going to let it go, and Colette was just so tired.

"Okay," she said, her voice a soft quaver. She couldn't fight anymore. She would have to talk to someone, if for no other reason than just so he would stop looking at her like this. But as soon as she agreed, she immediately thought of her mother, locked up in a psych ward for decades, talking in circles, nobody listening, nobody believing the things that she said.

I can't end up like her.

~

Dr. Brooks was speaking, and Colette stared at the woman. Her short bob angled perfectly to just reach her jawline, and her sharp features were in direct focus, but Colette couldn't concentrate on what she was saying. The doctor peered at her over her reading glasses, her pen poised over a notepad, both of her perfectly sculpted eyebrows raised expectantly waiting for Colette to respond.

"What?" Colette asked, embarrassed that she hadn't even heard the question.

"When was the first time that you can recall that you 'lost time,' as you referred to it?" Dr. Brooks asked again.

Colette gazed out the small window behind the doctor. The sky was blue, and the soft hum of the white noise machine in the corner of the office was so soothing, she felt like she wanted to lie down and close her eyes. She sighed and looked back at the doctor.

"I guess the first time was when I got locked in the doll store," Colette answered. "My mother owned this store, and I would go in with her sometimes . . ." She paused, hoping the woman wouldn't ask for more. She did not want to say more about that night; she didn't want to say aloud what she knew was true: that her mother had left her there on purpose.

When the doctor didn't say anything, Colette continued. "She thought I was in the car with her when she went home . . . but she had left me behind, and I . . . I stayed there overnight . . . alone." She avoided the other woman's eyes as she spoke.

She looked up to watch the woman as she jotted down notes. Even though she had been meeting the doctor for several weeks, Colette still felt uneasy. Something was holding her back from being completely truthful. She knew that it was partially her inability to truly remember and partially shame.

"What do you remember of that night?" Dr. Brooks asked.

"I just remember trying to get out and pounding on the door." Colette took a deep breath as she pushed away the images of the dark, dusty room with the broken dolls that were suddenly flooding her mind. "I was scared . . . and then I just remember being woken up in the morning by a police officer. My mother had called them to help find me." *Only after a truancy officer came to the house asking why I hadn't been in school for two days . . . again.* Colette shrugged and forced a fake smile.

Dr. Brooks put her pen and pad down on a glass table that was directly next to her chair and pulled her cream cashmere sweater tighter around her thin frame. As she leaned in, what smelled like expensive perfume wafted Colette's way.

"So like we talked about last session, when we were discussing what could be a potential diagnosis, this might be where your condition could have presented itself," Dr. Brooks said.

"Okay." Colette tried to keep the shakiness from her voice. "Or could that night have just been, like, so traumatic that I blocked it out?" Colette asked hopefully.

Dr. Brooks nodded. "It's possible, but the more we talk, the more I think it's not that simple. We will figure it out in time, but please know that whatever it is, it's treatable, and you will most likely be able to continue to live a normal life." The doctor's smile was soft and her eyes were kind, but Colette looked away.

"Can you dig deeper into some memories, maybe jot them down in a journal, so we can look for clues next session?" Dr. Brooks asked.

"Okay, I'll try to remember," she said.

Colette kept her head bent, looking down at her hands, which were twisted into each other, her cuticles raw and bleeding. Her stomach lurched at the thought of what could possibly be wrong with her. She had been afraid her whole life of turning into her mother, becoming an adult woman with no control over her mental health. She had convinced herself lately that she was fine, that she didn't have to worry about that anymore. But perhaps she had to worry now more than ever.

Chapter Twenty-One

GRETA

2017

Greta stood under the showerhead for a few extra minutes, letting the warm water comfort her as it cascaded over her shoulders. The shower had become a fleeting escape. Everything in her life felt routine these days: dropping the kids off at school each morning, texting Patrick to pick them up, and trying not to let work consume her like she often did when she was stressed out. She'd felt numb since losing her father and watching his secret unfold as his illegitimate child was named in his will, and shocked at how well everyone took the news. If only her own deep-seated secret could be as well received, she guiltily thought, but she was so exhausted by grief she tried to push it all aside and focus on her homelife.

She watched Patrick brush his teeth through the steamed-up glass shower wall. His freshly showered hair was a little longer and sexier than normal. Other women her age would kill to have a husband like him. She wished she could will herself to be more physically attracted to him. She was tired of acting. Was the distance caused by the secrets she harbored? *How much longer can I go through the motions?* she wondered.

Her rehearsed moans felt much less robotic after she had a glass of wine at the end of the week. Did all couples who were together this long experience the same choreographed facade? Maybe their disconnection was normal. Could he sense that when she closed her eyes, she fantasized that he was someone else? She worried that this lack of attraction might eventually outweigh the love she had for him. But until that happened, she would continue to remind herself that love was more powerful than passion.

She got out of the shower, wrapping a towel around her as Patrick gave her a peck on the cheek. He wasn't wearing his customary tennis shirt; instead, he wore a long-sleeve Vineyard Vines tee.

"Aren't you working?" Greta asked.

"No, I told you. I volunteered to go with the boys on their school field trip."

"Oh, yes, yes, that's right. I'll try to come by on my lunch break."

"That'd be great," Patrick said as he slipped on his sneakers. Greta thought they looked too much like something a teenager would wear, but she said nothing.

She kissed him goodbye and the kiss felt genuine. She still loved him—very much, really—but a disingenuous feeling always bubbled just below the surface. It was as if her father was partially right and she was starting to outgrow Patrick. In the beginning she'd had the need to have a young, attractive guy by her side, but now she craved a deeper, more intimate connection with someone who spoke her language. When she was with Jack, she felt as if he listened and didn't chalk her up to being "too uptight" the way Patrick was doing.

Greta slipped on a flattering gray suit and Ferragamo heels, which she had purposefully bought because they didn't show the logo. She didn't feel the need to be flashy like her mother and sister, but she was still drawn to quality and designer items.

On the drive to work, Greta thought about how sweet Patrick was. The week before, he had surprised her at work, showing up unannounced at her office with flowers. It was moments like this that kept pulling her to him, keeping her attached, but still, she vacillated between leaving and staying. Those moments plugged the holes of doubts in her mind, making her feel loved and accepted. Patrick was different from the guys in her male-dominated workplace; he was fun to be around, he was caring, and he was thoughtful.

At work, she sipped coffee as she walked to her office, smiling at coworkers as she pretended not to notice their eyes often wandering onto her long legs. She sighed as she leafed through the reports on her desk and realized all the work she would need to make up if she took part of the afternoon off. She had already decided that she would spend her lunch break going to the lake; she was making an effort to be a more involved mother now that her boys were older.

~

"I'm taking a long lunch. Patrick and the boys are on a field trip, and I promised I'd stop by," Greta said. She was unsure of why she was explaining herself to Jack.

"Okay, I'll be here late if you want to come back and do a work dinner."

"Maybe," she said, winking before immediately wondering why she had confidence with him and not with family life.

She entered the campsite's name into her Range Rover's GPS, sipping a Diet Coke and eating a Kind bar on the way, excited that her small lunches over the past two weeks had helped her lose that one last stubborn pound. It was worth skipping lunch to show her boys that she cared.

Ed Sheeran's "Thinking Out Loud" blared from the car's speakers, and Greta sang along, nodding her head to the music. The song drowned out her work and homelife burdens so much that she put it on repeat, feeling light, lively, and hopeful. She opened the window and let the wind blow her long auburn hair in all directions. The lyrics reminded her of her younger self: the woman who first fell in love with Patrick.

Before long, she was at the camp's entrance sign. She parked, hopped out of the car, and walked to the lake's edge, her designer heels digging awkwardly into the dirt. The afternoon light was reflecting off the lake, making her pause for a moment to appreciate nature and the beautiful mild weather.

She looked for Patrick, Logan, and Brayden and spotted them in the distance. She recognized Patrick's relaxed, almost bouncy gait. He walked like a college athlete, and she thought about how his walk was similar to how the boys strutted. All three had a little skip to their step. Patrick was high-fiving the boys as they jumped off the dock, Brayden in a poised dive and Logan in a cannonball, splashing everyone around him. Greta felt a pang at the boys' connection with their father. When she'd go out of her way to leave work early and pick the boys up from school, she'd purposefully ask them how their day was. When they'd respond "fine" or "good," she wasn't sure what else she could do.

They finally saw her, and she waved as she walked up to the campsite's information center to use the restroom before going to say hello. It was a dismal restroom that smelled like a combination of wet bathing suits and grilled cheese. While she was lining the toilet seat with tissue, a few of her sons' room moms walked in and started talking about Patrick. She froze.

"Love that those twins' dad came," one woman said. "He's *so* good looking."

"Yeah, he's like the only hot dad in the school," the other woman agreed. The sound of running water blocked out the first woman's response.

Greta was torn between pulling the stall door open to put them in their place and remaining hidden until they left to avoid the drama.

"His wife's *much* older. Not sure what he sees in her. She's a wicked workaholic and doesn't seem interested in her kids."

"Yeah, I never see her at the school, but she's loaded."

Greta flushed the toilet. She had heard enough. She flung the door open and just missed the gossiping women, who were already out the door by the time she marched out. She ran her hands under hot water and used her elbow to try to get soap out of the broken dispenser, which was nearly empty. Waving her hands in the air to dry them, Greta began walking down to the docks feeling both sad and irritated that her lack of maternal instinct was showing.

She decided that she was not going to let these mothers convince her she wasn't enough. They might think she was not up to par when it came to being a helicopter mother, but Greta gave herself a lot of credit. Her best friend at her kids' age was her driver to and from prep school; at least she was here and showing her boys she cared. She had to let what they said about her go and not let their little crush on Patrick get in the way of her recognizing that she was doing pretty well. If anything, it made her want to find him and make some sort of public display of affection.

She reached the lake's edge and took her heels off, debating whether to walk along the dirty sand or out onto the dock. She vaguely recognized a few students playing on a nearby playground and waved at some teachers she knew but wouldn't have been able to name. She envied all the mothers who were so well connected with the school, but she also wanted to get back to work.

She saw four boys and Patrick on a floating dock about ten yards out. Patrick spotted her and swam over. He pulled himself up onto the dock where she stood and shook the water out of his hair. He gave her a kiss, and she noticed his nose was even more sunburned than normal. She was happy she had come to see them.

Greta looked around, wanting those room moms to see her but also feeling awkwardly overdressed as she held her dress shoes on the dock in her gray blouse and skirt suit. Patrick didn't seem to care, though.

"Thanks for coming," he said. "The boys are having a blast!"

"Why aren't they closer to the lifeguard?" Greta inquired.

Patrick shrugged as he looked back at them. "I don't know. Keep an eye on 'em; I'm going to hit the head."

Greta watched some of the boys swim from the floating dock to nearby kayaks. It looked like Brayden grabbed one and shared it with his friend and took off. Another boy grabbed the other one and paddled off, leaving Logan alone on the floating dock. Then she watched Logan jump into the water and swim toward the boy. He had taken off his T-shirt and his body was tan, and it was the first time she noticed he was becoming muscular. Suddenly, Logan grabbed the kid off the kayak and started pushing his head in and out of the water by his hair. Greta's jaw dropped and she shouted, "Stop!" *What was Logan doing this time?* Was he mad that the kid took his kayak? She looked left and right for Patrick, and her heart felt like it had skipped a beat when she saw that Logan was now holding the kid under the water.

Greta yelled, "Logan!" She yelled again, "Brayden!" hoping he could help. "Isn't there a lifeguard? Help!" Her yell was now a full high-pitched scream. Greta's muscles tensed, and she kept screaming her sons' names.

She could see Brayden and his friend playing together, their hands lifted over their heads as they faced away from the action. Brayden and his friend were farther out on the lake, oblivious to the attempted drowning. Why were they just goofing around when Logan was acting like this? Greta looked out and the boy's face was still submerged under the water, his hair in Logan's grasp. She realized they probably couldn't hear her as she screamed, so she began waving her shoes in a crisscrossing motion, her face turning red in frustration. She didn't want to jump in the water in her work clothes.

She screamed again as her whole body cringed in horror, "Logan, stop! Lift him up!" But her son wouldn't let up, and Greta's insides froze. She had no choice. She jumped into the water and swam out, and just as she reached the crime scene, Logan lifted the boy's head up with a laugh. The boy gasped for air and coughed water out.

"Logan!" she shouted, now two feet in front of him, treading water. The boy continued to gasp for air and was now slumped over the edge of the kayak.

Logan was smiling, and Greta was just as disturbed with the smile as she'd been with what she'd witnessed. The boy still wasn't breathing right, and Logan's eyes looked happy and she didn't know why.

"Oh my God, are you okay?" Greta said to the boy, feeling dizzy as she continued to tread water in her work clothes.

Brayden and his friend paddled over and looked as scared as she was. Her mind flashed back to when Logan had pressed the ski pole into his brother's body. Emily's comment about him misbehaving on the boat. It was all flashing around in her mind. She began to sweat, despite still treading water in the cold lake.

"Mom, you jumped in?" Brayden asked.

"Yes, your brother almost killed this kid," she said, pointing in disbelief, fury, and horror.

"Max wouldn't give me the kayak!" Logan barked.

"Are you sure you're okay?" Greta asked the boy again. She grabbed his hand and swam the tearful child to shore as Logan followed in the kayak. She encouraged him to apologize, but that didn't even seem like enough.

"Logan, get out of the water with me and make sure your friend's okay!" Greta shouted back into the lake, where her son still lingered.

"He's not my friend," Logan said.

"Logan, what is wrong with you? You almost killed that kid!" Greta wanted to report her own son to the teachers. But then she looked up and groaned internally as she realized that the mother of the kid her son was bullying was the same mom that had been bad-mouthing her in the bathroom earlier and was now running toward her. But two wrongs didn't make a right, and Logan's behavior was alarming.

The woman came running up to Greta and said, "What happened?"

"Well, your son wouldn't share the kayak so I guess Logan held him under. I'm sorry," she said, shivering and horrified by the entire ordeal. The woman's face was bright red.

Greta added, "Maybe it's normal boy stuff?"

The woman responded, "Well, maybe you don't know this because you are never around, but this isn't *normal*."

"Well, I jumped in to save your son too," Greta said, realizing she had a habit of being defensive and the woman was right, but she couldn't explain something she didn't yet understand. Why was her son exhibiting this "lashing out" type of behavior?

Shame washed over Greta and she wanted to disappear. She yelled, "Patrick!" She finally spotted him on his way back toward her, but he had missed the entire fiasco. The mother stormed off with her son still in tears.

"Oh my God, Patrick. Logan just bullied that kid," Greta said, pointing over at the boy and his mother, still shaking. "He took his kayak, so Logan held him under the water!"

"Max? Oh, his mother's a Greenwich socialite. Who cares? He probably started up with Logan. I told him to stop being so shy and stand up for himself."

"This wasn't standing up for himself. He was drowning him!" Greta snapped.

"That's so funny that you jumped in. Bet the kids got a kick out of it."

"Patrick, you aren't listening. He scared the shit out of me. He was holding him under for like three minutes!"

"Max is a crybaby," Patrick said, looking over at the other boy. He continued to explain, "The pediatrician said we aren't supposed to referee, we need to let kids work out fights. I don't think there is much we can really do, ya know?"

"What the *hell*?" Greta said, fed up with his denial as she yanked the towel he was handing her out of his arms aggressively.

"I'm sure it's fine," Patrick said.

"Yeah, well, it wasn't *fine*. It was fucked up!" Greta said, feeling furious. She grabbed her Ferragamo shoes off the edge of the dock, where she had tossed them before diving in. "That was *not* funny! He has like . . . anger issues. We need to take him to see someone, he needs a professional. Maybe our old marriage therapist can make a referral." Greta regretted that she had skipped so many of their therapy appointments. It was hard with work, tennis matches, and exhaustion.

"Calm down, Gret, he doesn't need *therapy*," Patrick said. He looked chastised but then winked at Logan, and Greta's blood began to boil.

She opened her mouth, but nothing came out. She was too furious to speak, and Logan was still floating around on the kayak with a puzzlingly blank expression pasted on his face. Patrick stretched a hand toward her and squeezed her shoulder, but she cringed.

"Greta, it's just boys being boys. They mess with each other all the time."

Greta knew what he meant, but she also knew what she saw. "I'm leaving," she said, handing the towel back to Patrick and leaving as fast as she could in her sopping-wet suit. She dreaded the fact the gossiping mothers had another failure of hers to track.

In the car, she was overwhelmed by the sinking feeling that Logan was suffering from some sort of developmental issue, and she hated she couldn't talk to Patrick about her concerns. The thought gutted her and was another reminder of her father's prior comments regarding Patrick's immaturity. She had liked that he was more happy-go-lucky, but maybe he was *too* type B—not serious enough for their life now.

She blasted the heat and drove to her house to change. She called the school and texted Jack to confirm that they were working late and getting takeout. Maybe he would be a comfort to her stress. She pulled into her driveway, left the car on, and ran inside to change, then drove back to work, reapplying mascara at a stoplight.

She was still so angry with Logan and with Patrick and realized she could not ignore her son's violent behavior. She began to wonder about other things people had said to her through the years. Teachers, Audrey, and her sister had subtly tried to warn her that something was off with Logan, that perhaps he provoked fights. She knew he had a shy demeanor, but today she had witnessed an even scarier type of quiet. It wasn't just the drowning; it was his overall affect. He showed no remorse. It was as if he still thought he was right in hurting the boy because he took the kayak. She was torn between wondering if her son was nuts or if she herself was overreacting. Therapy meant the doctor might ask about his genetic history. But was Logan's behavior out of control because she wasn't going to risk that? She knew something was wrong; he acted younger and quieter than his peers—angrier. But she had no idea why she was the only one seeing it and was starting to resent that she couldn't share any of this with Patrick.

She dialed Patrick.

"I called the school to ask if Logan's been having any issues."

"Oh my God, Gret, why?" Patrick said.

"I don't think you discipline him enough. He really hurt that kid."

"Do you know how many fights I got into in high school?"

Greta couldn't picture Patrick fighting and almost chuckled. "You did?"

"Yes, babe, I did. He's fine."

Greta realized that Patrick's voice was a comfort; she'd have to let it go. Perhaps she was just exhausted from wrangling with her own grief and her fear was getting the best of her. When the teacher called her back, she let it go to voice mail. She hoped that Patrick was right. Boys fight, she told herself. Why would she start digging around for a pill that might be hard to swallow? She needed to just enjoy the good life.

Chapter Twenty-Two

COLETTE

2017

As she made the trip to see her mother, Colette wanted to feel something. But try as she might, she was detached from it all. She hadn't seen her since that one time she went with Aunt Lisa. She had sometimes thought of it but could never bring herself to make the trip again. Plus she knew that her mother could contact her if she wanted to and never had. Not once. She tossed a stick of gum in her mouth and chewed nervously as she drove down the Merritt Parkway headed to Middletown, Connecticut, listening to her aunt warn her over speakerphone not to get her hopes up.

"I know," Colette replied. "I'm not."

"I wish she could give you the answers you're looking for, but the last time I went to see her, she wasn't doing well."

"It's really fine; I get it. I'm way overdue for a visit anyway. You know, since I turned forty, I feel a greater urgency for clarity. I just want to try to figure out if my infertility is hereditary," Colette explained.

"I totally understand," Aunt Lisa said. "And I support you completely and am here for anything. I love you, honey. Good luck today, and whatever you find out, just remember that you are strong, Colette; you will get through this."

Colette hung up and couldn't help but feel frustrated. Lately she felt as if everyone was speaking to her like she was crazy, and she was getting tired of it. She hadn't told her aunt about her meeting with Rob or her therapy appointments—no need to worry her—and yet Aunt Lisa's tone made it clear that she was in fact concerned about her. Vic, her therapist, and now her aunt. She was desperate for clarity. She needed to see her mother one more time; she wanted proof that the underlying fear and worry keeping her up at night weren't valid. *"You're nothing like her."* Her father's words from his deathbed rang in her ears.

The irony wasn't lost on her that she was reaching out to her mother for answers. Colette wanted to talk to her mother about her life. Of course, she knew better than to expect a heart-to-heart with someone she barely recognized, but she was cautiously optimistic that she might learn at least a little today. She knew her mother's schizophrenia had meant she had delusions, and when she wasn't on medication it was difficult for her to distinguish reality from hallucinations. She also knew people with it often had trouble concentrating or responding to questions in a logical or coherent manner, so she was keeping her expectations low. But she had to try. She needed answers.

She thought back to the last day she had spent with her mother before she was put in the institution. That day, and night, in the doll hospital were the most traumatic hours of her extremely painful and lonely childhood. Much like the day Colette had gotten her job or the morning she had woken up in her drug dealer's apartment, there were a lot of details that escaped her. Dr. Brooks had suggested there was a small possibility that it could be a type of dissociative amnesia called localized amnesia. Somewhat common when something traumatic or stressful happens, the brain protects itself by not remembering the details. This combined with her alcohol and drug use was a recipe for disaster. But that was the best-case scenario; she knew that. The other option was too scary to consider. Colette pushed it out of her mind. She didn't want to think about why she couldn't remember. It didn't matter. She just wanted to put the pieces together now. If she could just remember and learn more about how she got to this point in her life, maybe she would be okay.

Going to therapy had awoken something in her. Memories came when she least expected them, more frequently than ever before. Maybe because she was speaking with Dr. Brooks regularly about her childhood, and about her struggles in adulthood, something was happening to her brain. Suddenly she couldn't stop the onslaught of flashbacks. Wisps of a life that didn't seem like hers floated in and out of her consciousness. Flashes came that seemed like she was there but just outside of herself. The images and recall were often jarring and unpleasant, and they left a gnawing ache in her stomach that she couldn't seem to shake. Each week that she met with Dr. Brooks, she found she was unearthing chunks of her childhood, and her life, piece by piece.

Colette sighed as she pulled into the parking lot. The sky was gray, and raindrops had just started to fall. She grabbed the bottle of pink nail polish from her purse and put it into her pocket along with her ID. She glanced in the back seat and was relieved to find a jacket. She shrugged it on as she made her way to the front door, and the faint smell of cigarette smoke hit her. Confused, she lifted the arm of the jacket to her nose and inhaled. Stale smoke was embedded in the fabric, and she dropped her arm quickly to get away from the stench. *That smell keeps following me.*

She took the jacket off as she approached the front of the gray building—it looked as bleak and depressing as it had last time. A shiver ran up her spine as she considered for the first time the reality of her mother's life. *She's been locked up for more than three decades.*

Her hand shook as she signed in at the front desk. *Just stay calm. I might not get all the answers I'm looking for today, but anything will be better than living my whole life in the dark.*

More than reaching out for guidance or support, Colette wanted to know about her mother . . . well, becoming a mother. Fertility wasn't genetic, but Colette had dealt with guilt and self-loathing about her fertility—and if she had done something to cause it by having an abortion, having her eggs harvested, or doing drugs for so many years. And after she turned forty, she began trying to come to terms with her childhood, her inability, so far, to become a mother herself, and with her own potential diagnosis. For Colette, the prospect of having her own child had always seemed like a chance to right the wrongs of her own upbringing, but now she was wondering if maybe she just needed to come to terms with her mother, her childhood . . . her own mental health. Maybe she had to forgive her mother, understand her more, and then her body would let her conceive. She never verbalized this idea to Vic because it sounded ridiculous, but she was out of ideas. And desperate. Maybe she wasn't meant to be a mother, and that thought had prompted this, her first visit with her mother alone, her first visit at all since 2010.

Colette was already drained, emotionally and physically, but she was good at putting one foot in front of the other, which was what she did now. Once inside the lobby, she saw those dolls, so eerie and triggering on her last visit, were gone. She breathed a small sigh of relief as she stood awkwardly, waiting for her mother to arrive. She looked around the dingy lobby, the linoleum floor worn in patches and a sad plant in the corner, its leaves drooping and brown at the edges. A large shelf on the far wall was filled with dusty, neglected books, and Colette pretended to glance through the titles as a way to avoid the unsettling gaze of an elderly man in a wheelchair petting a cat.

"Oh my, you look beautiful," Connie said as a nurse guided her into the room and sat her down in a chair.

Colette reached over to give her an awkward embrace, and her arms were shaking and starting to feel numb and heavy. Already her mother seemed more lucid than she had been during their last visit, and Colette felt a small surge of hope. Yet she couldn't shake the fear that overcame her as the nurse left them alone. She was glad she hadn't forced herself to visit more often; it was too torturous. Colette sat across from her mother on a couch.

"I wanted to talk to you about when you were pregnant with me," she said, rushing to the topic at hand. It was a clumsy approach, but she had no idea how long her mom would be clearheaded.

"What about it?" she asked somewhat gruffly. "I hated being pregnant, and your father always yelled at me for smoking." Her face scrunched into a grimace. "Do you smoke?" She gestured to the patio in front of the building. "Wanna go outside? You can just wheel me out." Her eyes lit up at the idea.

"No, I don't smoke," Colette said, pushing her jacket behind her. She pulled the nail polish from her pocket. Her mother looked upset, so Colette plowed on. "How about I paint your nails?" she said, reaching for her mother's hand. The palm was rough, and her cuticles were chewed and raw—much like Colette's often were. She had little bits of nail polish on each nail, just like last time, and Colette was happy she had remembered. She opened the bottle and started to paint as her mother watched.

She kept her eyes down, focused on her task. The fumes hitting her were a welcome scent to cover the institutionalized smell of the lobby.

"Remember when I was little and I wanted to do rainbow nails like Punky Brewster?" Colette asked as she painted.

"No," her mom answered.

"Well, I did, and you let me. We went to the drugstore and bought five cheap polishes, and you painted my nails red, yellow, pink, purple, and blue. Everyone was so jealous . . . nobody else's mother would let them do it." A sad smile tugged at Colette's lips at the memory. She looked up to meet her mother's gaze, and she had a wide smile across her face.

"Ha!" she said.

Colette kept painting in silence and then spoke again.

"I came today because . . . well, I just wondered . . . did you want to be a mom? Were you and Dad trying to have me?"

Connie stared at her daughter for a few seconds. "Nope."

She didn't know a word with such soft sounds could be so barbed. "So you didn't try to get pregnant with me?"

Her mother's eyes couldn't seem to stay in one place, but she still seemed tuned in to the conversation. "It was just one night. Your father was drunk, and he forgot to pull out. And then I was pregnant. Neither of us had ever said the word 'baby' to each other—even as a nickname." She snorted a bit at her joke.

Colette squirmed on the couch cushion, wanting to get the imagery of her father "pulling out" out of her mind. She blew lightly on her mother's wet nails.

"And then me and your father . . . we never tried again, if you know what I mean." Connie leaned forward as she spoke the words softly, her eyes still flitting about. She reached out and touched Colette briefly, then the couch itself, then her chair's armrest.

"Okay, thanks," Colette said a bit distractedly, reaching for her mother's other hand, pushing away the feelings of disappointment flooding through her.

Colette looked at her mother, who was still touching her chair's armrest and the couch, alternating gently, running her fingertips on just a few inches of one before going back to the other.

"Careful, Mom, your nails are wet."

Connie lifted her hand in the air and admired Colette's handiwork. "Oh, they look bee-you-tiful!" she gushed.

Colette twisted the polish cap back on and put it back into her pocket. Her fingers brushed against something, and she pulled out the *C* necklace that Aunt Lisa had given her for Christmas years ago. The pain of her mother's words made her clutch the necklace in her palm, but she forced herself to stand.

"I almost forgot. I brought you a gift," she said.

Colette walked to the back of her mother's chair and held the necklace in front of her face, moving her thick, wiry hair out of the way to clasp it. Her mother looked down and touched the pendant.

"This was your necklace. Aunt Lisa gave it to me, but I thought you might like to have it back." Colette felt a weight lift as she walked back around the chair. She was happy to be rid of the necklace, as it stirred up too much and her mother would enjoy it more.

"I wore it a lot since I got out of rehab. I thought of you whenever I wore it. Maybe it's good luck?" Colette tried once more to engage her mother in a meaningful conversation.

This time, her mother spoke as though she hadn't heard a word Colette had said. She caressed the necklace and gazed at her daughter.

"I was never meant to be a mother," Connie said. "I always knew there was something wrong . . . with me or the world or both. Bringing a child into it, passing that on, was not something I ever wanted."

It was possibly the kindest thing her mother had ever said to her. Yet it caused a tumult of emotions to go through her as she pulled away from the dingy building her mother called home. Maybe she shouldn't have a baby. She was making progress with Dr. Brooks, but her mental health was still not under control, and she didn't know if she might have to start to take medication. Plus, even with medication and Vic, why would she want to put a child through any of the trauma that she herself was working so hard to overcome?

Chapter Twenty-Three

GRETA

2017

Greta unfolded a piece of loose-leaf paper she'd brought from home to work and reread Logan's messy handwriting: *Mom, I hate this summer camp. I'm afraid of my counselor hurting me. Come pick me up!*

His letter really disturbed her, but she wasn't sure what to do about it. Should she go and pick him up, or would making him stay at the camp be the best parenting move? She hoped they were teaching him the golden rule. The camp brochure explained that its goal was to build confidence and self-esteem while living away from their parents. When the twins got back from camp, she would tell Logan she was proud of him for sticking it out. She missed them.

Jack popped his head into her office. "You bringing Patrick tonight?"

She shook her head. "No, he's away."

"Oh. Where's he at?"

"East Setauket, at a Professional Tennis Registry training," she replied, aware that he didn't likely care but was asking to be polite.

"Wanna go together, then? My wife's away too, visiting her folks."

"Sure." Greta tried hard to ignore the flutter in her stomach. She felt so disconnected from Patrick after him undermining her worries about Logan, and she'd become even more numb after losing her father. She'd been devastated that she'd never really made things right between them and had ended up embracing those aspects of herself that were a bit like her father—to the detriment of her marriage perhaps. On the one hand, they'd stopped bothering with therapy and had settled back into a pattern that had her feeling as if Patrick were more of a roommate than a husband who really listened. On the other hand, her success at work—and her flirtation with Jack—was flourishing. She'd tried to resist her attraction to Jack for years. Her building resentment toward Patrick, mixed with grief, caused her to just give up. Part of her wondered why she hadn't caved sooner.

"Okay, I'll pick you up early, and we can grab drinks before we go."

On the way home, Greta stopped at a boutique and splurged on a sexier-than-she'd-planned-to-wear backless dress with a subtle surplice neckline. She also made a last-minute appointment with her favorite makeup artist, Lisa, who lifted her spirits for the first time since her father had passed and talked her into a new red lipstick to complete her stunning look.

When Jack arrived to pick her up, Greta felt like she was going on a first date, which wasn't helped by the look on Jack's face as he took her in. He drove them to the station, and they took the train into the city. The sign at the entrance of the Mandarin Oriental hotel confirmed they were in the right place: *Institutional Investor*'s HEDGE FUND INDUSTRY AWARDS. The event space was decorated, with a stage in the front of the room. Greta and Jack immediately found the cocktail waitress. They bumped into a few colleagues and networked, but mainly they talked and flirted with each other. The energy between them had shifted completely, and Greta wondered if it was because she was letting her guard down, too weary to fight off her natural instincts anymore, or if it was because her whole family was gone, no one there tonight to help ground her in her reality.

Just as the winner of Macro Hedge Fund Manager of the Year was being announced, Jack leaned in. "I've heard these speeches before. Let's go."

Though caught off guard, Greta got up smoothly and followed him out of the ballroom and into the adjoining lobby. Alone at last, he grabbed her and kissed the nape of her neck. Already flushed from her three martinis, she felt like her entire body was on fire, desire pooling in her stomach. She liked Jack's drive, his ease with taking charge like this.

He pulled back to make eye contact meaningfully, and then, without saying anything, they walked outside and she thought about how guilty she felt, but at the same time she felt heard for the first time in forever. He looked amazing in his Armani suit, the New York City lights as a backdrop. They boarded the train back to Greenwich hand in hand, standing against the train window, their bodies close. The anonymity was like a drug, making her as giddy as the heat from him pressing against her. Greta's body was tingling from the inside out, as if a weight inside her were finally lifting.

"What perfume are you wearing?" Jack whispered in her ear, his facial hair gently scratching her skin.

"Fucking Fabulous," she answered, suddenly feeling a little shy about her new Tom Ford perfume.

"You smell like my Porsche." When he squeezed her butt, the silliness disappeared and she felt herself clench in response, her lust getting the better of her. He pushed her up against the wall of the train, blocking her from view, and slid a hand up between her legs. She squirmed, double-checking that they weren't causing a scene on the public train, and nearly gasped as he moved her lace underwear to one side. He pressed a finger against her, then one was inside her, and then another, moving them in until she moaned effortlessly, like she hadn't in so long.

"Oh my fucking God," she moaned under her breath.

Jack ran his other hand along the opening of her dress, between her breasts, then wrapped his hand around the back of her neck, pulling her toward him. All the while, she ached for more of him. He relieved her tension with his other hand, then moved the underwear back in place, gently rubbing her clitoris over her panties as her nipples stiffened against the thin material of her dress.

She felt eyes on her and pushed him away. "Stop—we can't do this here." They may not have known anyone on the train, but she couldn't do this in view of anyone. It had been a turn-on briefly, but she couldn't get caught on someone's phone recording or something equally as horrifying. Thoughts of Patrick swirled in her head—she knew she shouldn't be doing this. She was essentially risking her entire life, her world, the one she'd stood behind so staunchly, refusing to give up and praying no one would ever find out.

But she didn't care. She was transported back to prep school, when life was less complicated. She hoped they would pick up the minute they arrived at their stop.

"Are you okay? I know we're crossing a line."

Greta realized he was probably worried that she was drunk or feeling taken advantage of. "I'm better than okay," she said. "It's just . . . public." She gave him a small smile and he pulled her close to him. "Our stop." She nodded at the door and reluctantly pushed away from him.

They were the only ones to get off, and there was no one waiting at the station. Finally, fully alone, they headed toward the parking lot but didn't even make it to Jack's car. He leaned up against the red Greenwich train station wall, unzipped his pants, and picked her up right there, in the dark parking lot, hiking up her dress, ripping her underwear off, and pressing himself inside her.

"I'm scared someone will see us," she whispered through a moan.

"Who cares?" He hiked her skirt up higher, but she pulled it down again and wiggled out of his hold, pulling him gently toward his car.

They barely got to the driver's seat before his pants were all the way to his knees, and he unzipped her dress so she was totally naked in the front seat of his car. The smell of leather, cigars, and her candy-scented perfume heightened her arousal. Jack was practically frantic with desire, busy sucking her nipples into his mouth, then laving her neck with his tongue. Greta had never been this turned on, and she couldn't believe this was all happening in the front seat of his Carrera.

When it was over, Greta felt ashamed she'd been unfaithful, but it didn't dampen her hunger for him. She pulled her dress on as Jack hiked his pants back up over his hips and started the car. She peered over at him, wondering if he felt the same blend of relief and regret and desire she did. She'd already crossed a line, so now she felt as if she might as well keep going and allow herself to continue to feel young and really seen, heard, and appreciated for just one night.

After a long stretch of silence, he grabbed her hand. "I want you again, Gret."

They'd waited just long enough for thoughts of her sons to creep in, but before a pit could even form in her stomach, her lust smothered it. She was happy. "I don't want this to end either."

He still had one hand on her thigh, only taking it off as he shifted gears. But when he pulled into her driveway, put the car in park, and politely leaned over to kiss her goodbye, Greta felt a sharp stab of disappointment that he was being so chaste. "I meant I don't want this to end tonight," she said, reaching over and taking the keys out of the ignition.

She pulled him into the house, and this time, his clothes as well as hers came off piece by piece. Their trail of discarded attire began in the entryway, wound through the kitchen, and ended at the sofa—much more comfortable than the car.

She'd had this chemistry with Patrick in the very beginning, before infertility, motherhood, but it had never been this intense. Would it be so exciting with Jack if they weren't both married? Probably not, but she wasn't sure she cared at the moment.

Jack took her from all directions, sometimes teasing her, sometimes being playfully rough as years of sexual hunger were sated. She was sore from him being inside her for so long, but they couldn't stop. While they were still in the throes of heated sex, Greta's cell phone rang and interrupted their flow. She tried to ignore it, but when the ringing cell moved to the house phone, it officially became a buzzkill.

"Do you need to check that?" Jack panted, and she nodded.

Disentangling herself, she walked naked over to the entryway and looked at her phone. It was the boys' camp. Her neck tensed in concern. She quickly looked at the typed-out voice mail description: "Brayden was involved in an archery accident and we had to call an ambulance. He's in the hospital. One of the counselors accompanied him in the ambulance . . ." Her eyes widened and her hands would not stop trembling.

Before she could react, the phone rang again—Patrick. She cleared her throat, suddenly shaking, praying he wouldn't be able to hear her betrayal through the receiver. He didn't even say hello. "The camp just called. Brayden is in the hospital."

"I know, I just got the call. I'm sure it's fine; they just have to take precautionary measures." Greta's heart was racing—she couldn't stop thinking about what she'd just done, her emotions hard to pin down now that she'd been interrupted, but guilt became all-encompassing. She rushed Patrick off the phone, telling him she was heading out to meet him at the hospital immediately and wondering if this was a case of instant karma.

Jack had clearly heard enough to realize their evening had come to a screeching halt. The after-sex glow was certainly wearing off, and she thought it was probably for the best. She didn't say a word as he backed out the breezeway door in his untucked shirt, holding his shoes. "I hope everything's okay," he said quietly, but the look he gave her said *I know we just made a mistake.*

Greta prayed for her son, consumed with guilt as Jack left her house walking backward at this late hour. After quickly changing into jeans and a T-shirt, she called the camp as she pulled out of the driveway as fast as she could drive without losing control of her car. She caught a glance in the mirror and was disgusted by the smudged eye makeup that signified her reckless night. She rummaged for a napkin in the glove compartment and wiped her eyes hard, hoping Jack's smell wasn't on her. She trembled as she thought about her son and worried the world was somehow punishing him for her indiscretion. She had been working so hard to find a camp that improved kids' social skills, thinking it would help her sons to get off video games, and now it seemed as if all her efforts were backfiring.

Someone at the camp finally answered and she identified herself.

"Oh, yes, Mrs. O'Brien. I'm so sorry. From what I could piece together, Brayden snuck out of his cabin and went to the archery field. He was . . . well, he was struck in the knee by an arrow. One of the other boys called for help, and we called an ambulance. From what I understand, the arrow was still in his leg when the ambulance picked him up, and it's pretty serious."

"Oh Jesus Christ, his knee? Will he be able to play tennis?" Greta asked, imagining the worst. "Why were they up? Wasn't there a counselor in his cabin watching him? Who's the kid who shot him?" Her worry and uncertainty were making her feel a mix of regret and rage.

"Mrs. O'Brien, it was just an accident and . . . and it was Logan who shot him."

Her mind needed a moment to recalibrate before dread overcame her. "Was he devastated he hurt his brother? Did he act upset?" she said, realizing she was revealing some of her concerns publicly.

"Yeah, I'm sure he feels bad," the counselor said.

She was shaking as she threw her phone on the passenger seat and prayed this counselor was right. Her emotions were running high, and she regretted sending them to this camp. It was another item on her list of regrets at the moment, which now had "adultery" at the top, knocking "lying to my husband about our sons' conception" out of the first spot for the first time ever. She was filled with unease.

She stopped at a Dunkin' Donuts drive-through for a large coffee and called the hospital to get an update. Brayden needed emergency knee surgery to remove the arrow and debris; they wouldn't know until they were in there what would need fixing immediately and what may need follow-up surgery. She wanted to make sure it wasn't just a resident operating on her son's knee, so she called Patrick, who was going to get there a little ahead of her. "Don't let some intern touch his knee; we need an orthopedic surgeon, a great one!"

"I agree, he needs the best surgeon. I might have to name-drop that my wife is a Walsh. He needs to be able to play tennis in college," Patrick said.

For once, she and Patrick were on the same page. Regret poured through her veins—the details of her evening with Jack rushed back into her consciousness. She vowed never to let something like that happen again. Never.

She'd been silent so long, he probably thought she was angry, and she heard him take in a long breath. She hated herself right now; the only words she could get out were "I love you."

"Love you too," he said.

She hung up and sipped her coffee as she drove toward the Adirondack Medical Center. She'd had three martinis at the dinner, but that had been a one-hour train ride and five hours of raw shame ago, so she arrived at the hospital exhausted and chewing gum to cover any smells she hadn't been able to register on herself. Guilt ridden, she stood farther from Patrick than normal, but he was so focused on

Brayden he didn't seem to notice. She wasn't sure if the tension was due to the raw nerves between them about Logan's behavior or the stress over Brayden, or if she was making mental excuses for selfishly straying away from it all.

Eventually, early the next morning, Brayden came out of surgery, which had gone well. The arrow and debris had been successfully removed, and they didn't foresee any other necessary surgeries, though the doctor warned that Brayden would need to rest in the coming weeks. If he did everything they recommended, though, he'd be back on the tennis court in no time.

A camp counselor had finally shown up with Logan a few hours before Brayden was out of surgery, and after hearing from the doctors, Patrick took him home. Greta stayed and wheeled Brayden to the rehab facility, where she'd spend the night in an adjoining hotel so she could help out. Work would have to wait.

~

"Do you think Logan feels bad about hurting Brayden?" Greta asked Patrick hesitantly over the phone as she sipped coffee in her hotel room before heading down to watch Brayden do his PT.

"Oh yeah, Logan was upset this morning, it was a total accident," Patrick said. Greta wasn't sure if her own guilt was letting her believe Patrick or if it was indeed just an accident.

She realized she'd taken her grief too far by allowing herself to have an affair that made her, for just one moment, feel like she was still a prep school girl with two parents at home. If she hadn't needed to rush to her son's rescue, she would have just stayed swept up in that moment. She knew she needed to work on being a better communicator with Patrick, and she'd need to tell Jack that their encounter was a huge mistake and hoped that he agreed.

She said, "But I think we need to talk to him about not being reckless in general. He can get hyper and not seem aware of his actions, you know?"

"He's not hyper. I sat and played Othello with him right before camp. Anyway, I'm going to have to register a substitution for Brayden. Do you think we can take Zeke to the competition?"

"Um, maybe Logan shouldn't play either. Do you think competing is important when Brayden's hurt?"

"He'll be back on his feet in no time. Logan's been working so hard for this," Patrick said.

"Okay, yes, bring Zeke. I've gotta go see Brayden, and the doctor said he can come home in a few days. I was on the phone with him before I called you, and he's all set up to complete his PT at home. I actually hired a physical therapist to come to the house so we don't need to drive him there. He's a family friend and he's self-pay; he doesn't take insurance, but he's the best in Greenwich."

"Great!" Patrick said.

Greta was happy that he didn't say anything snarky about her connections. She hung up the phone and thought back to the chairlift episode when the boys were nine, and then she thought of when Logan had nearly drowned that kid on the lake and how he showed no remorse. She was happy that Patrick said he felt bad about hurting his brother. Maybe despite the accident, the camp had helped him develop more sportsmanship. She'd decided she was going to let her worries go and focus on getting Brayden back on the court. She hadn't made time to play tennis with her father, but she could make time for her sons.

～

Patrick asked Brayden if Zeke could play for him in the tournament, and Greta made the reservations for them to fly first class to Florida.

She had taken several days off from work so they could all be together. Brayden's knee was healed up well but still not strong enough to play. She hoped he wasn't jealous of Zeke for taking his spot, but she was happy they were all going as a family.

Logan and Zeke were competing in the doubles championship in the Junior Orange Bowl tournament in Coral Gables. The twins had done well the previous year, but the goal this time was to place in the top three. Their first match the next day was practically a gimme, and they won in straight sets. At the courts for the second match, Greta sat next to Brayden, who seemed upbeat for someone watching a competition he should have been playing in. She was so proud of how well the three boys had gotten along on the plane, and while she'd been meaning to have a heart-to-heart with Logan about the accident, she thought she'd wait until the competition was over.

"I'm sure it's hard for you to watch," she said to Brayden, gently patting his uninjured leg.

"No, I get really hot playing. It's fine, and it's fun having Zeke with us. Thanks, Mom," Brayden said.

"Do you really think it was an accident?" Greta bravely asked.

"Yeah, totally, why?" Brayden said as he gave a shrug worthy of a preteen and Greta fell into another round of second-guessing herself.

"Okay, well, I was thinking of having Logan see a therapist," Greta said, shocked she was sharing this with her son instead of her husband.

"A shrink?" He laughed. "He has no time. We have tennis practice every day."

"Don't be silly. We can find time if he needs it," Greta said. "But I'm glad you think it was an accident."

Brayden scoffed. "Maybe he hurt me because he's jealous I'm better."

"Do you think so?" Greta gasped.

"I'm kidding, Mom!"

"Oh, okay, and who cares who's better. You are both *so* good." She understood Brayden, though. She hated whenever Emily seemed to be better at something—or maybe it was just Emily's attitude about it that she hated.

"Logan asked me why you even came," Brayden said.

"Because I'm your mom." She felt a little back on her feet now. Why had they been talking about that? Was it *that* strange that she showed up for her kids? Or had he gotten so used to her not being at tennis matches that he was lashing out, like she used to do with her own father? Or maybe his rude behavior was another example of needing that therapist.

"Do you wish I came to more matches?" Greta asked.

"No, I don't care. It's fine to just have Dad here. We're used to it." Brayden got up and went to sit next to Patrick by the fence. Greta knew his moodiness was at least partially because he wished he were playing too. Maybe she'd even deserved his attitude a little because she hadn't made going to his tennis games a priority until now. She hoped that over time he'd warm up to the idea of her being more involved and interested.

Despite Brayden's lack of appreciation for her, she was glad she'd come. She had convinced Patrick to stop giving them sugary sports drinks and try her packets of probiotic/prebiotic blueberry- and lemon-flavored water and had made sure they ordered blackened chicken Caesar salads at the Biltmore instead of the fast-food diet Patrick allowed, so she felt useful. She had also booked the hotel's massage therapist to knead Logan's and Zeke's elbows and shoulders after matches and was going to make sure they soaked in the hotel's hot tub and got to sleep at a decent hour that night. Patrick would have been perfectly happy staying at a Holiday Inn and letting the boys share a bed, fall asleep with the television on, and wake up with their Beats headphones still in.

"Patrick, it's so hot and I'm getting red. Do you and the boys have enough sunscreen?" Greta called while applying SPF lip balm.

"Yeah, they tan well," Patrick said, ultrafocused on Brayden and Zeke setting up to play. She wondered if he questioned why the boys tanned so well when she was so pale but hoped he assumed they were blessed with an even more olive shade of skin than his.

"I'll be right back, I need to freshen up," she said, not even sure if Patrick could hear her, and snuck up to their air-conditioned hotel room for a quick moment of solitude and to reapply more sunscreen. She'd be back in plenty of time to see the majority of the match.

Greta went into the bathroom and locked the door even though no one was around. She splashed some cool water on her face, hoping it could somehow splash away her mistakes. She toweled her face dry and applied some zinc on her nose. She didn't feel the need for lots of makeup because she was tired of constantly pretending she was perfect. She grabbed a few different visors to see which one looked best with her outfit and settled on one more quickly than she had in the past. Who cared if the Ritz-Carlton visor matched or not? It was just to protect her skin from the sun, she told herself. She was proud she resisted the urge to check on her phone how the market was doing and wanted to get back out to the court to see Logan and Zeke. She thought about her father and wished he were alive; perhaps she could have let go of her grudge and invited him to see her son play. She wondered if he was ever as guilt ridden as she was right now and, giving him the benefit of the doubt, mentally forgave him.

She looked at the Ritz visor in the mirror and realized she still struggled to strip herself completely of the pampered, entitled mark that growing up a Walsh had left on her. She wasn't all the way there, but at least she was right then. She whispered to herself, "You're not a horrible, selfish person; you just made *one* mistake that will never happen again." She vowed to foster more warmth in her home when they returned from this trip. She really felt a shift away from being a Walsh and a deep desire toward finally being Greta *O'Brien*.

She walked briskly from the hotel room back to the courts. They had just begun their match, and she tried to keep her mind focused on it. She gave Patrick a few thumbs-up signs when they made a good point.

They won the first set 6–1, lost the second set 2–6, and played a sudden-death tiebreaker. By the end of the match, Greta was on the edge of her seat. She watched Logan and Zeke go back and forth, trying to get the two-point lead required to win the match. She wondered if all their matches were this intense and felt proud.

It was match point and Logan's turn to serve, and he squinted against the late-afternoon sun, tossed the ball up in the air, and faulted. On his second serve, he tossed the ball, swung, and shanked it, putting it wide. Greta looked right at Patrick, who was shaking his head slowly, and took a long exhale as she said to him, "It's okay, it was a great match," but was equally upset when this victory went to their competitor. The boys left the court with discouraged expressions until Brayden ran over and they banged his crutches and their rackets together like boys their age do.

Over dinner, Patrick seemed unable to keep from bringing up the details of the match. "Sucks to lose on a double fault," he said.

Greta was ready to kick him under the table for making Logan feel even worse, but her son just shrugged. "If they're going to let noises like that interrupt a match, I'm not going to take responsibility."

Zeke laughed, but Greta's brow furrowed. "What noise?"

"Serving lessons when we get back, and we don't make up excuses," Patrick said.

"The sun was in my eyes, Dad," Logan said angrily. "And there's no way that loudspeaker didn't bother other players."

Greta picked at her salad and glanced over at Patrick, who was watching Logan as he threw his food on the plate and stalked to the hotel pool.

"He should finish eating before going in the pool," Greta said.

"Let him go," Patrick said quietly, but Zeke and Brayden couldn't hear, as they were hurriedly shoving their last bites of food in their mouths. Patrick excused them to join Logan in the pool.

"I think it's rude to leave the table before we are all finished," Greta said.

"It's not dinner at your parents' house—it's the pool, Gret."

"They don't even wait until we're all served to start. They need better manners."

"We can deal with it at home. He just lost a match and wants to play with his friends."

"You're always dismissing me about Logan," Greta said.

"Huh?"

"Yeah, and not just leaving the table. Like in general. I wish you'd take some of his behavior more seriously. We need to teach both of them responsibility. I was thinking of giving them chores."

He chuckled. "It's hard to make them do stuff you don't even do. When's the last time you did a chore?"

"Well, I'm an adult, Patrick, and they are kids."

"Okay, but we have cleaning ladies and nannies. What chores would they even have?"

"I don't know, maybe you can teach them to mow the lawn or bring some of the firewood that's delivered in and stack it by the fire. Or should I be asking them to put their washed and folded laundry away? Maybe we can at least take something away when they're bad, like the PlayStation. I want them to have consequences when they act up, especially Logan. Like when he hurt that kid kayaking, I think we should have grounded him. Maybe he needs therapy? I'm worried," Greta said defensively.

"Therapy?" Patrick chuckled. "That's very Greenwich. A kid dunks his friend in the lake and now he needs *therapy*?" he mocked.

She shot her sons a worried look and wondered how she would ever get him on board without at least exploring if they could do more as parents. She hadn't felt like a team before her affair, and while she'd accepted that Jack wasn't the answer, there was still a problem between them.

As she and Patrick finished dinner, she watched her boys, Brayden sitting on the edge of the pool and letting his feet dangle in the water since his stitches weren't out yet. Zeke soon had a small crowd around him, making friends with other kids from the tournament, but he always tried to get Logan to join in. Logan alternated between staring off into space and trying to play games that he could only get the younger kids to play. Greta's worry continued to grow.

"He's still struggling with showing emotion properly," she said to Patrick. "The teachers say he's quiet, but I think something else is going on. He seems off in outer space, just staring with that blank expression, and I don't think he has a lot of friends."

"He's got his brother and Zeke. How many good friends do kids need? I'd rather him have a couple of friends than be into partying or something, ya know?" Patrick said.

"Do you think we should offer to pay for Zeke to go to private school? I think I can get a tax deduction, so it will feel like pennies."

"It might feel like we are *buying* him friends," Patrick said.

"They're already friends. It was just an idea—to get him out of his shell more. He doesn't seem to have any friends at school except for Brayden, so it might be nice to have Zeke there with him at school."

"Sure, if an extra fifty thousand a year feels like pennies, then why not? He'd be a great addition to the tennis team," Patrick said as Greta assessed if there was any sarcasm in Patrick's voice and hoped there wasn't as she played along.

"Okay, I'll call his mother when we get home and let her know we'll pay."

"Maybe just make it an anonymous 'scholarship' so our sons don't know you did this."

"Sure," Greta agreed, happy to be on the same page with Patrick for once.

This gave her hope. If something was wrong with Logan developmentally, Patrick would eventually see it. She told herself they were making progress and she was working on potential solutions. Logan was probably fine, she told herself, and since the boys were occupied, she'd have to go upstairs with her husband and try to wipe away the memory of her mistake with Jack.

Chapter Twenty-Four

COLETTE

2019

"Colette!" Frank bellowed from the front office. "Get me the Anderson file!"

She rolled her eyes as she stood up from her desk chair for the fifth time in the past hour. She found the file, walked into his office, and tossed it on his desk. They had been working around the clock on a case that involved a young man accused of murdering his parents as they slept. The young man's defense attorney was attempting to prove to the court that his client was not guilty by reason of insanity, alleging years of abuse at the hands of his father that had caused a drug addiction. The case hit close to home for Colette, considering her childhood and her addiction issues. And now, having done research for Frank, her desk was piled with pages covering similar cases where the defendant's attorney had used drug addiction as part of their defense. To be able to use the insanity defense in Connecticut, the defendant could only be on drugs that had been prescribed and used as directed; otherwise, the onus was still on the person who used the drugs. They'd have been better off with a self-defense argument, but since Frank was the prosecutor, he wasn't going to offer that up to the wet-behind-the-ears public defender.

"Anything else you need before I head out?" Colette asked, glancing at her iPhone. If she didn't leave the office soon, she'd be late for her anniversary dinner with Vic—they'd been together nine years, and she was not going to miss out on celebrating a milestone she'd once thought she'd never achieve. She saw two missed calls from Vic as she shoved her phone in her pocket, praying that Frank would dismiss her.

"You can go," Frank said distractedly as he riffled through the file she'd found for him. Their relationship had shifted after a while—she'd proved to be a great paralegal, both in his medical cases and others.

The past that haunted her during the first year of their business relationship had melted away over the course of their decade working side by side. He still frequented the Branch, and she suspected he'd replaced Bunny with an untold number of women over the years, but it wasn't her business. Frank would never change, but she had learned a lot, was making a decent living, and loved the work.

Colette called Vic as she rushed to her car, and he answered on the first ring. Before he could speak, she said, "I'm on my way! So sorry. I needed to do a few last-minute things. Are you at the restaurant?" Getting into her car, she glanced at the dashboard and saw that it was 6:20.

He laughed a little. "Um, yeah, for almost a half hour."

"I'll see you in a few," she promised.

A quiet calm came over her as she entered the restaurant and saw the man who was her best friend and husband patiently waiting for her at a small table by the bar. He had stood by her through so much, especially during the past year, as she grappled with her health and continued to dig into her past with Dr. Brooks.

She leaned down to him and gave him a kiss on the lips. "Thanks for waiting, baby. Happy anniversary."

He hugged her tightly and then softly caressed her belly. After so much heartbreak, she was just weeks away from giving birth to their son. Most days, so full of joy and hope for the future, Colette questioned whether it was all really happening. When Dr. Brooks had promised her that she could lead a normal life, she hadn't believed her, but now her dreams were coming true. She was pregnant. She'd been so worried for the first six months, but now she was actually convinced it was going to happen.

They enjoyed their much-needed date, knowing that once the baby came, they wouldn't have much time alone. They engaged in their favorite topic: baby names. Vic was pressing to name his first son after himself and his father before him: Victorio De Luca III.

"It's too grown up," she complained. "Baby Victorio" sounded ridiculous to her.

"My mother would be so excited," he said.

"Lisa has a friend whose son is a third, and they call him 'Tripp.' If we call him by his nickname, I'll agree," she said, smiling as she forked a bit of tiramisu into her mouth.

"Hmmm . . . will my mother approve of this?" He smirked. After a couple of seconds, he agreed and Colette cheered, thrilled that their dinner ended with the baby name issue finally resolved.

When they got home, she lingered in the baby's room before heading to her bedroom to change. After spending a solid year mourning the loss of her eggs—not to mention the years before that mourning her miscarriages—she had used her anger and bitterness to figure out what was going on in her life, what had happened.

A part of her knew those eggs were not something she should have used. She wanted to know what had happened with them, but Dr. Brooks and Vic often reminded her that this line of thinking would not benefit her at all and could jeopardize her well-being. The eggs were gone, and even if she had a way of finding who had used them, she wasn't sure finding her biological child (or children) being raised by someone else would help at all—more likely it would send her into a deep depression and challenge her sobriety.

Once the eggs were taken out of storage and sold, they were given a number under the donor system. On a day when she was feeling particularly strong, she'd gone to a local tattoo shop and gotten a cross inked on the inside of her wrist with the egg donor number listed on Dr. Erikson's paperwork. This small act had served as closure. She was comforted when she looked at her tattoo each day, a memorial to her unknown babies. She struggled with her sobriety during those months, but Vic had helped. And once they had given up trying, had let go and let nature take its course, at forty-two, finally just enjoying the joys of a happy marriage and life, she'd gotten pregnant.

After changing, she found Vic on the couch flipping through the television channels. She leaned over and kissed his cheek.

"Will you be mad if I cut our date night short and go to bed?"

"No, babe, go ahead; I know you're tired," he said, finding a baseball game to become engrossed in.

Exhausted and grateful, Colette headed up to their bedroom, hoping she could sleep through the night. After she got her pillows arranged—she needed two to prop up her swollen feet now and a body pillow to get her any semblance of comfort with her huge belly—she grabbed her phone to set her alarm and saw she had missed calls from Frank.

"Ugh," she moaned loudly. She was never off duty, and this case was making it hard to balance her homelife and work. Frank had left a rambling list of files he needed and tasks for her to complete first thing in the morning in his first message. The second message, difficult to decipher because of the noise, told her he was calling from the Branch.

"Colette! I'm with Melissa. She's asking for you!" Frank practically shouted, his tone markedly different from the first message. "I forgot to tell you. We're hosting a small breakfast meeting for the new hires in the morning. Can you pick up bagels and pastries on the way in? Thanks!"

Colette tossed the phone on her bed and set her alarm for twenty minutes earlier than usual. She was so happy she had left her old life at the Branch behind. She drifted off thinking about her baby being born with soft brown hair, golden skin, and deep, inquisitive brown eyes.

Chapter Twenty-Five

GRETA

2020

Logan and Brayden were playing basketball in the driveway despite the cold weather. Their dark tans had hardly faded on their olive skin, and they had grown more muscular in the last year. She couldn't believe they were in high school now. Greta stole a quick look at her pale arms. She always wondered if anyone, especially Patrick, had ever questioned why she looked nothing like her sons.

She gathered materials for carving pumpkins and carried them out to the back deck, waving goodbye to the cleaning ladies as they pulled out of the driveway. Patrick came out back a few minutes later, finally done with tennis lessons for the day and drenched in sweat.

"Grab me the paper towels," she said, looking up from the news-paper-covered picnic table.

"Don't the boys want to help?" Patrick asked.

She sighed and looked down at the pumpkin guts all over her hands and shirt. "I think they're too old to care about this stuff anymore. I want them for at least one photo; we can take it on my phone. I don't even care if they're dressed up. Would you hand me one of those knives?" She gestured toward the block on the table. "The tools that came in the kit aren't sharp enough."

"My mom loves carving pumpkins," he said as he handed the knife to her. "She made me do it with her every year, even when I came home from college." He gave her a quick kiss on her head. "Happy anniversary, babe," he said, then went upstairs.

"Ah, you too, honey," Greta said and was proud that despite their difficulties they were still under one roof. She wished she had done this with her sons when they were younger; it felt like they had shared everything special with Lucia, and now here she was, carving alone. Work had been stressful following the recent blowup in treasuries, and her carving felt cathartic. She and Jack practically ignored each other now, and while she was happy she'd chosen family, she did miss having a close work confidant. It was as if as soon as she began really leaning into motherhood, her teenagers hardly needed her.

She finished up and headed upstairs to chat with Patrick, who was getting out of the shower. She handed him a towel and said, "I wish I had listened to your parents and put the boys in confirmation classes, and maybe we should have gone to church more like our parents did with us."

"I can't. Do you know how many clinics I have on Sundays? It's fine," Patrick said, giving her a peck on the cheek as he dried off and got dressed.

Greta knew their school was guiding them academically but didn't want to overlook her sons being spiritual, knowing right from wrong, but they were older now, and it seemed too late.

"I have a makeup appointment with Lisa at the house. She's coming soon." She caught a glimpse of herself in their bedroom mirror and laughed at the wet seeds coating her clothing. "Clearly, I need to change before that, though. I think I'll show her a photo of Nicole Kidman from *Moulin Rouge!* so she can do my makeup to match. Oh, I bought a black top hat too."

Patrick chuckled as he pulled on his pants. "Good. Maybe I can tie you up later."

Greta was continuing to be sexual just enough to ease the tension, but she was racked with guilt over never enjoying it and wished it didn't feel like an obligation versus a connection. Their communication had suffered as well. She knew how much she was keeping from him, how big the lies were, and she couldn't shake the feeling that he *must* be lying to her about something in retaliation. For the last six months he'd been especially distant. She shifted topics. "Have you seen those small patchouli candles I bought from the florist? I bet the cleaning ladies put them away. They're always putting my shopping bags in random places." Greta pulled on a warm knit dress. "Try and find the candles while I'm getting my makeup done upstairs with Lisa."

Brayden was coming up as she was going down. "If you're making us go to this dumb party, can we at least bring Zeke? *Please?*" he asked.

"If he doesn't have plans with his family, it's fine." The party was with a small group of neighbors, but Greta was glad they'd included the boys on the invitation because she didn't want them trick-or-treating this year. Bringing one friend felt fair; they could handle one low-key Halloween. Besides, she wasn't sure she wanted it to just be her and Patrick if he was already making "tie her up" jokes; she wondered if she and Patrick would have anything to talk about once the boys were in college. Maybe that was what would finally break them—they'd no longer have the obligation to stay together for the boys, and the one thing—well, two—they had in common would have moved out.

She rushed back into the bedroom to tell Patrick about the change in plans.

"I'll go pick up Zeke and his bike and bring him here," he offered. "Can I borrow your car?"

"Sure, good idea. Thank you. Lisa's here and my costume's already hanging up. I'll be ready soon. Bye!"

~

Two hours later, after making Zeke take photos of the family in front of their lit jack-o'-lanterns with her phone, they were on their way to the Halloween cocktail party up the road. The back seat of Greta's Range Rover was too snug to fit three athletic boys, so Patrick gave them the house's address and let them ride their bikes.

"It's going to be so dark, and cold . . . ," Greta said.

"It's down the road," Patrick said. "If you weren't in heels, I'd have us walk too."

Once they arrived, Greta made sure to get photos of her and Patrick all dressed up, posing with her *Moulin Rouge!* dress and red drink. There were Halloween masks and creepy gloves available for the guests, a mock trick or treating candy graveyard, and a kids' costume parade that Greta knew her sons and Zeke had likely grown out of but was adorable nonetheless. She noticed the boys mingling with older kids by the fire and was impressed with the individualized s'mores kits on display. They hadn't been out in so long, and the heat lamps made it quite comfortable. Greta was happy with all the compliments she was receiving about her long red dress and youthful lash extensions.

"She takes this holiday very seriously," Patrick said, winking and holding up his drink to toast an adjacent couple. Greta was enjoying festive hors d'oeuvres and a third blood-red martini when she was interrupted by Zeke approaching.

"Um, the guys left a while ago on their bikes. I'm gonna go meet up with them."

Greta turned to Patrick, her brow furrowed, then looked back at the boy. "I'm so sorry, Zeke. It's rude that they just left you so soon after arriving. Sure, go meet up with them."

Then Greta looked at Patrick. "I told you we shouldn't have let them ride bikes."

Zeke shrugged. "I don't mind. They just biked over to the tennis club," he said, pointing down the street.

"Okay, call us if you need anything," Patrick said, and turned back to their friends.

"You sure you don't want us to drive you? We can leave now," Greta offered. Without the boys as a buffer, maybe it was time to call it a night.

Zeke said he'd walk, and Patrick and Greta made the rounds to say good night shortly thereafter. She wasn't concerned—they were teenagers, after all—but she was a little irritated, leaving their friend and not even letting her and Patrick know.

Patrick was designated driver, so he drove them home, making it clear what he wanted by grabbing her breasts over her tight red costume as they walked into the kitchen from the garage. She had hoped the alcohol would help her be frisky and the sex not just feel like an obligation, but being in the kitchen triggered a memory of her hot night with Jack three years ago, and the guilt was like throwing cold water on her. She was glad they had maintained a great working relationship and she was over him, and she'd started seeing little signs of him trying to get ahead at any cost. She wanted to get ahead via hard work, not shortcuts. She'd buried the fantasy of them ever being more—below all the other lies that existed between her and Patrick—but now it was suddenly in the forefront of her mind.

Patrick's hands were everywhere, and instead of getting her in the mood, they were making her feel squeamish—and like a terrible person. "I'm just going to change into something more comfortable," she said, wiggling free.

"Maybe I should pay you for sex," Patrick said suddenly. "You're always suggesting ways of righting wrongs with money. Let's try that. Besides, you love money—clearly more than you love me." It was obvious his sarcasm was covering up his real anger.

"My God, Patrick. It's not my fault that I know how to make money! What do you want me to say? I hate that you're starting a fight!" Greta said. She knew, though. She knew he was smart enough to have realized at some point in the last three years, when her moods had swung from overly sweet to lashing out because she couldn't take it anymore, that something was wrong that was probably never going to be fixed. Something shifted after the affair, and the more Greta pulled in, the more Patrick pulled back. Jack was part of it, losing her dad as well, but when it came down to it, she'd never been able to put her finger on it being a single thing, a single fix. And because of that, she'd never brought up any of it.

"Maybe we should think about a break from each other," Patrick said matter-of-factly.

Cold fear washed over her, and she gaped at him.

"I feel like you're keeping something from me," he continued. "I have no idea what it is, and at this point, my imagination may actually be worse than the truth, but it just . . . it tortures me."

Greta froze and wondered what he suspected. Her blood ran cold as she worried her lies were more transparent than she thought—that this was the beginning of a discussion about the end.

Divorce—the word seemed heavy in her mouth, like she wouldn't be able to just say it, let it roll around her tongue, without it manifesting. Was that really what he wanted? Was it what she wanted? Deep down, she didn't think it was. She still loved him, loved their boys, loved parenting with him, but the lies had become recalcitrant.

"I'm sick of you never wanting me." He said it quietly, calmly. Which made it so much worse.

Greta was gutted, a hollow carved out of her belly, and she suddenly remembered standing in this very room that night with Jack. She thought that after so much time she'd let it go. But perhaps her mistakes were still haunting her.

"I just feel like I'm not a priority," Patrick said.

"Sorry. Let's go talk upstairs." Greta sighed, hoping Patrick would follow her and she could prove everything was fine between them. Just as she made her way from the kitchen to the foyer, she noticed red lights beaming and disappearing through the window.

"What's going on?" Greta said as she realized the lights circling were coming from *her* driveway. She looked out and confirmed it was the police as she simultaneously worried about the boys still being out. She had a gut feeling this involved them somehow. "Patrick, have you heard from the kids?"

The doorbell rang.

Greta slowly opened the door and Patrick was now right next to her. Patrick's eyes were wide and he asked, "Can we help you?" He was ashen.

Greta thought about when the camp counselor had called to tell her about the arrow accident and had déjà vu. The officer's expression was sullen. She and Patrick were both still. They instinctively grabbed each other's hand, and she gave Patrick's a squeeze.

"Mr. and Mrs. O'Brien?" she said as they nodded. "My name is Officer Carr. Are you Logan and Brayden's parents?"

Greta nodded and held her breath for several seconds.

"Logan O'Brien is at the police station. Your other son has been badly hurt, and he has been transported to Bridgeport Hospital in an ambulance. You can proceed to the hospital, but you'll need to come into the station when you're finished. We're sending one of our detectives there to meet with you."

"Is Brayden okay?" Greta said as her stomach clenched.

"We don't know anything at this time," the officer replied. "I think it's best you get down to the hospital as soon as possible."

Officer Carr walked back to her car, shut the door, and pulled out of their driveway as if she had just delivered a package.

Greta's heart raced as she grabbed her phone and dialed her son's cell, getting only his voice mail as she pulled on her pumpkin gut–stained sweatshirt over her red dress and ran out the door.

Patrick was right behind her. He jumped in the driver's side, barely waiting for her to shut her door before peeling out of the driveway.

He was taking deep breaths, probably trying to avoid hyperventilating, but his panic was palpable, almost another passenger in the car—it was keeping hers company. "What the fuck happened?" he bellowed as he sped through a yellow light.

Greta dialed the hospital, holding her breath as she waited for someone to answer. It was an exercise in futility, though, as she was rerouted ad nauseam until finally speaking to someone who would only confirm that their son was a patient there but they "could not disclose other information over the phone." Just before she started to lose it, Patrick pulled into the ER. lot.

Inside, at the desk, Patrick yelled, "Is my son alive? Where is he? Where is he?"

He paced back and forth as Greta reached for his hand. She was able to muster a slightly calmer voice as she said, "We're looking for Brayden O'Brien. Actually, his legal name is Patrick: Patrick Brayden O'Brien. I was just on the phone with someone who confirmed he was here but wouldn't tell us anything else."

The receptionist looked down at her computer screen and told them he had been transferred from the ER to the hospital's burn center. Greta was trembling as she and Patrick plowed straight ahead; she was unconcerned about causing a scene. While uncertain of the details, she knew it was serious.

Chapter Twenty-Six

COLETTE

2020

Colette's eyes were heavy as she read through court documents at her desk. She stretched in an effort to wake up her sluggish body; chronic exhaustion was taking its toll. She woke up frequently in the middle of the night from a veritable laundry list of issues: panic, cold sweats, hearing Tripp's cries, night terrors. The loss of energy was like nothing she had ever known. During her pregnancy, Colette's fatigue had been rough. It was nothing compared to what it became after giving birth, and almost two years later, she still couldn't seem to fully rest. She'd gone to the doctor so much, trying to figure out what was wrong with her, yet she had few answers, too many prescriptions, and a continued lack of real rest. But she pushed through.

She held her face with her hands and leaned forward, desperate to finish proofreading the documents and turn them in to Frank. When she dozed off, she stood and read while she rocked back and forth to try to stay awake.

Finally finished, she popped her head into Frank's office and announced, "I'm heading out. Just emailed you the documents."

He grunted in reply, too immersed in work to look up, and she closed the door behind her. As she walked outside, the crisp fall air hit her face, giving her a bit of energy.

The sun had long since set as she pulled into her driveway. Children ran across her front lawn; their squeals of excitement and the sound of their little feet storming across the fall leaves made her stomach clench. Sadness sometimes hit her at the most unexpected moments, and she couldn't gain control of her emotions, no matter the million reasons she had to be grateful and happy.

Vic opened the front door, smiling, as she approached. "You're home," he said. "I took care of everything. There's dinner for you, in the fridge, or some leftover trick-or-treat candy if you prefer."

Colette smiled. He knew her so well, took such good care of her. For her to not even make it home on Halloween . . .

She shook her head. She hadn't even realized it was Halloween until she had gotten to work and saw the date on her emails. How would she ever be a good mother if she couldn't even keep track of and manage the basic holidays for children?

She had always been a witch or a ghost for Halloween. Her father had never made costume shopping a priority, and she had dug into the back of her closet each year searching for her witch hat or an old sheet to whip something together at the last minute. She didn't really remember Halloweens before her mom left, but when she cleared out her father's house, she had found a picture of herself dressed up as a cat, sitting in her mother's lap when she was probably five or six years old. Confirmation that her mother at least made an effort that one year.

Once she was old enough, her father would drive her down their long, winding road to the center of town and drop her off to trick-or-treat with her best friend, Kelly, who always had an amazing homemade outfit. One year it had been a beautiful Princess Leia costume, her long brown hair tied up in buns on the sides of her head, her gauzy white dress making her look like she was straight out of the movie. Colette had felt ashamed wearing her black dress and old witch hat, wishing she had a mother like Kelly's.

She was miles away from being as perfect as Kelly's mother. There was just so much these days that didn't lend itself to her being present and available. Exhaustion and depression plagued her daily, not to mention her work schedule.

As she slid inside, past Vic, she pressed a kiss to his cheek and pulled her shoes off—she didn't want to clack around the house in work shoes past bedtime. Vic, having to get up early, gave her a long hug and another kiss—this one lingering on her mouth—and went to bed, after which she set up camp on the couch with what was left of a bag of Kit Kats to think about her son.

She took deep breaths, battling her intense feelings of guilt and the sense that she was a failure. Postpartum, it turned out, was a mess of emotions, and it felt like she'd spent all her time since then trying to hold back her tears at something or another. Now, as Colette fought to stay awake, the late news came on, a reporter speaking live in front of a tennis club about an accident. But her eyelids were heavy, and she gave in. If she stayed up much longer, she'd begin to dwell on the past and become maudlin anyway, so she clicked off the TV, happy to have Halloween behind her.

She stopped in Tripp's room. She picked up the *Corduroy* book from the small shelf built into the wall. She flipped through the pages mindlessly and then put it back. She pulled open the second drawer of the dresser/changing table, pulling out the Halloween costume she had joyfully purchased so long ago—a tiger onesie she hadn't remembered until late today, hadn't called Vic to tell him about, another thing forgotten, another item to add to that list. She stared at it for a few minutes, then heard Vic calling her name.

Surprised he was still awake, she laid the costume back in the drawer and went to bed. Lying there, in the protective arms of her kind, decent husband, she told herself tomorrow would be better. That was the mantra: get up, try again, focus on the good.

She and Vic had just recently started talking about the future. Was trying for a second child too unrealistic? Was adoption something they might consider? But the thought of checking that box, twice, that read "former addicts" seemed too daunting to even think about. All the while, Colette found herself more than once a day feeling her mouth water, dreaming of a drink or a pill . . . anything that might dull her senses. But thankfully Vic never wavered. Despite their struggles, the uphill battle that had become their daily life, he was her rock.

Sometime in the night, she heard Tripp crying, and her eyes flew open and she sat straight up in bed with a start before realizing, once again, that her baby wasn't with her—her baby wasn't there at all. His birth had been difficult, and she'd suffered from placenta previa—the placenta covering her cervix—which had put her life in danger and required an emergency C-section. She'd talked to many doctors afterward, started going to meetings more frequently again, saw her therapist almost daily, but she'd struggled so much: with her addiction, with her loss, with her depression. After all, they'd lost baby Tripp before she'd ever heard his real cries.

Chapter Twenty-Seven

GRETA

2020

They'd been directed to the burn and trauma floor and quickly put on personal protective equipment in order to enter through the glass doors. Patrick was now bracing himself with both hands on the edges of his chair as they stood outside the burn center area, where worried-looking doctors and nurses were treating their son. The air was filled with the sickening, heartbreaking stench of burning flesh.

A nurse emerged from Brayden's unit to update them. "Ninety-eight percent of his body has been burned, he lost oxygen, and his internal organs are very weak, but the doctors are doing all that they can."

As she slumped over in a chair, Greta looked over at Patrick, who was equally wobbly. The color had drained from his face.

"I'll bring him some water," the nurse said, pointing at a pale Patrick. Motioning to another nurse behind her, she said, "She'll show you to your son," as if she were passing a baton in a relay race.

"Mrs. O'Brien, I'm so sorry. Please come with me." The second nurse took off slowly but determinedly down a short hallway. Greta left Patrick in the chair, following the woman until they came to a stop outside a treatment room. "You can't go in. His immune system is too compromised with his skin so damaged. But you can see him through the window."

Greta, eyes open wide, stared through the glass. This couldn't be real. Most of her child's body was wrapped in gauze—what she could see looked dark, charred almost, and she could make out some ragged locks of brown hair and his toes. She flashed to his sweet little feet. Doctors and nurses were racing around, tending to his damaged body, and suddenly the thought of the pain he was in overwhelmed her and she was afraid she'd be sick. She looked for chest movement, but all she could see was the stillness of layered gauze.

The whiteboard on the wall used his legal name, "Patrick O'Brien," and again she flashed to him in the NICU, fourteen years earlier. The doctors had called him "a little trooper," her Brayden. She briefly thought about her other son, stuck at the police station, and she wiped the sweat on her palms onto her thighs as she grasped to get one deep breath.

The hospital staff's pace slowed as one person changed the fluid in a bag and nodded distressfully at the other. Brayden had always been her easier son, the one who got good grades, made friends easily, never caused a fuss. Yes, he was rambunctious like any young boy was and ribbed Logan like any brother did, but he was always just so . . . smooth sailing compared to Logan.

The commotion in his room came to a sudden halt, the doctors and nurses retreating one by one from Brayden's body, as if choreographed. The foul smell of burned human flesh was repugnant. The main doctor pulled down his mask, his face pinched, as he obviously pronounced Brayden's death.

Greta collapsed, tears streaming down her face. She tried to suck in a breath and was unsuccessful, hyperventilating by the time the doctor came out of the room. He stood close, shaking his head slightly as he delivered the news that would change everything, but all she could hear was a dull roar in her ears. Only a few words came through: ". . . injured in the sauna . . . cuts on his neck and arms . . . third-degree burns . . . too much for his organs . . ."

A pit formed in her stomach and then nausea and dizziness spread through her as she gasped to get air. Her entire body was wrenched with such intense grief that it made every muscle in her body tight. The tightness turned to shaking as tears consumed her. She couldn't comprehend that her son was really gone.

Maybe the fact that it had taken so long to become a mother was a sign she shouldn't have become one. She knew she was too focused on her career, her flirtation, showing off . . . it all seemed so frivolous, grotesque even. She wanted to go back in time.

Nausea suddenly swamped her, and Greta ran for a bathroom, just barely collapsing in front of a toilet before her stomach emptied itself violently. She cried and lay on the cold tile floor, unable to move. This was punishment—for all her lies, for her selfishness, her apathy toward motherhood.

She got up and splashed ice-cold water on her face over and over, shocking and punishing her skin. The swollen, hollow eyes didn't look like her, but she knew this would be her new normal, reality from here on out.

A pounding on the door made her jump. "Mrs. O'Brien?" They weren't going to let her be.

"Just a second," Greta called, slowly wiping her face one last time.

Before she'd even made it to the door, the voice commanded, "Mrs. O'Brien, come out. Immediately."

The floor felt like quicksand, but she opened the door and stepped into the hallway, and she felt like she was going to faint as she took in the next words she heard.

"I'm Detective Morales. I have a few questions."

Patrick came racing down the hall, running toward Greta with outstretched arms, shaking. He pulled her close to him.

"I want to talk to Logan," Patrick said, as if he were grasping for the words.

"Detective Morales," the man cut in. "I'm so sorry for your loss." Patrick let go of Greta just long enough to give the man's hand a quick shake. "Logan is being interviewed at the station."

"And Zeke? Were any of their other friends with them? Are they okay?" he asked, rapid-fire. He seemed to be more in control than when they'd first arrived, which was good because she was having trouble following any train of thought.

"We believe we know what happened. At present, your son's friend, Zeke Davis, is at Greenwich Hospital, being treated for his milder injuries."

Greta pulled on Patrick's arm and she looked at him, imploring. She wondered how Zeke was but was more focused on her own sons . . . one of whom was gone. As the terror of it all sank in even deeper, she knew she *needed* to be with her only son. Thankfully, Patrick understood.

"We'll let him rest and go to the station. We need to see Logan," Patrick said. He gently guided Greta out of the hospital and to the car, Morales following them the entire way.

Outside, the man handed Greta his card. "I'll follow you to the station. He has the right to an attorney."

Greta registered that what he said should have been a surprise to her, but she was numb and slid the card in the back pocket of her pants, her movements mechanical. Patrick put his arms around her and squeezed gently but firmly, and it dawned on her that she was shaking.

Patrick slid into the driver's seat, and they drove in silence for the twenty-nine-mile drive, which felt like an eternity. Greta kept leaning her head out of the window, unsure whether she was going to throw up. As soon as they entered the building, an officer greeted them and ushered them toward a back room while Greta just prayed.

Here, finally, she was able to see her only living son. She saw her boys separately all the time; they weren't attached at the hip. But here, now, seeing this closed-off room where Logan was being held, away from his brother's . . . body that was in the hospital, it felt like a dark omen. He was alone, without his twin, and would never be with him again. It was a disconcerting dichotomy, her looking through another window at one of her sons tonight, this time into what looked like an interrogation room instead of a hospital room.

There were several officers in the large open area, and their desk signs revealed various titles—sergeant, inspector, and superintendent—but Greta didn't know who to ask for help. She noticed Logan was sitting in a small room off to one side. He sat in a metal chair, looking down, picking at his hands, and humming ever so softly as he swayed back and forth. He didn't seem afraid or upset; in fact, seeing him so out of it and glazed over was almost as disturbing as seeing Brayden so bandaged and burned. She was desperate to understand what was going on inside of her son.

Greta and Patrick were finally allowed in the room where Logan was sitting. She leaned down and hugged her sole surviving son, now her only child, which stopped him from swaying.

Patrick took a turn embracing him. "We're taking him home," he said assertively.

Greta was still confused why they were all there, why Morales had mentioned a lawyer. Had someone *attacked* her son? Was this not a horrible accident . . . or was it purposeful? She feared that her undercurrent of worry had just manifested into a nightmare.

"I'm sorry, but Logan will be remaining at the police station," Morales said. The crowd of uniformed officers dispersed, leaving behind a man and woman not in uniform sitting on the opposite side of the table from Logan but behind it, as though they'd been observing, and their uniforms were slightly different.

"What is going on? My son just died! We need to be home and grieve, to arrange . . . to . . ." Greta ran out of steam. Logan didn't need to be home to plan a funeral, but she wanted him home, wanted to know what was going on.

"Your son is being placed in temporary custody. We'll have him in a holding cell here for the day before transferring him to the juvenile detention center in Bridgeport tomorrow. You can come back with his attorney later today."

And before she understood what was going on, Logan was escorted away by the differently uniformed guard, and she and Patrick stood there alone. Greta had so many questions. Tears ran down her face as she thought about her only child, who'd come into this world with a brother and was now alone. Her heart raced but her body remained frozen.

Patrick turned to Morales. "Did he witness something? I'm afraid we're still not following what happened. Can someone *please* explain what the hell is going on? We have one son who just died and another who seems catatonic. What's happened?"

Greta realized Patrick was right. Logan's eyes had been unseeing, almost otherworldly looking.

Morales took a deep breath. "We're not entirely sure at this point, but it looks like Brayden's . . . condition may have been caused by Logan."

Greta swayed on her feet, dimly aware of Patrick holding on to her. It wasn't registering that she was awake and this wasn't all a bad dream.

It had to be a mistake. This couldn't have happened because of some ridiculous fight between brothers, some terrible act that one twin committed. It couldn't . . .

"He's just a kid," she said quietly. "I'm sure he didn't . . . that it was . . . Oh my God."

The detective looked at her grimly. "He hasn't spoken so far, but based on a witness statement and video from the tennis club, your son's been arrested and will be charged according to the recommendations of the state's attorney."

Greta's tremors had transformed into overarching and paralyzing guilt that left her in so much shock she could barely absorb that the officer was saying that her one son was being charged for *murdering* his twin brother.

Chapter Twenty-Eight

COLETTE

2020

Colette shot up in bed and listened for her son, and it took a moment for it to sink in that it was her grief, yet again, waking her . . . a presence all its own. According to her phone, it was 4:03 a.m. She could try to go back to sleep, but she knew she couldn't quiet her mind again. She longed for Tripp. She pictured herself holding him, his gorgeous face beaming up at her, his brown eyes with light and life behind them.

After fifteen minutes of staring at the ceiling, she gave up and got out of bed, despite the overwhelming exhaustion that hit her as she shuffled down the stairs toward the kitchen. She took her meds and flipped on the local news as she poured herself a cup of coffee. Vic had left an hour earlier to be on-site for a masonry job in Massachusetts, so at least the coffee was fresh. After the weather report, a "breaking news" banner hit the screen.

"We are live in Greenwich, Connecticut, where a grisly scene unfolded last night at the Beachland Tennis Club," the newscaster reported. "Three boys were involved in what appears to be a tragic death. One of the boys is said to have died in a sauna after being locked inside for approximately ninety minutes. Authorities say the fourteen-year-old was rushed to a nearby hospital and pronounced dead shortly after arrival. A thorough police investigation is underway."

Tragic and grisly. How awful, she thought. The camera switched to a medical expert, who began speaking about the dangers of saunas when not used properly, explaining how a human body would react to being in the heat of a sauna for an extended period of time, citing dehydration, heart attack, and/or third-degree burns as the likely cause of death.

Taking a sip of coffee, she jumped and nearly spilled it when her phone rang. So much for a quiet morning before work.

"Colette, sorry to wake you," Frank said by way of hello. He had a bit of sleep in his voice himself. "We gotta get down to the police station."

"I was already awake. What's going on?"

"I don't know all of the details, but I got word that we need to head down to the station. A Patrick O'Brien died last night after being burned in the Beachland Tennis Club's sauna; it's all over the news. It's unclear what happened, but it seems like some sort of foul play. We need to be there for witness statements from the brother." He sounded weary. "I need you there to work with me on this, talk to the forensics team and the medical examiner. A third kid has already made a statement but has been taken to the hospital. It's . . . complicated."

"I just saw it on the news. I'll be there in a half hour." She took two quick swigs of coffee before making her way upstairs to throw on some clothes and brush her teeth.

Dread consumed her the closer she got to the police station, roiling her stomach. Years of nursing, being a medical paralegal, and even her time as an addict had made her numb to a lot of things, yet she hadn't hardened enough to be unaffected by a young kid getting cooked in a sauna. Especially with her own losses, she found sometimes her job was becoming too much to take emotionally. She couldn't imagine the world of pain the mother of these two precious boys must be experiencing.

But her medical expertise would be pertinent as the case unfolded, and she would have to hold it together today, as she was about to be faced with the deceased's brother and his parents, all in the throes of grief.

Frank met her in the parking lot, still wiping sleep from his eyes. "I don't think we'll have to do much. Everyone's probably just in shock and confused, but we need to be here to get some preliminary facts."

Within five minutes, they were seated in an interview room. Colette's stomach turned over again, making her wish it had occurred to her to at least put a piece of toast in her stomach as opposed to all that coffee and nothing else.

She knew how this went, though: an officer would be speaking to the brother first. They'd be listening, in the room, but wouldn't be engaging. Colette nervously picked at the raw cuticle on her thumb until it started to throb. She sucked on it and glanced over at Frank while he looked at his phone. Finally, an officer led a handsome young man with his head down into the room. They sat on opposite sides of the table, but it lacked an adversarial feel that was always shown on TV, possibly because the door was open and other people were around.

"I know this is difficult, but our first task is to get as much information as possible about what happened," a female plainclothes officer said. "I'm Officer Reed, and we just need you to tell us what happened last night."

The teen continued to look down, silently wringing his hands. Colette watched the boy, wondering what was going through his mind. His long fingers were entwined, rubbing frantically at each other. He thrust his thumb into his mouth, biting the sides, and she felt a pang, seeing this clearly lost teenager chewing his nails like she and her mother did when they were nervous.

The line of questioning started off pretty standard, but Colette could sense a turn as the questions persisted. Officer Reed's tone became more loaded with disbelief as the boy sat silently, refusing to answer questions or numbly grunting "I don't know" and "I don't remember."

They were interrupted by another police officer who asked to speak with Reed outside the room. When she and the officer returned, her face was solemn.

"Logan, I'm afraid we're going to have to take you into custody."

Colette was confused by the sudden mood shift in the room. The police officer reached behind Logan and pulled him up from his chair by his arm, but someone stilled him.

"He can wait until his parents get here," Reed said. "The kid's not going anywhere." She aimed her voice at the tape recorder she'd turned on and acknowledged at the start of the proceedings. "This is Officer Reed, and we're now stopping the interview of Logan O'Brien, as it has come to our attention he is a suspect in a suspicious death. Interview will commence when a lawyer or guardian is present."

Frank and Colette exchanged glances. Things had certainly taken a turn.

It didn't take long for the parents to show up, and Colette considered the couple. The father was wearing an Under Armour hoodie and a US Open cap with a brim that was curled enough that it hid his eyes. The wife stood next to him, staring straight ahead, one hand clutching her husband's forearm. She was wearing a dirty sweatshirt and what looked like a red costume underneath, her swollen eyes smeared with the remnants of lots of eye makeup.

Both of them hugged their son, but the boy didn't register their presence. Colette gazed thoughtfully at him as he was finally escorted out of the room. In the hallway, the young man turned and locked eyes with her, and her blood ran cold. She was losing her mind. She needed to get home and get some sleep.

Those eyes, their rich brown, their long lashes, the slight downturn at the outside edge that gave them that puppy-dog look—they looked so familiar and she wasn't sure why.

Chapter Twenty-Nine

GRETA

2020

By the time they got home from the police station, Greta felt like she was walking underwater. She and Patrick fell onto the sofa, moaning in mutual grief for one son's death and their other son's arrest. A weight seemed to press on her chest, robbing her ability to breathe normally. It was all too much to comprehend.

"I'm going to try to talk to Zeke. See if he can explain what happened," Patrick said.

"I'll go with you." She looked around and tried to get her bearings, shuddering as grim reality sank in deeper. The last twelve hours had not been a bad dream. Her son's death had not been a night terror. Her head also hurt so much that she had to press on it to try to relieve the physical reminder of the horror and fury she held inside.

She mustered up enough energy to make coffee. Patrick fought to keep his eyes open, downing a cup as soon as it was brewed. "Let's go. I hope the hospital lets us into Zeke's room."

Greta nodded, took a few swigs from her mug, and walked toward the garage, coming to a halt at the sight of Brayden's shoes by the door.

"I can't do this." She wailed as she collapsed onto the bench by her son's shoes.

They decided Patrick would go and talk to Zeke in person, and she could stay and wait for the call from their attorney, whom they'd left a message for. Greta heard the car screeching out of the driveway, and she worried that Patrick shouldn't be driving in his state of mind.

Greta dialed Manny again; it was just past seven, so it was no wonder she could still only reach his answering service. She dragged herself into the shower and just stood awhile, the hot water mixing with her tears. When she got out, she struggled into her robe and opened her phone. There were already news reports showing the Beachland Tennis Club, reporters swarming out front. That'd be her house soon.

Before she could get sucked into the macabre spectacle, her phone rang.

"Manny. Thank you for calling. I'm sure you've heard about the teenager . . . killed in the sauna. It was . . . our son Brayden." The words were making her sick, so she'd rushed them, speed somehow offsetting their reality briefly. "And . . . and they have Logan in custody. Can you meet me at the police station?"

"I can go there right now," Manny said. "Where are you?"

"Home," she said. "But I . . . I need to regroup. And I want Patrick with me; he's trying to get more information from the friend they were with, Zeke. He's at the hospital."

Manny cleared his throat. "It may be better if Zeke doesn't see him. If Zeke was there, he's a witness, and Patrick talking to him could look bad to the prosecution."

Greta remained silent, words like "witness" and "prosecution" making her feel like she'd been plunked down in a *Law & Order* rerun. Finally, she said, "Can we meet you there in an hour, when Patrick's back?"

"Absolutely. I'll see where the investigation is and keep you updated. I'm so sorry for your loss, Greta."

His condolences solidified this nightmare in a way the officers', doctors', and nurses' hadn't—she knew this man, and his apology congealed the grief in her stomach. She couldn't accept that one son was dead and perhaps at the hand of the other. The emotions were too raw.

She stared at the phone still in her hand a few moments, working hard to overcome the nausea, then dialed Patrick.

"Did you see Zeke yet?"

"Yes. Well, no. I'm here and he's stable, but they won't let me talk to him because I'm not family," he said.

Greta wanted to scream. It didn't matter that Manny had told her it was better if Patrick didn't speak with Zeke. She couldn't fathom any of this and wanted answers.

Patrick was practically hyperventilating as he said, "Do you think Logan locked him in as a joke and didn't realize he would die?"

"Zeke's a big kid; maybe he did it and Logan couldn't fight him off? And now Zeke's lying," Greta said. She thought back to all the times she'd noticed Logan's behavior was off, but regardless, she'd never imagined that meant he was capable of killing anyone, especially his own brother, so she had to grasp for blame elsewhere even though she *had* seen gradations of aggression that worried her.

She had turned the TV on earlier and now saw another news alert. "Channel 5 Breaking News. One fourteen-year-old has died and one is injured in what looks to be a freak accident at the Beachland Tennis Club involving a sauna. Police are continuing the investigation."

"The news is saying it's an accident," Greta said.

"Jesus. I don't know what to believe, but I can't stop crying about Brayden. We should have picked them up from the tennis club as soon as Zeke told us they biked there," Patrick said through sobs.

"Don't blame yourself," Greta said, trying to convince herself to do the same thing. "And why is the news speculating about our son's death? It's private! What's wrong with people?" She could feel herself on the edge of hysteria.

Patrick let out a long, dejected sigh. "I'm coming home. We can go meet Manny and get to the bottom of this." Greta heard the car starting. "I got the chills going back into a hospital. I can't . . . I can't believe Brayden's dead. I'm going to throw up."

"I know. Be careful driving. Please," Greta said, the desperation in her voice evident, but she couldn't stop it. The fleeting thought of something happening to Patrick nearly sent her into a tailspin.

As she hung up, Manny was calling back. "I'm so sorry to share this, but they have video of the incident, and it's . . . *very* incriminating. Logan seemed off. Did he drink or take any drugs last night that you know of?"

"No," Greta said, "but there was alcohol at the party. I suppose they could have snuck some." She thought of her own youth and realized she and her friends did stupid things when they drank, but she had a sneaking suspicion that this wasn't alcohol or drugs, that it was something much worse.

Manny didn't answer. "I'm going to need to see you and Patrick as soon as possible. Right now, the state's attorney is saying they're going to charge him with second-degree manslaughter."

"Oh my God!" *Manslaughter*—the sound of it was grotesque.

An image of poor Brayden's burned body flashed in her head, and she realized she wasn't sure she could stomach a video. She had to speak to Logan. She wanted to hurt him and apologize for never getting him the help he needed all at the same time.

"Do you think he didn't understand what he was doing?" Greta asked, struggling to keep her voice from wavering.

She wished now that she'd pushed harder, ignored Patrick's lack of concern, sought out a therapist. She was too selfish, too worried about having to confess the truth about a donor egg—the life she'd worked so hard to create was now shattered.

"It doesn't matter what I think. My job is to defend him. Right now, the first hurdle we have to tackle is that I have to petition the judge to have him transferred to juvenile court." Manny said all of this calmly, which should have helped, but it almost made her more upset. "If anyone fourteen and older is charged with certain crimes in Connecticut, they're automatically tried in criminal court. This has already hit the news, and getting the judge to agree to transfer him down to juvenile court will be an uphill battle."

"I can't hear any more of this right now. We'll be there as soon as we can."

She hung up and turned the TV off, waiting for Patrick in a silence that seemed to throb around her. When he pulled into the driveway, Greta ran to meet him and jumped in the passenger seat. Before he could put the car in reverse, she laid her hand on his forearm. "I think Logan killed Brayden." She couldn't believe she'd said it out loud.

Patrick gave her a long look, his eyes somehow getting sadder the longer he looked at her, though no moisture appeared in them.

"Manny said they're charging him with second-degree manslaughter."

"Fuck." Patrick stared straight ahead.

"And that it's automatic that he'll be tried as an adult," she wailed.

Patrick hugged her tightly, then put the car in gear. When they got to the station, they were briefly allowed to see Logan, who barely spoke, though this time he seemed to be coming out of his emotionless state, and the confusion in his expression was evident. For now, they decided to avoid watching the video, and Manny explained that the first thing on their plate was probably going to be a petition to let Logan come home while awaiting trial, then asking for a juvenile court trial. In the meantime, he said, they should go home, get some sleep, and grieve the loss of Brayden.

The next couple of days were a fog of grief and unreality. Greta threw out the condolence cards unopened. She resented the obligation to thank people who sent things in an effort to comfort her. These people who were on the fringes of this, who sent cards saying how sorry they were and gossiped about it when they were behind closed doors, their lives would return to normal—Greta's and her family's never would.

She drove forty minutes away to buy groceries, just to avoid the stares and the whispers. She continued to work after the funeral but knew she needed an exit plan, to focus on the upcoming trial. She thought about the ceremony they'd had. She let her sister plan everything, which turned out to be a small, private funeral—again, to avoid people judging her, to avoid the looks and the incredulousness, the vicious rumors, the gross people who just wanted to horn in on attention and grief by pretending they were closer to the family than they were. The image of Brayden's casket being dropped into the ground haunted her. Logan didn't attend the funeral because he had been placed in a juvenile detention center and wasn't allowed to leave. All she remembered about the funeral was hardly making eye contact with Jack, and his wife and her mother complimenting her black dress, and Zeke offering such young, innocent tears. Greta was surprised he'd even come after all he'd been through. Patrick's parents hardly said a word to her, but she found their silence more comforting than her own mother's frivolous comments scattered amid her pain.

After the funeral she went into work and packed her desk up. It took so long that all the offices around her had their lights out. She called Jack to discuss a few projects before she left.

"Sorry it's late, but I wanted to explain the files I left on your desk," she said, her cell phone on speaker. She wanted to make it quick and get back home.

"Greta, take as long of a leave of absence as you need," Jack said. "*Gret,* I'm here, the company's here for you whenever you're ready." The tension between them seemed to temporarily be put into perspective.

"I hope you'll be coming back, eventually?" he said.

She couldn't tell if he meant it or not. Part of her assumed he was happy to be taking over her clients, but she no longer cared. Getting ahead meant nothing to her.

"I need to focus on Logan. *Goodbye*," she said and pressed the hang-up button quickly.

Greta went back into Jack's office and as she was sorting paperwork to put into his files, she saw one dated back to before the Kentucky Derby party where her father was arrested. It was a file from the FBI, and it included her father's name. She leafed through it as her jaw dropped.

Jack had taken a plea bargain. All this time she'd blamed Bianca, but from what she was reading, she realized for the first time that Jack was the real whistleblower.

She called him back, confronted him. "I can't believe you lied to me about this for all these years, and you let me sleep with you!"

She thought back to times where she should have been smarter and listened to her gut—Jack's coordinated rule violations, corruption, and greed. She had never used her head, only her heart, and he never deserved the friendship she gave him.

"My mother was right about you!" she lashed out as he remained silent on the phone line.

Every bit of her admiration for Jack was shattered. Greta realized that *he* was just another blurry part of her life that was finally coming into focus.

"I'm so sorry," he said.

"I pity that everything you have is based on deceit!"

"Are you going to tell our—"

"No, I'm not telling Teiking. I won't even give you the satisfaction of telling our boss you're a fraud. Reporting you would be easy. I'd actually prefer you to have to live with your lies. *Trust me*—living with your inner demons is much worse than being behind bars!"

"I was young, and I didn't know what to do. I'm sorry I hurt your dad."

"It's not my dad; you hurt me!" Greta said, angry but proud she could admit vulnerability.

She confidently ended the conversation. "I'm never coming back to work with you here." She hung up, and her nausea turned to numbness as she realized she had bigger problems that actually deserved her attention.

Part of her was relieved she'd never have to question her decision to leave work for good. She noticed the cleaning lady in the office and apologized for never asking her name until tonight.

"Thank you," she said as she gathered her things and headed home.

"You're welcome, Greta, have a good night," the cleaning woman said.

~

Everything that had happened before—the IVF, her new half sister, that night with Jack—seemed to have been wiped away, and, along with it all, Greta's personality had been irrevocably changed. Before, details, success, maintaining control of situations had been so important. Now, she'd lost one of the most important things in her life, and so little else mattered. Her energy was spent caring about her one living son and keeping him out of prison. So she went through her days on autopilot, a quieter, softer version of her old self.

She had no doubt that Logan had done it—Manny had convinced her of that—but she still had no idea why. He'd hardly spoken, the silence infuriating but also depressing. It gutted her that he was so incapable of connecting with her or Patrick, that he'd prefer to keep them in the dark about whatever was going on, whatever had gone on that night. She grappled with her son's unconscionable act of violence, but right alongside her anger was an unexplainable sense of forgiveness, slowly enveloping her as if, despite the pain she felt, she couldn't just stop loving him.

In the months that followed the funeral, her routine was to open her eyes and enjoy that brief moment before she remembered it had all really happened and another heart-wrenching day was ahead of her. Then she would let the tears spill. She spent any energy she had trying to research anything she thought might help Logan's legal team. Her mother came by often, as did Audrey, dropping off food and magazines and bottles of wine she didn't even have the energy to open. She couldn't fall asleep without a sleeping pill, and even Patrick borrowed a few.

Though they slept side by side, the tension that had come to a head just before that fateful night now stretched silently between them. They each ignored it, unable to muster up the energy to discuss anything else so emotionally draining, but it meant they processed their pain in isolation. Greta was numb all the time, and if Patrick laughed at a television show, she resented that he was even temporarily okay without Brayden alive, even for that second. If he cried too much, she felt like he wasn't being strong enough. Once the journalists got tired of camping out in front of the house and the trial itself became a more interesting future prospect, he would work outside again. Sometimes she would watch him from their bedroom window and wonder what he thought about as he pushed the mower, expressionless.

Sundays were the hardest. If she dared drive anywhere, she was sure to see families walking together. She started scheduling the cleaning lady that day just so she had someone to talk to, and when she left, Greta mostly stayed in bed. Her dark moods were occasionally interrupted by glimpses of light when she came across something that reminded her of Brayden: a silver spoon she found tucked away in the junk drawer engraved with his name, the family photo on the wall featuring his angelic smile, the tennis rackets hanging up in the mudroom.

One day, alone at home, she was overwhelmed once again by the depth of her loss. It was like losing a limb, like having it ripped off your body, she thought. After never feeling like motherhood rested easily on her shoulders, the depth of her pain was a horrifying reassurance that she loved her boys to the depths that only a mother could. In the midst of her anger and grief, there was also so much guilt for the anger she felt toward Logan. Anger and confusion intermingled, all laden with guilt for his conception, her deception, and her longing to go back in time and erase her lies. It occurred to her at least once daily that this could be her fault in a different way, could have something to do with the fact that she used a donor egg.

She walked into Logan's bedroom and looked around at the detritus of his life—antique rackets picked by the decorator hung along the wall behind his bed, his plaid bedding coordinating with the window treatments, tennis trophies, and various books on his desk. She picked up one dusty book, *Arthur Ashe on Tennis*, and flipped to the front, where her father had written to both boys. It said in beautiful cursive handwriting, *Dear Brayden and Logan, Off the court, Arthur was good, often great, but even he was not perfect. Regardless, this was one of my favorite books and a good reminder to take his advice: "Start where you are. Use what you have. Do what you can." Love, Grandpa.* She wished she'd read this inscription sooner, but she took a deep breath and realized that all she could do right now was start where she was and take one step at a time as she dusted off the book jacket with her unmanicured hands. Then she looked at her son's sketchbook and was in awe as she wept at the intricate drawings.

Greta walked down the hall to Brayden's room but couldn't bring herself to go in, standing in the doorframe before collapsing onto the floor. Pain jabbed her chest on each exhale—it felt like her heart was physically breaking. One of the babies she'd worked so hard to bear was now buried underground; she hadn't been able to save him.

She looked at his trophies and wondered why she'd pushed him so hard, wishing she could go back in time and say "I love you" more often. She paced around, and tears continued to stream from her eyes.

She'd just read a grief book that explained forgiving your child's murderer didn't have to be part of healing, but for her the murderer was also a son. Greta knew the only way she would be able to go on living would be if she let go. Her body was still so angry, but her heart was healing in a way that could only be explained as unconditional love.

She wished she and Patrick could sit and cry together, forgive each other the way she'd just forgiven Logan. She had accepted that grieving was a solitary endeavor, but when her sister rang the doorbell, she didn't just take the box of Danish and push her away. She'd been ignoring the media still periodically perusing their home, but she decided to invite Emily in.

She peeked out the side window and then unlocked the door and gestured her in. Emily was dressed up, wearing red lipstick and a short black skirt and looking like an Audrey Hepburn replica. She was graceful, poised, and holding a white box tied with string from the bakery. Greta was wearing Patrick's sweats that were too big on her and knew her eyes were likely swollen, but she didn't care.

Emily came in and set the baked goods on the counter. "Mom said all you're eating is a scoop of peanut butter, and you need your strength for the trial, so I'm taking you out to lunch."

"Em, I can't," Greta said, plopping back down on the sofa next to the kitchen counter. "Thanks for bringing food. Patrick appreciates it too."

Greta burrowed deeper into the sofa and listened to her sister's kitten heels clicking on the wood floors as she ran upstairs and back down. Emily reappeared next to her holding a jean skirt and leather slides that Greta barely remembered owning. Most of her clothes were designer suits—now sitting in her closet during her leave of absence from work.

Emily's voice was forcefully chipper. "And after lunch I got something for you, so bring the sweats and I'll pack these." She threw a pair of Hunter rain boots into an empty canvas bag that was hanging in the mudroom.

Emily reached for Greta's waistband, trying to tug her sweats off and help her put on the jean skirt. "I'm taking you out to lunch; you need some real food. Come on, put this on and I'll get you a steak at MacDuff's."

"God no, we could run into Jack. And why do you care if I wear Patrick's sweats to a restaurant? This town has made you all so insane."

Emily ignored her insult. She pulled a tube of lip gloss out of her pocket and rubbed it on Greta's lower lip. "Your lips look dry. I thought you guys were friends. Has he not been supportive? I saw his wife at Pilates and—"

Greta held her hand up to stop her. She buttoned the jean skirt. In some ways, it was nice that Emily was making small decisions for her. "I'm just such bad company," she confessed.

"You need vitamin D," Emily said, pulling on Greta's arm. Emily dragged her out the front door and into her new BMW. She buckled her in and said, "Where can we get you a steak? A drink, we need a drink."

"Can we go to L'Escale? Hopefully it's all out-of-town tourists. I can't deal with people. I've never hated this town so much."

"Okay, we'll go there, but none of this is your fault, and if anyone even looks at you otherwise, that is their problem."

"Thanks. I just don't have the energy. And it's not just seeing people. Every time I go out of my house, I see things that remind me of Brayden. I went to CVS to pick up my prescription. I had a scarf around my face, oversize sunglasses because I was so worried about someone seeing me and offering condolences while they secretly judged me, and then I saw a bag of Chessmen cookies, Bray's favorite, and had to run back to my car."

"I would have picked up your scrip," she said, putting her hand on Greta's knee.

When they got to the restaurant, Emily said, "Let's self-park so you don't have to answer if the valet guy asks how you're doing."

"Yes, and maybe we should get it to go."

"Let's sit outside and see how you do. The sun will be good for you."

"Okay." Greta sighed. She had known this day of leaving her house would come, but she hadn't realized how hard it would be to sit through one lunch.

Emily held her hand, practically holding her upright, and then whispered to the waitress as if she were sharing that it was a kid's birthday. A young hostess escorted them to a table in the sun, and the waitress came over with two drinks and quickly took off, as Emily had likely instructed.

"To one step at a time," Emily said, lifting her glass. Greta lifted hers too. A tear rolled down her face. She was touched by the effort Emily was making.

Greta chuckled. "I didn't even know I owned a jean skirt."

"So what's up with Jack? Is he upset you left work? He's got to understand you need to focus on your family. Mom worries that you're not sleeping. She's been so worried about you, honey."

"Well, I wish she'd come by more, or call Logan, instead of asking me if I need a pedicure where she knows I'll see people."

"She'd take you to a New York spa if that's the issue. She'd totally get it."

"Oh God, Emily, it's more than that. I'm working morning, noon, and night on the trial. I'm just sick of the rat race, and now that I know that Jack's the one that ruined Dad's career, I'm done with him. I'm not going back to work after my leave of absence."

Emily gasped as Greta continued. "I figured it out when I was putting my open client files into Jack's desk. He admitted it, but I was so consumed with Logan, I practically just let it go."

"What an asshole," Emily said.

"This solidified the end of our friendship," Greta said as Emily continued nodding in disbelief.

"It's not important now," Emily said, her maturity impressing Greta.

"I know, right? My life looked so fucking perfect, and then it just blew up!"

"Greta, don't say that, and stop shutting Mom out," Emily said, tears now making her perfect makeup drip down her face. "You are going to get through this."

"I'm not doing it on purpose. I mean, what would you do if Connor was in a jail cell? Would you just go get a pedicure with Mom?"

"Greta, I know it sucks, but Marshall says you have a good chance." She put her hand on top of her sister's.

Emily ordered chilled lobster, mussels Provençal, and oysters for them to share along with two more drinks. She slurped up the rest of her first one, exhaled, and asked, "Does Mom know Jack tipped off the Feds?"

"No, I'm not giving her the satisfaction of being right. I guess he was involved in the corruption, too, and likely took a plea bargain. But can you believe he had the nerve to show up at the derby party when he knew Dad was going down?"

"I'm so glad you guys didn't get married."

"Me too, but I cheated on Patrick with him," Greta said. She was surprised she was sharing this with her sister at a time like this. "Makes me sick to my stomach that I did it."

"Oh my God! Were you and Patrick having problems? When? I'm shocked."

"Not everyone has to be having problems to do stupid, hurtful things, Em. I used to justify Dad cheating on Mom with Bianca because they had problems and Mom never showed him appreciation, but I think sometimes people do stupid things for no reason. I still can't believe that Dad had a kid with Bianca."

Emily buried her face in her hands and then said, "I know. I feel like we never talked about it much after you told me at Dad's funeral. I can't believe Bianca had the nerve to come. That was crazy. Poor Mom."

"Mom's always alluded to her being pretty aware of Dad's secrets. Maybe she's accepted her."

"Yeah, I'm not talking to Mom about it. And all of this has put it in perspective too. I'm letting it go. I'm putting my energy on my nephew, and you." Emily squeezed both of Greta's hands.

Something was shifting between them. At first Greta was just getting things off her chest, but now she was glad she'd chosen Emily to reach out to. After facing tragedy, she was grateful to still have a sibling and wanted to reestablish a more genuine connection.

"Years ago, Dad asked me to hide some paperwork for him, and I noticed an extra 529 fund and thought it was suspicious, but he was in so much trouble with the law I never brought it up. Then I tried to just focus on my own family and issues and pushed the suspicion away, and then when Dad was dying I saw that he was still in touch with Bianca, and he admitted that her daughter, Valerie, is his."

"I'd heard Bianca had a kid. I just never paid attention to who she was." Emily slapped her hand on the table. "Have you met her?"

"No, I saw her name in the will. But now I have too much on my mind to even care," Greta said, chugging down her second drink. She was second-guessing telling Emily about knowing for so long. The last thing she wanted was her sister angry she hadn't shared sooner when she needed to put all her energy into freeing Logan.

"Absolutely. Focus on Logan." Emily touched her forearm as the waitress set plates of food in front of them. "Is there anything I can do? Marshall might be able to help. Anything?" Emily squeezed a lemon over an oyster and held it up to her sister. "I know you haven't eaten well in months."

Greta muttered "Thank you" and then said, "Emily, maybe Marshall can help, but you are going to be completely shocked when I share something with you, and the *only* person who knows is Audrey. It's just that I need your advice."

"What is it?" Emily's face flushed, and she looked genuinely concerned as she leaned in.

Greta looked to her left and right, and then, in a low monotone voice, she began to spill her entire hidden past. "Remember Dad's derby party when he was arrested? I'd just gotten back from Sweden . . ."

She explained how she was already pregnant, and how on her second date with Patrick, he had explained he would never adopt.

"I was just so in love and so scared to lose someone who seemed like so much fun, and anyway, one lie led to the next and I told him it was his, and then after I miscarried, we were just cursed with infertility from then on. After the pregnancy loss, I was never attracted to him sexually, and our whole marriage felt like a sham."

"Now you're exaggerating because you're grieving," Emily said, holding her cloth napkin across the table and wiping a tear on Greta's face. The waitress approached their table, and Emily snapped, "Everything's good," to get rid of her.

Greta continued to pour out her secrets perhaps as a subconscious practice run; she knew she might need to confess to Patrick soon. "Well, nothing worked. We had failed IUIs, failed IVFs, and I think it was God telling us we shouldn't have . . ."

"Greta, I knew you had help, but don't blame infertility for what happened. Lots of my older friends have had help. You and Patrick will get through this."

"No, you don't understand. I used donor eggs."

"You did? Why didn't you just tell me? What's wrong with that if you couldn't get pregnant? It makes sense that you'd do what you need to do to become a mom. You could have told me this."

"No, I couldn't. Because when I broached the subject to Patrick, he said, 'No way,' so Dr. Erikson and I did it behind Patrick's back. He could probably lose his medical license, and Patrick would one hundred percent leave me if he knows I've been lying to him our whole life, and now *this lie* feels like it's destroyed our family."

"This wasn't your fault," Emily reiterated.

Greta sighed. "I know, but it feels like it. I mean, I'm not the mother you are, but I saw so many things about Logan, especially, that I questioned. He was obsessed with counting things, obsessed with fire detectors, wiggled his hands weird, and I saw him being more and more aggressive as teenage hormones kicked in. I knew something was off with him. He pushed Brayden skiing, was getting into fights, you saw him on your boat . . ." Greta pressed another cloth napkin to her eyes as tears streamed down her face.

"My God, it's not your fault. And this might have nothing to do with you using a donor."

"But what if it does?"

"I don't know. Do you want me to ask Marshall? Do you know who the donor is?"

"No, it was an anonymous donor. I'm planning on confessing to my lawyers. It could be what saves Logan from being sentenced." Greta pressed on her temples. "Should I tell Patrick?"

Emily looked straight into Greta's eyes. "Feels like a bad idea with Patrick's grieving. It's *too much*. Marshall said you guys need to present as united, loving parents, and this might make him aloof. It might not be the right time."

"Oh my God, I agree."

Greta wasn't sure if she wanted to try and save her marriage, but she knew she wanted to save her son.

"I get it," Emily said. "I know everyone thinks he's a great guy, but I knew you weren't happy. I'm sorry you were married to someone you had to be fake with."

Greta sighed again. "You don't think I'm horrible?"

"Are you kidding? I've *always* looked up to you. Especially now!"

Emily flagged the waitress over, handed her a credit card, and wiped Greta's eyes one last time before she lifted her up and guided her back out to the car.

"Trust the lawyers, and let's just keep praying for Logan. I know you are working your ass off, and I've *always* admired how smart you are. You can do anything you put your mind on. I have a really good feeling you're going to win this case, honey."

Emily popped open her trunk. She pulled a pair of leggings up under her skirt and slipped on boots, then hopped into the driver's seat and handed Greta the canvas bag so she could change.

Greta wasn't sure what was going on but obliged her sister. She was feeling so much lighter after confiding in Emily about everything.

"I'm taking you somewhere, to get your mind off the upcoming trial, just for an hour."

"I can't. Lunch was good, but I need to get home and work on more research," Greta said, pulling down the visor and looking in the mirror. "Oh my God, my eyes are still so swollen."

"I'm not taking no for an answer," Emily said.

Greta pulled the Hunter boots on, still curious about what her sister was up to. When she looked up, she realized they were pulling into Kelsey's stables, where they had both ridden horses growing up.

"Em . . . ," Greta said, feeling touched.

"I thought it would be therapeutic to ride, get you strong for the trial. Breathing is good," Emily said. "I called, and Kelsey said we can take a trail ride for as long as we want."

Greta saw the owner from afar. Kelsey had grayed but still had the same gentle smile as she approached them. "It's good exercise for the horses," she said, and Greta was happy she didn't bring up anything else.

Greta liked that she was helping Kelsey's horse get exercise, and she knew the horse would help her in return, clearing her head.

Emily eagerly hopped out of the car, ran around to open the passenger-side door, and handed Greta a riding helmet. She pulled Greta out and up to the stable entrance.

Emily saddled up two horses, and they mounted and began to ride off into the woods, which were a deep, lush green.

For the first time since she had lost her son, Greta smiled and took in nature. She remembered that she did have one happy memory from childhood: riding horses here with her little sister. She had been envious of Emily, never knowing the envy was reciprocated until today. Her jealousy transformed into appreciation. She felt relieved to have someone—at least one person—on her side.

This support allowed her to believe she *could* still save her son. She'd carried him, given birth to him—she wouldn't turn her back on him now.

Chapter Thirty

COLETTE

2020

Colette could barely keep her eyes open. She had gotten through the meeting at the police station on pure adrenaline and hadn't slept well since. The cloud of grief and horror that had filled the room, the eeriness of the boy and his silence, the guttural sobs and pleas coming from his parents—it had all hit her like a ton of bricks. She was haunted by that fleeting moment when she had stared into the boy's eyes and seen something so familiar, but she knew she was suffering from lack of sleep.

She had gotten to the office that first morning, bleary eyed, barely able to see straight, and gone right into Frank's office. Frank had been peering at his computer screen with a stricken look on his face.

"What is it?" she had asked, sensing his despair.

"This kid . . . the whole thing was caught on the club's surveillance camera. He is totally fucked," he said, leaning back and running his hands through his thinning hair. "You have to watch this. I'll send you the file. He fucking fried his brother in the sauna on purpose. The poor kid cooked to death at the hands of his twin brother." He shook his head with disgust.

"So if it's caught on tape, then case closed—he pleads guilty, right?" Colette had asked, having no idea just how complicated the case would become.

"First off, I'm assuming they're going to petition the judge to have him released to his parents' custody while awaiting trial, and then they'll ask to have him kicked back down to juvenile court." Most juveniles were released to their parents during trial rather than having to stay in a juvenile detention center, Frank explained; this case, though, wasn't like most offenses. "If we stay in criminal court—and I hope we do—I'm betting they'll plead not guilty by reason of insanity so the kid can go to a mental health facility instead of spending the rest of his life behind bars. You'll be spending all of your time going forward researching this kid and proving that he is violent and killed his brother."

The overwhelming sadness Colette had felt for the defendant's family since day one had only increased daily as she immersed herself in the case. Frank had shared that the family hired Manny Cashvan, a colleague of Frank's with a lot of extremely wealthy clients. But he hadn't tried many cases of manslaughter, and none involving children, which made Frank hopeful about winning.

"I don't think even the Walshes' money can buy his freedom when our evidence is this clear cut," he said, tossing a bunch of files on the desk toward her. "Here are the preliminary statements and the police paperwork. Dig into medical records to be sure there isn't a history of mental illness." Frank had been talking a mile a minute that first morning, and Colette's anxiety bubbled.

"I have a bunch of other casework to do," she said, trying to avoid the assignment, but Frank wasn't having it.

"You're off all other cases for now, and we'll file continuances to buy time or I'll give them to some of our more junior prosecutors so we can focus on this. It's a huge case; it's on every news channel, including national news. We need to win this, Colette. This could be the biggest case of our careers. The pressure is on."

Sick to her stomach just from anticipation, Colette had reviewed the surveillance video right away. The images were jarring, and she sometimes wished she had never seen them. It was grainy, but she watched as Logan carried a fireplace poker toward the sauna. He casually stuck it through the door handle and then, seemingly calmly, waited. After a few minutes, Brayden's face appeared in the small window—at first looking annoyed, then screaming, begging, going from angry to terrified to desperately banging on the glass on and off for, according to the tape, approximately twenty-five minutes. She was grateful the video had no sound.

At the twenty-five-minute mark, Logan left to go hit balls, as they had verified by another camera. The time on the tape ticked away, Brayden periodically coming to the glass to peer out and bang on it. At about forty-five minutes, a rock bounced off the glass inside the sauna. Then more. At around fifty-eight, it started to crack. At sixty-nine, the glass shattered. Two more rocks were thrown through the glass, knocking out most of the remaining shards that had been in the frame. Brayden was seen trying to claw his way through the tiny opening, and even from the angle of the video and an obscured view of his face, it was clear he was incredibly weakened. The inside of his arm pressed against the broken glass, and blood gushed down the front of the door. At that point, he stumbled out of view and didn't come back for fifteen minutes. At minute eighty-four, Logan returned and looked at the broken glass, rocks, and blood with seemingly little interest, stepping through it all to peek through the window, most likely seeing his brother unconscious, dying on the sauna floor.

At eighty-six, Zeke Davis appeared, took a quick assessment of the scene, and started toward the sauna door. Logan picked up one of the sauna rocks and lobbed it at Zeke, who ducked and continued forward. The next one hit him squarely on the knee, causing him to stumble and grab his knee, yelling something. Logan's movements throughout were stoic, robotic even. He picked up one last rock and threw it, hitting

Zeke squarely in the head, and the boy fell, hitting his head on the floor. It took only a few seconds for the boy to sit up, looking stunned, and scramble to his feet. At eighty-nine, he ran out of the camera's view, and Logan sat in front of the sauna door and looked straight ahead. He appeared to be speaking to somebody, though without audio, it was hard to say if he was speaking to himself, his brother, or someone no one else could see.

Fear rippled through Colette as she watched the boy's lips moving. Ten minutes later, paramedics rushed into the scene. Colette pressed pause, sickened—if the boy didn't have a mental illness, he was a cold-blooded killer. His erratic behavior, the mumbling to himself . . . it all made her flash back to her mother's behavior.

~

Colette's head was pounding as she woke up after yet another restless night of sleep and realized it was already morning. She needed to get ready for work. The case was taking over her life. As she brushed her teeth and changed, she thought about the boy. He seemed odd; she'd felt nervous in his presence, but she was still shocked, even weeks later, when she thought about how he could murder his twin brother. The mere thought of what could have happened in his life to bring him to that point made her head spin. And it made her question her desire to bring a child into this world.

She spent each day reviewing the paperwork Frank had given her, all standard. Apparently, the boy had been more responsive during questioning with his lawyer present. Logan had told police that they had been hanging out, playing tennis, and that Brayden had headed down to the sauna while Logan stayed back to hit off the ball machine.

She flipped through to the statement given by an eyewitness. The boys' friend, Zeke, had made a very different statement regarding the night's events. The police had visited him in the hospital, where he had been admitted for observation. He claimed he'd found the boys in the locker room area, where Brayden was locked in the sauna and had tried to escape by breaking the glass window with a sauna rock. Blood had stained the door around the tiny window, and Logan was standing still outside the door, watching. When Zeke tried to get near the door, Logan had screamed at him to go away and picked up the rocks Brayden had thrown through the window and hurled them at his friend. Zeke was eventually hit in the head by one of them and fled for his own safety, calling his mother, who called 911.

Frank had given her a list of records they needed to subpoena: both boys' cell phones, the parents' cell phones, school and medical records. She emailed Logan O'Brien's attorney, requesting he set up a preliminary meeting with his client or his client's parents to go over these things. As she hit send, it occurred to her that these parents had to host one son's funeral while trying to get the other one out of jail, parents of both the defendant and the victim. It was like a Greek tragedy.

The O'Briens' attorney had put in a special request with the judge the morning following the incident that Logan be held in the local psychiatric hospital until trial. Frank was right—they'd blown past the idea of having him released to his parents' custody, apparently understanding the slim chances of that and laying the foundation for their insanity plea.

Frank had argued that Logan was a danger to the community due to the depraved nature of the crime and that there was no history of mental health issues in his past. The request was denied, and a hearing was set to address the defense's motion that the case be tried in juvenile court.

~

"Your honor, Logan O'Brien is a child, and he just lost his twin brother," Manny Cashvan said.

"At his own hand." Frank's tone bordered on incredulous. Colette had heard him do it before, toes right up to the line of dramatic interpretation and legal argument.

"Enough," the judge said. "There were two motions filed today, and I'm only going to entertain one. As you know, Mr. Cashvan, felonies that mean classifying the child as a serious juvenile offender are tried by the Superior Court for criminal matters at the state's attorney's discretion. Your motion asking for what would essentially be a second transfer has been thrown out. I'll hear you on the motion of a closed courtroom."

The O'Briens had either been prepared for that outcome or were medicated, as they had very little reaction as their lawyer continued. Colette peered at the mother, wondering, as she had so many times, how she was able to even get out of bed in the morning.

"The O'Briens are a prominent family in Greenwich, and this story has already been splashed across the media both locally and nationally." Cashvan looked down at his notes. "One national show has dubbed our underage defendant the 'Sauna Slayer.' His mental health is precarious, his parents' home has practically become a campground for the media, and it seems unnecessary and prejudicial to open the courtroom to the public just so the salacious details can feed the twenty-four-hour news cycle."

The judge waved him off. "Enough, Mr. Cashvan. I agree. But in accordance with not making the closure broader than necessary, we will be allowing a set number of reporters into the gallery, no cameras, no recording equipment, no public."

∼

Colette immersed herself in not guilty by reason of insanity cases. The nature of this research kept her up at night. She couldn't help but think of her own mother and her illness, and how it may have contributed to

Colette's struggles with addiction and her current mental health concerns. In each case, she thought of the mothers of the victims as well as the accused. All these people were once someone's innocent baby. It scared her to think about how fragile the human mind could be. Especially since she had firsthand experience with her own mother. She found herself thinking that her mother hadn't been so bad after all—at least she hadn't killed herself or others like the people she had researched.

Colette's sleep was still disturbed, and she kept up on her medications. Most important, since her work seemed to keep her busy at all hours, were her own doctor appointments. There was a lot on her plate, and if she didn't keep up with everything, especially everything that happened after she'd lost Tripp, she was in danger of a relapse. So she meditated; when appropriate, she medicated; and she worked.

As the subpoenaed documents came flooding in, she was surprised to find that there was zero evidence of mental illness or any history of any real violence in Logan O'Brien's records. He was an average student for most of his academic career—though clearly struggling more recently, with one of his report cards containing two Fs: one in honors math and one in honors language arts. The notes from a parent-teacher conference revealed that Greta, his mother, had hired two private tutors to help Logan with a few subjects off and on over the years. Aside from that, there weren't too many absences or anything that was even noteworthy in his school files. His medical records were boring and revealed nothing. He had never been prescribed medication or sought counseling of any sort. The parents' and brothers' cell phone records were a litany of boring messages about tennis, dinners, and work, with a random meme or YouTube video link (normally to someone falling and hurting themselves or to more tennis).

She dug into researching the grandfather's incarceration, but it seemed pretty straightforward—textbook white-collar crime—nothing that would have any bearing on his grandson's case or his mental health.

There was an infamous 2013 case, when a teen was eventually sentenced to two years in jail after killing four individuals in a drunk driving accident, which Colette thought could be relevant to Logan's defense. Prosecutors had sought twenty years, but the teen had received no prison time after a psychologist testified that he was a victim of "affluenza": a product of wealthy, privileged parents who'd never set limits for him. Colette bristled, as she read the reports and articles, to think that someone could be born and bred so entitled that they would stop at nothing to get what they felt they deserved . . . even murder.

After reviewing Greta and Patrick O'Brien's financial records and private lives, it seemed like Logan might, indeed, be a victim of his upbringing. She wanted Frank prepared for any angle.

As she worked into the night for the third month in a row, she pored over Logan's medical records, looking for anything she might have missed. Then she found something—when he was a year old, he had experienced seizures. She Googled "seizures in babies" and found that it was sometimes hereditary, but there were no follow-up notes in his file, which she found odd. Greta had been forty-two when the twins were born. Colette pondered the likelihood of Greta having twins naturally at that age.

Frank had scheduled a deposition with the O'Briens the next afternoon. She would make sure he asked about the discrepancy between Logan's blood type and his parents', as that could lead to a totally different hereditary trail to look at for mental illness. They needed to be prepared to counter any evidence the opposing team might present to get this kid off by reason of insanity. Colette turned off the voice deep inside her that said *something's not right* and focused on the task given to her by Frank. Whether he was mentally ill or not, her job was to prove that he wasn't.

～

The next day, the couple came into the conference room timidly, seemingly shell shocked and raw as they sat at the table facing Colette and Frank, Manny next to them. Frank started with a series of basic questions about more recent events, with a focus on ruling out motives—a tournament Brayden couldn't play in, an argument they'd had at school. There were no clear signs of mental illness or a history of violence—there'd been no incidents that had made either parent get doctors involved. The husband did offer a note from a teacher ten or so years ago, in preschool, who'd mentioned developmental testing, though it'd never been done.

Eventually, Frank turned to her. "Colette, do you have any questions?"

She had to ask about their genetics; she hadn't mentioned it to Frank, but he was giving her the opening. "There was just one thing." She shuffled some papers to put off the inevitable. "I noticed there was a period of time when Logan was a baby that he experienced seizures." She looked up expectantly and locked eyes with Greta O'Brien. The woman stared back at her, her gaze suddenly icy, and Colette felt as though she was almost daring her to continue. "It seems as though the doctor's findings were inconclusive and there was no follow-up."

Neither of them responded. After a minute of silence, Patrick spoke up. "That's not a question, but yeah, we were told that some kids have febrile seizures. He grew out of it; he hasn't had a seizure since he was little."

"Hmmm, okay," Colette said, busying herself writing notes. A little embarrassed at her weak phrasing and him calling her out on it, she decided she had to throw it out there and see if it stuck. "Sometimes this type of inconclusive medical history indicates . . . well, I just have to ask: Are both boys your biological children?" She searched their faces for some sort of reaction.

Mrs. O'Brien's eyes had widened but her jaw had clenched, making Colette think she was surprised but also pissed. "Yes," the woman bit out. "They're our children. Why would you ask such a thing?" She'd looked mad at first, but now she seemed flustered.

Colette didn't know what it meant, but she felt like it wasn't as cut and dried as the woman was implying. Looking down at her notes, she said, "All right, thank you," slowly crossing out *adopted?* and writing in *but something else?*

Chapter Thirty-One

GRETA

2021

Greta was exhausted from running back and forth to preliminary depositions. She was too tired to even think about how to broach the donation issue with her lawyer. Maybe it was selfish to focus on her own guilt when she should be keeping her focus on what was best for her son. But she couldn't help but wonder how things would turn out if Patrick ever knew the truth. She also wondered how the boys would have responded if she'd sat them down and told them they were donor conceived. Would it have changed anything? Was her lie the reason she'd never sought help? She wondered. What had seemed like the biggest deal in her life—losing Patrick—now seemed minor. For the first time, instead of looking at using a donor as a shortcoming, she'd looked at it as having gone beyond herself to create a family, a family she was still fighting for.

Her son was being tried as an adult, but apparently that could work in their favor—Manny had told them that they couldn't have Logan plead not guilty by reason of insanity in juvenile court. It had something to do with children not being diagnosed with mental disorders very easily.

They had a hearing in juvenile court on Logan's competency to stand trial, which could have backfired on them. After an initial period of flat affect and near catatonia, he had seemed relatively like himself again, which may have made it harder to prove he couldn't stand trial and participate in his own defense in juvenile court. Now, in criminal court, Manny just had to show that Logan had not been in possession of his full faculties at the time of the incident. Greta didn't know if this was really easier or harder; all she knew was that she had a hard time seeing her only living son in a detention center. And she still could not understand what was happening to him—what had happened to him.

Thankfully, Zeke's mother had said they were not pressing charges and would do what she could to support their family. She felt like Logan had had a psychotic breakdown because it was so uncharacteristic of him. She'd known him for years now, so this carried a lot of weight—at least for Greta and Patrick—though it didn't stop the prosecution from subpoenaing Zeke. He was the only eyewitness to the attack, and Logan had also injured him, so they couldn't stop that from happening, but as long as Manny did a good job on cross-examination, it could work in their favor.

Greta was hounded by the media at every turn and unable to concentrate. She further extended her leave of absence from work and was even beginning to negotiate a severance package. She started taking early-morning walks and meditating; perhaps her antidepressants were working. She couldn't shake the feeling of strangers stalking her, snapping photos as she got into her car and then tailgating her. She and Patrick hardly speaking was just salt in the wound; they were no longer even sharing a bedroom. Most nights, Patrick fell asleep in the living room with the television on while she was upstairs on her laptop, researching anything that might help Logan's case.

She desperately wanted to stay married, though now for entirely different reasons than before. It no longer mattered for herself, for her own sense of success or love—now she thought it would help the judge see that Logan came from a stable home. She made an extra effort to connect, buying Patrick things, cooking every night, but she felt stonewalled by him most of the time.

"Did you like the beef stew? Your mom dropped it off," Greta said, not saying anything about the alcohol on Patrick's breath.

He ignored her.

"I have a video call right now with Logan. Do you want to sit together?" Greta asked, sad that Patrick was so aloof overall but knowing he'd want to be on the call.

"Sure," he said and scraped a chair across the floor and sat two feet to her left.

Greta looked at the scratch marks the chair made on the floor and couldn't believe all the little things that she used to let bother her. She reached for Patrick's hand as she nervously dialed into the detention center, which only allowed video visits at this time.

Logan's image popped onto the screen and Patrick sighed. Greta caught a glimpse of the outside courtyard, basketball hoop, and chain-link fence topped with barbwire that made her cringe every time she drove by the facility. He looked pale and weak, and his expression was empty. He was wearing a shirt she'd dropped off that already looked oversize.

"How are you?" she stupidly began.

"Hi," Patrick said as he moved his chair closer to Greta.

"Good. They let me draw on my wall since they figured out I'm a good drawer," Logan said. Greta didn't understand how he could be doing anything other than feeling guilty.

"Oh, can we see it?" Patrick asked.

Greta realized the video visit was set up in an unused room and the background of the video wasn't his actual cell.

"Yes, I'll ask the guard," Logan said as his face disappeared from the camera and his live image was replaced with a photo of Logan, signifying he'd turned his camera off while he walked to his cell.

Greta whispered to Patrick, "He doesn't seem that upset. Are they giving him sedatives? He seems tired."

"No idea," Patrick said, practically expressionless. "Greta, I'm sorry I downplayed the ski incident, the camp, everything."

"It's not your fault," she whispered but was happy he said something and wasn't just shutting her out. Logan's face finally reappeared, and now he was in his cell and a guard was sitting next to him.

"Here," Logan said, pointing at the wall that was covered in exquisite detail. Greta noticed an intricate drawing of a hand grasping bars that created an instant pit in her stomach. She noticed rows of lines, with every fourth line having a scratch through it, and assumed he was counting the days until his trial. He had also sketched the "Go to Jail" Monopoly square, and one red image really stood out; it read BROS, and underneath the graffiti lettering it had an image of the Mario Brothers, but instead of the faces looking like the red-and-green cartoon, it looked like Logan and Brayden. Greta's heart practically stopped.

"Looks good," Patrick said, his voice cracking. Greta noticed a tear falling down Patrick's cheek as he wiped it away.

"Do you miss him?" she couldn't help asking.

"Who?"

"Your brother," Patrick barked as his eyes widened.

"Yeah. Can he come visit me here?" Logan said, and Greta really sensed that he didn't know Brayden was gone. It was as if he'd blocked out everything.

Greta's gasp matched Patrick's.

"How can they put him on trial?" Patrick whispered. Tears continued to stream from his tired-looking face.

Greta looked right at Logan and realized that until now she hadn't looked deeply into his eyes and really tried to see and understand him.

The pit in her stomach grew as she thought about them labeling her son, who had no idea what he'd done, an adult. She said goodbye and slammed the laptop shut, wishing it would all go away. Tears streamed down her face as hard as Patrick's, and she assumed he was as sick to his stomach as she was. She wiped her tears off with her hand.

"I'm sorry," Patrick muttered again.

"He doesn't seem to remember hurting Brayden." She choked up on his name.

"You mean killing him?" he said, his voice now colder.

Greta's breath caught. "I just wish he could explain it."

Patrick remained silent.

"But we need to talk to each other," she said, reaching her hand out toward him, but Patrick flinched as if he'd done enough warming up for one evening.

After a long silence Patrick said, "This sucks."

"I know! But please don't shut me out," Greta said through heavy, flowing tears.

~

The only consistent thought that kept running through her mind was the boys' conception. Now, as she continued to think about it, she wondered if this would finally be the time when it would all come out. Was there a link between Logan's behavior and his conception? Maybe washing the sperm? Maybe destroying that third embryo had done something? Maybe the IVF drugs were the culprit?

Greta didn't even know what she was looking for but scrolled through every scientific website she could find related to IVF anyway. She ordered dissertations on mental illness and IVF treatments in older mothers and joined a chat group to ask a mother with twin autistic teenagers if she had undergone IVF. She reflected on Logan's current odd, lethargic demeanor and searched websites to find a reason for his psychotic outburst. There had to be something she was missing. She longed to link his behavior with something diagnosable.

And then she saw it: New Research Shows IVF Kids Are Twice as Likely to Have a Mental Illness. Could this help their case? Greta printed several similar scientific articles to take to Manny. Another article said the correlation was even higher. She searched for symptoms of childhood mental disorders, reflecting upon how quiet and sleepy Logan had always been. Now she had more questions than answers. Was it the drugs? Her age? Mixing her biology with someone else's? She wished she could call Manny now, but it was the middle of the night. She wanted to know if he could use this information, blame the IVF for what had happened.

Greta decided Dr. Erikson had been money hungry as she thought back to how he'd suggested IVF—an expensive treatment—without ever mentioning the risk of mental illness. He'd convinced her to use a younger woman's eggs, had probably taken advantage of someone who needed money.

Her terrifying research led her down yet another internet rabbit hole, to a website of mothers commiserating over their teenagers with autism hitting puberty and becoming more aggressive. These women lamented how their children lashed out verbally and some violently. Why was no one else paranoid about her assisted reproduction? Feeling herself teetering on the edge of mania, Greta gathered up the printed articles and put them in her bag to take to Manny in the morning, finally forcing herself to try to get a couple of hours of sleep.

~

The months had passed quickly—more quickly than they had thought possible at the beginning, when every visit to Logan, every person wanting to give condolences, every meeting with cops and lawyers seemed to drag on. As the final month before the trial came to an end, Greta prayed every day that Manny would get her son out of the god-awful facility he was being kept in. At this point, Logan had been forced to see a number of health-care professionals, had numerous tests run, but the results were sent right to their lawyers.

She grabbed a coffee at Starbucks, noticing that, even as long ago as that night seemed now, many people still stared and whispered. The difference between then and now was that she no longer cared. She took her coffee to a table and called Alyssa, Manny's paralegal, and asked to schedule a meeting. There was something she finally had to come clean about. She'd lived through confessing to her sister, and this information might help her son's trial.

"Of course," Alyssa said. "I have a short conference call now, but come by at tenish."

"Okay, thanks."

Greta walked into Manny's office around ten, catching her reflection in the glass below the CASHVAN & GOLDSMITH LAW sign. She looked like a sad, low-rent version of herself, but she had for quite some time, if she was being honest. Certain things had just lost their importance once they'd lost Brayden.

Alyssa greeted her warmly but professionally and waved her into the familiar conference room. "Before we get started," she said, "I know you asked for this meeting, but we wanted to let you know we got Logan an appointment with Dr. Brown. She's the top psychologist in Connecticut, and she's meeting him today or tomorrow."

"What's she going to do?"

"Well, she'll evaluate him and hopefully testify that Logan most likely has a mental disorder. The state has already sent over their psychologists and psychiatrists—their experts that will claim the opposite."

"Haven't we already done this?" Greta was being polite—she knew they had already been through this multiple times.

"Yes, but Dr. Brown is the best in the state. We have doctors who we know are willing to diagnose minors with mental disorders, who tend to lean toward that in general in their practices, and we have them on our witness list. But Dr. Brown would make it carry more weight with the jury."

The jury—a whole other worry that she had no control over whatsoever, of course. Her son's fate was up to a bunch of strangers Manny and the state's prosecutor would be picking soon. The thought that it was all still happening made the latte in her stomach sour.

Manny entered the conference room. "Good morning," he said, then got right down to business. "We wanted to let you know we got some updates on the opposing team's testimony. Some witnesses have been dismissed. Should I tell you now, or do you want to wait until you're with Patrick?"

"No, tell me now."

He nodded. "We received more forensic reports that show Logan's fingerprints on the poker, though the video already showed this. It isn't a make-or-break piece of evidence, as we aren't saying he didn't commit the crime; we're arguing that he wasn't aware of his actions. The biggest issue is the interviews with the boys' camp counselors; we'll want to look those over. The opposing team is trying to say you ignored prior violence."

"Logan accidentally hit Brayden in the knee!" But as the words came out, her face turned red, and she realized it could easily look like they had ignored his violent behavior. It had been an early sign of what he was capable of. He'd never actually expressed regret or said he was sorry. Why hadn't she made Patrick wake up and face this with her? Her desire to smooth things over, to see their sons succeed at tennis, to avoid talking about tough subjects with Patrick had made her ignore Logan's odd behavior. She could see clearly now that he *had* done it on purpose.

Greta shook her head a little, dispelling the memories so she could focus. She couldn't fall apart now. She had to get Logan help, not abandon him to prison, and she had to do that any way she could. "Well, I wanted to show you these insanity cases and this research on IVF and how it's linked to mental illness." She pulled the papers out of her bag.

Manny looked at the studies. "Greta, you've been sharing this type of thing with us for the last six months or so, and while I understand your need for an answer, for something to blame for this, infertility is a billion-dollar industry. And the field doesn't have much regulation. There is no government agency that is empowered to crack down on these giants based on how many kids end up being diagnosed with something. The studies you found just aren't enough data. Correlation isn't causation; it could be that affluent older moms just report autism more frequently. Data for the entire industry needs to be collected, and we can't do that in the next few weeks, so we need to table this. We need to stay focused on facts that might prove Logan was suffering from a mental illness, not hypotheses."

Greta had only a moment to feel disappointment before he plowed ahead.

"On the subject of fertility, Alyssa has pointed out some inconsistencies in Logan's medical records. The doctor's report stated that his blood type is AB, but you are an O positive?" He had the good manners to look a little chagrined, but he was also a successful lawyer for a reason, and he held her gaze steadily in his as he said, "It means the twins can't be your biological children."

And there it was.

Dizziness hit as her stomach lurched and her throat constricted. After years of subterfuge and outright lies, of being scared one of her sons or her husband would find out and it would shatter her family, now her family was in fact shattered, and they had this to deal with on top of everything else.

"May I please use the restroom?" Greta asked, suddenly rising to her feet.

Alyssa grabbed her elbow. "You don't look well. I'll come with you." They walked together down the hall, and after entering the large restroom, Alyssa said bluntly, "I'm sorry, but if you want us to free your son, we need to know everything."

Just thinking about confessing her secret caused her entire body to freeze. Alyssa had it wrong, and Greta knew she had some explaining to do but stumbled on how to say it, any of it. She wanted to keep her secret and save her son, but she knew she couldn't have it both ways. She'd told Emily, but she wasn't ready to tell Patrick, especially publicly. It was bad enough she had hidden it from him, but to share now felt like an even deeper betrayal than him never knowing. She definitely never imagined breaking this promise to herself by telling her sister and now telling a stranger.

Nausea overcame her as she realized how long she'd lived with this secret. She thought back to how her best friend, Audrey, had been so judgmental about keeping this from Patrick, but Greta was now disgusted by how her secret was the seed of destruction in her life. She needed to tell Alyssa. If there was any way it would help Logan get the help he needed, she had to try and make things right for the first time in her life.

Greta remained still and listened to Alyssa speak in a soft, comforting tone. "Lots of clients have shared similar issues to yours. They have had affairs, and we can be discreet, but we need to know about your children's heredity so we can get the facts right in the case. We're searching for proof of mental illness, and considering how few doctors feel comfortable diagnosing a kid of fourteen, correct genealogy is more important than usual." She paused and, when Greta said nothing, continued, "Greta, this kind of thing happens *all the time*. We aren't judging you. We just need to know to have a shot at winning this."

Greta took a breath and finally let the secret out. "The babies are Patrick's and . . . I used donor eggs . . . and I . . . I never told Patrick." After so many years of holding it in, the weight veritably flew off her shoulders now that it had been shared with someone else. The feeling was so sudden, she felt like she might collapse, as if the secret itself had been holding her up.

"Okay, I'm familiar with how to get in touch with donors," Alyssa said. "I'll need your paperwork, for the donor number. If you could call the doctor again and be sure he's aware we have permission to access your files and that the donor has permission to contact us and you, that'd be great."

"Patrick doesn't know about the donor," Greta said again. Part of her was relieved that one more person knew, and it wasn't really in her hands now if her husband finally learned the truth—though that didn't mean she wasn't feeling nauseated about it. "Please don't use this information unless it's the *only* way to save Logan," she said. Dizziness overcame her as she realized that once this lie was out, Patrick would leave her. This was the final nail in the coffin for her family.

But maybe it would save her son.

Chapter Thirty-Two

COLETTE

2021

The week before the trial, Colette was exhausted. She'd worked seemingly nonstop for months, and now, with it looming, she was torn. She knew how much winning would mean for Frank, but she couldn't help but feel sorry for the O'Briens. Though she'd dealt with so much pain on her own path to motherhood—a destination she still hadn't reached—she couldn't imagine what Greta O'Brien must have been going through, knowing one child had killed the other, mourning and raging and struggling to forgive because of a deep love all at the same time.

At home that night, she flicked through the mail, her eyes catching on one piece in particular: Dr. Erikson's office and the Edison Fertility Bank. The doctor she associated with heartbreak. A pit formed in her stomach, but it didn't stay there long. It started to rise almost immediately, making her unsure whether she was going to be sick or cry. She knew it couldn't be good news.

"Sweetie, did you want pork chops?" Vic said, clearly having asked already.

She met his eyes. He was adorable—a little rumpled, already ready for bed, having just waited up for her to get home to see her briefly before he had to go to sleep. Their schedules were so rarely fully in sync, but he was so understanding, so supportive. She wouldn't have gotten through her missing eggs or her miscarriages, losing Tripp, and most importantly, her diagnosis without him.

Dr. Brooks had pushed her hard to examine the key occasions in her past where she had lost time. She had asked her to really dig deep, to face the harsh realities that surrounded those episodes. It hadn't happened overnight. It had taken a long time for Colette to face her past. With her pregnancy and her loss of Tripp, she hadn't been able to force herself to do the hard work required of her. But with her doctor's help, she had little by little been able to fill her journal with memories and put the pieces together.

Colette had forced herself to think about the time her mother had set her tree house on fire, the time her mother had locked her in the doll hospital, her abortion, her father's death, and most importantly the time her eggs went missing. She had rummaged through all her paperwork, any evidence she had for these events. The most glaring proof that each moment shared was the signature scratched onto each document. The police reports, the abortion paperwork, the autopsy, and the egg-donation papers . . . they all shared a signature that Colette could not remember once using in her life. "C. C.," the name she hated most, the nickname her mother had given her, was signed on every single document during times of trouble. Every document that Colette had no memory of signing. Working on the case had really brought some of her worst memories to the forefront, and she finally had the courage to face them. When she had brought her journal to her doctor and they had pored through it together, the answer was clear.

The next appointment she had gone to, Dr. Brooks had seemed apprehensive but firm in her delivery. Colette couldn't catch her breath as the doctor told her the news.

"Colette, I am so sorry, but you have DID, which is dissociative identity disorder," the doctor had said, leaning over to grab her hand and give it a tight squeeze.

Colette's hand lay limp in the doctor's, her body and mind numb. She couldn't imagine that her worst fear, what she had prayed against happening her entire life, was coming true.

"I promise, I will help you get through this," Dr. Brooks said. "And I encourage you to seek support through NA regularly and call your sponsor daily to avoid relapse while we work through this together."

At these words, an overwhelming sense of relief tumbled through Colette. The diagnosis was jarring, but it allowed her to put her lifelong fears of what was to become of her to rest. Dr. Brooks assured her that they would come up with a comprehensive plan that would include medication and therapy to control her condition. Instead of living each day feeling afraid of a diagnosis lurking in her future, she finally had answers.

Colette had suspected it after investigating and discovering C.C.'s signature. But in the weeks and months following her doctor's confirmation, she found herself spiraling deep into a pit of despair that she couldn't imagine ever digging herself out of. This couldn't be happening. She had only ever wanted to be "normal." And now genetics was playing a cruel game with her fate. Her knee-jerk reaction was to take a pill, or a drink, anything to numb her feelings of hopelessness.

The diagnosis rocked Vic's world too, and Colette had feared he would leave her, but he had stayed, strong and steady. He'd been there for her through it all, everything that came after, even when it threatened his sobriety because hers had been threatened.

Colette's diagnosis of DID had been an absolute blow for both of them, but they worked hard to remain stable and immersed themselves in education around the disease. Colette Catharine Richards De Luca had just one other personality state she and Dr. Brooks could identify: C.C. Richards. It was tough, protective, chain-smoking C.C. who had emerged after one too many abusive episodes from Colette's mother. Colette had taken the blame the time her mother had told the police she had started the fire in the tree house and kept her mouth shut to teachers, her father, Aunt Lisa, and anyone else who questioned the safety of her homelife. This fact had comforted Colette in her journey to acclimate herself and accept her diagnosis. This other personality, or "alter," was protecting her. It was her body's way of blocking out anything that could potentially harm Colette.

After the terrifying time at the doll hospital, C.C. had been the one to finally tell the truth. In an effort to protect Colette, she had told the kind policeman why she was locked in the back room of the doll hospital, which had resulted in her mother going away and her father coming back to care for her. The C.C. who had protected her from the terrifying doll hospital had taken over on more than one occasion when she found herself in precarious situations with her drug dealers and was the one who had signed the abortion paperwork. When her father was dying, the nurse had said she knew what to do. Colette had interpreted that as meaning she should sit with him, be with him. It was C.C. who had interpreted it as "help him end his misery" and had poured the heroin Colette had found at her dealer's house earlier that day into a shake and fed it to him. C.C. also had conveniently been the one signing the paperwork for her father and checked the box that said "No Autopsy Requested."

And most important in Colette's deep dive into her illness and her alter, she realized with absolute horror that in fact it had been C.C. who had sold Colette's eggs. This act had likely been performed as a means to prevent Colette from ever having to face motherhood, to protect her from her deepest and darkest fears. But she would never fully understand C.C.'s motives or thought processes.

For years, she'd suffered blackouts on a regular basis that she thought were brought on by her drug use and drinking but were actually C.C. She'd experienced depersonalization as well—the feeling of being outside her body, a mere observer—especially when she'd performed sexual favors for drugs. But what it came down to was that the greatest fear she'd had as a child—being like her mother—had come true. They may not have had the same diagnosis, but that was splitting hairs as far as Colette was concerned. And what she had been most afraid of for all her adult life—not becoming a mother—had been part of what caused her greatest trauma. But then, most moms would probably say that—when you have a child, part of your heart lives outside you.

Without a word, she held the envelope out to Vic.

He stepped forward and squinted, understanding dawning in his gaze when he saw the return address. "You want me to open it?" He set the plate of cold food down on the table. He took it from her and ripped it open, the proverbial Band-Aid gone. She kept her eyes on his, watching as they flitted back and forth at a seemingly frantic pace, taking it all in.

"I . . ." He looked up at her, eyes wide. "You have to read it. I think . . . I think they're asking you to testify . . . in the case you're working on."

That was a curveball. She'd been expecting something more personal, more revealing of her past. Her hand shook as she took the letter back from him, her eyes raking over the information—the donor number matched the one she had inked on her wrist, and the requested contact stated two names: Greta O'Brien and Alyssa Arthur at Cashvan & Goldsmith Law.

She gasped as the sudden realization shook her. Greta had used donor eggs.

She couldn't believe that it had been right in front of her the whole time and she had missed it.

Chapter Thirty-Three

GRETA

The Night Before the Trial

The kitchen clock flashed 1:00 a.m. She stood in the dark, thinking. It was the night before the trial, and she had just hung up the phone, a shiver enveloping her body.

Greta's eyes fell on the bundle of sage on the kitchen counter that Audrey had given her. She fumbled in a drawer and found a lighter, then ignited the dried leaves and placed them on a ceramic dish. She began praying, praying for Logan from the deepest recesses of her heart.

It was hard to process the information she had just been given from Alyssa while simultaneously worrying about Patrick being blindsided by her biggest lie. She was annoyed he was asleep, but she had to wake him up. It was time to confess.

She had imagined this moment—drumming up the courage to confess—so many times over the years, but she had never thought it would be like this. Emily's voice echoed in her head telling her it was too much, and part of her wanted to let Patrick take this bullet of truth in the courtroom tomorrow. But it felt cruel to do that to him. It would be worse than the original lie, to let a stranger tell him what she had done. And now that she knew it was coming out, she had to wake him and admit her mistake.

She tapped on his shoulder, her insides squirming. Patrick wriggled around and woke easily. "Is it time to get ready?"

"No, no, you just fell asleep on the sofa, but there's something I need to talk to you about."

Her addiction to perfection now felt like a compulsion to keep this secret.

"What is it? I'm just as scared as you," he said.

Why did he have to utter his most gentle words right before this blow? Greta reminded herself he was hurting too, but her grief seemed even more toxic. Her confession came out slowly.

"Patrick, when I was younger, I brought my best friend to my dad's office. I remember she was so enamored by his big leather chairs. She made photocopies of the grade-school magazine we'd invented. Being there reminded me of when I'd been younger and used to see the drawings I'd made for my dad, crumpled up in the trash. Anyway, while Carole Ann was busy putting the gossip column together, I overheard my father telling Bianca he loved her and wished he didn't have a family."

Patrick put his hand on Greta's shoulder and squeezed. She couldn't avoid the truth any longer. She knew she was stalling. "When I heard my father say he didn't want us, it made me want to do family differently. But then it was so hard . . ." Her words were replaced with tears. "And when I met you, I just forced it, and . . ."

She couldn't tell him about faking the pregnancy, but she believed her first miscarriage was punishment for her lies, and she hadn't learned her lesson. She clenched her stomach, the knots she felt more painful than bleeding into the tub the night she had lost her first biological child. She had never really mourned that loss until very recently.

"You went through a lot to give me a family," Patrick said. "The doctor's visits, the shots, they didn't go unnoticed. I think about it too."

"You could have told me you noticed the effort back then. All I felt was pressure."

"I'm sorry. It's just that all our friends were having kids, and I didn't get why it was so hard for you."

"Well, I'm older than you, and you were so mean when I brought up adoption."

"You didn't want real kids?"

"I wanted to be loved, I wanted a family, but you made me feel like without biological kids, I wasn't enough. It hurt."

"I never said that," he said, wiping a tear from Greta's face. "Well, it is what it is, and we did it, and I fucking hope that, for once, your money can get him out of this, because if my son's in jail for the rest of his life, I'm going to kill myself."

"Our son," Greta said, his tone making her slow the confession once again. She felt the same disconnection with him that she had tried so hard to ignore.

"Patrick, I lied."

He quickly shifted into a full upright position, sitting on the couch, his eyes wide open.

"Our sons were conceived using donor eggs, and Alyssa has found their donor. It's going to come out in court tomorrow."

Greta winced as Patrick's angry words spilled out. "What the fuck are you talking about? You aren't our kids' mother?"

Greta had said "their donor," not "their mother." *She* was their mother.

"I didn't know what to do. You pressured me to want a perfect family."

"Me!" he snapped. "*You* wanted all this perfect shit." He pointed at the tall glass vases, a Steuben sculpture of tennis players etched in glass, and the picture frames that adorned the living room.

She continued: "And it wasn't working. You saw me suffer miscarriages, failed IVFs. Dr. Erikson said this would increase my chances, and I knew you'd say no! What the hell was I supposed to do, Patrick? You looked so disappointed when I had that miscarriage, like it was all about you. I knew you'd leave me if I didn't lie!"

"So you trapped me. Is that even legal, to hide you didn't have your own kids?"

"Patrick, the thing is, they couldn't be more my own. And the fact that you can't get that, can't see that, makes me know this marriage is over. The fact that you are making this all about you, again . . ."

"I should have never underestimated you Walshes," Patrick said, his voice stone cold.

His words stung, but she meant it when she said, "I'm not like them."

"You're just like them," he snarled, his own grief likely feeding his anger. Greta was more than willing to be his temporary punching bag. The bruises were less hurtful than she had imagined. She realized perfection hadn't caused her powerlessness—loneliness had. And she knew in this moment that a person could be married with children and still feel alone.

"I'm sorry, Patrick. When I bought the eggs, my walls were crumbling, and then the only thing I knew how to do was grab a brick and try to build something. Now I know it was wrong, and we're sitting in the middle of this nightmare, and all I can do is fight like hell to save my son."

"Our son," Patrick said, his voice cracking. "I don't know if I can even go tomorrow. I can't hold your hand and walk into the courtroom and pretend we're a united front when all I feel for you is disgust."

"I'm sorry I lied."

"I can't go."

"You have to come to court, not for me, but for Logan."

"I just don't know if I can be as fake as you."

Patrick got up, walked across the room, and threw a family photo of them against the wall. Glass shattered into a million little pieces as Greta sobbed.

He opened the front door and slammed it behind him. Greta exhaled. His car screeched away, but this time shame didn't overtake her. She had just faced her biggest fear head-on, and while she hoped that Patrick would show up in the courtroom, she didn't regret warning him of what they would need to face, together, to save their only living son.

~

The next morning was the first day of Logan's trial, and Patrick pulled into the driveway an hour before they needed to leave. Greta didn't even ask him where he had been. They got ready in silence and then drove in together, parked, and walked hand in hand as the lawyer had instructed up the steep courthouse stairs, ignoring the media. Greta whispered, "Thank you." She had dressed impeccably and had bought Patrick a striking suit in gray, hoping to appear nice but not too overbearing or coming off as rich, aloof parents. It was the most she'd thought about clothing since that Halloween last year, when she'd gotten that fancy costume and had her makeup done. Her former lifestyle now nauseated her.

She sat near Patrick in the hallway outside the courtroom, nervously tapping her foot. Manny and Alyssa arrived, both looking polished and more professional than the opposing counsel, she thought, but that made sense when she thought about the state's attorney's salary versus the one Manny must have earned in private practice with Greenwich's elite as clients.

Patrick squeezed her hand, and when she looked at him, he gave her the weakest smile she'd ever seen. But it made her heart nearly burst. Everything else in their marriage they'd messed up, but this—this, they could do together. She was grateful that following her confession he'd even shown up, and a part of them seemed united.

Their sole focus was Logan: getting their son a not guilty by reason of insanity plea and getting him the help he so desperately needed.

Despite the fact that he'd murdered Brayden, Logan was still their son. She vacillated between grief for one son and her instinct to protect the other. Right now all Greta could do was pray that he'd be mandated to live at Lakewood, a mental health hospital in Connecticut.

When it was finally time, Greta and Patrick walked into the courtroom still holding hands and sat down behind their legal team. Greta had taken a moment to direct a glare at the television crews spaced apart outside; the media ebbed and flowed, but she'd never forgive the people who had referred to the story of her family's tragedy as "sibling rivalry gone too far" and called Logan "the Sauna Slayer." She was grateful Manny had managed to get the courtroom closed to the public.

Greta felt like one giant raw nerve, a rush of anxiety nearly overwhelming her when she thought about looking at the strangers in the jury box who were there, literally, to judge her child. It was all profoundly surreal. Not long ago, from the outside at least, their lives had seemed enviable: money, looks, all of life's comforts, twin teens with the promise of bright and shiny lives, a handsome, athletic father and a pretty and successful mother. But Greta knew they weren't those things—or at least, they weren't *only* those things. Below the facade they were also a family with two young boys whose mother was too busy for them most of the time, one son who clearly had problems they had been too preoccupied to act on, a wife who'd cheated on her husband, who'd based their entire relationship on a lie, really—one drunk night of fun had turned into a backup plan for an unwanted baby, which had turned into a backup plan for her life. Put like that, she wondered if she didn't deserve this.

Now, they'd suffered a tragedy, lost a child, viciously ripped from them by their surviving son, destined to go down in history as a modern-day Cain and Abel saga. Greta knew that if the accused were not her own son, she wouldn't have felt an ounce of pity for him. Grief oddly had some positive qualities that surprised her. It was as if she could breathe more easily because of her sons. Sensing Brayden's presence became part of her breath, and her desire to make Logan a priority finally felt natural, an exhale unlike anything before the tragedy.

Logan entered the courtroom in the clothes they'd brought for him to change into—nice but not too nice—and sat six feet in front of them. Greta felt dizzy when the judge came in and began his initial comments: "Logan O'Brien is here today, being charged with second-degree manslaughter . . ."

It felt like the room was closing in on her, and she grabbed Patrick's arm and took a few deep breaths, unsure of what was about to happen. The prosecuting attorney stood up and walked toward the judge as he began speaking. While she sat there, ostensibly listening to Frank Marciano's opening remarks, she replayed all the times she'd said "maybe later" when Logan asked her to play a game. Now it was too late. Even if they got the best possible outcome, it meant years in a mental-care facility for her son.

~

For the first few days, the state's attorney called his witnesses to the stand: psychologists, a few teachers, poor Zeke, their family doctor, and camp counselors. Listening to them say they had never seen any signs of mental illness and couldn't think of any reason why Logan would act violently against his brother was reassuring until she realized they were, of course, laying the groundwork to make the defense's plea seem implausible. They described Logan as a "loner" and "painfully shy," reminding Greta of how people described serial killers. She cringed internally.

Behind her sat only a few supporters: her in-laws, her mother, and everyone who entered the courtroom needed to be screened. Greta was grateful that it was closed to anyone else. She still hadn't spoken much with Patrick's parents—she hadn't had the energy or the focus—but she was grateful to have their attempts of support. As she stared at Logan, this killer she'd raised, she took in his appearance—his once olive skin was now pale; his eyes had dark circles; his clothing hung loosely on his frame, and she realized she should have bought him something new instead of bringing old clothing. Despite living his last months at the center, where he certainly wasn't getting the physical activity or nutrition he needed, he'd grown, and she saw his pants were a little too short for him now.

A camp counselor was talking now, telling the story of Logan shooting Brayden in the leg with an arrow. Greta thought about when he had held a kid underwater and how her own embarrassment had prevented her from doing more after the incident. She pushed the thought away; she couldn't keep blaming herself.

When Mr. Marciano pushed the counselor, he confessed that he thought it might have been done on purpose. Logan was a novice archer, and accidents can happen; however, Brayden had been standing quite a way off from the target, which meant it would have been very hard to misfire that much and perhaps it was intentional.

"Objection, Your Honor," Manny barked. "Speculation."

"The witness is an expert marksman himself as well as the person who trained the defendant," Mr. Marciano responded. "Surely he can speak to the likelihood of misfiring, if not actual intent."

His point had been made regardless, and Greta hadn't been able to keep her eyes from straying to the jury, to see what their reaction was. She had to keep reminding herself that they weren't denying that Logan did it; they were just trying to say he didn't understand what he was doing. The state's attorney's opening statement echoed in her head: *extreme indifference to human life.*

She couldn't let her mind go there. These were just words he was paid to say; it wasn't the truth. Her son wasn't a psychopath. The state's attorney and the witnesses he called made Logan out to be an affluent, jealous, spiteful murderer with a history of violence. The arrow shot into his brother's leg, the school field trip—these were true stories, but they were only pieces of the whole picture.

Chapter Thirty-Four

COLETTE

Wednesday, Third Day of Trial

Colette pulled on her lucky black suit as she gazed at herself in the mirror. Her eyes looked weary, and the concealer she had applied had not hidden the dark circles and puffiness. The suit looked like every other one she owned, but it was the one she had worn the first time she'd been the lead paralegal on one of Frank's big cases, and they had won.

She hadn't had long to process everything, but she was proud of herself. Her mind had buzzed and she had tasted the powder of a pill on her tongue, fantasized about the beautiful feeling of mind and body numbness that she used to crave. But she wasn't that person anymore. She was strong; she had been through so much. Today would be one more tough day in her life, and she would persevere.

She tugged on the right jacket sleeve to cover the tattoo on her wrist, then changed her mind and pulled it up for a moment, tracing the black-inked numbers tattooed on her skin with her finger. Her brain didn't have the capacity to insert all this new information into actuality; it was too big, too life changing. It was jarring enough to find your biological children after years of grief and learning to "let go and let God" and coming to terms with the loss, but learning they were the murdered and the murderer, the victim and the perpetrator? It was incomprehensible, like seeing the two sides that have constantly warred within you springing to life outside your body, Athena springing from Zeus's head—only this felt like one child from her addictions, her mother's illness, her heartbreak and one from her hope.

Colette blinked back the raw emotion, swiped on some lip gloss, and pulled her long hair into a low bun. She was queasy as she headed downstairs to get her things, but she forced herself to eat a banana with her coffee. She glanced at her phone, saw the time, and called out to Vic.

"I'm ready," he said, walking down the stairs. He'd taken the few extra hours of sleep he'd been given by going to court with her today instead of to work, but he still looked slightly off to her. She quickly realized it was the suit—she hadn't seen him in one since they'd had the service for Tripp. And yet despite all they had been through, even now with this mind-blowing news, he was there . . . for her. Standing in his suit, strong and ready to support her. A feeling of gratitude tumbled through her, temporarily taking the place of her frazzled nerves.

Her stomach flipped. If that letter hadn't reached her, she knew that Frank would have had a great shot of putting Logan O'Brien away for life—though she'd always been torn about that prospect and now had no desire for that to be the outcome.

In criminal cases, the prosecutor was required to disclose all their information to the defense as long as the defense was regularly filing discovery requests. So while the defense was entitled to know about the prosecution's case before trial, the prosecution did not have the same luxury, which meant that while Colette's name would have appeared on an amended witness list filed sometime this week, it would have appeared along with her doctors' names as well and perhaps would not have registered with Frank so close to trial, especially without Colette herself there to highlight the meaningful changes in the massive amounts of paperwork that accompanied such a trial. It was a little bit underhanded, but she had no choice. She would resign as soon as this was over.

As she and Vic struggled to get through the dozens of reporters and cameramen camped out in front of the courthouse, no one paid them much attention. She was well known around the courthouse by the local reporters, and she wasn't noteworthy at this point to anyone else. It still felt like having to run the gauntlet just getting into the building to be rid of them, though, and when they got inside and had to go through security, she wasn't sure whether it was Vic's hand or her own that had made both of their palms so sweaty.

Through security, they walked into the courtroom, Colette guilt ridden just seeing the back of Frank's head. It all made her feel terrible, and she wished there had been a way for him to not be blindsided by it in court, but there wasn't. It was going to be one hell of a blow. It'd been one hell of a blow to her.

Outside of the immediate future and this trial, Colette had no idea what she was supposed to do, how she was supposed to go on from here. She was used to having setbacks, emotional kicks in the pants that had made her up her drug use when she was still using and increase her trips to NA meetings nowadays. But this was different. This was the answer to a lifelong desire for children of her own wrapped up in more contradictions than she'd thought possible. She was a mother; her eggs, which she'd finally accepted were gone and she'd never know how or why, had suddenly been tracked, and she now knew they had become beautiful boys—twins. Twins she would never be a real mother to because they had one. They had a woman who had wanted them so badly she had looked outside her own biology for help; had carried them, birthed them, and raised them. And now one of those boys was gone forever, a soul she'd never get to know, and the other may have been suffering due to something she passed along.

She worried her whole life about becoming her mother, and though she hadn't, she did suffer from a similar disorder. She was nothing to that poor boy, nothing more to his parents than an egg donor, but she was faced with the clear and undeniable fact that she had passed along something that they had not known about. Colette's own diagnosis had taken far longer than it should have—her fear of the truth, her denial, her addictions, and cloaking her symptoms had created the perfect storm for her to hide from it—but at least she had been aware it was a possibility. This family had clearly been blindsided in the most awful way.

Last week, she had had a long conversation with her therapist and had tried to start working through her crushing guilt. It felt like it was her fault. She had set this in motion during an episode. But her illness was not about fault. It was an illness. And she was working hard to keep in mind that blaming herself was the same as blaming anyone for being ill—she wouldn't do that. No one would. Yet it was hard to push the what-ifs out of her consciousness. Her biggest one was what if she had never fallen in that snowy street in New York? Would she have never gotten addicted to drugs? Stayed married to Rob? Used her eggs as they were originally intended? Given birth to one or two or three beautiful, healthy children? But she forced herself to remember that this line of thinking would do nothing but hurt her. She had to let go. But being here in this moment, ready to testify about something this young man—her son—did, seeing his parents, their sadness and fear, it was hard.

The noise in the small courtroom increased as it filled up with court staff, attorneys, family and friends of the accused, and several reporters. Colette decided to still sit on the side of the prosecution, and Vic followed her lead. The jury was brought in, and when the judge entered the room, silence rippled through the small crowd.

The air in the room shifted as Logan O'Brien was escorted to his seat. Her heart pounded, guilt spreading out from her core as she watched. She felt almost like she knew him—after spending so many months interviewing people he knew, digging up details of his life, and of course having the almost uncanny moment of connection when she'd looked into his eyes that first day at the police station. It now loomed large in her mind, spoke to her of some primal knowing, as if it had been trying to tell her that this boy, this teenager who'd been a rising tennis star, had had a twin brother whom he'd killed, this boy was . . . *hers*.

After sitting through a tense morning when she didn't particularly notice what was going on, her anxiety too high for that, she filed back in after a brief lunch recess and sat on the defense's side, next to her doctor, who was also on the witness list for today. Colette gave her a reassuring smile as Manny Cashvan stood up to call his next witness—a fertility expert. Frank looked over at her with confusion right before the judge returned from his chambers and the bailiff said, "All rise." Colette looked away from Frank. He would figure it out soon enough.

As the testimony began, they discussed genetics and what it meant when egg donors and sperm donors passed along their genetic makeup (good or bad) to the children conceived. He outlined the flawed guidelines and laws that were in place to protect prospective egg recipients and cited numerous cases where genetics had negatively affected children born via IVF.

The fertility expert was dismissed from the stand, and Manny Cashvan said, "The defense would like to call Colette Richards De Luca to the stand, Your Honor."

She closed her eyes and took a deep breath. *I can do this. I'm strong and I will survive this. And I have to do it. I have no choice.*

Frank whipped around and found Colette, clearly confused before shooting to his feet. "Objection, Your Honor. There was no notice of this witness."

"We sent over the amendment Monday morning, Your Honor," Mr. Cashvan stated. "We'd actually included her on the witness list before arguments started, but we didn't fill in the name until Monday morning. The notice was sent over to Mr. Marciano's office and received by Colette De Luca herself."

"Noted," the judge said.

Colette stood up without making eye contact with Frank and made her way to the stand. She had given him the new witness list right before trial in a folder, but he hadn't noticed the amendment. It felt like she was walking through water, the slow-motion sensation, the silence pounding loudly in her ears, the heaviness of gravity. She concentrated on just making it to the seat. Once there, the defense attorney asked her to identify herself to the court.

"My name is Colette Catharine Richards De Luca, and I work for the state's attorney's office as a paralegal."

"Objection, Your Honor," Frank said, throwing his hands up with exasperation. "A paralegal at the state's attorney's office cannot be called for the defense."

"Your Honor, Mrs. De Luca will not be speaking as a paralegal."

The judge called the attorneys to sidebar, speaking in low susurrations, before motioning them back to their tables and stating, "Overruled." He looked down at Colette curiously.

Colette had worried about this moment, worried that the judge would not allow her to testify. She breathed a sigh of relief.

"Mrs. De Luca, can you explain to the court what your experience has been with infertility?" Mr. Cashvan asked.

Colette took a deep breath, exhaled, and began telling the courtroom full of strangers about her first marriage, her unintended pregnancy, and her egg freezing. When she concluded her story with the forging of her signature on the paperwork to sell her eggs, several people gasped.

"Your Honor, I am presenting exhibit twenty-seven to Mrs. De Luca," the defense attorney said. He handed a paper to Colette and a copy to the judge. "Mrs. De Luca, can you please tell me what you see before you?"

"This is paperwork from Edison Fertility Bank that outlines the purchase of frozen eggs from donor 96360," Colette said, reading as she'd been instructed.

"And who was the recipient of these eggs?"

"Greta O'Brien." Colette spared a glance at the O'Briens—the husband looked poleaxed and the wife as though she'd just learned someone else had died.

"If you flip to the next page there"—Mr. Cashvan pointed to the papers in Colette's hands as he handed the judge another sheet—"you also will see exhibit twenty-eight from retired fertility doctor Dr. Nathan Erikson. Can you read the report from the fertility doctor outlining a procedure done for Greta O'Brien?"

This was beyond her knowledge, but he needed someone to read it into evidence, someone the jury could listen to. She cleared her throat. "Dr. Erikson obtained twelve donated eggs from the Edison Fertility Bank. Per the request of the client, the donor was anonymous and only listed by number. Mrs. O'Brien had these eggs fertilized with Mr. Patrick O'Brien's sperm, and then Dr. Erikson chose the best four to implant. After three successfully attached to the uterine wall, on medical advice from Dr. Erikson, the patient opted for selective reduction, which resulted in two healthy fetuses from the same donor." Colette tried to hide her own surprise at the news that they could have been triplets.

The lawyer pressed on. "I'm now presenting exhibit twenty-nine, Your Honor," Mr. Cashvan said as he reached for two papers on his desk and again handed one to the judge and one to Colette. "It is an affidavit stating the identification of the anonymous egg donor associated with 96360. Can you read the name for me?"

She sat up straight and looked Mr. Cashvan in the eye with as much courage as she could muster. "Colette Richards."

The courtroom erupted in murmurs and cries. The judge slammed down his gavel to quiet everyone, and Colette watched as Frank shuffled through papers, frantic to find the paperwork for exhibit twenty-nine.

"Are you absolutely positive about this identification?" the attorney reiterated.

"I'm one hundred percent sure," Colette confirmed, pulling up her sleeve to reveal the donor number branded on her wrist.

"Let the record show the witness is showing a wrist tattoo with this exact number. Mrs. De Luca, thank you."

Colette didn't want to think it, because he was a decent lawyer and, in this instance, was trying to help a kid, but she thought he looked a little smug as he turned to Frank. "Your witness."

Chapter Thirty-Five

GRETA

Third Day of Trial

As Mrs. De Luca testified, the moment Greta had been afraid of for sixteen years had come. It had felt like her insides were being scooped out, her lungs trying to fly out of her chest. But she was still breathing—her hand pressed to her chest at least assured her of that much, as she could feel her rib cage expand and release. She tugged on her blouse, stuck to her skin with a cold sweat.

This was it: her nadir. She'd lost one child, the other was on trial, and her biggest secret was finally out. Patrick knew—Patrick, who had gone from not being able to hold back the anger in his face to clearly upset to radiating the same relief she was feeling, yet still unable to look at her. Poor Patrick. She hadn't even had the guts to look at him while the woman was talking, her hand holding his becoming more and more rigid. He had eventually shaken off her grip, but it was okay—everything would be okay. She'd faced her biggest fear and was still breathing, albeit short breaths. She knew she'd finally done the right thing by telling Alyssa and warning him the night before the trial. It didn't matter that her in-laws and mother were likely judging her harshly; they had just witnessed her confession, publicly, and would hopefully understand that though she had held this truth from all of them, she'd shared her secret when it really mattered, when it might save their grandson.

The prosecutor asked a few sputtering questions and quickly sat, the judge telling Mrs. De Luca she could now step down.

Manny stood again. "We call Dr. Gabrielle Brooks."

As Mrs. De Luca returned to her seat, she passed the doctor, the woman giving her a warm look as they did. What had just happened, Greta had been prepared for—at least in some sense. She'd known it could happen—probably would happen—ever since she'd confessed what she'd done. She'd gotten used to it, though, that feeling of balancing on a tightrope constantly, always being phony. When she really thought about it, she'd been doing it for years before. Her family was so far from what they presented to the outside world that she'd basically been raised in that mask, worn it so long she was a little surprised it hadn't just become her face, surprised she could still tell the difference. Whatever happened with Patrick was secondary. Her face was bare now, vulnerable under the gaze of others for the first time she could remember. And it had helped Logan, *would* help him. Finding her way through life, learning to be truthful, and becoming her actual self would be difficult, but she now had faith.

What she hadn't been prepared for was the effect seeing this woman—Mrs. De Luca, Colette—would have on her. The woman had been her dirty little secret, and while Greta herself was okay being exposed, her first reaction to Colette in the flesh was unkind. This woman should have been in the shadows, not walking around in a beautiful black suit, looking demure and put together.

But a pang of a deep emotion Greta could identify only as love exploded in her chest. She wouldn't have had her boys at all if it weren't for this woman. This woman whom she had purposefully *not* thought about, tried to never wonder about, because it brought her lies closer to the surface. She could never have imagined her sons' biological mother, but she saw her boys in her—Logan more than Brayden, though they both had her eyes. The woman had ragged cuticles, like Logan. She even brought her hand to her mouth as Greta watched, beginning to chew on her thumb in a similar way to her son. Their son? God, this was confusing. There were too many emotions rushing through her, so much on the line and so much being exposed, that she felt frantic, unable to pin anything down. It overwhelmed her to the point that it didn't occur to her what was happening on the stand until she heard the name of the egg donor again.

"And, Dr. Brooks, you are currently treating Mrs. De Luca, is that correct?" Manny was asking.

"It is. She's given me permission to discuss her mental health in court today, as well as her history."

"And she's sacrificing her job for her testimony." He turned briefly and shot Mrs. De Luca a smile, causing Greta to turn and look as well. "If we can briefly discuss the importance of establishing a genetic history for my client, can you speak to why it's so difficult to prove insanity in court?"

The doctor recrossed her legs, and a sinking in Greta's gut outweighed everything else she'd been feeling. Of course—Manny and his assistant had said they'd reveal all this only if it was necessary. That meant something in the IVF or DNA had caused . . . had contributed to . . . Oh God.

"Well, it's important to understand that 'insanity' is not a mental health concept. Psychiatrists and psychologists, we don't call someone 'insane.' That's a legal distinction alone. We have categories of mental health issues: dissociative disorders, stress disorders, anxiety disorders, and so on. But we don't have 'insane.'

"Beyond that, as Dr. Brown said in her testimony this morning, it's incredibly difficult to diagnose an adolescent with a disorder. Adolescents' brains are still forming, changing, evolving, and they're doing this constantly, so if the brain itself isn't done changing, how can we diagnose? Making it even more difficult is the fact that mental disorders do not come with simple tests. It's not like a blood test or even a brain scan can tell us what's going on. Meaning, we diagnose people based on their behavior. Adolescents often act without reason and have issues with impulse control or an inability to think reasonably. These are all mainstays of being a juvenile, so it gets difficult."

Greta was lost somewhere between grief and relief. She glanced at the jury, and they seemed open to what this doctor was saying, but this meant her decision all those years ago to give Patrick "what he wanted" instead of admitting her own fertility problems had been the first step in creating her family and also destroying it.

Manny had his hands in his pockets—his casual, relatable stance—as he asked, "And so that makes genetics more of a factor?"

Dr. Brooks nodded and Greta couldn't look away now. "It does. It means that, instead of looking only at what Logan did when he was seven or ten, or even just before Halloween of last year, we should also look at the likelihood that he will suffer from a mental disorder as he gets older. If he has a higher likelihood, it means that his behavior has a much higher likelihood of having already been affected by it. However, on the positive side, it also means he has a better chance of responding to treatment now, while his brain is still developing."

Greta noticed Patrick's face was pale, and he had dark circles under his eyes that were worn from more than the sun. His blank expression made each line look as if it were a reminder of the combined mistakes they'd made. She saw he was suffering, and part of her wanted to explain that the lie she'd begun their relationship on had grown into a web of other lies with using donor eggs in the middle of it. But he wouldn't even look at her.

"I see," Manny replied, nodding. "That's fascinating. So if Logan's genes on the donor's side show that type of likelihood, to use your word, it's more likely he was unaware of the consequences of locking the sauna door or was having an episode of some kind, and he's more likely to respond positively to psychological care."

"That's correct."

"And what does his donor side look like, genetically speaking?"

This time, Dr. Brooks made eye contact with the woman who'd just testified before answering. "Colette Richards De Luca's mother is a diagnosed schizophrenic who has been institutionalized since 1984."

Greta was sure she'd misheard. Why had Manny not told them about this? Alyssa at least could have warned her. It briefly flitted through her brain that Manny had warned her once that she was paying the bills but that Logan was his client, and she wondered if Logan had asked his lawyer not to give her a heads-up, a small stab back at her for the secret she'd kept from him. But that seemed like a wild thing to concern herself with at this moment. Keeping track of where she felt the blame was falling was like watching an expert playing the shell game for her mark.

"And Mrs. De Luca herself?"

Greta held her breath. Lawyers didn't ask questions they didn't know the answers to. He was waiting for a reveal that would affect the jury and their case.

Patrick turned and whispered to Greta, "This better help the case." He squeezed her hand, and she knew it wasn't to impress the judge. He was praying too.

"After many years of struggling with addiction, Colette suffered a few episodes, to use your words"—the woman gave Manny a wry smile—"totally sober and realized something not caused by drug use was affecting her mental state. We spent months going over her history. During her addiction, she'd had a number of blackouts and periods of not remembering, which she'd assumed were due to drug use. Unfortunately, while drug use doesn't trigger these types of episodes, it can mask them, so it took a while to unpack, but myself and a colleague who came in to give a secondary diagnosis agree that she has, and is currently managing quite well, dissociative identity disorder. Her diagnosis was likely caused from the early childhood trauma she endured."

And for the second time that day, even though she'd known it was coming, the bottom dropped out of Greta's world.

Chapter Thirty-Six

GRETA

2021

After Dr. Brooks's testimony, It didn't take Manny long to wrap up his arguments. Greta and Patrick went home together, and he'd asked her nothing, said nothing. He'd simply started packing his things. There was something freeing about the painful truth being out, and while she'd spent her entire marriage blaming herself for concealing a lie of this magnitude, she wasn't blaming herself as much as she'd always imagined she would. Just as she was able to see another side to her father's infidelity, to her son's aggression, she was able to see another side to her lie. A side that included self-compassion surrounding her desperate decision to conceive a child in the only way she knew how.

A few tense, silent hours later, Manny called them. The jury had come back.

Greta saw Colette as soon as they walked into the courtroom, but she had no ability to process her intense emotions, so she sat. Manny assured them it was a good sign that the jury was back that soon, then ignored them to talk to their son, as was only right. Logan had been relatively unemotional during the entire thing, but she assumed it was due to the massive amounts of antidepressant drugs they'd had him on while trying to diagnose him. She wanted to tell him that she was sorry she'd never gotten him the help he needed but trusted that they'd grow close enough to have that conversation someday.

The jury filed back in the room, then the judge directly on their heels, calling them to order as he sat. Greta felt like she barely had the time to breathe before he asked, "Lady foreperson, on the count of second-degree manslaughter, how does the jury find?"

The woman stood up and opened a piece of paper. In a strong voice, she said, "The jury finds the defendant not guilty by reason of insanity."

Patrick turned to Greta, pulled her to him, and gave her a long, hard kiss. It wasn't romantic. It wasn't a sign of forgiveness. Greta recognized it for what it was: the last kiss they would share, but also a promise that they would be able to put their son first when dealing with each other.

She pulled back to look him. "I will never apologize for having them." Her voice broke and his green eyes—those eyes she'd loved from the first—widened just a fraction, the surprise obvious. "But I am sorry, so sorry, I never told you."

He gave a tight nod and released her, and she thought she saw in his gaze that he recognized this was not only their last kiss but also the last time she would talk about the boys' conception. They'd all need time to come to terms with it, but now they had that time—and their son did too.

A few weeks ago, maybe even a few days ago, she would have wanted to sue the fertility clinic for giving her no information regarding her egg donor, for wrongful birth, failure to investigate, and fraud. But it would have been a knee-jerk reaction for Greta—to blame someone else, to threaten to sue. Listening to the judge sentence her son to time in a mental health hospital, it was clear that she'd first blamed herself, then Patrick, and then poor Colette, but then arrived at a place that superseded blame. She'd made peace with the fact that she'd faced something that went against the natural order of things. Greta had never imagined outliving her son.

As the judge banged his gavel to indicate that the case was over, Greta turned and saw tears in Colette's eyes. Before she could lose her nerve, Greta slid out of their row and approached her, fishing in her purse.

The woman was holding the hand of the big handsome man next to her, Greta assumed her husband, and looked at Greta with trepidation. Greta extended her hand, a business card between her index and middle fingers, proffering it to the woman.

"I can't do this today. I just . . . can't." Greta's voice shook, and she saw her hand was shaking a little as well. "But soon, you'll have questions—I'll have questions—and maybe we can . . . talk."

She turned before Colette could respond and joined Patrick where he was talking to Manny and Logan. Manny was explaining that, of course, Logan would not now be released, but he would be transferred to the hospital within forty-eight hours and Manny would be petitioning the court to get Dr. Brown into the hospital for initial diagnosis and treatment, so the O'Briens would feel confident he was getting the kind of help he needed.

When they walked out of the court, it was into a sea of journalists yelling for their attention, but they pushed past them, declining to comment. They'd leave them for Manny and Alyssa because they were also walking into a completely unknown future and lives that looked nothing like she had imagined—nothing like they'd been two years ago, a year ago, even yesterday.

They weren't ever going to look like the perfect family again. Greta knew that pangs of grief would be ever present. She also trusted herself more and made a decision that despite everything she'd endured, she'd focus on gratitude. Gratitude for having a second chance at motherhood, with Logan. This time around she would be able to act freely, incorporate compassion, and embrace imperfection.

Epilogue

GRETA & COLETTE

Logan was eventually given a tentative diagnosis of childhood schizo-phrenia when he was admitted to Lakewood, and though Greta did her research and found out that symptoms varied widely at such a young age, she let go of placing blame for not having gotten help sooner but still wondered if she could have prevented this tragedy. Each visit to Lakewood made it clearer that, eventually, their lives would have been irrevocably changed anyway due to Logan's illness, but she couldn't forgive herself for what happened that Halloween. At first she'd blamed her past, and then she blamed the present. She blamed herself—and Patrick. They'd bought too much into their own hype, into their own story that their lives were wonderful and perfect, as were their children. They had ignored the signs that he'd sent because they couldn't manage to tackle parenting as a team. She hadn't trusted her intuition, and perhaps subconsciously feared the lie that she'd worked so hard to bury might sneak its way to the surface. Greta was now able to recognize her son was ill, not a bad person.

Colette did eventually call Greta. She'd let a few months pass, which had given Greta time to get used to Logan at Lakewood and establish a new routine, a new life in many ways. She and Patrick had separated, then divorced—mostly amicably. The route to Lakewood, which she went to regularly to visit Logan, had her drive by O'Brien's Performance & Pro Shop, formerly the Beachland Tennis Club, which always filled her with grief and bittersweet pride. Patrick now owned the building where their son had died; he'd taken the club that no one wanted to go to after Brayden's death, renovated it entirely, and now ran one of the most successful tennis clubs in the Northeast. It had inspired Greta to continue to give up the person she had been with her disguise and her lies, with all the trappings of a perfect family and a perfect job, and figure out who she really was: a single mother to a teenager who needed some help managing his mental disorder.

That's when Colette had reached out, and it'd been perfect timing. Colette was also experiencing a shift in her life. In the wake of the trial, Frank had fired her before she had even left the courtroom.

"I knew that was coming, but I hope you understand . . . ," Colette had said as she watched Frank shove papers and folders into his briefcase.

He turned to look at her. His brow was furrowed, but there was a softness behind his eyes, and he peered at her. "I get it, Colette, you had no choice, it's your kid. Maybe someday I'll forgive you for ruining the biggest case of my career," he huffed as he pushed past her to leave.

She had exhaled with relief as he did so, and realized in that moment she needed a break. After coming up for air, in the months following the trial, Colette had reflected on her career and her next steps. What she loved most about her job as a medical paralegal was her ability to help people, and she realized that she didn't necessarily have to spend hours on end in Frank's office to do that. She had made a decision to help the O'Briens and make a difference in their life, and it had given her a feeling of purpose. After a lifetime of mistakes and doing the wrong thing, she wanted to continue to do something that would give her this feeling.

Though she'd thoroughly enjoyed her time as a medical paralegal, Colette decided that it would be easier to accept that at her age, with her medical history, she would never carry a baby, never give birth. She decided that she would at the very least enjoy doing something that involved caring for children. That's what she'd been doing when she reached out to Greta: volunteering with children through the National Alliance on Mental Health. She still had her nursing license, and that and her own experiences, both with her mother's illness and her own, were quite a boon to kids who were struggling. It was that which had given Colette the idea to start a program to benefit children.

Greta still felt the need to be a project manager, but making tons of money for other people no longer appealed to her. Though she no longer harbored any illusions about what kind of a man her father had been, she still didn't want to work with the man who'd tried to ruin him—he made her feel a little disgusted after that night anyway, as she'd always felt Brayden getting shot with the arrow was somehow cosmic payback. Without her father to pressure her and without her sons and husband to help her show off all the trappings of that life, her endless hours at that job weren't even appealing. She'd changed irrevocably in the wake of everything coming to light. Besides, it was as fulfilling to be the head of a nonprofit as it was to be a hedge fund manager. And that's how the Brayden Richards Foundation was born.

With Brayden's 529 and life insurance, they'd funded the foundation's beginnings: helping young adults and children who dealt with mental illness, either their own or in their household. After the trial, Emily and Greta had a heart-to-heart and agreed that down the road they would reach out to their biological sister and welcome her into their family of imperfection if she wished to meet them. Emily had explained that she always viewed Greta as perfect, their dad's pride and joy, and Greta admitted to Emily that while she was older, she always felt as if she were in Emily's shadow. Now they could see each other's strengths, and one of Emily's was being there for Greta. Bringing her muffins on days she could hardly get out of bed and taking care of all the details that overwhelmed Greta. For the foundation, she'd handle the numbers.

The following year, Emily had butted in and done what she did best: she had hired photographers and planners and thrown a ribbon-cutting fundraiser, getting them more capital than they knew what to do with at first for their relatively small foundation. Greta continued to be a money master, building their stable of services when necessary and investing it where it did good *and* earned dividends. Colette stayed with the mental health services they provided. They saw each other when needed, often only at board of directors' meetings and fundraisers. They took solace in the awareness of the other, and Greta kept Colette updated on Logan's progress, but they didn't spend a lot of time together.

It was for all these reasons that it was a surprise for Colette to see Greta on that fine spring day. They had a rhythm to their work, their lives, and this was a bit of a departure.

"Hey, what are you doing down here?" Colette asked, shoving a piece of her hair that had escaped her ponytail back from her face. She was cleaning up one of the playrooms they used for the younger kids. Greta looked so chic and put together in comparison to Colette. She was even dressier than usual, in a gorgeous pencil-skirt suit, while Colette wore jeans and a sweatshirt that felt grungy from the day she'd had running around after kids and cleaning up. "And looking so spiffy too." Colette pulled at her shirt and gave Greta a rueful smile.

Greta looked down at her clothes and waved off the comment but smoothed down a nonexistent wrinkle in her skirt nonetheless. "I had some things I needed to do in person. I had a court hearing with DCF today, hence the outfit."

Colette was intrigued. DCF, Connecticut's Department of Children and Families, was the department that the Brayden Richards Foundation did much of their work with. There were other nonprofits and after-school programs that BRF worked with when they could, but since their work focused on children with known mental health issues, many of the kids they worked with were in the foster care system and, due to those mental health issues, harder to find permanent placement for. They worked with a large group daily, helping take some of the burden off already overpopulated homes and centers. Colette knew she wasn't supposed to have favorites, but one of the kids they'd been working with for the past few months was a precocious five-year-old whose father was unknown and whose mother was in a mental health facility.

Yes, it was partially that little Gloria reminded Colette of herself, her own situation, but Gloria was also the sweetest kid—she had thick dark-brown hair, big green eyes that sparkled when she laughed, and a disposition that would put most nuns to shame. The other day, they'd had a birthday party for one of the kids, and one of the other workers had brought in a bunch of fun hats for the kids to wear. Gloria had put on a pair of cat ears from the bag of silly headwear and climbed into Colette's lap as they sang "Happy Birthday" to the little boy. Colette had had a jolt of déjà vu thinking of the photo of her and her own mother when she was little, that Halloween when she'd been dressed up as a cat but was too young to remember—the photo was now framed at home. The moment with Gloria had inspired such a familiar and familial feeling of comfort for Colette that she hadn't wanted to let the little girl go.

"DCF, huh? Are we starting another program with them, or was it just about funding and keeping our government and private donations in their own lanes?" Colette didn't really understand all that—the funding aspects—but then, she had no reason to since Greta was there.

"No, it was more . . . personal than that." Greta had a grin that Colette had rarely seen the woman wear. A few times, when Logan had come to the center with supervision and engaged with the younger kids, Colette had seen this smile, but that was about it. Greta wasn't maudlin by any means, but she wasn't someone who beamed a lot—and that was the only way to describe what she was doing now.

"Put that down and come over here. I need you to sign something." Greta pulled some paperwork out of her bag and flapped it at Colette, who dropped a doll into a bin and approached.

Colette gave her a cockeyed grin. "What is going on?"

Greta handed her the papers. "Just read it."

And that's when Colette saw it: Colette Catharine Richards De Luca and Victorio De Luca II were being given temporary custody of Gloria Michele Mercer—and based on pending check-ins, permanent custody. This time, she was sure her heart had exploded. Colette had tried—and tried and tried *and tried*—to become a mother. Because of the placenta previa and complications during the C-section, her doctors had suggested she not try to get pregnant again, and she'd been unable to find an adoption agency that was okay with her mental illness. They had signed up at a bunch of agencies but hadn't been chosen. Though they both provided documentation that they had been sober for many years, that they had a stable home, for one reason or another, families never chose them. Colette couldn't blame them . . . on paper she and Vic looked like they had a lot of problems, but she knew it was hard to show on paper what their hearts felt. One agency had said she could sign up and wait for a pregnant woman to choose her and Vic, but that had seemed unlikely, that a woman would choose someone with DID—even DID that was fully in hand through meds and therapy—to raise her child. She'd failed at every turn. And now . . .

Her vision swimming, one hand on her chest to assure herself her heart was still intact, she looked at Greta. "How?"

Greta gave her a sly smile this time. "Well, it turns out that the Walsh family name still has some pull around here. Between me and Dr. Brooks giving statements on your behalf, DCF was more than happy to let you take care of Gloria. You'll be able to take her home tomorrow, after you and Vic fill out some more paperwork. They're at your house now, doing the at-home check to dot all the i's and cross all the t's."

This was unbelievable. For so long, she'd been fighting through the arduous process and hoping for a family of her own, to be a mother, and now, for it to happen in this way . . . her joy was beyond imagining. "So Vic . . . knows?"

Greta nodded. "I'm afraid so. I did have to take away the pleasure of you getting to tell him so he could help with the inspection today. I wanted to tell you myself, alone." Now Greta's eyes looked a little watery as well.

"But why?"

Greta felt a little panicked, and it must have shown, because Colette put her hand out, her fingers barely skimming the fabric of Greta's suit jacket in a soothing motion.

"No, not why did you tell Vic. Why did you do this? I . . . I'm so grateful. So unbelievably, amazingly grateful . . . but why? I'll never be able to repay you."

Greta's anxiety eased but her heart still pounded, the adrenaline in her system taking her from anxious to joyous in a fraction of a second. "Colette, *you* made *me* a mother." They looked into each other's eyes far longer than they ever had before, both women's raw emotion on display. "The very least I can do for the woman who made me a mother is to help her become one."

Colette, whose life and family had started out so sad, so twisted, and Greta, whose family had looked so picture-perfect from the outside but splintered in so public a fashion, had both finally found salvation. It was as shocking to them as it was to anyone else that they'd found it in each other.

BOOK CLUB QUESTIONS

1. The theme of this book includes "striving for perfection." Have you ever experienced knowing an individual or family that you considered "perfect," only to find out that the perception did not match their reality?

2. Were you surprised to learn that the book was written by two authors? Could you tell the difference in voice or writing between the two POVs?

3. In the book, both Colette and Greta hide their struggles with infertility. Why do women so often feel isolated and ashamed when they experience this?

4. Greta committed several dishonest and deceitful acts. As a reader, could you relate to her choices, and could you forgive her in the end?

5. Greta's choices and addiction to perfection for her family and herself were fueled by her upbringing and environment. Have you ever experienced this in your circle or felt this drive for perfection yourself?

6. Were you surprised at the outcome of the trial? Did you agree with the judgment?

7. Do you think that Logan's violent crime was solely the

result of a predisposed mental illness, or was it also the result of his upbringing?

8. When women face assisted reproduction, how can they capitalize on available science and technology without infringing on their morals and ethics? When does science go too far?

9. In the end, Greta pulled some strings to enable Colette to adopt a child. In your opinion, should people who are diagnosed with mental illness but are medicated and stable be given the chance to have a family?

10. Should children who are conceived via assisted reproduction be told the truth about their conception?

ACKNOWLEDGMENTS FROM KRISTA AND NICOLE

We want to thank all the authors who were so generous with their time and support, especially Mark Sullivan and Lynn and Val Constantine. To our Lake Union/Amazon team, Danielle Marshall, Melissa Valentine, Tiffany Yates, Nicole Burns-Ascue, and Jon Ford: thank you for your support and patience with us throughout the publishing process. To ThrillerFest: this event absolutely changed our lives and gave us an unbelievable opportunity. Thank you so much to Gotham Writers and the Manuscript Academy, which we listened to throughout this process, and a special thanks to Julie Kingsley for giving us some immeasurable writing tips. To all our beta readers and the numerous people who provided us with feedback and answers during our endless research: we appreciate you. We appreciate Rory Wells for helping us with our legal scenes. To our amazing first editor, Gretchen Stelter: thank you for sharing our vision for this book and making our manuscript sparkle. We are forever grateful for Victoria Sanders & Associates and the endless support and guidance from our superstar agent, Bernadette Baker-Baughman, who never gave up on us. Words cannot express how important you all are to us.

FROM NICOLE

Thank you to my mother for telling me that I was a good writer from an early age, giving me writing prompts, and telling me to "go write a story." That gave me my early start to ten thousand hours of telling stories and writing. Thank you!

Thank you to my father for always pushing me, even as an adult, to be better. Even when I asked you if you read this book and you said, "Well, I read a couple of pages, but I stopped . . . because it was really bad." This type of brutal honesty—which will likely result in some sort of therapy at some point—also serves as a catalyst for me to work harder. Thank you.

To all my amazing beta readers: Anne, Tiffany, Sarah, Veda, Jen, Amy, Erin, Linda, Cristy, Aunt Sue, and Aunt Jacky, our very first reader. To Kelly, for reading and for introducing me to the real Jewett City and letting me put my spin on it. To Ally, for teaching me all about life on the streets. To Craig Raabe, for helping a random girl who was emailing and calling with questions about juvenile murder trials. To Laura and Rachel, who in the very early days of my research and writing shared valuable insight on the frightening realities and psychology behind violence and mental illness in children. To Lauren Levinson, my very first editor and the first person in this industry who believed in my voice.

To all the readers of my blog, which I started over ten years ago to tell my stories of motherhood and to hone my writing skills. So many of you loyally tuned in each week, sending me messages, thanking me, and sharing that my stories were helping you to not feel so alone. Every single word of support gave me the confidence to keep writing and to ultimately go out on a limb and write this book. Thank you.

To Krista: Thank you for joining me on this journey. So much of this project from inception to today was paved with your ideas (starting with a vision board in 2017 that I rolled my eyes at the whole time). I have learned a lot from you since that first day we met in the hair salon, and I look forward to many years together writing, laughing, and playing tennis.

To Danny and Sean: thanks for being the best two kids a mom could ask for, and thanks for providing solid blogging material for ten straight years.

Dan, thank you for your endless support. Even when I decided to start a "funny" parenting blog ten years ago, after you had told me time and time again that I was not one bit funny, you still were supportive every Sunday night so I could "do my blog." I have always known that you would support me in whatever I wanted to do. That feeling, knowing that you have my back, no matter what, is priceless and has helped me to get here. Thank you.

FROM KRISTA

Mary Louise Bidwell was my first reader and biggest fan; thank you for always believing in me. I'd like to thank Noah Ballard, Matt Keller, Alicia O'Hara, and my life coach, Amy Cotter, for helping me gain the confidence to pitch this book and pursue a new passion. The book's inspiration came from my best friends, Lisa Len, Christine Keller, and Danielle Sanderson, and our endless conversations on infertility through the years.

I'd like to thank some of my early beta readers—Kristina O'Connell, Erin Trimyer, Summer Land, Barbara Coppa, Lisset Wells, and Lynn Wells—for your honesty and insight and for reading those early copies and still believing in the story. Thanks to my behind-the-scenes early editorial support from Elizabeth Conard and Katrina Oko-Odoi. Thank you, Melyssa Smith and Kaleea Alston-Griffin, for your unwavering encouragement. Thank you to Danyale and Ryan for cheering me on. Thanks to my sisters and mom for putting up with my storytelling all these years. Mom, your *Today Show* vision helped us keep going when the going got tough.

Thank you to Babette Maxwell, who published me in *Military Spouse* magazine, allowing me to first see my name in print many years ago. Thank you to Sue Hoppin and Wendy Poling, who provided additional platforms and opportunities for me to write to the military-spouse space, a community close to my heart. In hindsight, this is what began my interest in writing.

Nicole, thank you for encouraging me to try writing fiction for the first time. I couldn't have picked a better partner in crime. This roller coaster was way more fun with you by my side, and I look forward to writing more books, laughing, and traveling to fun places to do "research."

My amazing kids, Alexa, Elijah, Lucas, and Sierra: you were all so supportive during my long hours behind my laptop and ate way too many peanut butter sandwiches over the last year.

To my husband, Rick: our morning coffee ritual and *endless* conversations about this book mean so much. You truly helped every step of the way, and I'm so grateful for your coaching, support, and love. Thank you.

ABOUT THE AUTHORS

Photo © 2020 Bella Blue Photography

Addison McKnight is the author of *An Imperfect Plan* and the pen name of Nicole Moleti and Krista Wells. After over a decade of writing non-fiction, their common interest in women's emotions and the cultural obsession with perfection sparked an idea for this debut novel. With six jobs and six children between them, they wrote their first book on Saturday nights and on the sidelines of their children's games. They reside in West Hartford, Connecticut, with their families.